Praise fo

THE EUL

"*The Eulogist* is a moving story, beautifu

—Amitav Ghosh, author of *Gun Island*

"Gamble seduces with her rich, rollicking portrait of life in Jacksonian Ohio."
—*The New York Times Book Review*

"In the Givens siblings, Terry Gamble has created a vivid and fierce-souled trio who navigate some of the strongest crosscurrents of American history. This is an inventive, spirited, and captivating story."

—Jessica Shattuck, *New York Times* bestselling author of *The Women in the Castle*

"A captivating historical novel of family loyalties and conflict, and the borders between freedom and slavery, *The Eulogist* is a searing portrait of the Ohio Valley and its pre-Civil War turmoil with beautifully drawn characters. Highly recommended."

—Paulette Jiles, author of *Enemy Women* and *News of the World*

"A sprawling yet richly drawn family saga." —*Kirkus Reviews*

"This gripping historical novel follows an Irish-American immigrant family as they search for their place in the free border state of Ohio, and the momentous choices they must each make in the face of the insidious reach of slavery. An essential read."

—Lalita Tademy, *New York Times* bestselling author of *Cane River*, *Red River* and *Citizens Creek*

"With more twists and turns than the Ohio River, *The Eulogist* brings us to the source of our nation's spirit, introducing us to characters we won't forget, no matter whether we loathe them or love them, culminating on a pitch-perfect note: forgiveness."

—Sally Cabot Gunning, author of *The Widow's War* and *Monticello: A Daughter and Her Father*

"A standout depiction of family dynamics." —*Publishers Weekly*

"This is history at its liveliest pace, its most surprising turns, and its strangest twists in the narrow borderlands between antebellum north and south. *The Eulogist* challenges us to engage with both the living and the dead, the loved and the betrayed, the captive and the free. I am convinced by every irreverent, astonishing thread in this tale."

—Linda Spalding, award-winning author of *A Reckoning*

THE EULOGIST

ALSO BY TERRY GAMBLE

Good Family

The Water Dancers

THE EULOGIST

Terry Gamble

wm

WILLIAM MORROW

An Imprint of HarperCollins*Publishers*

A hardcover edition of this book was published in 2019 by William Morrow, an imprint of HarperCollins Publishers.

FIRST WILLIAM MORROW PAPERBACK EDITION PUBLISHED 2020.

The Library of Congress has catalogued a previous edition as follows:

Names: Gamble, Terry, author.
Title: The eulogist : a novel / Terry Gamble.
Description: First edition. | New York, NY : William Morrow, [2019]
Identifiers: LCCN 2018018492| ISBN 9780062839893 (hardcover) | ISBN 9780062839909 (paperback)
Subjects: | BISAC: FICTION / Historical. | FICTION / Cultural Heritage. | FICTION / Literary. | GSAFD: Historical fiction.
Classification: LCC PS3607.A434 E85 2019 | DDC 813/.6—dc23
LC record available at https://lccn.loc.gov/2018018492

ISBN 978-0-06-283990-9 (pbk.)

20 21 22 23 24 LSC 10 9 8 7 6 5 4 3 2 1

To Peter, the love of my life

THE EULOGIST

CHAPTER 1

Anything untethered washes down this river. Old stoves, felled trees, derelict cows. A spring surge might bring a smorgasbord of candle crates and errant knickers, while autumn eddies snatch a mud-caked doll or blackbird, its wings splayed and broken. Just last week, one of Mary's girls informed me a house had flowed right past.

How big a house? I asked.

I told her I once saw an entire encampment that had washed away, carrying with it men, women, and children. I once saw a riverboat explode, raining body parts on the Kentucky and Ohio shores. Long ago, I saw the body of a man fleeing slavery who drowned while trying to reach the other side.

But people tire of my memories. I am eighty-six and nearly blind, and people wrongly regard me as a spinster. I overheard Mary promising her husband that, as soon as I'm gone, they'll move to California. California! It seems the Givenses are always pushing west. Over seventy years since we left Ireland—poor Ireland, impoverished by the falling crop market. If you happened to be on the banks of the Ohio in 1819 when we drifted past, you would have seen a father, a mother, and three children with the erect bearing of the privileged. Look more closely and you would have noticed our frayed clothes, my brothers' pants too short, my dress hanging limply on my ungenerous chest. At fifteen, I must have looked a sight, having wailed across that ocean—a six-week passage of wailing and puking, and wouldn't you have wailed if you were pulled away from that bonny youth who had kissed your unkissed mouth with such urgency as to make you want to lie right down and unbutton something?

We were Ulster Plantation Irish, which is to say that we were Scots. We had come to America to pray and to prosper. Come to America because America wanted us—this too-new country with land and trees to spare, but not enough people. I can see him now—my father standing at the bow of the flatboat he had christened the *Ark of the New World* but which to us felt more like the belly of the whale. Josiah Givens—a man of strong conviction and tepid Calvinism, whistling a passage from the *Eroica* Symphony and wishing he had more to show for himself.

"Ye shan't be finding many symphonies here," said my mother, resting a hand on her queasy stomach. "Ye'd be hard-pressed to find a fiddler."

It wasn't just seasickness that affected her, but the twinges of an early pregnancy going awry. Having lost four already, she knew she would lose this child, leaving only three—James, myself, and Erasmus.

It was early autumn. Our father had hired a pilot to navigate the rocks and fend off pirates who would rob and possibly murder us. By now we had grown accustomed to the animal carcasses and half-eaten limbs that washed down from the hinterlands. We scarcely noticed the stench until James shouted, "Look, Da! 'Tis a body in the snag!"

Dazzled by the sun on the water, we followed the direction of his finger, hoping it might be a felled tree since there were so many being cleared. The figure's head dipped below the surface, its bloated chest lifted, its arms flung wide as if to embrace the sky.

"Lord help us," said the pilot. "Niggers clogging the river."

I gaped at the body.

"You're not even going to pull him out?" I said to the pilot, tapping my parasol upon the deck. In Ireland, we would have helped anyone—even a Catholic—but you'd think this was a sheep for how little vexed he was.

"And what then, missy?" said the pilot. "We haven't time to bury it. And why bother? If someone comes by and thinks they can fetch a price . . . well, then." The pilot spat. "In the meantime, my contract is to deliver *you*."

"I feel sick, Da," said Erasmus.

We had all been sick. Nothing stayed down after that first week out of Belfast, and now our mother, wan and edgy, spent most days on her cot. So many long days staring at the horizon, and my saying, *There! Land!* But it was only a fogbank teasing us until—finally!—Nova Scotia.

We arrived in Philadelphia diminished. Halfway across the Atlantic, paralyzed by doldrums, the crew of the schooner *Lucretia* had pitched our piano overboard. And then to have my mother's trunk of good dresses and most of our books stolen off the landing in Philadelphia. We had watched as seven shirtless black men had loaded onto a stagecoach what was left of our belongings. It scarcely mattered that we still had our Minton china and our silver candlesticks.

Hottentots. That's what they were to us. My skin had burned—mostly from the sun, and there was Jamie jabbing me in the ribs, pointing at a half-naked Negro and saying, *Livvie, did you see* that?

Honestly, Jamie, this is America.

America—where it was said that the Indians were cannibals.

Every day on the river, we would see distant fires clearing forests for settlements. We'd heard tales of a comet and how an earthquake had reversed the current, reddening the river with iron-rich soil. Now at sunset, the smoke rendered the sky hellish and glorious as Dante described, *The Divine Comedy* being my only salvaged book other than the Bible. With the strange weather and the crops failing, the Book of Genesis had collided with the Book of Revelation, and portents could be gleaned in anything.

"You saw that body, Josiah," said my mother. "What next?"

A flock of geese blackened the sky. To the south lay Kentucky: slave state. To the north was Ohio: free. We drifted past limestone escarpments restraining forests of beech trees ten hands wide. "This is ours," said our father. "Our new Eden."

IT WAS FORTUNATE Erasmus vomited. Had he not done, we might have kept floating, floating, floating—past Indiana and Illinois, into the Mississippi, all the way down to New Orleans.

By morning, he was talking in gibberish, swearing that small, rabid creatures were tearing at his skin. He swam in delirium, alternating between the conviction he was the baby Moses borne by water into a strange land, or damned for abusing himself, and not just on the passage over, but on the flatboat with James and me sleeping beside him as he carried on with despicable and furtive abandon. *Salt,* he said through parched lips. *Brimstone.* When the fever broke, he rose from his cot, beheld the new city, and announced to us all, *I am saved.*

We all felt saved. Cincinnati was a village on the verge, the Queen of the West, the North's last bastion before the frontier. Flophouses and whorehouses had sprouted up. Packets of tobacco and indigo, rice and cotton heading north, pens of pigs and crates of produce heading south. Into this Babylon we alighted—a mosquito-infested backwater at a bend in the Ohio that muddled up rich, poor, black and white, fifteen versions of English, a growing German population, and a smattering of French.

And on every corner, a preacher.

The streets will flow with blood, the preachers said.

Which was not far from the truth. Blood and bones clotted the streets and creeks downstream from the slaughterhouses. The carrion was the worst near Bucktown, where the Negroes lived—those who had been given up or sold free or who had stolen themselves out of slavery until no one cared to find them.

Thou art dead in sin, and only by divine hand will thee be converted, said the preachers, damning the populace with their cheerful theology.

After enduring a few nights in a hotel, we moved into a boardinghouse where, for a dollar a week, we had two bedrooms and access to a privy that served half a dozen domiciles. The water pump was down the street, and twice a day I carried buckets for drinking, bathing, and cooking. In the bed we shared, my mother tossed and groaned. I was sure she would be fine. Our father had promised.

Yet when the baby came, it was stillborn, and soon thereafter, my mother died, the stench of her necrotic womb so foul that the landlady, one-eyed and irritable, threatened eviction.

"Mrs. Humphries," my father said, squaring off with her in the hall. "My wife is dead and my younger son isn't right in the head." Met with her intractable stare, my father added, "We will pay you in advance."

Humphries eyed him with her single orb, knowing that the silver candlesticks would soon be hers. "Then bury her quickly. I shall not abide with the smell."

"And where exactly shall we bury her?"

We were not yet attending church, but laying my mother's body to rest seemed imperative enough to join one, and so the following day we were in a pew at the First Presbyterian, our father's hat in his hand as he explained our plight to the minister. Alas, said the minister, our story was all too familiar. The best he could do was direct us to the immigrants' graveyard, our mother being the first of our family to die upon American soil. In that unhallowed grave we buried her along with my lifeless baby sister—a plot of land far from any church, unwelcoming as the anteroom of Purgatorio.

We had neither the time nor the means for lengthy mourning. Within weeks of our landing, a bank collapse had ground all enterprise to a halt. The fires of brick kilns were extinguished. Nails went unhammered. Chisel ceased to meet stone. Even the wealthy were reduced to chopping wood and bartering livestock. At night, my father, whistling with less conviction, counted the last of his coins with James gazing on as if he were willing those mounds of silver to multiply.

"I found a job," said James. "It doesn't pay much, but the work is steady."

"Steady work in a city brought to her knees?" said my father. "And what is that now?"

"With the chandler Midas Barker. I'll be fetching animal castoffs for tallow."

"'Tis a pissman's job. Leave it to the scum."

"'Tis we who are the scum, Da. Look at us."

My father ran a coin up and down between his fingers. "You were a scholar, my boy. Your mother was right. You could have gone to Trinity."

Our father started to weep in a silent way that frightened me more than his graveside wailing.

"We'll make the money, Da," said James.

It was the obsession of every immigrant. Ambition—along with its sullen sibling, thwarted plans—was thick as miasma in the valley. Our father had hoped to speculate in real estate or at least buy land to grow hops. Unable to raise more capital, he would try his hand at several enterprises—cobbling and lathe turning—each of them failures.

In the spring of 1822, bitter and despairing of making a living along the Ohio, our father grasped at the promise of fecundity in the alluvial deltas of the Mississippi. Three years to the day of our arrival in Cincinnati, our father pronounced the three of us of age and booked himself passage on a steamboat heading south, assuring James that he would one day return after establishing a distillery.

"Look after Olivia and Erasmus," our father said to James. "Make sure you remain Christians of some description, and read anything you can lay your hands on so as not to become illiterate as Americans clearly are. And James—you should by all means marry, but only when advantageous. If all else fails, make as much money as you can and purchase passage back to Ireland to secure assistance from my scoundrel of a brother who stole the estate out from under me."

Our father waved his hat from the upper deck of the *Mississippi Queen* that would be stopping in Louisville, St. Louis, and Natchez before putting in at New Orleans. We never learned if he had made it all the way to New Orleans or disembarked along the way, for that was the last we saw of him.

CHAPTER 2

1828

We are not impoverished. We are reduced," James said—an assessment I found a little rich given that we often could not make rent and had to plead with the ghastly Humphries. Out of desperation I had placed a notice in the local papers soliciting students whom I could teach to read and write and do simple sums. *If promising,* my advert read, *I shall teach them Latin.*

It was six years since our father had deserted us, three since James had gone into business for himself. Each morning, James rose before dawn, packed a scrap of bacon, donned his hat and coat, and walked the half mile to his workshop. By six A.M., he would have stoked the fire and commenced to render lard into tallow and stearic acid. The air in his workshop was so stifling that I would not have wondered if he had fallen into the vat and become a candle himself.

He was very proud of his new spinning machine. Braided wicks were much improved over the old simple strands that needed constant tending. *The candles I sell are good burners,* James pronounced, so full of self-importance. *And I don't overcharge.*

Housing his enterprise in a tiny building in the yard of a pork broker close to the creek, James nailed up a sign with the grand inscription

GIVENS AND SONS—although he had no sons to speak of. Not even a wife, though by then he had met someone.

Well, not *met* exactly. Spotted.

He had considered speaking to her, but it was difficult to clean up and look one's best after toiling over grease. Poor James. His skin was constantly smudged from smoke, his hands and forearms marred by burns. Verily, he looked a wreck. This after working fourteen hours a day, six days a week, observing the Sabbath less from religious leaning than from exhaustion.

Still, he told me, he would *like* to have a son. Our younger brother, Erasmus, was an uneven employee given his fondness for drink. Had Erasmus *not* been our brother, James would have fired him, but to his credit, James could no more forsake his family than he could forsake a god in whose existence he only partially believed. If he thought about it (which I suspect he seldom did), James would have said his religious views consisted of a Divine Creator who, having accomplished His task of Creation, had moved on to another enterprise, leaving Man to fend for himself as he, James Givens, surely did.

Once we concluded our respective obligations—James his boiling, I my tutoring—we would meet each other on the landing, fleeing the reek of Mrs. Humphries's cooking to make our way across the broad, dirty streets.

On that day late in April, James was already checking his watch, his face compressed with irritation.

"Are you tapping your foot for me?" I asked while trying to catch my breath.

"'Tis Erasmus. He was supposed to be back with a load."

It was Erasmus's job to go from door to door to collect meat scraps and bones for rendering.

"Perhaps he was held up at the docks," I said, knowing full well he was probably buttoning up his pants as we spoke, assuring some Mollie she would be paid soon enough.

"I will give him an earful," said James.

Yet when Erasmus put his mind to it, he *was* a good producer. Even James reluctantly admitted that our brother could have been the best scrapper in the city. He could talk a housewife out of her rolling pin, procuring a payload worth of scraps in one afternoon that could have fed a family for a week. Girls and women were always falling for him. Even from the start when we arrived in Cincinnati, and Erasmus was frail and sickly, there was something sweet and charming about his face. Some said his eyes were womanish, but that made him all the more appealing, for pretty eyes are rare in a man, and women like to look at them.

But pretty or not, he was just as apt to turn up empty-handed, infuriating James. Like his former employer, Midas Barker, James ran a tight ship, insisting that a day's batch of candles must run on schedule to meet each evening's demand for light. No candles, no money. I admonished Erasmus, but even then I was disinclined toward mothering, so it had fallen to James to be parent to us both. No wonder he was yearning for a wife.

Heading across the muddy swath teeming with barkers and boatmen, James muttered as we picked our way through the jumble of draymen and carts, dodging ruffians and feral chickens while men in suspenders loitered by storefronts, smoking cigars and greeting us with a tip of their hats. It was a hodgepodge of humanity unheard of in Ireland. Black, red—even yellow. I could not help but stare.

"We are set for candles today," said the gnomish clerk at Merkl's paper shop. It was James's practice to make several calls before we took our meal.

"Then place an order for tomorrow, and I'll throw in a couple extra," said James.

"You're an ambitious young man," replied the clerk, who had an unattractive growth on his forehead. "But no more than Barker, I'd say." His eyes drifted over to me and settled. "Is this the missus?"

"Heavens, no!" said I.

"Barker's candles are burned up in half the time," said James, pegging the clerk for gullibility.

"You don't say," said the clerk. "Well, the sooner the second candle's done, the sooner I'm home to bed." To my horror, he leered at me.

"Then save my candle and relight it," said James. "It will not disappoint."

The clerk, who hadn't taken his eyes off me, said, "No, my lad, I'm sure it will not." Turning back to James, he tapped the blossom above his eyebrow. "You'll go far if you don't extinguish yourself too quickly."

"Mark my words," said James. "I intend to light up Cincinnati."

"Really, James," I said after we left. "What a demon."

"Oh, he will buy some candles. Just you wait."

Another whistle. A carriage hurried past. Taking my brother's arm, I accompanied him to the next shop and the next, three more before heading home. I could see him making mental lists: extra candles for all the customers next week; hire another apprentice to replace Erasmus; try his hand at soapmaking to better wash off this infernal grease.

"James," I said. "A note has come from the minister's daughter inviting us to tea."

He looked at me sharply. "Reverend Morrissey?" he asked. I nodded. "And his daughter?" Again, I nodded. His features melted from pleasure into worry. "And how to be presentable?"

A printed bill, dancing merrily in the breeze, affixed itself to the front of James's shirt. He snatched it off and read aloud: "'*100 Dollars Reward! Runaway from the subscriber on the 27th of January, my Black Woman named Bee, standing about four foot eleven, with black marks on her cheeks* . . .' By God," he said. "'Tis far better to deal in tallow than in human flesh."

"Tch," said I, echoing his disapproval.

Crumpling up the bill with a grunt of disgust, James used it to wipe the grease from his face before tossing it away.

I WAS PUSHING what I thought to be a carrot about my plate, hoping we might have pie for dessert, when Erasmus finally appeared. Everyone stopped talking as they took in Erasmus's sorry state—all grease and wayward hair with a look on his face that betrayed mischief.

"The pigs got the goods," he said, gripping his hat and avoiding James's glare. "I came up empty."

I stabbed an onion that rolled away. James cleared his throat.

"'Twas the pigs!" said Erasmus.

Said James, "'Twas Barker's nephew sure as soot, for he knows your ways, Erasmus, and you are easy enough to snooker."

It had been a great disappointment that three years prior Barker had chosen his nephew over James as successor. That the nephew was dim and shiftless added further insult, and soon thereafter, James had set out on his own.

"I shall fetch twice as much this evening," said Erasmus, his expression darkening.

"Then you'd bet' get going," said James in a tone.

I retrieved the onion from the edge of my plate. Every day since our father had left, the three of us, at James's insistence, sat together for the afternoon meal whether or not we were speaking. "You were with those women."

Erasmus looked at me with some amusement. "And who are *you,* Livvie, to cast aspersion when you engage so little with society yourself?"

I was used to his chiding me that I was too tall, too thin, that my temper, like my hair, tended toward the red. Erasmus saved his flattery for others. As for me, I've never been one to preen for a compliment, even as a girl when preening seems to be the way and at my prettiest back in Ireland before we crossed that swollen sea.

A day like this could end in thunder, another fact of Ohio I had never grown used to, like that day the pigs got into the boardinghouse and knocked over the table before Mrs. Humphries herded them out, shouting *suey! suey!*, and all my pupils were shrieking and hooting, and even my brothers thought it was funny as though we had never lived in a lovely house with beautiful things on an estate in Ireland.

Remembering the feeling of another's lips on mine, I fanned my face. A pool of fat that had congealed on the plate. In my opinion, Mrs. Humphries's larder offered more than enough inedible parts to stock James's cauldron for a month. Some mornings, Erasmus came home slam-into-the-wall drunk, and I had to get up and shut the door so my pupils would not see him. Then Mrs. Humphries would swoop down, banging on the door and screaming, *Your brother is at it again!* And out he would go onto the street with the squalid pigs and back to the landing, where boozing and spitting were as natural as prayer.

It was not just Erasmus who drank. Everyone knew whiskey was safer than water seeing as how some took sick after drinking from the wells. Some men seemed able to drink and keep working, but there were hordes of sots sleeping in alleyways or wedged between sacks of wheat. More than once I had to step over an inebriate sprawled in the road like a pile of manure.

"The pigs indeed." I sniffed.

"You watch," Erasmus said. "One pass down at the docks, and I will fill up the 'barrow. Heck, I'll take their old shoes and dead passengers. There is nothing I can't boil down."

THERE WAS NO SIGN of Erasmus for the next two days. More often than not, we knew better than to worry. But this time, our brother returned in a bad way—bruised and cut, looking like Lazarus before he met Jesus.

"Say nothing," he said to James and me at dinner. "I have heard it all."

James opened his mouth and closed it. There were people you knew better than to associate with, but that did not stop Erasmus, who was drawn to the disreputable like a moth to flame. He would find the wrong girl attached to the wrong man or the wrong man attached to the wrong deal and come out the other end with wings as scorched as Icarus.

"I have met a preacher," Erasmus said. He had a shiner, and the cut on his lip was still bleeding. "A Methodist."

"Oh, this is rich," said James. "And what has the poor man done to deserve the likes of thee?"

"I have been listening to him," Erasmus said. "I took his tract."

James looked at the folded paper as if it were a rotting fish. "Does it promise to cure your dipsomania? Or rid you of the clap?"

"It promises to save my soul."

"Does it, now? Well, so do the Catholics if you pay them enough."

The tract was printed on a cheap stock and featured a clumsy drawing of what purported to be praying hands but which looked more like a mollusk. *Salvation is available to anyone,* it read. *Anyone can repent!*

As Presbyterians, we had been raised with the assurance of our own election at the expense of everyone else, who would be going to hell, and better them than us.

James said, "So repent and get on with it."

Which was very like James to say. And very unlike Erasmus to do.

"Sam Mutton said . . ." began Erasmus.

"Mutton?"

"'Tis the preacher's name."

"'Tis a ridiculous name," said James. "The next thing we know, you shall be becoming a Mohammedan or a quaking cracker. These preachers are everywhere, Erasmus. And contributing what?"

"You are not listening to me."

"Open your eyes."

SEVERAL WEEKS LATER, with my cloak wrapped around me, I walked with purpose as though I had an appointment, pausing as a shepherd coaxed his woolly procession across the cobbles. I had decided to go see this preacher Sam Mutton for myself. As a girl, I had pointed out to the minister in Enniskillen an inconsistency between the Book of Job and John 1:18 as to whether one could see God. The minister had marched me back to the Grange and demanded to see my father, who whacked my hands with a spoon.

Who shall marry a girl like this? my father asked my mother after the minister had left.

Amid the crates and barrels of the landing, peddlers hawked cornhusk pipes and furled tobacco on pavement littered with tattered bills. Negro women balancing baskets on their heads moved like swans amid locust swarms of children carrying letters and hustling for change. Through the mayhem, I spotted a black-hatted figure poised on a crate. He was wearing too-short pants and a too-big coat, his wide-brimmed hat slipping below his brows. When he spoke, he punched the air as if jousting with an unseen adversary.

"Oh, we all know too well the sins of Eve," the preacher exhorted as I drew in closer, his eyes trailing across the crowd and, for a moment, alighting on me.

Oh, to have *some sins,* thought I.

"But ever since the Fall, we have been waiting at the garden gate, asking to be let back in."

I expected hokum and was not disappointed, for Sam Mutton went on to claim that we had a choice one way or another in our own salvation. Good deeds and right intention—not election by God—were the surest path to heaven.

A choice indeed! thought I. Pulling my cloak about me less for warmth than as a shield against such outrageous theology, I scanned the faces until I made out Erasmus, who was intensely focused on what was being said.

"There are those who would tell us that God has already stacked the deck," said Sam Mutton. "But I say this is balderdash. For who among us separates our children thusly, or lays a hand on one simply because he is not the other?"

I lifted my skirts and barreled through the crowd until I came up alongside my brother.

"Livvie?" said Erasmus. "Are you spying on me?"

"Just curious."

And I *was* curious. For two weeks, Erasmus had been sober as a brick and a diligent worker. James had been silent on the subject, but he, too, was taking note. I was certain that, at any moment, Erasmus would fall, for he was a chronic backslider and weak of will. If this fool of a preacher could sway him, I wanted to meet the man.

The preacher's hands were twitching. "So if thou art cast off, is it not of thy *own* doing? And so should it not be of thy own doing that, like the Prodigal, you can *choose* to return to God?"

There were murmurs among the crowd.

"He speaks of me, Livvie," said Erasmus. "Of *me*."

I sniffed. Surely Erasmus's lurch to religion had sprung as much from expedience as a call to redemption. His notion of godliness was wispy as clouds. At this moment, the promise put forward by this preacher named Mutton held more allure than knocking on the doors of slaughterhouses and evading debt collectors.

"Erasmus," I whispered, "you are going to be late for work. If James has his way with you, you'll meet your maker soon enough."

But even when he was a child, claiming to have visions—or more recently in the thrall of women and liquor—I had never seen a look on his face quite like this: a mix of rapture and serenity like an infant's comtemplation of its mother's breast, eager, hungry, avid. In truth, it scared me, for as my father once said, Erasmus was not altogether right in the head.

CHAPTER 3

1828

It was the steamiest of days—the kind that dampens the lightest muslin as soon as it touches your skin. Even the river seemed stupid in the heat. Slow flowing and sluggish, it meandered past banks of cicada-infested trees. Cincinnati, Sabbath-silent but for the occasional hymn, had surrendered to its lethargy.

For days we had been hearing rumblings about "the coloreds" and the "city going to hell," and was it any wonder with so many of them settling here, and now the Germans were arriving and, worse, the Catholics. If there were to be a riot, it shouldn't have surprised me in the least, and I would gladly have joined in if someone had given me a stick.

I stared out of the window of Hatsepha Peckham's book-lined parlor, my needlepoint in my lap like a sleeping cat. The little crisscrosses upon my canvas were intended to tell a story—one that I could display to a prospective suitor and say, *See? Here on the upper corner? That's a daisy.*

But I have never felt any particular ardor for daisies. They were simply easier to stitch than roses.

But you must *have a flower in your sampler,* Hatsepha Peckham had told me with resolution bordering on fervor. *It would be unwomanly to omit them.*

Doing needlepoint with Hatsepha Peckham made my head hurt, but she was the closest thing I had to a friend. As Erasmus had so baldly observed, I seldom went out in company. Hence, James pressed for my acquaintance with Miss Peckham, saying it would do me good. Do *him* good, more likely, given that the business of her father was coal, the mining of which necessitated the purchase of many candles.

Hatsepha was telling me that I should get a maid as my coiffure was compromised. Would that I could afford one. In Philadelphia and Boston, ladies employed dressers to do their hair, but there were few maids in Cincinnati, even with half the girls so poor and ignorant you would think they would jump at the chance.

"Indeed I should," I said to Hatsepha with as much courtesy as I could muster. Church all morning, and now an endless afternoon of visiting and stitching. If previous horrors were any indication, Hatsepha would soon rise to the piano and sing.

"Tell me," said Hatsepha, pretending to focus on a fancy threaded detail, "why does your brother James rush off so quickly after church?"

Had I told her James had hurried back to his workshop on a Sunday to preserve a day's worth of candles from softening, Hatsepha would have been appalled. In her mind, it would be an affront to piety to toil on the Sabbath.

"He was not feeling well," I said.

"Not well? Why, he looked in the pink even before the Creed."

Clearly, she had her cap set on my brother. Hatsepha, with her wide, bland face and badly spelled name that gave a nod to the female pharaoh Hatshepsut. Today, her head was a bowery of satin roses stuck all about. I fancied a swarm of bees might rush through the window in a frenzy of pollination.

"Of course James is *well*," I said quickly, not wanting her to assume he was in need of nursing.

"But you *said* . . ." Hatsepha shook her head. The roses quivered.

Phantom bees flew up. "I couldn't help but notice he was staring at Julia Morrissey."

Now I understood the invitation to stitch. A little stitchery and spill the beans. But there were no beans to spill since James would tell me nothing.

I murmured that James was merely paying his respects to the minister's daughter.

I wanted to say, *You may be rich, you silly thing, but that girl has thrice your looks*. Nevertheless, Hatsepha seemed appeased by my answer. She said, "That Reverend Morrissey makes me quake in my pew."

"Imagine being his daughter."

"And have that man glowering at me over breakfast?" She shuddered. "And poor besides? No thank you."

I drew my needle through the canvas, pulled it taut. Indeed, it was known that half the male congregation was in love with Julia Morrissey. "Her impoverishment will serve her well, don't you think? No threading *that* camel. Heaven is positively panting for her."

Hatsepha bit her lower lip. I almost regretted toying with the woman. *You have a mean streak*, James often told me, *wider than the river.*

"Father says that prosperity is a sign of God's approval," said Hatsepha, her lips thinning to a small moue of sanctimony.

My canvas had all come loose in its hoop and was puckered at the edges. Feigning a gaiety that I was sure rang hollow, I said, "Then He undoubtedly approves of the Peckhams!"

I am very sorry to say that Hatsepha beamed. Oblivious to irony, she persevered. "I went up to Maysville last month," she said, her voice dropping as if to include me in a secret. "All the new styles are in. And the bonnets? Have you seen such extravagance?"

"Only on you, Hatsepha."

"You don't think they're too large? People might talk."

Talk, talk, talk. How was it that a city built only decades earlier in the spirit of progress could so quickly succumb to manner and habit?

"But *you*, Olivia! You don't care about such things. I hear your younger brother has run off into the wilderness, but *you* haven't even mentioned it."

Which was true. I had not. Perhaps I was embarrassed. Or perhaps the omission stemmed from my own misplaced hope that Erasmus would come to his senses. My eye settled on the spine of a book that read *Piety and Proverbs*. "One need not go so far to find oneself in the wilderness."

"Is that biblical?" Hatsepha said. "Because you are always quoting something, though I know not what. I daresay it surprises me, for I have scarcely seen you pray. So tell me, has your brother turned into a primitive?"

I regarded my shoes. They were practical leather boots—not the fine silk shoes Hatsepha wore. In spite of brushing them daily, I could not absolve the effects of manure and slop.

"You make him sound like an Indian," I said. "He has . . . well, he has become a Methodist."

"A Methodist?" Hatsepha's eyes bulged.

Until that day, I had never been inclined to defend Methodism—or any religion, for that matter. Still, I shrugged as if becoming a Methodist and riding off into the woods was as common as shopping for hats.

In truth, there had been a terrible row between James and Erasmus when Erasmus told us he had been saved.

Saved from what, you horse's ass? said James. *Your creditors?*

After several weeks of piousness, Erasmus had succumbed to his ways and showed up looking a sight (so badly banged up that I feared he might expire), begging James for the money for a horse.

You're out, Erasmus, said James as he laid out the bills. *I'm done.*

The next day, Erasmus had left Cincinnati with twenty dollars in his pocket and a thirdhand Bible, mounted on a swaybacked, half-blind, ill-christened horse named Abel. It wouldn't be the last time James would bail out Erasmus. As I watched him ride away, heading toward the wilderness, I imagined him sauntering through the arched cathedral of trees, liberated by faith and a little bit of currency. *Alleluia,* he would say, fresh and free of sin. *Alleluia.*

"Tell me, Olivia, do you play?"

"Pardon me?"

Hatsepha smiled. "Piano?"

"Alas," said I, my gaze drifting longingly once again toward the books. "No more." Our piano lay at the bottom of the ocean, a casualty of capricious winds. That I had once loved to play, and had done so with some élan, I did not mention. Again, embarrassment. That and the defiant refusal to admit that, in coming to America, our family had lost nearly everything.

"But then, you must start up!"

She was indomitable. I tried to protest, pleading lack of practice. But Hatsepha wasn't having it. "Everyone plays," she said, determined to prove I could be as conventional as she. Or if not conventional, that I, like Erasmus, could at least be saved.

She jumped to her feet and took my hand. Resigned, I followed her to the piano, where she directed my index finger to middle C. Together, we sounded out the note.

CHAPTER 4

1828

James had been scrubbing. Mostly his face and hands. Like most everything in Cincinnati, the brush was a by-product of pigs—in this case, hog bristles that chafed and scraped until James looked more bloodied than cleansed.

"Goodness, James, are you walking down the aisle?" I asked from the cookhouse doorway.

It was a joke between us since neither had prospects. Today was out of the ordinary since we were invited to tea at the Parish House. James had donated a fortnight's worth of candles (which sounds more generous than it was since summer's light was upon us), and the minister's daughter, Julia Morrissey, had sent us an invitation out of thanks.

"Here. Let me," said I, striding across the room.

James's arms and back were muscled from wrestling pots. Stocky like our father, he was freckled all over and reddened from the brush.

"You have been mortifying your flesh, James," I said, using my fingertips to smooth the waves in his hair. "I shall call you Archbishop Becket."

"You'll call me no such Catholic folderol, especially in front of the Morrisseys."

"Still," I said, our eyes meeting in the looking glass as James cinched his trousers, "you are looking quite the dandy."

NEITHER OF US followed the sermon closely. Morrissey's lectures were, for the most part, grim screeds that made me flinch. And James kept looking at his pocket watch. When we stood to say the Creed, I recited Ovid.

"Ecce metu nondum posito."

More than one Cincinnati matron stared.

James clenched his jaw as we left the church. "I suppose you find it amusing to utter Latin in a Protestant church."

I might have apologized, but when we arrived at the refectory, most of the parishioners looked as relieved as we to be done with Morrissey's brimstone for another week. James's eyes darted about. It was a sea of hats—high ones on the men's heads, voluminous ones on the women's.

"Law," said I, still partial to simpler attire. "We might as well move to Timbuktu for all the strangeness here." I touched my fingers to his sleeve. "And you still have grease under your collar, James. You will never get a lady to give you a second look."

From across the room, we heard a female voice. "Mr. Givens! Olivia!" Hatsepha Peckham strutted over.

James looked stricken, but when he spoke, he was formal and polite. "Miss Peckham."

I was rendered mute by her ensemble. An entire flock of red-feathered fowl had been slaughtered to crown her with the Burning Bush.

"Not scurrying off as usual?" Hatsepha Peckham said to James. She barely acknowledged me. "Did you have a biscuit? I made the buttermilk ones. Well, my girl did. She has a hand with pastry."

James demurred, but I took two.

Hatsepha looked him up and down. "You are quite thin. But then, I heard you have been ill . . ."

"Excuse me?"

"Why, your sister said something just last week."

"My sister says a number of interesting things," said James, a sidelong glance at me.

Hatsepha leaned in, the brim of her headgear knocking him on the brow. When James made a motion to step away, she clutched his forearm. "I understand you are coming up to the Parish House for tea, as are Father and myself. I am so pleased," she said. "So pleased."

"Mmmm . . ." said James, extracting himself.

Later, as we walked toward the Parish House, I said, "Hatsepha Peckham has you in her sights, James. Tell me, is it mutual?"

"Hatsepha Peckham? Goodness no."

"Well, you are certainly dressed as though you are trying to impress someone."

James took off his hat and ran his fingers through his hair until it stuck straight out, fortified by beeswax. "If you must know, Olivia, I am hoping to approach the minister's daughter."

"Julia Morrissey?" Julia Morrissey of the wickedly lovely hair and much-commented-upon eyes. "Ha! I knew it, I knew it, I knew it," said I, skipping ahead. Often James scolded me for being childish, but that day my giddiness was contagious, and he had to smile as if his hoped-for alliance held out the promise that our family might actually make traction in this new world to which we clung as tightly and tenuously as barnacles.

"I shall distract Hatsepha," I said. "I shall ply her with bonbons while you converse with your paramour. Hatsepha shall be none the wiser. Although I must say, she watches you like a hawk. Do not think you have fooled her. She knew even before me where your interests lay."

"I do not understand women's minds," James said.

"Do not sound so morose, Jamie. And for goodness' sake, talk about something other than candles."

"What do women want to talk about?"

I threw up my hands. "Hats, apparently. Or their children. Or other people's children."

I looked up at the Parish House with its joyless windows. Out of nowhere came a thought of Erasmus. Two months since he had left us and still no word. Almost every day, I would go to the landing, hoping to find that preacher again. Surely Sam Mutton would know something. The landing pulsed with the usual riffraff and mélange of humanity, but there was no sign of the scarecrow Sam who had been railing from a soapbox.

Pardon me, but do you know a preacher named Sam Mutton? I had asked upon catching the filthy collar of a boy carrying valises to a waiting dray. *You've seen him about, I'm sure. The one who speaks of forgiveness?*

The boy eyed me evilly. *Them's that's preaching here is always talkin' crazy. You don't need to go far to hear sech manure as spews from the likes of them. Why, I's heard hell described fifty differnt ways. So which un is it, ma'am? You tell me.*

"I miss Erasmus," I said to James. "Oh, I know it is all nonsense. But of the three of us, he knows how to talk to ladies."

"I would not call it talking," said James. "And I would not call them ladies."

We entered the clammy, occluded halls of the Parish House, where Ephraim Morrissey lived with his daughter.

"Lasciate ogni speranza voi ch'entrate," said I, reciting Dante.

"'Abandon all hope ye who enter here,'" said James. "Indeed."

In spite of the June heat, there was a fire in the grate. I groaned, but James, showing restraint, bowed before the Reverend Morrissey and thanked him for his sermon.

"I believe you checked your watch," said the reverend, who up close was no lovelier than in the pulpit. Pouches, like little sacks of wheat, dangled beneath eyes radiating retribution. "Not once, but thrice."

Said James a bit too quickly, "'Tis a chandler's habit to time the cooking lest the pot boil over."

"Yes," said a woman's voice behind us. "Candles, Father. A bushel for the church, Father. For which we can thank this gentleman."

The lovely Julia Morrissey—and she was so pleasing to look upon that I might have envied her but for her demeanor that seemed unconscious of the fact—touched her father's arm. She smiled at James, her bright eyes eerily similar to her father's except that the light in hers seemed anything but damning.

James stammered out something about making plenty of candles, that it was nothing really, and I thought, *On my grave, do not get him started.*

"I do not believe we have formally met," said Julia Morrissey. Her voice was honeyed and vaguely southern but so lightly touched as to avoid the twang that demands twenty minutes to utter a sentence.

"I know who you are," said James.

Julia did not seem to notice his bluntness, but the reverend cleared his throat. He had no discernible mouth, yet his lips curled into what would be a smile were it not so reminiscent of a grimace.

"James Givens," said James, holding out his hand. Julia extended hers, and he pumped it.

Really, Jamie, thought I, for she clearly expected him to kiss it. Now it lay limply in his. I noticed his nails were not entirely clean.

I cleared my throat. James, coming to himself, presented me as his sister, Olivia Givens.

Julia Morrissey turned those eyes on me, and for a moment I felt what James must have felt: that to be seen by eyes such as these was to be appreciated and reflected back in some imagined glory that, once conceived by Julia Morrissey, could be altogether possible—so possible, in fact, that I, too, found it difficult to speak.

The Reverend Morrissey, on the other hand, continued to regard James with the cool appraisal of Saint Peter assessing heaven's new arrival. Were it not for a couple approaching with an infant in tow distracting the reverend, James might have bowed again and beat a retreat from father and daughter alike. Instead, he seized the opportunity to turn to Julia and say in a rush, "You have such lovely skin, Miss Morrissey. I am hoping . . . well, I've been experimenting with a soap recipe that will be kinder to tender skin. I . . . I would be honored if you would try it."

It was not a bad effort, considering, and his earnestness was not lost on Julia Morrissey, who replied graciously, "Seeing that my father disapproves of warm water in the bath, I shall be more than happy to at least have pleasant soap."

Her quick look over her shoulder at her father did not escape my attention.

In truth, James's soap recipe was in need of improvement, having burned his skin through an excess of lye and later causing an explosion when his proportion for glycerin went awry. I scanned the room for Hatsepha, who any moment could descend like a vulture after carrion. But she was nowhere in sight. Relieved, I turned my attention back to James, who was blushing, and Julia, who said, "You were so kind to donate your candles. I wish we could enjoy them longer."

"Longer?"

"Have you not heard? My father is taking a position in Kentucky. I am afraid our days in Cincinnati will be coming to an end."

Only I would have noticed the falter in James's smile, and this because of the stirring in my own stomach.

"Times are changing, Mr. Givens. Out with the old, they say. This is such a progressive city, do you not think? My father frightens people.

Oh, do not protest. I am well aware. I live with him. I know his views. But I *did* quite like it here."

She had the saddest look, like Persephone in winter. Her distress matched James's, though I suspect for different reasons. Looking from James to me, she said, "I am sorry we will not be better friends."

No sorrier than I. With a dip of her head, she turned back into the roomful of guests.

James gripped my arm a bit too tightly. "Did you know Morrissey was leaving?"

James looked inconsolable, so in an attempt to cheer him, I said, "Can you not propose on the spot?"

"We have spoken but two words."

"In many places they arrange marriages," I said. "And why not? You think everyone just falls in love? I was in love when I was fifteen, and where am I now?"

A nice wife for James, and our life would be set.

"Remember what our father told you, James. Marry well and, if possible, above your station."

"Our father," said James with a snort.

"Too charming by half," said I. And for a moment, my thoughts returned to Erasmus. "Speaking of charm." I jerked my head toward Hatsepha Peckham, who was heading our way.

CHAPTER 5

1828

Several weeks after James made the formal acquaintanceship of Julia Morrissey, a gentleman called on me. We had struck up a conversation at the market two days prior, but I had not given it another thought. The man had made such a slight impression that when Mrs. Humphries announced I had a caller in the parlor, I thought she was joking or that one of Erasmus's creditors had arrived to collect an outstanding obligation.

"Phinneaus Mumford, ma'am. We met last Saturday morning."

"Ah," I said, racking my brain. Had we talked about tomatoes?

Phinneaus Mumford took his place in a Windsor chair. He had a neatly trimmed moustache, finely combed curls, and a rosebud of a mouth. Never had I seen lips so unappealing. Were women here at such a premium that I, Olivia Givens, of unremarkable countenance, should be somehow in demand?

I composed myself on the settee. I concentrated on Mr. Mumford's feet that were turned inward, pigeon-style. His teacup clattered.

"You like it here?" he said.

And to think I had been merely civil to him at the market.

"At the boardinghouse?" My eyes grazed the clock.

"Cincinnati, I mean."

"We have been here for nearly nine years," I said, and tolerantly, in my opinion, for his tone implied that my accent betrayed a recent arrival, yet there are accents far thicker than mine.

"Yes, but . . . you're from Ireland."

I held my breath for a second, exhaled loudly. What was Ireland to me but a boggy land from the past? I regarded the fabric of Mr. Mumford's coat and trousers. The colors were not quite right. No doubt the cloth was piece-dyed and would soon fade. "What do you do, Mr. Mumford?"

"Me? Well, ma'am, I'm a surveyor. I make maps."

This sounded promising. A maker of maps might be just the thing. After all, there was a whole frontier to explore, and I, for one, was willing.

"So you go into the wilderness and count the hills and plot the streams and . . . ?"

"I ensure the streets run square."

"Ah," said I, slumping a little. "Well, they do, don't they? Not all hodgepodge like in Ireland." Again, I glanced at the clock, but there was no mercy there. "And where do *your* people come from, Mr. Mumford?"

"Mine? Why, I'm Ohio born. But my parents came from Virginia."

"And before that?"

"Virginia."

"And before that?"

"Virginia."

"Ah. Do you read?"

"Books?"

I smiled with such exquisite patience that he must have taken my expression as encouragement, for he perked up and pressed on. "I read the papers. Front to back. I'm interested in politics." He leaned forward. "I'm thinking of running for office."

"No!" said I. Through the window I could see an old Negro whipping a horse that was refusing to pull a dray.

"'Course it'll be easier to sell myself if I have a wife."

"Ah."

"So I'm in the market." He puckered and moistened those rosebud lips.

At that moment, I longed to be back on the ship in the middle of the Atlantic, unfettered by the obligation to marry. One of the sailors had made a loop in the halyard and hoisted me up, shoving me hard to leeward and sending me out over the water. Although my dress had flown about immodestly, I had cared not in the least. For that brief, thrilling moment, I had grasped the line, spun and soared.

I knew what I was supposed to say. Hatsepha Peckham had instructed me about how to maintain the interest of a suitor.

"I suppose you will want to look at my sampler."

"Well, I figgered you could sew." Mr. Phinneaus Mumford put down his teacup with a little chink of expectation.

Outside, the racket persisted. The whipped horse was now rearing back, its eyes bulging horribly as it struggled against the bit.

"Honestly," I said. "How people treat their creatures. Can you not make him stop?"

Mr. Phinneaus Mumford said, "It is best to leave others to their business."

Perhaps Mr. Phinneaus Mumford had an unseen quality I had yet to appreciate. I said hopefully, "I wonder, Mr. Mumford. Do you own a piano?"

"Ma'am, I live in a hotel. I possess no furniture."

"And yet you are in the market for a wife. When we met each other, I thought you were shopping for tomatoes."

I longed for Erasmus, who would at least see the comedy in the situation. *Livvie,* he would say, *I believe you have an appointment with the doctor. That terrible rash on your hands* . . .

"Tell me, Mr. Mumford. What recommends you?"

He was clearly taken aback that so plain a woman should request he make his case. "We Mumfords have been in America for four generations. I've got people in Virginia. You're . . . well. Miss Hatsepha Peckham said you had no prospect of attachment."

"Did she? How remarkable. Did you court her first?"

"Well, I . . ."

"She's awfully rich."

"Yes, I . . ."

"Perhaps a little stout, but should she abstain from butter and cream . . ."

"I did not . . ."

"Good breeder, I would imagine. I, alas, have no meat on my bones. You want to have a look?"

I stood and rotated, ever so slightly lifting my skirts.

Mr. Phinneaus Mumford departed soon thereafter.

CHAPTER 6

1828

Opportunity was as scarce as it was fickle, and though Mr. Mumford was not what one would call a catch, I was well aware that he could be my only fish. I did not need James to remind me, though he most certainly did.

What were you thinking, Olivia? Could you not have been more cordial to the man?

The twin perils of spinsterhood—poverty and charity—loomed like the summer heat. I believe I might have reversed myself and exerted some charm were it not for Erasmus's return.

I had sponged myself off beneath my nightdress, tied up my pantaloons, and slipped into a chemise and two petticoats before stepping into my dress. Twisting my pigtails into loops, I went down to a breakfast of lard-soaked eggs after which I arranged chairs in the parlor to face the mantel in front of which I set an easel and a slate. The children I tutored were of various ages, woefully ignorant of sums and grammar, not to mention history, verse, or Latin. I was not partial to children, but funds were short, and I refused to take in sewing. Still, when faced with the sullen pout of a reluctant scholar, I could feel Opportunity dim to the point of extinction.

It was on such a dimly lit day (no sun, no gaiety) that I heard a pounding at the door. The lesson had already been interrupted by the lunatic landlady shrieking about a roguish rooster. The whoops of Mrs. Humphries and the cackles of the indignant bird had been enough to wake the dead. From the back of the house, Mrs. Humphries was still cursing, though the rooster had grown abruptly quiet. Now with her girl busily tending to the landlady's wounds, it was left to me to greet our caller.

"Excuse me," I said to a pale-lashed youth named Colin to whom I was teaching the Latin verb *vincere*. Snapping my primer shut, I rose. When I opened the door, my heart began to pound. "Land sakes," I exclaimed. "The Prodigal!"

Erasmus looked as peaked as an Ohio winter.

"Has nothing changed in these six months?" Erasmus said, jerking his head in the direction of Humphries's outrage.

Then we were in each other's arms. Through his woolly coat, I could feel his ribs. When we released each other, he coughed.

"You are ill."

"Where is James?" Erasmus asked once he managed to regain his breath.

"Where do you think?"

I did not tell him that poor James had been pining over the soon-to-depart Julia Morrissey, having spent the last month navigating Presbyterian Cincinnati only to have the lady elude him by chasing after a wayward child or grabbing a platter to refill.

Do I smell like a hillbilly? James had asked after his last muddled attempt at engaging Miss Morrissey.

But Erasmus truly *did* smell like a hillbilly and worse—as if he had absorbed every odor of wood and swampland, highway and bog.

"Have you been sleeping in hay?" I asked.

"When lucky." His eyes were moist and yellow.

My wan little scholar was staring gape-mouthed at Erasmus from behind the settee.

"Colin," I said. "That is all for today. Head along home now."

With a hoot, he rushed out the door, but not without one backward glance at Erasmus, who, in his black coat and hat, looked like a crow.

Erasmus slumped to a stool by the fireplace and was warming his hands from the coals. He removed his hat. Out tumbled shoulder-length, unkempt hair. His whole body seemed to thaw.

"Almost six months, Erasmus! And not one word!"

"Livvie," he said, "let me catch my breath."

WHEN HE LEFT CINCINNATI, Erasmus had but one sermon to his name, and this he'd perfected, ridding it of all lofty language and lowering the tone so as not to offend any howling Methodist he might meet in the thick of the forest. It was a simple sermon about Hell and Salvation, composed of words that Every Man could understand: a litany of slaughterhouse-inspired images complete with eyeballs melting, sizzling flesh, and disembowelment.

For months, he had traveled road and path and untrammeled woods, hundreds of miles, evangelizing to as many weary, isolated souls as he could find before his overly zealous conversion of a smithy's wife forced him to flee New Richmond.

"'Conversion'?" said I, my eyebrow raised.

Finding respite across the river in Kentucky, he had come upon a village that had one modest church, a dry-goods store, and a platform from which to auction crops and flesh. Tobacco and hemp greened the fields as far as the eye could see. The people were friendly, and their accent gentle, so that when they inquired of his business, Erasmus could understand them and they him even with the remaining bit of Irish that strapped his tongue.

Do folks here know the love of God and Jesus? Erasmus had asked of a cobbler while dipping a cloth into a bucket to wipe his neck.

That they do, sir—only it's most likely the ladies who are intimate with either.

Erasmus had nodded, for it had been his experience that the women seemed happy for an excuse to stop their laundering, mending, or churning for a spell. Some of them even redid their braids as he talked to them of the Lord, their faces intent on his, their lips parted. *Not often we get strangers in these parts,* they'd say. *That last preacher was dang near fifty.*

The village lay at the juncture of farmland and thoroughfare. Mules, crops, and slaves heading south; cotton and rice going north. Below a platform outside the cobbler's shop, a crowd was assembled, straining their necks and talking among themselves. *Not worth much,* someone said. *A lean crop, if you ask me.* Hearing somebody cussing, saying, *Here now, you stand still,* Erasmus had spotted a black woman atop the platform. She wasn't much to look at. A short leg had made her posture crooked. The auctioneer praised her docility, giving her a pinch every time she tried to move away. Her hands dangled at her side, but there were bruises on her wrists. People milled about. Some of them reached to touch her. *Scrawny,* one man said to another. *Sickly-like.*

The bidding started, but in a desultory fashion, so that the auctioneer became impatient. A man approached from the crowd—probably the seller—and whispered something in his ear. When the auctioneer spoke again, he extolled the woman as a breeder. *Look here,* he said, pulling up her chemise, *as full of milk as a cow in spring. There's more to be had, and she'll feed others till her next one comes.* The auctioneer had squeezed her breast until her clothes were soaked clear through.

Erasmus paused. "What if that had been you, Livvie?"

I shuddered. That was *not* me, would *never* be me, but I could not rid myself of the image.

After leaving the auction, Erasmus had ridden along hemp fields, stopping at a well pump along the edge of a field where ten or so slaves tilled the soil. The women kept their eyes averted, but a couple of the men looked up.

Hail, brothers, said Erasmus, *have you heard the Good Word?*

Hain't heard one good word from a white man, muttered one of the younger men.

An older woman shushed him.

Mistuh, you got something to eat?

In the land of milk and honey, no man will go hungry, Erasmus said.

We's heard all about that milk and honey, and we is wondering when we might get us some.

Then you must follow Jesus, Erasmus said, almost convincing himself as he launched into his sermon, exhorting them to remember Sodom and Gomorrah and how the sinful cities burned. He exhorted them to remember Moses and the Ten Commandments. He exhorted them about the flood. He was right in the middle of exhorting them to drop everything like Simon Peter and walk away to follow Jesus when the overseer rode up and got wind of his exhortations. Erasmus was in full force with a story about Potiphar, who freed his slave, his *Lord sayeth*s and *Praise Jesus*es coming fast and loud, and why shouldn't they, like Potiphar's slave Joseph, be set free? Sweat had gathered beneath the brim of his hat. He barely noticed the overseer until the man on the horse shouted, *Hey there!* and whipped the ground.

"Did Sam Mutton really think I could reach these sorry souls?" Erasmus asked during a pause in the story.

The slaves had gone back to their tilling. The man on the horse jerked his head. *Ye best be going,* said the overseer. *Next time I see you talking to my folks here, I'll have you arrested for inciting slaves.*

"And then what?" I asked, horrified at the picture my brother was painting.

"More of the same." In many fields, he could see the bent backs of men, women, and children culling and weeding as he rode through farmland, turning finally into woods. Dismounting by a stream, he had tied his boots to his saddle and led his horse to the water. Mosquitoes harassed him, his feet stank from his boots, and he was allover itchy from sleeping in a hayloft several nights before. The mud in the stream was warm and soft as a feather down mattress. Back on the shore, he picked off leeches, watching the blood trickle down through the hair on his calves.

That night there was little moonlight, yet he could see every detail of pine needle, of bark, of scurrying night creature. The tall pines groaned, obscuring the stars. For lack of anything better to do, he knelt and prayed.

It was during that camp he'd started shaking, gripped by freezing so profound he lay convulsing on the ground, wrapped in a blanket, ice flowing in his veins. When the sun was high, he began to burn up and became desperate for water.

He was halfway into the stream when a man found him and dragged him out. With lips that were nearly purple, the man said, *I thought you was a corpse.*

He nearly was, only this time there was no fever-induced vision of God in a column of smoke. So befuddled was he that at first Erasmus didn't notice the man going through his pockets and his knapsack before tossing it down.

You as penniless as me, said the man, disgusted.

"I was sure he was going to kill me," said Erasmus.

Perhaps the man was the Devil. Black as the Devil he was. Metal bands gripped his wrists, each with a chain link dangling like a jewel. Leaden-eyed, he was unshaven and nearly as emaciated as Erasmus.

Have you come to slay me? Erasmus said, clutching the blanket, his teeth chattering. Around the man's matted hair, the air seemed to shimmer.

I's as good as dead myself, said the man, raising his banded hands above his head as if pleading for release.

Have ye repented? Erasmus managed through shaking lips, making a silent deal with God if only he were spared.

The man stared down, studying Erasmus like a word on a page. *You that preacher that come by our field.*

Erasmus coiled himself into the blanket even tighter. He weighed his answer, feeling his life might depend on it. *I am,* he confessed, swearing he could hear Jesus sigh at his stupidity.

The man's eyes narrowed. *Overseer shooed you off.*

Erasmus had read some abolitionist letters and could quote a line or two. This moment seemed as good as any to preach abolition, for hadn't Sam Mutton told him to understand the varied needs of his congregations so that he might better light the candle of Jesus in their hearts?

Thy color is not the mark of Cain, brother, said Erasmus through his chattering teeth. *Rather, it is the effect of climate.*

Getting no response, he pushed on, quoting Acts. *God hath made of one blood all nations of men. Wheresoever we find a man, let us treat him as a brother without regard to his color.*

The man looked at him as if he were a simpleton. *Got any whiskey?* he asked.

Alas, I am a preacher. This said piously if regretfully.

No money. No whiskey. You a po' excuse for a white man. Arms crossed, the runaway slave assessed Abel, who was tied to a tree. *If I heft you on that sorry ol' mule, you can show me the way north. If anyone aks, I's yours.*

Erasmus doubted that anyone would believe a Methodist minister would actually own a slave, but he figured it could save his life if they could just get to someone's house or farm. The manacles dug into his ribs as the slave heaved him onto Abel. It was midday, and the sun filtered through the pollen of the forest. Even in his weakened state, Erasmus could read the moss on the trees that told him which direction lay north. North would take them to the river in a day or two of walking.

This way, brother, Erasmus said, jerking his head east.

You sure?

Erasmus said he'd bet his life on it.

For half a day they walked. When they spoke, it was in curt sentences like, *My wife was sick like you.* Or from Erasmus, *And where is your wife?* To which the man responded, *Back on the farm.*

Children?

Six. One dead. Two sold. Three still living with us, thank the Lord.

After that, they walked in silence. Erasmus could sit almost erect now, his thoughts clearing to the point where he could make a plan. And here was the plan he made: to return the slave to the farm he came from, to explain to the owner that the man should be allowed to stay with his wife, and that Erasmus, as a minister of God, wanted to make sure the union was honored. Surely the family would understand.

You must be missing your wife. And if I say so, my guess is that she's missing you.

The man began to weep.

"You *did* take him back?" I asked, feeling a newfound compassion.

"I did, Livvie. I did."

"And then what?"

Neither of us had noticed James standing by the parlor door. We started at his voice. "So have ye converted the masses, then?" said James.

"Alas," said Erasmus, rising to greet our brother, "only one."

CHAPTER 7

1828

Reluctantly, James rehired Erasmus, and for a while, our younger brother was diligent in his efforts. But if James hoped that Erasmus had exhausted his sprint into evangelism, he was sorely disappointed. By August, Erasmus had recovered from the ague and was once again robust. And with robustness came the spirit. Before we knew it, Erasmus had taken Sam Mutton's place on a soapbox on Sundays.

"Oh dear," said Hatsepha after church. "Was that your brother I saw down at the landing shouting 'Alleluia' like a madman?"

I pretended not to hear.

"Now, your *other* brother," said Hatsepha, jerking her head at James, who was shadowing poor Miss Julia Morrissey with the tenacity of an alms seeker. "I believe he has had a conversion of his own."

Indeed, James was hoping to impress Julia Morrissey by singing hymns in a full-throated manner that did not become him.

"I told my father that James Givens has indeed changed his ways," Hatsepha went on. "He sings with such gusto. I believe I even saw his lips move when we said the Creed."

James had, in fact, been reviewing accounts in his head. *Ten crates of tapers to Mitford, five to Warren. Six dollars, twenty-four cents.* But far be it from me to disabuse Miss Hatsepha Peckham.

"But I won't miss that Reverend Morrissey," Hatsepha said. "Awful man." Then slyly—"And your brother James? Shall he miss the Morrisseys?"

I could see Julia Morrissey on the church steps kneeling down and fussing over some children. The tableau was endearing—her glorious auburn hair swept back, lace clustered about her perfect neck.

Hatsepha and I watched as James broke away from a group of gentlemen and headed toward her. I wondered if he could feel our eyes penetrating his back as Miss Hatsepha Peckham did some calculations of her own.

IN OCTOBER, Erasmus announced that he was off again—this time to a revival in Kentucky.

"I tell you, Erasmus," said James, fed up with our brother's unreliability, "I'll not be hiring ye again."

"And what about me?" I said, hands on my hips. "Fine for *men* to go off and explore the world. Or drag their families across the sea."

"Souls, Livvie," said Erasmus, "thirsting for hope."

"Pshaw!" I said. "Good riddance. You will not be seeing me at such a spectacle."

Perhaps it was because Erasmus had one too many times needled me for being solitary, but when the day came and my younger brother was saddling up his nag, Abel, I found I could not bear another evening in this parlor, starved for conversation, waiting for some maker of maps to come along and deem me worthy to bear his brood. Though I had no stomach for making goggly eyes and writhing about, I decided to cast away caution and asked to tag along.

"But, Livvie," said Erasmus. "Abel can barely carry *me*. And who will you bunk with?"

"Mrs. Humphries has that old cart in the back of the privy. The wheels work. All it needs are reins. And aren't these gatherings about love and generosity? And shouldn't such generosity extend to *me*?"

"James won't hear of it."

"Oh, a fine specimen of hypocrisy you are. You, who has never cared a whit when it came to James's opinion."

"Very well," said Erasmus. "But do not blame me if you contract the ague."

"It shall be worth it. Besides," I said, my eyebrow arched, "how are you to know if the soul that is saved might not be mine?"

"DON'T WORRY, JAMES," I said to my glowering older brother. "I shall watch after Erasmus and he after me."

James's mouth tightened. No doubt he thought that, once we loaded cart and horse and valises onto a wobbly ferry, we mightn't return. And to compound his wretchedness, the Morrisseys had departed Cincinnati the prior week. I waved at him as our little barge pulled away from the landing.

How the river had changed since we had traveled down its course just ten years earlier. I felt as if I was given a front-row seat. A filigreed, double-decked steamboat swanned past us, its decks glutted with gorgeously attired passengers who barely noticed a preacher and his sister with their pitiful wagon and their pitiful horse on the nondescript ark below. My neck ached from looking up. I could not wait for the day when I could take a trip on one of these majesties—maybe up to Pittsburgh.

We disembarked at Augusta about ten miles upriver, hooked up the wagon to the nag, and started down the cobbled road. The pretty town of Augusta gave way to woodland and then to farmland worked by slaves. I tried not to stare at the dark figures, bent like commas in the field or standing by the road, leaning against stumps or fences, watching the parade of visitors.

"They look sapped," I said, remembering the scene that Erasmus described. "Poor things."

"Kentucky," said Erasmus, "is a whole different story from Ohio."

I, for one, did not ken to the idea of owning and selling people like livestock. It was generally ill-regarded back in Cincinnati, though if you raised the topic, everyone became fascinated with the weather.

Already we were falling into the company of other pilgrims: two elderly women, a hatter from Maysville.

"Hail, brother," said a farmer who was managing a pair of draft horses that pulled his family in a wagon. "Hail, sister." He took in Erasmus's coat, the wide-brimmed hat and collar. "You must be heading to the revival."

"Indeed," said Erasmus. He leaned over to me and, in a low voice, said, "I know your mind, Livvie. But at least try to muster some enthusiasm."

"Hail," I said flatly, thinking Erasmus's unusually stern tone sounded remarkably like James. "Alleluia."

"Alleluia!" said the farmer, echoed by his three towheaded children.

The air was rife with pine and tobacco and harvested hemp. Autumn thistle nipped at Abel's fetlocks as we fell into a companionable trot. Whole families—including slaves, chickens, and sheep—joined the procession as if everyone had heard the call. For an entire day, in wagons and on foot, upon horses and mules, we swarmed the road as it diminished to a lane, a trail, a field, hooves and wheels pummeling the sod and grinding it to dust.

"Heavens," I said, fanning myself with my bonnet, "what a horde." I nervously eyed the hatter from Maysville, who had joined us some miles back. Riding alongside us, he had been prattling on to Erasmus that he was fleeing persecution.

"What is it that persecutes you?" Erasmus asked.

"Demons," said the hatter.

"Demons?" said I, looking at the insects buzzing about his face. "Why, sir, 'tis flies."

"Flies to you," said the hatter with an evil look.

He pulled ahead and was replaced at our side by a slave chauffeuring the two old women in a carriage who had been traveling for days, having heard about the revival from a neighbor who heard it from a seed salesman who read it on a flyer in Versailles, Kentucky.

"Have you heard the Word of the Lord?" they said cheerfully, leaning forward in the carriage.

"Alleluia," said I.

There was talk of little else.. Who would be preaching? How many people might gather? Whatever glory awaited us was sure to pale in comparison to the shared confections of our speculation.

And then we were upon the revival camp—a vast field already dotted by tents and reverberating with the din of sawing and pounding, shouting and song. Erasmus scanned the landscape, trying to find a pattern in the chaos or at least a face he recognized. Then he spotted the farmer we had hailed on the road, who, with his three children, was setting to string a rope between some trees and build a shelter.

"Hail, brother," said Erasmus, navigating us to the site. "We are wondering if we might keep you company in this paradise?" He jerked his head at me in the dray beside him. "A little tabernacle for my sister."

The farmer, whose name was Fenton, looked at the oldest girl, who shrugged. "My wife says it is all right. You and I can sleep out under the stars 'less it rains."

His *wife*? The girl looked barely sixteen—and already a mother of two! "Thank you kindly," I said, dismounting from the carriage with the help of Fenton. I was coated with dust and needed to relieve myself, but I could see little prospect of privacy.

As if he read my mind, Fenton said, "They've set latrines up yonder. You might want to keep Caroline company."

Thanking him, I walked with his young wife to a sheeted area that enclosed a series of holes in the ground and buckets of water. It made the amenities at Mrs. Humphries's seem luxurious, but I was so happy to be away from that boardinghouse that I gathered my skirts up around my waist and squatted. Seeing as Caroline was squatting next to me, I said, "How long have you been married?"

"Four years," she said. With her dress pulled up, I could see her burgeoning belly and knew she was with child.

"Fenton looks a bit older than you."

She did not seem to take offense. Just stood up from where she was squatting and fixed her pantaloons into place. "Old enough to be my daddy. But then, my daddy and ma are dead, as is Fenton's first wife and family. So me and Fenton . . . we started over. Praise be to God."

"Praise be to God," said I, though given the death of Fenton's family and Caroline's parents, I was unsure as to what we were praising.

We walked back to the camp, where Erasmus and Fenton had managed to wrestle a couple of tarps into not-half-bad shelters. Fenton was describing how his family, along with several others, including Caroline's parents, had been scalped and left to die. "You know, Brother Erasmus, if it weren't for the comfort I find in the Word, I fear I might not have been able to carry on. Four girls and a boy—all dead. A wife so lovely it would make you weep. That was the end of Illinois. You can have Illinois as far as I'm concerned."

Erasmus took a tobacco leaf out of his pouch and deliberately rolled it. "Well, you have a lovely wife now," he said. "Young."

That evening after we had eaten a meal of fried corn and stew and were walking back toward the tent, I grabbed Erasmus and made him face me. He had an inch or two on me, but I could rear up, and that evening I did, looking him so hard in the eye and stating in no uncertain terms that he would not abuse the friendship of farmer Fenton no matter how young and comely his wife, no matter how many sidelong glances she tossed at him, no matter if she thought Erasmus was the Second Coming.

"Livvie, I have no idea what you are talking about."

I narrowed my eyes. "Look, Erasmus, these people have a second chance. Do not go saving one soul too many."

FOR THE FIRST FEW DAYS, I watched Erasmus around Caroline like a raptor. Once or twice I saw his eyes linger and imagined him imagining her. At night, I slept on hastily made beds of straw next to Caroline and the two children. The ground was hard, and the ignominy of lying among strangers took me back to the tight quarters of our Atlantic crossing. We ladies did our best with our hair and the cleanliness of our garments, but in the end, we sacrificed our comportment and made do with the dirt and the flies and the shocking lack of privacy.

In the morning, I helped Caroline with the wash and tending to the children. Children have always been drawn to me, though I know not why. I was fierce and ill-tempered, and my resemblance to a hawk had been remarked upon more than once. Nevertheless, there was excitement—the excitement of expectation. Even *I* felt it, though I was sure I had nothing in common with most of the assembled that were hoping for Second Comings or at least an assurance that Jesus had not plain forgotten them like a hand-me-down pair of gloves.

"So do you really think the spirit comes into you, Caroline?"

"Oh, who knows?" said Caroline as she busily chased the toddler who, but for being a boy, looked just like her. Her calico skirts twirled around and settled. "But Fenton puts it in me either way."

That old goat, I thought. But a flash of envy swept through me.

"Sister," said Caroline, "have you ever . . ."

"No," I said quickly. "I am unmarried."

"But your brother's mighty fine."

For the first time, I discerned keenness in eyes that had otherwise struck me as dull. I said, "He *is* my brother."

To which she said, "And we are all in the wilderness."

ALL THE NEXT DAY and the day after that, the racket of call and response, the hollers of hucksters calling to a captive audience of pilgrims, the songs of worshippers threatening to ignite the sere grass. I expect there were a thousand people and from all over, given the different accents. Indians, too, and Negroes, some even of the free variety, who had started their own churches in the North. I tagged along after Erasmus as he visited every camp, looking for affiliation. At night, the fireflies competed with the glow of lanterns and cook fires. A makeshift band of a banjo, a harmonica, and a fiddle sounded out the notes of a melodic and righteous God.

Praise God from whom all blessings flow . . .

Sparks flew. Leaves reddened, the damp air presaging winter. I pulled my shawl tighter around my shoulders. There were several men looking at me. *Dear lord,* thought I.

It looked like half the population of the border states had congregated, if not to worship, then to socialize in what might otherwise be a bacchanal, had more liquor been available. This little city of tents was teeming, and it was easy to get lost. Turn this way, and you would end up with the Baptists. Miss your lane, and some Holy Rollers would have you in their midst. I came across scenes I shall never forget: men blessing women in overly familiar ways; the next moment, someone crying out praise, or just crying out, weeping, apparently, from joy.

In the end, it was not Caroline whom I had to watch. On separate platforms, groups of preachers teamed up to damn or save our sorry souls. I have never heard such palavering before or since—*Amen!* and *Glory!* and *Sweet Jesus!*—a frenzy, mind you, completely without restraint.

Born of sin, ye are. And but for the Lord's forgiveness, in sin ye shall die.

I was crammed between Caroline and one of the ladies from Versailles. Erasmus stood at the back of the tent in hope of special vantage from which to study the orators. Tonight's fare was Presbyterian, but it was no Presbyterianism I recognized. The first man who took the stage began to pace back and forth and query the congregation. Had we looked into our souls? (Evidently, we had not.) Did we know Jesus as a friend? A personal friend? Really? How? If we thought we knew Jesus, was it not possible that it was Satan in the *guise* of Jesus—a wolf in sheep's clothing—for hadn't we all sinned by gambling, swearing, whoring, drinking, cheating, and thinking unclean thoughts? (I confess to the last in this litany.)

Did we *want* to know Jesus?

Those among us who were most eager (assuredly not I) were invited to the front to sit upon the "anxious bench" while a succession of preachers worked their magic. The second preacher took the stage, and I gasped, for there he stood in all his ghoulish glee—no one better suited to treat us to images of hell, for he was so well versed in the subject that I suspected he might have actually visited the place—Ephraim Morrissey, the pious purveyor of pornography packaged as preaching who had left Cincinnati two weeks earlier.

"Those who will not repent shall be eternally damned," Morrissey roared, ". . . in tar-laden air that shall choke the breath . . ."

I was stunned to see him, for I was under the impression that he had left to take up a new congregation. Next to me, Caroline began to squirm. She had not yet risen to the anxious bench, but her discomfort was palpable. With each acid word, I could feel her sweet ardor succumb to Morrissey's tongue. Conjuring from Deuteronomy, "the waste howling wilderness" and "the teeth of beasts and the poison of crawling things," he exhorted that many of us were already condemned with no hope of redemption.

"You are shaking, sister," I said to Caroline.

"And you are not?"

Dusk now. On the face of the reverend, torchlight rendered the terrain of Hades. The crowd was in his thrall as if mesmerized by the bared fangs of a snake. Looking into each of us, he said, "The Devil will push himself into the boudoir of your wives and daughters, seizing their weak souls, possessing them for himself . . ."

Then we heard it.

"Alleluia."

It came from the back of the room. A shuffling as some turned to see who had tossed this white stone into Morrissey's murky pond.

"Alleluia."

"Oh dear," I said, for by the second time he spoke, I knew it was my brother. He was striding down the aisle, a look of determination both in his gait and on his face.

Please no, I thought.

"Calm yourself, Brother Ephraim," shouted Erasmus, bounding up onto the stage. He took the Reverend Morrissey by the shoulders, affronting the older man to the point of dumbness. Then he turned toward the crowd. "We must all thank the righteous reverend, but I bring good news. Behold, the Lamb of God!" Sweeping his gaze across us, Erasmus cried out, "Lo! I come to speak of salvation, not tribulation. The time of the singing of the birds is come!" He raised his arms. "Alleluia!"

A murmur of confusion erupted all around me. Caroline said, "Sweet mercy. Is that your brother?"

Erasmus cleared his throat. His eye bored into every individual in the first row. His voice brimmed with emotion as he shouted even louder, "Alleluia!"

This time the crowd responded with a tentative "Alleluia?"

"Jesus died so that God may shower us with His mercy. And there shall be upon the fields a great flowering of hope. Alleluia!"

With more certainty now—"Alleluia!"

"What?" said Morrissey.

"Jesus suffered on the cross so that we could rise. And the angels will come to lift us up. The time is nigh. Alleluia!"

"Alleluia!"

"For the year of jubilee is come!"

"Alleluia! Alleluia! Alleluia!"

Even I joined in, albeit weakly. By the fifth alleluia, many had begun to weep in response to Erasmus's promise of joy on earth in spite of Man's lowly condition and horrible sins if only they would come to Jesus, come to Jesus, come ye sinners, come.

And out of the crowd she came, her arms thrust forward, her palms turned upward as if she was pleading—the beautiful girl who had won the heart of James. Her transformation was so extreme that I barely recognized that gracious creature. Her auburn locks had descended into chaos, her lovely eyes gone wild. So possessed seemed she that, had I been a Catholic, I would have crossed myself. As it was, I could only gawk while one by one the congregation took note of her, the last one being Erasmus, who was so busy issuing glad tidings that he was unaware until she was only feet away. Upon seeing her, he paused but a moment before his torrent of words increased in pace and volume like a river after a squall. He spared nothing, even as Julia Morrissey crawled onto the stage and knelt before him, shoulders convulsing. Indeed, were he to lie right down then and there and personally bestow rapture upon the prostrate woman, I would not have been surprised. But Ephraim Morrissey stepped in.

"Daughter," said Morrissey gruffly, taking her arm. "Stand up."

But she did not stand. Instead she wrestled away from him and threw herself at Erasmus's feet. Erasmus placed his hand on her brow and lowered his voice.

"Come, sister. Come to Jesus."

The crowd let out a collective sigh as if they had all been taken in holy consummation and, indeed, in love.

Ephraim Morrissey glared, an inferno of rage just beneath his skin. "Beware, my son, or the land will vomit you out."

Erasmus took Julia's hand and helped her to her feet. "No more shall we quiver and quake before a vengeful God, for the Word of God is Love, and Love shall lift us up." Ephraim Morrissey opened his mouth to protest, but his words were drowned out as the captivated crowd burst into a rousing rendition of "Blow, Ye Trumpets! Blow!"

"Well," said Caroline, while everyone around us bellowed, "your brother sure has a knack."

CHAPTER 8

1828–1829

I plunked down on my bed and threw off my hat. My hair was a sight, and my shoes were ruined, and I dearly wanted to boil some water and take a brush to my skin. Any minute now, James would return, and here I was, a heap of filth and disarray and no small situation to explain, though it hardly seemed up to me, but who else knew of James's intentions—and besides, James *would* hold me accountable regardless of anything I might say, whether it was to tell him how the Reverend Morrissey had blown smoke like the Devil, or that Fenton and the hatter had to intervene and hustle us out in the middle of the night, the marriage having been performed by a Methodist preacher from Louisville who, by last count, had hitched twelve couples in less than a week. No matter that Erasmus and Julia had known each other barely two days at the hour of their betrothal, and both believing that it was "fate"—a laughable view, in my opinion, having far less to do with "fate" than a pressing physical urge, the consummation of which, I am certain, preceded the nuptials, and me all stiff and cramped for having had to share the hard bench on the wagon ride home with yet another body who now occupied the only chair in my bedroom, staring out the window.

"Julia," I said to my new sister-in-law, who held a pair of gloves in her hands as if she was prepared to leave at any moment. "Were you aware that my brother James had set his heart on you?"

"Oh."

It was a punctuation—nay, not even that, for an "oh" that carries the weight of a question mark or an exclamation would have an inflection—*something*—that betrayed emotion. This was an "oh" so devoid of compassion or shock or dismay that I suspected she was unable to *place* James or could hardly recall having met him. That she was drained and spent, to my mind, hardly excused her, for I was girding myself to intercept my brother, and not with happy news.

And so, when the time came, I met James at the door, having prepared a little speech about how Erasmus had not known of James's infatuation (would it have mattered?) and how it was in the passion of the moment that Julia had been swept away (*such* passion, I might add, that any memory she might have had of James paled like the flick of a match to the roar of a forest fire).

Instead, I blurted out, "Erasmus has taken a wife . . ." but was unable to finish, for James had already entered the parlor and beheld Julia, a look of delight infusing his expression to such a degree it would break your heart.

"Miss Morrissey?"

"Oh," said she, and this time she could not quite hide the dawning realization of her betrayal, intentional or not, for had not James Givens paid close attention at church socials, taking special care to seek her out—although, truth be told, there were so many gentlemen in Cincinnati who pressed their case upon Julia Morrissey, yet none of them, not one, including James, stirring in her the inexplicable lurch of longing that Erasmus Givens had when he stood up to and so passionately contradicted her father.

Everyone else seems scared of my father, she told me on the ride home. *And with good reason,* she had added without elaboration.

I wished that I'd stood up to Ephraim Morrissey myself, but confronting ministers has never served me well.

Erasmus set down his pipe and took Julia's hand. "James, I have wonderful news. Miss Morrissey and I are married."

James made a sound—something between a cough and a retch. He stared at Julia so long I thought he was having a seizure. "Married?"

"Brother," said Julia, extending her hand.

James wrenched his gaze from her to Erasmus. "To you?"

In the light of the parlor filled with Givens candles, Julia's hair was more burnished than ever.

"On Sunday," added Erasmus as if this explained it.

James crossed to the fire. It reflected in his eyes and, for a moment, turned them red. "Well then," he said, clapping his hands and blowing on them as if overtaken with a chill. "Congratulations. Congratulations to you both."

"Jamie," I said, staring at those wax-blackened hands. They were beautiful hands, their long fingers once intended for paging through books, not for manual labor. He stared at the mantelpiece that bore a pair of his most exquisite candles. With two quick bursts of air, he blew them out.

OTHER THAN HER APPARENT ARDOR FOR ERASMUS, it was not clear what had compelled Julia Morrissey to so abruptly and radically leave Ephraim Morrissey. It was generally agreed that only a nefarious situation would allow for a young lady to defy her father. As such, speculation was rife.

They say he beat her. They say he used her as a wife.

Still, said many, her duty *was* to her father.

And then there was Erasmus and the fact of his unsuitability. Most agreed that if she *had* to marry a Givens, James was the more respectable, having at least a business with prospects and a sober demeanor, neither of which could be said for his younger brother.

Yet Miss Julia Morrissey had married Erasmus, a man of words and poetry and grandiose claims of Paradise. Indeed, I could hear them reading aloud the Songs of Solomon. Solomon and the erotic breasts of love. Their heads would bend together, Erasmus would say something, and Julia would laugh about "hair like goats." Had he truly been like Solomon, Erasmus might have compared Julia's hair to a deep forest on a summer's night flecked with stars and lightning bugs and the lust-filled smoke of campfires.

Read me that part again about the lover's breasts.

"*. . . thou art fair, my love; yea, pleasant: also our bed is green . . .*"

Those early days of love. The way she looked at him, I could not help but wonder how it would feel to be regarded so.

Now winter was upon us, and we had taken refuge under quilts. I listened for the first bells of morning as I contemplated the acquisition of a sister. That I and not Erasmus would lie alongside Julia may seem unorthodox, but space was lacking, and so we had to double up. Nor should it suggest connubial interaction between the couple was negligible, for Julia was now with child. I shall not go into detail as to the arrangement, but suffice to say there *was* one, and those hours when James was at his workshop were the most fortuitous for Julia and Erasmus if inconvenient for me.

So there was I beside the sleeping Julia. James would be gone to the workshop, and soon I would rise and break the ice in the basin. The day was coming to life with the usual crowing, bleating, clopping, and hollering. I could smell bacon frying in the cookhouse. Mrs. Humphries made griddle cakes most mornings, but sometimes she made fritters from a recipe taught to her by a man passing through to Michigan. Still sore about Erasmus's reappearance, she would go on and on about how she had no use for these itinerants and why did he not settle down with a regular church, and what with his waking up the whole house on more than one occasion, croaking about redemption not to mention his nightly ranting brought on by recurring fever. Erasmus swore as soon as he was well, he would be on the road again in spite of his wife's condition.

In the meantime, Julia was either throwing up or wan with fatigue. James could barely look at her and never addressed her by name, but I saw how he fixed her candlewick and once brought her a case of Louisiana lemons to ease the sickness. Julia accepted these gifts with a smile that betrayed neither gratitude nor pity.

I untwisted my chemise and fought for a piece of the blanket.

"What is it?" Julia said as she rolled over onto her side. In the narrow bed, her rump pressed into me. I lay on my back, gazing at the ceiling. Julia's nightcap had come loose during the night, and the ribbons were tangled in her hair.

"Morning," I said, stating it less as a greeting than a fact.

Julia sat up. A ripe melon of a breast escaped from the front of her nightshirt. I tried not to stare. "I had the strangest dream," she said with a shudder.

I rose and fluffed the quilt, but didn't ask. Perhaps it was to Julia's better nature that Erasmus had appealed, but more than likely it was the promise of escape. That her father was stern was one thing; that he may have been a devil was another. Evil comes in many forms, as I since have learned. But the evil done to Julia by her father was never explicitly stated beyond rumors. Still, you could glean it from her manner whenever his name was mentioned, her refusal to set foot again in the First Presbyterian Church.

The air in the room was darker than the sky. With icy hands, I lit a candle. Behind me, Julia rebraided her hair. That she had such abundant hair was the least of my envy. On those afternoons when Erasmus managed to have the room while James was at work, the amorous sounds coming from the bedroom disturbed me far more than the sounds of Erasmus's delirium, and I burned with shame and desire.

You are so kind, Olivia, Julia often said. But what else is one to do when one has a brother like Erasmus, whose excesses and impulsivity had driven us to distraction ever since he was a lad? *You are a good Christian soul.*

You are a simpleton, I would say with a laugh, restraining myself from tucking a strand behind her ear.

I withdrew my arms into my nightdress and began to tie up my undergarments beneath the muslin. I had not wanted to tell her that being Christian implied faith in all sorts of things, many of which I found preposterous. Most of the "Christians" I knew affected sufficient piety to parade a new hat in church.

An extra room in the boardinghouse was bound to free up eventually. Until then, I would not complain. It was cold and drafty, and what was one more body if it kept me from freezing to death?

I had no sooner pulled on my dress when I heard two raps on the adjoining wall. With an embarrassed look of pleasure, Julia pulled her chemise together and slipped out the door.

JAMES STARTED TO MISS DINNERS ALTOGETHER, preferring instead to eat at his workshop or at one of the hotels or pubs. For his part, Erasmus was more and more in demand in the parlors of Cincinnati ever since the revival, preaching to ladies seduced by grace and forgiveness promised at such a low premium in so persistently gray a winter.

Chillier still was the pall that lay between James and Erasmus like the slick, frozen mud. That Julia and I ate more often than not in each other's company did not escape Mrs. Humphries, who compensated for her lack of an eye with an uncanny sense of the obvious.

"So," she said, sashaying by our table in the dining room, "he doesn't want you standing beside him while he spouts his spilth?"

Julia patted herself on her stomach. Were I Catholic, I might have likened her to Mary. "My husband is protecting me, Mrs. Humphries. When he speaks, there is often hysteria."

"Hysteria, is it? I hear what time he comes in. Preaching in Niggertown, I wouldn't wonder."

Whether Erasmus had been completely forthcoming about his past to Julia was doubtful, but Humphries was eager to drive it home.

"My brother is redeemed, Mrs. Humphries," said I, affecting both indignation and piety. "Not only does he embrace the Lord, but he embraces the fallen."

Mrs. Humphries turned to Julia. "And clearly prefers to do his embracing away from the presence of his wife."

IN SPITE OF JULIA'S GROWING BELLY, Erasmus continued to come to her in the afternoon after my pupils had left, leaving me to fend for myself with few friends and little ardor for stitchery. One gusty day in late March, I could bear their proximity no longer. Donning my jacket, I stepped outside. A cold breeze insinuated its way up the street from the river, masking the pulse of melting water. A dormant lust lay like frost on the cobbles. It lay between Erasmus and Julia in the middle of the night as their breaths threaded together through the wall. It lay in James and in me.

My breath came in puffs, and I warmed my hands beneath my coat as I headed down the road. I wanted to escape as quickly as possible, leaving Erasmus and Julia their hour together, longing to step onto a steamboat to be ferried away.

I had walked barely two blocks when I caught sight of James striding up the other side of the road. I wished I had worn a hat. And how many times had James scolded me for walking unaccompanied?

"Jamie," I yelled, but he didn't seem to hear.

Wrapping my cloak more tightly, I chased after him, but he had already pushed through the door of the boardinghouse. He was halfway up the stairs when I followed him into the hall.

"Jamie?" I called up to him, panting. "Home so early?"

He didn't break his stride, but answered over his shoulder, "Wonderful news, Livvie. Wonderful. I've hurried home to share it."

"But, Jamie!"

He had reached the upstairs hall, his hand already on the knob.

I charged up after him, my cheeks reddening. As he drew the door open, James stiffened and started to withdraw, but not before I saw his shattered face. Seeing me, he straightened.

"Come to the parlor," I said. "Sit with me."

The clock in the parlor ticked as we waited it out. Somewhere in the house, I heard a groan or a creak. A dog barked, and the girl pushed through the front door with a basket of squash and beans.

"Your news?" I said to Jamie. "Tell me."

He allowed himself a deflated smile. "Midas Barker," he said, naming his biggest competitor in the candle business as well as his former boss, who had passed up Jamie for his nephew, "has had to fold his business. Word is, all his accounts shall come to me."

CHAPTER 9

1829

We awaited the coming of Julia's baby by distracting ourselves with debates and lectures. That summer of 1829, culture and curiosity came over the city like the quickening of a maiden's heart. Cincinnati was overrun by fanatics and intellectuals trying to make their case: Caldwell's discourse on phrenology; Miss Fanny Wright on slavery and marriage; Dr. Alexander Campbell and Robert Owen battling the fundamental relationship between godliness and goodliness.

The first I attended was that of Fanny Wright—the Scottish damsel who had arrived in our country to cajole and reform, draped in Grecian simplicity of such looseness and comfort that I found myself breathing more deeply just looking at her. Everyone was uncertain as to what to make of such a specimen. While we women were wired, corseted, bustled, and laced, her figure was unfettered in a slender cut of muslin—out-of-date, to be sure, but daring in its refusal to buttress the body. Charmingly she spoke from the lectern at the hall, linking such sensible notions as personal responsibility and the nobility of man. These were favorite topics of late, along with Virtue and Heroism and Man's Agency in Redemption.

We all knew of Fanny Wright's views regarding slavery; indeed, many agreed, regarding the institution as distasteful to both the enslaver and the enslaved. But nods turned into expressions of bewilderment as Fanny Wright veered onto the topic of marriage. As a single woman, she could not be considered an authority, emancipated as she was from obligation.

But this did not stop her from opining. Marriage, in Miss Fanny Wright's view, was restrictive and demeaning. And not only that—it was cowardly. Why were men forced to resort to prostitutes, she asked of a stunned audience, except to satisfy a natural urge that was suppressed by enforced monogamy and endless childbirth? Marriage afflicts society as sorely as slavery, and since we must insist on procreating, then why not breed between the races, and thus alleviate the social ill of slavery and inequality once and for all?

At which point, many people rose and left the room.

"Fanny Wright buys up slaves like butter and sets them free," Hatsepha whispered. "And this abomination she calls a 'free love' colony down in Tennessee? It completely fell flat. Mosquitoes weren't the least of it."

Hatsepha nodded so vigorously in anticipation of my agreement that I refrained from telling her that Fanny Wright had struck a chord.

FOUR WEEKS LATER, we gathered again for debates, this time between Robert Owen, the Welsh reformer, and the arch-Christian Alexander Campbell. These arguments, so close in the wake of Fanny Wright, went on for days, this being the seventh and, mercifully, the last. Touted as an *Examination of the "Social System" and All the Systems of Skepticism of Ancient and Modern Times,* the debate boiled down to whether Christian belief was essential to a meaningful life. Campbell, a Christian, said yes. Owen, an atheist, said no.

"Lady," someone shouted. "Can you take off your hat?"

"I may expire," said Hatsepha, fanning herself with a pamphlet.

Torpor had taken hold of Cincinnati, as much of the mind as of the humors. A violent downpour in the morning had flooded the streets, washing a stinky soup of garbage toward the river. By afternoon, the sun had reappeared to further cook the brew.

Hatsepha Peckham's headdress—a cornucopia of feathers and lace—was so ambitious that it seemed the very symbol for our small but burgeoning city.

My attire, in contrast, was modest. A satin bow was all I could muster. I had come very close to being persuaded by Dr. Campbell. Indeed, I *longed* to be persuaded by his defense of Christianity. So much easier to subscribe to conventional thought and practice. But skepticism kept creeping back with the tenacity of a cockroach.

You think too much, Livvie, James would say. *You suffer from Opinion.*

People clustered in doorways and windows, and outside, too—all craning to hear the final to-and-fro and, with any luck, the final word. We were fortunate to get seats. "There's James," I said to Hatsepha, who was clinging to her hat lest the woman behind us wrestle it off.

The room was cleaved by gender—the men on the left, the women on the right. Across the aisle, James nodded at Hatsepha and me. He was taking extra care to be cordial to Hatsepha, hoping to ingratiate himself to her father that he might supply all the candles for the Peckham coal mines.

Hatsepha made a mewling sound.

"Some people!" said the woman behind us.

"Please, Hatsepha," I said. "The hat."

She stared straight ahead while the mayor introduced the now notorious debaters. Owen, a man of small stature and rigid tidiness, wore a trim beard and spectacles. In contrast, Campbell looked like a deranged bison with a hoary beard extending past his chest. The argument was clearly Campbell's to lose, for any concession to Owen would refute Cincinnati's whole way of life, just as any concession to

Fanny Wright's views on marriage would have undermined civilization as we knew it.

The audience leaned forward as Dr. Campbell took to the podium. Every time he evoked the afterlife, bonnets bobbed and men stroked their beards as if Dr. Campbell held forth on God's Own Truth.

Which, in fact, was Dr. Campbell's very claim.

When he finished his speech, the room exploded into applause, after which Robert Owen calmly took his place.

"Robert Owen is an ideologue," sniffed Hatsepha. "A charlatan. I can't imagine what he will say."

As Owen commenced to speak, I caught a glimpse of Mr. Phinneaus Mumford, my erstwhile suitor and maker of maps, who had managed a seat toward the front of the room. I wondered if he understood even half of what was being said, particularly the nuances of Owen's argument that virtue for virtue's sake was sufficiently compelling without resorting to threats of hell.

I could not help but agree with Owen that religion was divisive. The Methodists looked down their noses at the waterlogged Baptists; the Presbyterians scorned the Catholics; and no one put stock in the Quakers, who were, to a one, abolitionist.

"Even the Pygmies," Mr. Owen was saying, "have their own little gods."

"Pity he is such a good-looking man," said Hatsepha. "I suppose he will go to hell."

As shall I, I thought, quite certain that hell could be no worse than seven days of debates.

"We are ethical beings innately," said Robert Owen, "while God and religion only lead us to conflict. Dr. Campbell has misconstrued my words to equate marriage with prostitution . . ."—and I thought of Fanny Wright, whose point was exactly that—"and misses the argument altogether by ignoring my very premise that *without* the constricts and confines of the unnatural state of marriage, the very existence—nay, the very *need*—of prostitution will be rendered as unnecessary as a vestigial artifact."

Although in complete agreement, I shifted uncomfortably. One of my dimity pantalettes had loosened and was creeping down my leg.

"Really," said Hatsepha. "The man is mad." She fanned herself excitedly and scanned the room. "And what of the resulting pregnancies? Speaking of, I don't see your sister-in-law here. Nor your brother Erasmus. Are they interested in the topic?" Not waiting for my answer, she went on. "Seeing as your Erasmus is some sort of minister, I should hope so." She lowered her voice and eyed my other brother. "As for James . . . ?"

Before I could respond, Dr. Campbell started bellowing from the pulpit that Mr. Owen's principles of Right Living in a Natural State were "*unworthy, contemptible*—nay, *beneath* contempt—for such principles could equally be applied to a goat!"

Owen rose in indignation. "So you say, sir. So you say." He jabbed his finger at Campbell. "But I dare you, Reverend, here and now before this audience, to *prove* the existence of God."

Proof that Jesus had died for our sins? A few in the audience gasped.

Campbell, unwavering, brimming with scorn, seized the opportunity. Clutching the edge of the podium, he leaned toward us, his eyebrows practically on fire. "Let *all* those in the audience who have been *swayed* by Mr. Owen's remarks that Jesus is unnecessary rise from their seats."

The next thing I knew, Hatsepha was clutching at my skirt, trying to pull me down. Heads craned. Murmurs rose to a din. I felt my pantalette release and drop to the floor. In the intervening chaos, two more people shuffled to their feet. I felt a thousand eyes on me. Viewing all of this from aloft, Campbell waited serenely, but in the end, only three of us were standing.

"And *now*," continued the gratified Dr. Campbell before Owen could object, "let *all* those who are in support of the *Truth of Christ* show *their* faith by rising."

Immediately the rest of Cincinnati stood. In the midst of thunderous applause, I, now seated, glanced furtively over at James and recognized in his look at least a week of silent dinners.

Neither of us noticed the gentleman standing at the back of the room, taking it all in, taking particular note of me.

"My dear Olivia," said Hatsepha, rushing me out of the theater in such haste that I was unable to retrieve my pantalette. "You might as well move up to Fanny Wright's colony and live like a rustic for all the suitors you shall receive henceforth."

CHAPTER 10

1829

As Hatsepha had predicted, the rest of the summer was an arid desert in spite of the humid weather. No one called at the boardinghouse. No one spoke to me at the market, although I was stopped in my tracks at seeing Ariadne Pritchard wearing my errant pantalette as a tucker about her neck.

James did not speak of it, but several merchants had dropped their orders with Givens and Sons—and just when the business was doing so well. Such was the sensibility of Cincinnati that a woman of contrarian opinion could drive away commerce like pigs before a stick.

Julia, in the meantime, had taken to bed. Sleeping beside her was difficult, for she was agitated and fearful about the coming childbirth.

"I keep having dreams."

Had I been raised on lurid prophecies like those advanced by her father, I, too, would be having dreams.

"Julia," said I, rising to dress, "you have neither been cleaved by the Devil, nor is your imminent labor punishment for your sins." I may have said this with some impatience and little sympathy. So full was I of Fanny Wright's words and attitudes that I had to bite my tongue from adding, *And what did you expect from marriage?*

And now here we were, prostrated by heat and the dullness of our existence, and Mrs. Humphries in the kitchen frying something foul. Little wonder Julia was melancholy. And where was Erasmus that he should leave his wife to languish?

Spotting a stack of my brother's clothes that Julia had laundered, I reached for his shirt and britches. Julia laughed and covered her mouth as I pulled on the garments that fit me quite well once I tucked in the shirt.

"'O come,'" I sang, prancing about and waving Erasmus's hat, "'let us make a joyful noise unto the rock of our salvation!'" I spread my arms. "Alleluia!"

It was immodest to brag, but I quite captured Erasmus in manner and tone. "You goose!" said Julia, but for the first time in weeks, she smiled.

AND LIKE THAT, I was given my first taste of liberation. Taking shelter in the privy the following day, I drew off my clothes and undergarments and pulled on the costume I had paraded for Julia. Stashing my bundle of skirts and petticoats behind the henhouse, I made for the street, hat pulled low, hair pushed up, stockings and britches shoved into the top of worn but heavy boots in which I managed an ambling stride. With such little subterfuge, but helped by my height, I became a man. No one heckled me. No gossip nipped at my feet.

On that first day, my foray was brief and modest. A trip to the landing—with which I was already familiar—yielded such pleasure from being able to look brazenly into storefronts, to step into a tobacco store, to walk by Merkl's lascivious clerk without so much as a second glance from him. For the first time in my life, I flagrantly read the want ads as if they were mine to answer.

"Got to have more meat on your bones for that job, boyo," said a ruddy roustabout who looked too porcine to be literate. He nodded at the illustration of a hog. "Gotta weigh more than them oinkers if yer gonna hoist 'em up," he said, poking me in the ribs.

Defiantly, I tore down the bill.

Walking down Cherry Street, I saw a Choctaw wearing buckskins and an epaulet-capped jacket such as Napoleon might have worn. The Indian's head was shaved but for a topknot of hair, his fierce nose glinting with a golden hoop.

The third or fourth time I ventured out, I mustered my courage to visit Bucktown, where pickaninnies scavenged through the garbage and the coloreds lived ten or more to a room. Whites, too, who had come from the East, or from Ireland, or from Europe, looking for something better. And I saw women and girls (and possibly some boys) advertising themselves to passersby.

"Come here, Pretty Face. You there! Handsome! I'll cook your biscuits."

Realizing she was talking to me, I blushed like a girl, pulled down my hat, and hurried on.

But it was up in the hills that I felt the keenest pleasure. I climbed a steep path, unencumbered by pantalettes, petticoats, or corset, making my way into fresher air and farmland from where I could see all of the city and Covington across the river, the steamboats and ferries, canoes and rafts, smokestacks and roofs, and the wide expanse of Kentucky. I breathed in the summer air and fanned myself with Erasmus's discarded brim—escaped as if from bondage, splay-legged as a boy, giddy with perspiration.

My antics were cut short the following week. It began as a too-hot day in a chain of too-hot days. On the street, there were conversations beneath the conversation, another tongue altogether. And now someone was wailing in the house or out on the street—

impossible to tell in the nonstop noise. Everybody was hammering or carting goods through the dust, and all day long men were yelling like jackals, and if they weren't yelling, they were spitting, and if they weren't spitting, they were drinking, and if they weren't drinking, they were eating meat. The smell of it was constant. Cooked meat, rotting meat, bleating-grunting meat.

The moaning coming from upstairs could easily have been mistaken for the sound of a saw through a reticent piece of lumber. Gradually, the sound took on more human characteristics.

"Oh God, Olivia! Will you come?"

Dropping my book, I hastened up the stairs to find Julia collapsed in the hall, the floorboard drenched.

"Oh dear!" I said, nearly tripping, for the baby's arrival was upon us, and with barely a blanket knit and Erasmus so scarce these last few days. "Mrs. Humphries!" I shouted, sliding down the wall beside Julia.

"Pshaw!" said Mrs. Humphries, her one eye glaring as she waddled up the stairs, gathered Julia into her hefty arms, and dragged her to her feet. "Mrs. Givens," she said, "the baby is *coming.*" She said this as if Julia were deaf or foreign. At which point Julia screamed again.

"Get Dr. Orpheus!" Humphries shouted to the girl downstairs, telling her to make haste and not talk to anyone.

Only ten days before, the esteemed doctor, Silas Orpheus—according to Hatsepha "a man worth listening to" and "apparently without a wife"—had taken the lectern to discourse on the various causes of biliousness. I had commented that he seemed a trifle sure of himself, but now I wished sorely for his presence.

Humphries bundled Julia off to the room she had shared with me. An hour later, Julia was grasping the spindle bedposts, while I, in spite of my being a nascent atheist, commenced to pray.

"Forgive us our trespasses," I began—and meanly, too, for Julia had clearly never trespassed upon anyone—but Mrs. Humphries cut me short by ushering in the midwife. The look on the landlady's face was enough to shut me up, her brow raised as if to say, *It has come to this*, for I could not remember ever seeing a Negro in Mrs. Humphries's house.

"This here's Tilly," said Mrs. Humphries, jerking her head at the girl beside her. "The doctor sent her." She glanced at the bed, then at me, implying that we all deserved each other, and if Mrs. Givens's husband had not seen fit to be present, then it was meet and right that his child be birthed by a colored girl.

Julia let out with another awful howl, and Tilly dropped her bag and set to her.

"Where is the doctor?" I snapped, groaning with exasperation when Tilly said he was otherwise occupied with some problem down in Bucktown.

Tilly was neat-haired and simply dressed, and she wasted no time. She stroked and soothed Julia, who was now silent except for the occasional whimper. I counted the hours by the chimes in the downstairs parlor. By the time the streetlights were lit, no baby had arrived. Tilly, however, was calm. It was second nature, she said, touching the knotted scarf on the back of her head. She'd practiced on kittens and goats as well as helping her mother, who was a midwife herself. She was in the middle of telling me how her mother used to put a knife beneath the mattress to cut the pain of childbirth when Julia let loose with a holler that had Mrs. Humphries shrieking up the stairs that that baby better come and soon, as we would be out on the streets, baby and all, if we did not pipe down.

"Julia," I said, with her gripping my hand so tight it cut off the blood. I looked her in the eye. "You've got to have this baby."

Tilly reached between Julia's legs and told her it was time to push. Such grunting I have never heard, and soon I, too, was panting in solidarity. Time and again Julia tried, until, all at once, she let out a ghastly howl, and a baby's red face appeared. Tilly let go of Julia's legs to grab him. I nearly wept, and would have done if Tilly had not so swiftly placed the child in my arms and turned right back to Julia. I stared at the baby, and he at me as if *I* were his mother.

"What is it?" cried Julia.

"A boy!" I said, loving him immediately. He was covered with paste and blood, slippery as a trout, and with that bit of Givens severity in the downturned mouth. "A right pet fox."

"A boy?" said Julia, still panting with exhaustion. "A boy? Thank God."

She closed her eyes and settled into the mattress. Tilly gave her a sponging, then pulled down her nightshirt. I clutched the child until Tilly took him from me, making quick work of the cord with her teeth. So engrossed was I in his tiny feet and hands that I barely registered the shouts outside. The room was peaceful, the blood-soaked sheets and afterbirth the only evidence of what had transpired.

As Tilly laid the baby in Julia's arms, I wondered where Erasmus was and if Mrs. Humphries's girl had found him. But it was James who arrived first, smudged with tallow, his hat in his hand as he knelt beside Julia. Hard he looked at her, so hard that no one could have questioned his feelings.

"A boy," Julia whispered. She pulled back the shawl so he could see the little head that was slightly pointed and with a dab of gold hair.

The look upon James's face made a tightening in my chest, and I had to turn away. Watching from the window, I saw somebody run up the street and turn the corner. A few seconds later, three or four people followed. The shouting grew louder. Someone flew by on a horse.

"Goodness, Jamie," I said. "What is all the fuss?"

Slowly James rose, looking very tired. "'Tis nothing, Livvie."

The room darkened. I could not move from the window. The

clamor on the street rose and fell, started up again. Tilly lit a taper, going from one candle to another until the room was aglow.

It was nearly morning when Erasmus returned. Julia was asleep, the baby in her arms. James had gone to his room, I was curled up on the chair, Tilly lay on the floor. A few candles flickered feebly at the stubs.

I roused in time to see Erasmus slumping down beside the bed, reaching to touch the child.

"Shhh," said Julia. "It is a boy."

I pretended to be asleep, but I needed to relieve myself. I stretched and groaned. "Where on earth have you been?"

"There was a fire," said Erasmus. "I was in the bucket line." I recollected smelling smoke, but it had seemed the least of our concerns.

"Who is this?" said Erasmus, indicating the sleeping Tilly.

"The doctor's girl," I said. "Seems we have a hand-me-down."

"All right, then," said Erasmus, crawling under the sheets beside Julia. In the half-light, I could see he was grimy. Lord only knew where he had been.

Julia said, "Erasmus, you smell horrible." But she allowed him to move in close, and I knew I would not be sleeping in *that* bed for a while.

Donning my jacket over my chemise and pulling on my boots, I headed to the privy. It was already warm in the way of August mornings, and the smell was ripe. When I was finished with my business, I pulled my coat back on. My legs were exposed below the hem of my chemise like two sticks stuck into my boots. In spite of my regalia and unkempt hair, I paused at the front of the house and lingered on the door stoop, surveying the morning. Given all the shouting of the night before, it was strangely quiet except for a cow nudging at the window of a house, hoping to get fed. Even the pigs were absent, though an odor of burned meat permeated the air. I did not notice the figure coming toward me until we stood face-to-face.

"Why if it is not the unorthodox Miss Givens."

"Excuse me?" I said, tugging at the hem of my jacket as if a chemise minus petticoats, pantalettes, and a dress was the latest fashion.

"It is I, Dr. Orpheus."

The famous Dr. Orpheus, who only a week before had held forth upon biliousness. He looked a bit worn around the edges. And his clothing was disgraceful. Still peeved about his absence the night before, I muttered something about Hatsepha's assessment of him being a bit generous. That he might know *me* was not altogether surprising, for I had garnered notoriety as "The Woman Who Stood in Support of the Atheist Robert Owen."

"I've come to fetch my girl."

"A girl, I might add, to whom we are very grateful. Which is more than I can muster for you, sir."

A rider made his way up the street, his cheeks smudged with ash. He stared so intently that I grew embarrassed at my appearance. Worse—I recognized the rider as Mr. Phinneaus Mumford, who only a year before had come to call. How quickly word would spread that Miss Olivia Givens of already dubious character had been seen half dressed in public.

Silas Orpheus tipped his hat at Phinneaus Mumford and offered me his arm. To Mr. Mumford he said, "Miss Givens is just catching some air after spending all night delivering her sister-in-law's child."

"Oh," said Phinneaus Mumford, "well!"—as he gave his horse an extra kick to urge him to a trot.

I let go the doctor's arm and glanced over at his profile. He was not so very handsome, but his high forehead and grave, gray eyes gave the impression of intelligence. "I suppose I should thank you for what is left of my sorry reputation."

"Neither of us appears to have worn the night well," said Silas Orpheus.

"I had no place to sleep," I said. "When my brother returned, his place was with his wife."

"Then you haven't heard? Your brother . . ."

"My brother." I gave out a snort. "He *said* he was in the bucket line."

"Had he been in the bucket line, it might have helped." He studied me. "But you don't know?"

"Know what?"

Silas Orpheus removed his hat and said that it pained him to give me the news that the livelihood of our family—James's workshop with its two vats and fifty crates and five wheelbarrows and a horse cart, not to mention his already completed order for five thousand candles to be delivered to Midas Barker's former customers, situated as it was on the edge of Bucktown—had been besieged by rioters, who had burned it to the ground.

CHAPTER 11

1829

In the days that followed, the papers were filled with editorials pronouncing the riots "inevitable" due to tensions between the Irish Catholics and the free black population. Everyone was vying for jobs. Jasper Fry, a metalworker, had brought down an iron rod on Cicero Green, a former slave who hauled junk for a living. A group of white millworkers broke the windows of a house and set it on fire, chasing a Negro family as they fled.

The colored community was not alone in its suffering. Caught in the random cross fire, the charred remains of James's workshop yielded little that was salvageable other than the iron pot. His dipping racks had melted; all of his supplies had combusted. Knowing that there were others who had lost their lives in the melee, James spent little time complaining. Instead, he went straightaway to the Commercial Bank of Cincinnati and pled his case, and when that was refused, went hat in hand to the office of the coal-merchant father of Hatsepha Peckham to ask him to underwrite his business and guarantee the purchase of candles from a resurrected factory.

"It would save me all my customers, Mr. Peckham," said James. "And you would have a lifelong discount on candles."

"There is just one thing, Givens," Mr. Peckham said after James described how he had figured it out. "It will be difficult for me to convince my associates to hold their orders while you get set up along the canal."

Even before the fire, James had already staked out a future site better suited for expansion. He would hire on seven hands, all of whom were Scots-Irish and each and every one a good Presbyterian. These would be hardworking men that James could count on—not the Catholics who had haunted our family's concerns back in Ireland, or the Negroes whom James found too exotic to be collegial.

Mr. Peckham clasped his hands together while James, sitting across his desk, discussed the virtues of slow-burning candles as well as the potential for coal gas in domestic lighting. James was flattered that Mr. Peckham regarded his opinion so highly, for though James was a man of intelligence, there were many such gentlemen of Mr. Peckham's acquaintance.

"I'll have to stake my reputation as if you were my own son, if you get my drift," said Mr. Peckham.

James, however, did not catch his drift. "That's fine, Mr. Peckham, but your partners will have my word that I will have this operation up in no time."

"Then again, there's the matter of the loan."

"I am hoping you can put in a word with the bank."

"It's true"—Mr. Peckham paused—"I have quite a bit of influence with the bank."

"Well then, sir, I would be much beholden for any expediting you could yield."

Mr. Peckham rose, walked around his desk, and slapped James on the back. "That is the spirit. You get my drift. You will get the loan; I will secure the contracts; and you will propose to Hatsepha next Sunday."

"You have sold your soul," I said to James when he told me.

"What would you have me do, Livvie? I'm sleeping on a sofa in the parlor, the baby wails all night, and I have no possibility of capital other than what Peckham might avail."

"Hatsepha Peckham, James? Really?" I shook my head. "She probably gets into bed at night wearing flounces and a bonnet."

But I could see there would be no argument. James was right. We were a family of limited prospects. Without the workshop, we were penniless. Erasmus was broke, and tutoring barely gave me purse money. If James did not marry Hatsepha, I feared I might have to walk the streets.

On the fourth Saturday of October, we sat in the front pew of the First Presbyterian Church. Hatsepha looked like a doily in her wicker-puffed sleeves, her hair all loops and curls. Julia, holding the baby whom they had christened William, sat next to me. Usually silent as a monk, the child let out a sudden squall that interrupted the vows, muffling those spoken by James, who was already known for paying lip service to the Lord.

In the end, it was worth it, for Peckham came through. By the time the calendar turned the page on the decade, Givens and Sons was being rebuilt, and at a better location that would afford wider distribution for James Givens's cunning little wicks. That these candles eventually would be forgotten as the genesis of his empire I find a little sad, for it was said that everyone looked more beautiful by the light of a Givens candle, and I rue their passing to this day.

CHAPTER 12

1830

One early morning the following spring, I was walking home from the market when a cab rushed by. Laden with baskets, I nearly collided with the carriage as it sped around the corner. Carrots and apples flew into the air.

"Feckin' Betty," yelled the driver at me as the horse trotted on.

"'Feckin' Betty' indeed, you feckin' Catholic," I muttered as I picked up the fruit and vegetables. The Papists were arriving in droves to work on the canal and, in my opinion, bringing nothing but trouble.

From inside the cab, an arm emerged holding a cane that soundly rapped the driver, who reined the horse to a stop. The door of the cab flew open, and out stepped Dr. Silas Orpheus. "Are you hurt?"

"No thanks to your yahoo driver, sir."

"Why, it is Miss Olivia Givens, denouncer of the faith."

"Ha!" said I, retrieving a turnip. "Are you my religious conscience, Dr. Orpheus?"

"God save us if I am," he said, dismissing the driver with a wave of his hand. "May I walk with you?"

I straightened my bonnet, recalling the morning after William's birth when I had emerged in disarray from the privy. "You mock me, sir."

He picked up one of my truant apples and bit into it. "Miss Givens, I may think many things about you, but I would never mock you."

We walked together up the sidewalk past prim brick houses.

"It has been almost a year by my count, Miss Givens. How goes your sister-in-law? Is she well after the birth?"

"She would be better for the presence of her husband."

"I heard he was offered an appointment in the Methodist church. Forgive me, but your brother does not strike me as someone particularly well suited to the bureaucracy of the cloth."

"Indeed, he refused it. Why settle down when you can gallivant up and down the river?" I glanced at the doctor. His hair was the color of straw, but neatly cut—a bit of gray showing about the ears. "You seem to know much about my family, sir, while I know nothing about yours."

He waved this off. "I hear you tutor children. Tell me, do you teach them to be heathens?" Silas Orpheus went on. "The first time I noticed you was at the Owen–Campbell debates. You were the woman who stood."

My cheeks burned. I knew as well as anyone that no decent woman could pass muster socially without proclaiming herself a devout Christian. But there it was.

"If you asked my brother James for *his* account of that evening, he will tell you I must have seen a mouse and leapt to my feet."

"*Did* you see a mouse?"

"Everyone prefers a rodent to the alternative. How dreadful that I should think for myself and rise in support of Mr. Owen."

"But you *did* rise, Miss Givens. You did. Brava! I, for one, am in complete agreement."

"And yet *you* did not stand."

"I beg your pardon, there were no seats available. I stood for the entire night."

"Then you did not applaud."

"How would you have noticed?" said Silas Orpheus. "*Your* attention was on the mouse."

We had arrived back at the boardinghouse, where I continued to reside with Erasmus and Julia, who by then had a room of their own. James, now married, had absented himself. I did not miss the tension between him and Erasmus. As soon as James wed Hatsepha, Mr. Peckham insisted that his daughter and son-in-law move to the up-and-coming Key's Hill neighborhood, where the air was noticeably fresher. He proceeded to build them a house in the Empire style of such proportion that I, as befitting a spinster sister, could have moved in and scarcely been seen, but I demurred, preferring to stay in town rather than suffer Hatsepha at breakfast.

Before bidding me good-bye, Silas Orpheus hesitated. "Miss Givens, forgive my medical prurience—how is it that you became so bold?"

"You speak as though it is a pathology."

"It certainly is unusual in a woman." He crossed his arms and raised his eyebrow—either in amusement or appraisal. "I should like to feel your glands."

He must have taken my stunned silence as acquiescence, for he touched my neck. I recalled the day when Hatsepha's phrenologist had palpated my skull to determine my character and now wondered if Silas Orpheus could feel my pulse that was, at the moment, elevated. "And who prods *you,* Dr. Orpheus? If I may be 'so bold' . . ."

He laughed. "No lady you would recognize as such."

"Then perhaps you should confine your inspections to another sort," I said, pulling back.

"My interests range to *every* sort."

"Really? And in the evening? How do you amuse yourself?"

I was not sure I wanted to hear, for I had my suspicions. The brothels in Bucktown outnumbered acorns in autumn, and not only barkers and boatmen frequented them.

"In the evenings, Miss Givens, I steal corpses."

"TRY AGAIN, HENRY," I said. "You must carry the remainder like so."

The boy was less doltish than the others. The education of children was a noble endeavor, but it chafed at me. While I labored with my charges over simple tasks, James was poring over his ledgers, adding up the columns that attested to his wealth. Erasmus was often riding for days along the river, perhaps to seek out converts, while Dr. Orpheus, in flagrant defiance of the law, engaged in the most interesting pursuit of medical science. Such was the world of men.

"Very good, Henry," I said. "You are a good boy. But the day is done. Run along."

With a shout of glee, he rushed to the door. I wished I could run along with him. He flung the door open just as Julia arrived, holding her whimpering bundle.

"Oh, Olivia, would you mind?" She pushed William upon me so she could remove her bonnet. Her glorious hair was stuffed into a cap. Ever since the birth of the child, she was resigned to mortifying herself into homeliness. If I had half her looks, I would have paraded them—but dourness had settled upon her with marriage.

Erasmus, when present, seemed little affected by Julia's appearance. His awareness of his wife and child was as an afterthought. Certainly, he seemed fond, but his fervor was otherwise directed, though I knew not where. I saw the tracts he read. If we had been shocked by his impulse toward Methodism, the feeling paled in comparison to our concerns about his budding interest in abolition.

Don't let James see you reading that drivel, I had said more than once. *He'll have a fit.*

He minds his business. I'll mind mine.

"I ran into Dr. Orpheus today," Julia said, adjusting her skirts upon the settee and reaching for the child. "He asked about you." She looked at me slyly.

"Did he, now? And did he tell you he almost ran me down in the street?"

"Ah," she said. "Perhaps that's why he wants to call."

When she said no more, I said, "Julia!"

She laughed. "I believe he is calling this evening."

IN SPITE OF MY DESIRE TO AFFECT NONCHALANCE, I had on one of my two good dresses and my cameo pin when the doctor called after supper. He seemed as ill at ease as I. I had the impression he had little experience with light talk (which came at some relief to me since I was so poor at it as to be considered dumb). Stiffly, we cast about for common ground, with him finally asking about our passage some eleven years earlier, and me recounting the high point of my hanging from the halyard, my skirts flying up while the sailors looked on—a story that delighted the doctor, who then shared an escapade involving a burning barn. So convivial grew our conversation that it seemed quite natural for me to ask about the dissections. This resulted in his coughing into his hands and looking about before leaning forward and saying in a low voice, "I don't suppose you'd like to accompany me."

TWO WEEKS LATER, I alit from a carriage, allowing Silas Orpheus to take my hand. He was a slender man with attenuated fingers that he constantly ran through his hair. We huddled like fugitives—which of a sort we were. Ostensibly, we were going to the opera.

"Not terribly romantic, I fear," said Silas, holding a lantern as we entered a stark white room in the basement of the new medical college. He offered to take my cloak, but I pulled it tight.

"Why is it so cold?" said I. My heart beat with expectation. Not since Fanny Wright had given her astounding speech had I felt so invigorated.

"Well . . ." Silas cleared his throat. "Were it *not* for the cold . . ." He indicated the table at the center of the room, the mounded sheet draping it.

Had we been discovered dissecting an unauthorized cadaver, Silas Orpheus's career would lie in ruins. Religious belief had it that mutilated corpses could not participate in the Resurrection, but given the condition of most bodies after a day or two, I doubted many were fit for heaven.

"I thought your girl would be here," I said. "The midwife?"

"Tilly? Unfortunately, no. But if it doesn't make you squeamish, perhaps you'll be willing to step in?"

A little too quickly, I said, "Of course."

By the light of the lamp, Silas drew back the sheet to reveal the ashen body of a man, bearded with soot-colored hair and skin like wax. He watched my reaction closely. "You are a radical, Miss Givens. Most ladies would swoon."

I was prepared to feel dizzy like the time that the prognosticator at Trollope's Emporium studied my hand and told me I was destined to influence the lives of young people but have no children of my own. My nerves, however, remained calm—steadied, no doubt, by my fascination. "How did he die?"

Silas hung up the lamp to free his hands. "You remember the brick wall that collapsed day before yesterday?" He adjusted the man's head to the side. It was squashed like a pumpkin.

Everyone had heard about the accident—how a group of immigrants had perished when the mortar failed in the construction of a new hotel.

Buildings were flying up and toppling down in almost equal proportion. Now this poor man was, for the second time, a victim. Nameless, unclaimed, he had been snatched before burial by a couple of opportunists who had sold him to the porter of the medical college. This was good news for Silas Orpheus, who normally had to wait for a condemned murderer to be executed before being legally donated to science. The fact that most bodies were those of criminals assuaged some religious misgivings, but deceased convicts were in short supply. To avoid drawing attention to themselves, the "resurrectionists" hired by Silas Orpheus confined their searches to paupers' graves.

"May I touch him?" I said.

Silas nodded. I placed my fingers upon the face. Regardless of how this man had died, no anguish was apparent. He seemed peaceful—complacent, even. I might as well have been touching clay.

"These human remains are a gift to us," said Silas. "Clandestine gifts, but gifts nonetheless. As such, their lives shall have meaning."

"You imply no one would weep at their graveside." I considered telling him that my mother had been buried in such a grave, and that we had all wept profusely, but he was already opening his kit.

"I have a theory about disease in relation to the circulatory system," said Silas. He laid out an array of instruments: a scooper, a saw, three blades of alarming sharpness. "One thinks our veins might carry contaminates just as the river bears detritus." Pointing out the darkness of the lower extremities, the pallor of the face, he explained the postmortem pooling of blood. "It separates," he said. "Like oil and vinegar." Selecting a straight razor, he set to work with some urgency, all the while assuring me it was not much different from carving a turkey. "Did you know the word 'ghoul' is from the Egyptian myth about a cannibalistic grave robber?"

I stood very still, my breathing shallow. The kerosene light flickered. A drop of perspiration fell from Silas's brow.

No blood oozed from the incisions. With a metal instrument like giant forceps, Silas pried apart the ribs. "Look, look, look!" he said.

The heart was smaller than I would have imagined, dwarfed by the liver and the stomach. There was an excessive amount of intestine.

"You will need your handkerchief," he said.

I held the lavender-perfumed linen to my nose as he had instructed and tried not to look away as he cut into the bowels and bladder. Even through my handkerchief, I nearly retched with the smell. And yet I felt exhilarated.

Hours later, we stepped out of the building into the cold advance of dawn. A glum summer fog occluded the light. After the medicinal odor of death, the arousal of a new day held the promise of the living in the seasoned scent of river. Already, the city was bustling. While the night soilers were taking away chamber pots and emptying latrines, the grave robbers would be reinterring the remains of our autopsy, doubling up the purloined body in the respectable coffin of another.

I gasped for air as if each breath were my last, overcome by the surge of my own blood, my lungs expanding, my beating heart. Two years earlier, I had failed to sympathize with the outpourings at the revival, but here I was, witnessing my own conversion. How fantastic that life perseveres in the face of corruption. Someday it would cease. All passion, all curiosity, all experience . . . gone. But for now, I was ecstatic.

"I would give anything," said I, trying to catch my breath, "to participate in this again."

"Miss Givens," said Silas Orpheus, adjusting my cloak. "For the sake of propriety, I shall bid adieu before we reach your home."

THREE MORNINGS LATER, the docter once again called just as my pupils were arriving. I hastened him into the dining room and told him to speak quietly.

"Were you serious," Silas Orpheus said, "about your offer to assist?"

"More of a plea than an offer," I whispered. "But why don't you have your girl?" He looked perplexed. "The midwife . . ."

"Ah. Tilly. Alas, she was with child. I had to send her back."

Seeing my face, he explained that Tilly had been on loan from his brother in Kentucky.

"Indentured?" I asked, for indeed many of the English who migrated to America arrived beholden to their creditors and obliged to work it off.

"She is my brother's *property,*" said Silas. "As are her offspring." When I said nothing, he said, "Ah yes. The radical Miss Givens. No doubt you hold with the sanctimony of the North."

Summoning the words of Fanny Wright, I raised my chin. "It does seem obscene to own another soul."

"Why 'obscene' if they're fed and cared for? Oh, but I can read it in your face. 'Slavery is inhumane' and so forth. Never mind that I have spent my life with these people. Would you not concede that I'm more familiar with their humanity than you are?" Before I could answer, he changed the subject. "So tell me, Miss Givens, are you interested in my offer?"

I dropped my eyes. "As you say, the girl's fate should be no concern of mine." In truth I had given slavery little thought. *Choose your wars,* James would say. Opting for the moment to dismiss Tilly and her predicament, I immediately said yes.

AFTER THAT, Silas Orpheus called on Saturday evenings, purportedly for opera or theater. On the night of our fourth dissection, I donned my evening clothes in advance of a performance of *Hamlet*. As we broke off toward the medical school, Silas informed me the corpse we were dissecting was a woman. A female body was almost as taboo as that of a child. The only woman heretofore deemed so beyond redemption that she had qualified for legal dissection was an Englishwoman who had murdered her own children.

"But surely women suffer from maladies uniquely theirs," I said upon hearing how little study had been given to the female anatomy. "The benefits to science and therefore mankind must outweigh this superstitious nonsense."

"On this issue, I concur with your idealism, Miss Givens."

We descended into the basement of the lab. Silas pulled back the shroud to reveal a young woman whose pendulous breasts slumped to either side.

I tried not to gape.

As was our custom, we lit the lanterns, laid out the tools, nodded our heads in perfunctory and silent prayer. Clearing his throat, Silas picked up the scalpel and commenced to cut a straight line down the woman's abdomen. The flesh split apart cleanly. Once he breached the abdominal cavity, Silas tossed the scalpel aside and began to explore with his fingers. "Please note the condition of her uterine wall." If I had any illusion that Silas Orpheus regarded the female anatomy as more sacred than that of a man, I was quickly disabused. In the doctor's hands, the body ceased to be human and became as earth. With bloodied fingers, he gripped and lifted her pelvis. "As for the vaginal opening . . . what is this?" He let out a long breath. "Ah. This woman was trying to abort."

Curiosity overwhelmed my skittishness, and I peered in close.

With efficient detachment, Silas pulled apart her thighs and pushed her legs up until they assumed the skewed posture of a rag doll. I averted my gaze. When I looked again, he was removing an object with forceps. It was dark and spiky. "What do you think, Miss Givens? Thornbush? Thistle?"

I glanced at the woman's eyes that in life might have been lively with humor or sly with mischief. The hair was in braids. In all likelihood, the body was found in a pauper's grave.

"Whatever it is," said Silas, "this thing was meant to induce bleeding and no doubt caused her death. There's nothing much left of the fetus. I would say she succeeded in her effort, partially at least."

My mother had bled out when she was six months along with a stillborn child that had looked fully formed.

"A prostitute," I said flatly.

Come here, Pretty Face. You there! Handsome! I'll cook your biscuits.

Silas must have gleaned judgment in my expression, for he said, "People will sell anything if there is a market, Miss Givens." He dropped the thorny object into a jar, set down his forceps, and began to wash his hands in the basin. Feeling ineffectual, I tried to muster an argument.

"Would it were not the case," said I, "that women must be forced to sell themselves. Miss Fanny Wright says—"

Orpheus laughed at the mention of Fanny Wright. "Miss Fanny Wright is a bit naive, don't you think?" He turned back to me. We were face-to-face, close as air. He went on. "It is one thing to stand in opposition to Christianity as you have done. Another altogether to truly understand people too compromised to worry about the condition of their souls. If there *is* a God—and like you, I wonder—would He not want us to turn our efforts toward saving each other rather than madly fretting if we ourselves are saved?"

Out of the corner of my eye, I studied the dead woman. She had a turned-up, childish nose. Floating on her grayish skin was a smattering of freckles. I brought out my piece of lace and breathed deeply of the lavender.

I ARRIVED HOME to find Julia waiting at the top of the stairs.

"It is not what you think," said I.

"Hurry," she said, "before Mrs. Humphries sees you."

It was fine for Erasmus to stay out all night, but a single woman returning at this hour would be grounds for eviction.

Julia looked at me closely. "You took some care with your outfit, Livvie."

Indeed I had. Swallowing my pride, I had accepted Hatsepha's offer of finer gloves, a jeweled and feathered comb, a fan, and a necklace—all in the service of a masquerade of which Hatsepha was ignorant and of which she would have no doubt disapproved.

"Why, Livvie," said Julia, her voice rising in concern, "is that blood on your hem?"

CHAPTER 13

1832

Eighteen thirty-two began with one of the coldest winters I have endured. For two years, I had continued to assist Silas Orpheus in Tilly's stead. Every few weeks or so, a resurrectionist would procure a body, especially in the months when the ground was too hard for burials and it was easier to "nick a stiff" from the icehouse than dig up six feet of soil. In order to work in the basement, we piled on woolens of every description, our skin chafing under knitted garments.

It was in January when, as usual, I left the boardinghouse dressed in a manner befitting a prayer meeting and hurried to the medical college basement. My head ached from the frigidity. The lips of the corpse would be no bluer than mine.

"Who is it?" I asked Silas, who was standing over the table.

Betraying excitement, Silas pulled back the sheet to unveil the body of a Negro. We had never before had a black man on the table. In fact, it was commonly assumed that autopsying a Negro would avail few insights as to the afflictions of our own race.

"He was retrieved from the river," said Silas. "He must have frozen almost immediately. See how perfectly intact?"

I thought back to the floating body my family had seen when we first came down the Ohio. "A runaway?"

"Perhaps. He fell through the ice floes. The man who delivered him must have thought it easier to palm him off on me rather than drag the body back to Kentucky."

Normally, Silas would make a scalpel cut in the shape of a *Y* starting from each shoulder, meeting under the pectorals and extending to the pubis. This time, he started the incision behind one ear, drawing the blade across the top of the head to the other ear and peeling back the skin.

"What are you looking for?" I said. The dead man's skin was very dark and he had red-rimmed staring eyes as if he had gazed longingly at the sky as he sank beneath the surface.

Silas took out a saw. "Chasing down old wives' tales. Looking for clues. Very little work has been done on the African race, Miss Givens. One would think we might know more, given the investment and their proximity. But look at your face! Are you intrigued or appalled?"

Both, I supposed, though I flinched when he gave the saw an enthusiastic thrust that sprayed blood onto my smock. As he pulled off a section of the skull, I knew what he was after. Excuses. Absolution. Evidence of difference.

"It looks like any brain," I said when he was done.

ALL THAT WINTER, Julia had wrapped William in layers of blankets and muttered through chattering teeth, *Too cold! Too cold! We must pray for spring.*

Julia would barely let go the child, though William was nearly three. He would run to me when he saw me, and peer around the door when I had my students during the day. Some of the students called him "Silly Willy" and it stuck, and comically, too, for never was there such a sober child, yet still so free with affection. That Erasmus could father such a little judge caused no end of mirth, with

Julia often saying, "It shall be upon this boy that I shall rely, for his father is useless." She would lay her head on my chest in a way that comforted both of us, and sigh, "And yet Erasmus is so lovely."

Eventually, winter relented, but had we known that the severity of season augured worse to come, Julia mightn't have prayed so hard for warmer days, for with warmer days came the thaw, and with the thaw came a flood such as Noah might envy, breaching the banks and lapping all the way to Third and Vine Street, ruining domiciles, drowning man and beast alike. When the surge receded, it left behind a vile, odiferous sludge. Then came the boats, many of them carrying immigrants—not only English and Europeans, but refugees fleeing the eastern seaboard, escaping a new and horrible scourge.

Cholera.

The newspapers blasted the story of plague striking Canada and New York, now half emptied out. The presence and spread of the disease were blamed on the lower classes—those too dissipated of soul and practice to incur salvation and remain free of infection. Those who could flee did so. Some pulled up stakes and ventured to our little patch of "virtue," as Cincinnati was perceived to be.

"It shall come," said Silas Orpheus.

Of course he was right. It came, but not immediately. News spread about a New York that was brought to its knees, a Philadelphia that was stunned, a Washington that was in chaos.

During that spring and summer, Silas and I autopsied three cadavers to observe the rotten liver of the inebriate, the wizened cranium of the syphilitic, the clotted arteries of the corpulent. We sliced into the chambers of seminal vesicles, Silas joking that these were a man's treasure troves. *One swift kick by a horse in the wrong place, and they'll be crushed and rendered useless. My brother knows this only too well.*

The intimacy of our inquiries had afforded a peculiar camaraderie, though I still knew little of this man who was prone to irony and yet had a cool quality that I ascribed to his scientific disposition. Together, we focused on theories and suppositions, the peeling away of viscera, the exchange of conclusions, usually limiting our opinions to the task at hand.

Impatient with my ruse of attending prayer meetings and socials, I had once again taken to wearing pants and a coat purloined from Erasmus, ostensibly for patching.

On those nights when I snuck out, I returned with equal stealth.

It was on such a black night that Silas accompanied me after a particularly difficult dissection involving the extraction of tumors. The streets were empty. It must have been nearly morning.

"Have you a wife, sir?" I asked. In spite of our sharing the investigation of the most private parts of bodies, Silas would steer any inquiry about his family back to the circulatory system or the etiology of disease.

"Are you proposing, Miss Givens?"

Fortunately, he could not see me grow pink in the darkness. It was a warm night made warmer by the absence of breeze. In all our time together, he had never spoken of a wife or children, and so I assumed not, and though he had once accused me of boldness, I had, in fact, been too timid to ask.

The boardinghouse came into sight. With any luck, Humphries would be asleep, and I could creep in.

"I shall leave you here, Doctor, that we might continue this charade another day."

Clumsily, I pulled down my hat and strode away. I wasn't but forty feet when Silas called after me. "Miss Givens," said he. "I have neither time for a wife nor the means for children. I am a man of limited interests and singularity of mind."

So composed was I, and so determined not to betray relief, I did not break my stride. I turned the corner. In the window of the room where Julia and Erasmus slept, the glowing nub of a candle betrayed a vigil—not for me, but for the husband who might be out all night or gone for days.

The day had not yet dawned as I shut the door behind me. I am sure I looked more like a scarecrow than a man, for when the housemaid, Katy, saw me as she lit the morning lamps, she let out such a screech that I turned to see if something worse lurked behind.

"Oh Lord, oh Lord," said she. "Pray do not hurt me."

"You silly girl. It is I. Olivia Givens."

I pulled off my hat, and out tumbled my hair. But the girl could only gape, no doubt on account of the pants. I had forgotten about them, so accustomed had I become to the freedom of having legs. I would have given her a slap, too, but Humphries came running, her one eye racing about.

"What . . . is . . . this?" she demanded. I could not tell if she was more affronted by the unseemliness of the hour or my attire. Or perhaps it was the smell.

I strove to think up some excuse (helping my brother? breaking in a new horse?), but nothing plausible came to mind, so I instead rose up and turned the tables.

"How is it, Mrs. Humphries, that you have hired such a squawker that one cannot visit the privy without waking the entire house?"

"The privy?" said Humphries. "In that garb?"

"Whose business is it what garb I wear when risking life and limb to relieve myself?"

The eye narrowed. "Why not use the chamber pot until the sun comes up?"

"What a question," said I. "I suppose you want details."

"I suppose you want to explain that smell," said she.

"It is *your* privy," said I. "If it is unclean, am I to blame? And have you not read the notices about cleanliness? The plague is coming, Mrs.

Humphries. Mark my word. And if it comes to this house, you have only yourself and this girl to blame."

At which point, Katy burst into tears, providing me with an opportunity to sashay up the stairs.

After that evening, I did not hear from Silas Orpheus for almost a month. Accustomed to seeing him every few weeks, I worried that he might have become ill. Goodness knows we were hearing awful news from other cities, but I had no good excuse to send word other than feigning illness myself. Instead, I waited.

I was sitting in the parlor, a copy of Galen's medical treatise before me on the desk, when the doctor came to call. Katy showed him in and curtsied grandly, but I pretended not to notice. Silas glanced at the ancient book upon which my eyes were fixed. "I never cease to be amazed by your curious mind."

"You think all women are fools?"

"Only a fool would think it of you."

I scrabbled about for another path by which to vent my annoyance at the absence of the doctor. "Is our city so riddled with maladies that you can be so seldom spared to call on me? It must be titillating company—even if rigor *has* set in."

He sighed. "You have quite a tongue, Miss Givens . . ."

"I should think it my finest part. If you care not for my tongue, sir, then you care not for my eyes that see all too clearly. Perhaps you care for my too-big hands or my mannish height or my—"

Which is when he reached down and kissed me. Evidently, he cared for my lips.

I shall not say I found it unpleasant. I had never forgotten that kiss in Ireland—a taste of onions and grass. Silas Orpheus tasted like soap. And here I was at twenty-eight, practically ancient, unable to breathe, not to mention speak, and in the parlor of the boardinghouse, where anyone could walk in, as Mrs. Humphries immediately did.

"Well!" she said.

"It is not what you think," I said, pushing away.

"It is exactly what you think," said Silas Orpheus. "If she will have me."

This, of course, was quite impossible, as there had been no discussion. "Miss Givens!" said Humphries. "Surely, you could show some propriety."

"You must find me desperate, Dr. Orpheus. At my age . . ."

"Miss Givens," echoed Silas, and so plaintively, too, that blood rushed to my head along with the memory of my parents telling me I was a rude little girl for having spoken saucily to the minister. I lowered my eyes. Silas stood still as timber. "Will you, Miss Givens? Will you have me?"

Humphries gathered up her skirt and, glaring at both of us, flounced off to gut a chicken.

I HAVE NEVER BEEN one to pine for marriage, nor did motherhood enchant me. As I saw it, marriage was a function of economic dependence, and wrongly, too, since women rarely had money of their own. And though I was familiar with the sensation of longing, I associated it more with proximity to Julia. Perhaps it was her passion for Erasmus. Perhaps, too, I appreciated her loveliness with my own eyes. My ardor for Silas Orpheus sprang more from our shared inquisitiveness and from the freedom our forays provided, and I confessed as much upon the heels of his proposal.

"Think of our marriage as a way for you to dispense with subterfuge," said Silas. "You'll no longer have the need of such . . . costumes."

"I rather like the trousers."

"Then by all means, wear them. What do I care? You have a mind, Miss Givens. If it weren't for your sex, you would do well at medical school."

That he had a point about marriage benefiting our arrangement I did concede. His appearance was not displeasing. And I *did* enjoy our banter.

But despite my age, I couldn't have said yes even if I wanted to, for I was still under the guardianship of James, although I assumed my brother would be pleased.

I assumed incorrectly.

We called upon him in the office of his factory by the canal, James locking his thumbs as he heard Silas out. The bones of a fish and a brown apple core sat upon a plate that topped the papers on James's desk. "I think well of you, Silas. You're a good man. But what do you have to show for it?"

Silas leaned forward. "I'm not without means. There is my mother's legacy."

"Enough to live on?"

"Had I not lent it to my brother. However, I have full expectation of reclaiming it."

Silas's older brother, Eugene, had inherited the family farm ("Hemp," said Silas. "Horses and the like . . ."), but had a bit of a problem with solvency (James cleared his throat at this), and so Eugene had prevailed upon Silas to part with a not insubstantial amount of money that he had yet to pay off.

"But once he does . . ." said Silas.

"Once he does," said James, rising, "you will retrieve your legacy, and we shall hope for the best." And with that, we were dispatched.

As we made our way back across the dung-strewn street, I said, "Honestly. This from a man who married his fortune."

"He is just trying to protect you from opportunists such as myself." Silas raised his eyebrow and smiled deliciously. "Little does he know how you spend your evenings."

But I was not ready to be cajoled. My older brother's reservations only served to bolster Silas's case, in my opinion. Now I was thoroughly ready to say yes. I turned to him to say as much when we were interrupted by a shout.

"Why, Dr. Orpheus! If it ain't!" Coming toward us was a young woman with sunburned skin and yellow hair braided past her shoulders. "I known you for an Orpheus soon as I seen you!" said she. "And you . . . livin' away from Caintucky so long. Don't say you don't even recognize me."

"Madam?" said Silas with a curt little bow, raising his eyebrow at me in a question mark.

"*'Madam'?* Oh, dear me, no. I'm really jes' a chit, but you ain't seen me for ages."

"Forgive me?" said Silas.

"Why, 'tis Bella! Bella Mason! The overseer's daughter."

"Of course. Little Bella." Silas made a motion with his hand as if the last time he'd seen her she'd stood only yea high.

In truth, "little Bella" now stood nearly five feet ten and weighed, by my estimation, fourteen stone.

"What brings you to Cincinnati?" Silas asked.

"Sent by my daddy to find work," she said. "Not that there's anything that suits me. Ironing and such."

"Let me introduce my fiancée, Miss Givens." Bella gave me a nod and a tight little smile, but barely looked at me. "Tell me, little Bella, how goes it at the farm?"

"With your tarnal brother? Done let my daddy go a year now, and with a sorry excuse for a reason. I swan his darkies will be addled if that man don't get his house in order. But you know Mr. Eugene."

"And what mischief is he up to lately?"

She tried to look coy rather than eager. "Why, you cain't trust rumors."

"And what rumors are being spread?"

Little Bella spoke in a conspiratorial whisper. "That he up and gambled this year's hemp crop, for one. Broke as a skunk, and Mrs. Bethany don't know a thing, now that she's got a baby and all."

A moment passed before Silas spoke. "Hadn't gotten word of any baby."

Little Bella met his stare. "Well, it was quite an *anemic* pregnancy she done have. One day she takes to her bed, and next thing you know, voilà!"

I had to stifle a laugh. Ever since the visit of the Marquis de Lafayette, Kentuckians had taken to spouting little bits of French.

"You don't say?" said Silas.

After we extracted ourselves and walked some distance, I said, "Well, *she* was full of information."

But Silas had a look on his face as if his thoughts were far away.

THE DEVIL ARRIVED on a warm September day. The steamship *Sylph* pulled up to dock, disgorging a stricken passenger before pressing on to Louisville. Soon thereafter, a colored woman went "queer all over" and collapsed in the street.

In less than forty-eight hours, thirty people succumbed. The tenants at the boardinghouse gathered in stunned silence as the news trickled in. No one dared go to the market or wander down to the landing. By the third day, businesses were shuttered, and nary a horse hoof was heard on the road.

It was dusk when Silas called on us.

"Good God," said I. "Are you sick?"

"May I?" He signaled toward the parlor, where he slumped into a chair.

Brimming with questions, I sat across from him. Was it true that there were corpses piled by the river? Had the plague been spread through the sins of the poor?

"They die in front of my eyes. Nothing works."

He had tried everything he could think of—bleeding, cupping, tincture of calomel, strongly brewed tea. "You must leave," Silas said.

We could wait it out, I told him. I could assist.

"Assist?" He looked at me as if I was demented. "People are dropping like flies, Miss Givens."

"All the more reason to help."

"Have you no fear of death?"

"Only if I end up on *your* table," I said, and wickedly, too, for it seemed poor timing for a joke.

He laughed, for the moment lighter. Then seriously: "You must heed my words. Get your family out of here."

Of course he was right. We should have fled to the hilltop home of James and Hatsepha. While our neighbors were sprinkling their yards with lime and burning tar, lorries were pulling past. The worst horror was the children, many of whom had been playing in their cribs one morning only to be carted off in tiny coffins the following day.

The quiet was broken only by church bells.

By week's end, most of the ministers had fled, and it was left to Erasmus to convene the grieving in an abandoned meetinghouse. In spite of my irreverence, I joined them. What else was one to do?

"The grass withereth, the flower fadeth, but the Word of our God shall stand forever," intoned a subdued and weary Erasmus.

"Amen," said the gathered.

Silently, we left the church.

October arrived, particularly blue and clear. Cooler nights followed the warmer days of Indian summer. By the second week, the cholera had abated, resulting in much praising of the Lord until the third week of that month when the disease returned with a vengeance.

I awoke one morning to hear moaning from the adjacent room. I arose and grabbed my shawl, but just as I opened my door and stepped into the hall, another door swung open. Julia, clinging to the jamb, staggered to the banister, called out for Erasmus, and vomited on the floor.

I nearly swooned, so awful was the stench. Calling for Katy, I instructed her to fetch the doctor and hurry, too, for she was slower than the Second Coming.

By the time Silas arrived, Julia had nearly drowned in a torrent of sick and sweat. Wasting no time, Silas reached into his kit and took out a flask. When he pressed the medicine to Julia's lips, she shook her head and turned away.

"Mrs. Givens, you have to take this."

"I am dying," she said.

She drank and retched. Her bowels convulsed, sending a plume of diarrhea across the sheet.

Again, Silas administered the medicine. Again, Julia heaved.

"Why are her lips like that?" I asked.

None of us could bear to breathe the word "cholera," but all the signs were there. The diarrhea like rice water; the vomiting; the desiccation and blueness of her skin.

Dear God, I thought—and with no small discomfort. *Dear God, you know I am no believer. I am worse than Thomas. But please, please save her.*

"Save her," I said aloud with such vehemence that Orpheus looked alarmed.

Out came the blade.

I knelt by her bed and held her hand that was as dry as an autumn leaf. She looked so small amid those awful sheets. As Silas cut, and Julia bled, I beseeched in burning silence.

"Thirsty," Julia said. Her eyes were wild and hollow. "Where's Erasmus?"

But every time she drank, the result was catastrophic. Her breathing slowed to an unsteady rasp. I couldn't bear it. Where *was* Erasmus—my brother, this husband whom Julia worshipped? Whatever occupied him, I cared not—only that he would arrive in time to comfort his wife.

Morning found the house as quiet as a crypt. I awoke in a chair, knotted and aching. Silas was in the other chair, his collar loose, his mouth ajar. One of his shoes had come off.

First his fingers came alive, then his eyebrows. He smacked his lips. Open now, his eyes drifted about the room. When they settled on me, he came to himself and sat up. "Olivia," he said. It was the first time he had ever addressed me by my Christian name.

Then William appeared. We had forgotten all about him. My heart lurched when I saw his pale face peer around the door, his gaze drifting from me to his pallid mother, where it fixed. I jerked out of the chair.

"No, Willy. No," I said, reaching for him.

But he was already upon her, crying out, and I knew whatever Divinity I had prayed to the prior night had turned His back.

CHAPTER 14

1833–1834

James and Hatsepha's Key's Hill manse was a firmly planted house—columns like sentries, fruit trees espaliering over trellises like fingers, the rooms lit by mirrored shades and crystal diffusers and flickering wicks and gaslight, the smell of lemon oil that glistened on chairs and sideboards, the murmur of servants' German and butchered English, and all the while Hatsepha, her coiffure painstakingly constructed by her maid, alternately musing on how to improve her poor relatives or make us go away.

Humphries, of course, evicted us. Since no mortician would touch the body, Silas had attended to Julia with James paying for the casket. When Erasmus broke down at the graveside, James wrenched his Bible away.

You as good as killed her, James said to Erasmus, who, upon hearing this, announced he was too tormented to linger in Cincinnati. I bundled up the boy, and together we left that Hades of a boardinghouse with its black-draped windows, wreaths, and smoke pots to be absorbed like ink stains into James and Hatsepha's life.

William had gripped my hand when we first entered this palace and did not cry, even when James told him that he would have a room of his own. *There now, Willy,* I had whispered to the boy, who had always slept with his mother. *I shan't be far.*

With Erasmus disappearing after the funeral, the boy was essentially an orphan. Little matter that he had his aunts and uncle to look after him. He was so young, and his mother gone in a day. No wonder it took months before he spoke again.

A year passed. During that time, Silas became an infrequent visitor, usually sending notes. On those rare occasions when he made his way up the hill, I would catch him staring at me, yet when I met his eyes, they shifted to the spine of a book or a painting on the wall. I consoled myself in regard to his melancholy by blaming the cholera. He was used to death, he was used to illness—but never at such a scale of devastation.

'Tis up to you, Olivia, Erasmus had said before he departed. *I shall write,* but the only letter had come months earlier when he wrote to inform us that he had rediscovered the preacher Sam Mutton in an encampment outside of New Richmond, Ohio.

Each night, James would hold forth at dinner about the application of gaslight. *Distribution is the thing,* he said. *You cannot expand a market without the means to get there.*

Hatsepha would touch her hand to her head and complain about her maid.

Loath though I was to admit it, I was growing attached to William. When he finally regained his voice, he was a soft-spoken boy—shy, but with a gift for observation and prone to intelligent questions. Many of his queries began with "why?" or "how does?" He kept me on my toes, paging through the books of James's library for the answers to how a snake might slither, how crystals cast rainbows, how bees kept track of their hive. In the woods of Key's Hill, we found arrowheads and stones with the outlines of fish and other creatures too fantastic to name. And when Silas *did* visit, we would present our specimens.

When did it live? William would ask.

Before Noah, Silas would answer with a quick smile. *Before Man came into Eden.*

Sitting in a clearing overlooking the city, we would watch the smoke of kilns and tanneries spewing forth from distant stacks. We made little games of pebbles and acorns. I taught William his letters in the dirt.

It seems you are suited to motherhood, Silas once said as we watched William from the veranda.

Not I, I said, shrugging, but in truth, I took proud note of the boy's sharp eye for finding arrowheads and bits of bone, a butterfly wing, a geode the size of a robin's egg.

He shall become a heathen, Livvie, Hatsepha proclaimed. *I shan't have a little heathen boy in my house.* But even she grew besotted, her own pregnancies having withered on the vine.

And when James and Hatsepha spoke of adopting William, it seemed it would be for the best.

Summer came and went. September arrived, and still there was no word from Erasmus. I was not altogether sorry, for the cholera had drained our filial ties the way it drained the body. As far as we knew, Erasmus had vanished into the wilderness.

It was in October that James announced he had made a plan with his lawyer. He confided in me that, though years ago he'd reconciled at not having Julia, at least he'd have the boy.

Together James and I watched as William pushed a stone tattooed by a worm fossil across the conservatory floor. "William?" I said. The boy looked up without speaking, but when I motioned to him, he came over.

"You're a quick boy," James said, producing from his pocket a gold coin with a half-eagle imprint. "Look here. You needn't be playing with stones. You can spend this if you want. But better you should tuck it away." He stroked William's chestnut curls as if they were his mother's. "Think of it as an advance."

THAT SPRING, we greeted the thaw with bated breath, vigilant for signs of resurgence. But no pestilence came. The buds of spring burst forth with the zeal of the converted, and everyone seemed giddy.

When a letter came for me, I hoped to finally hear from Erasmus, but instead it was from Silas, who wrote:

Dearest Olivia—

I must return to Kentucky to tend to some business. Please tell James that it is my hope to return with my fortune. That you and I may resume our life as man and wife is my strong desire, for I remain—

In fondnesss,
Silas

I read the note several times—"man and wife," "fortune," "desire"—before slipping it into a drawer.

IN AUGUST, Silas Orpheus returned from Kentucky with Tilly, the colored girl. She barely resembled the young woman I remembered. This Tilly was hollow-eyed, downcast and slow, not to mention very thin.

As I sat on the veranda Silas told me of how his brother, Eugene, was still cash-strapped, and so had offered up the girl as Silas's assistant until he was once again flush. *They have taken her child,* he told me.

Listening, I found it difficult to breathe. There would be no fortune. No man and wife.

"That is not what I'm saying," said Silas.

"Then what?"

"There are poorer men than I, Olivia. I hope you will reconsider."

"CALL OFF YOUR ENGAGEMENT," said Hatsepha, "until the whole mess is resolved."

"And how would you resolve it, sister?" said I, pulling taut a strand of crewelwork as we sat together in the drawing room.

"Tell him to send the girl away, of course," said Hatsepha. "There's a perfectly good country for their kind in Africa. James and I have contributed through a society at our church."

I coughed as delicately as I could. I had read William Lloyd Garrison on the topic. Earlier that year, our very own Lane Seminary had hosted debates on the merits of abolition versus the recolonization of the slaves. I could see little difference between the colonized freemen shipped off against their will to deepest Africa and the manacled wretches sent down the river to a fate unknown. But Hatsepha, as a member of the Colonial Society, was delighted with the plan. Free the slaves and be rid of them, as if anything could be so tidily put back in a box.

But Silas Orpheus would no more consider liberating Tilly than giving a horse away for free.

"I told him to hire her out," I said to Hatsepha. "If Silas won't free her, at least the girl might buy herself."

"'Hire her out?'" said Hatsepha. "For what?"

I punctured the canvas. "Silas says she's very talented." Hatsepha raised an eyebrow. "Oh, stop gaping at me. For midwifery, of course. And evidently, for dressing hair."

"She shan't be doing *my* hair," said Hatsepha. "I'd fear for my neck."

I eyed Hatsepha's rather stout neck that was overly laden with pearls. It seemed to be growing fatter along with the rest of her. I wore a simple cameo, the only piece of my mother's jewelry that hadn't been stolen or sold.

I cleared my throat. "I know a number of ladies, myself included, who wouldn't mind their hair done if the cost is right."

"Well, I say you're awfully generous to that fiancé of yours. Goodness knows. But one thing's for certain," Hatsepha added, peeking at me across the length of table. "At least my German girl won't murder me in my bed."

HOLDING UP MY PARASOL AGAINST THE SUN, I knocked on the lacquered door. It took some minutes before it cracked open enough for Tilly to peer out at me.

"The doctor's out."

"May I come in?"

It had been nearly five years since William's birth. Tilly had grown lovely in a darkish way. Not so bad with her hair tied back. She wouldn't meet my eyes.

"Do you know who I am?" I waited. "You birthed my nephew. That night of the riots?" An almost imperceptible nod. "And do you know who I am to Dr. Orpheus?" Silence. "Well, evidently I am his fiancée, though we are never entirely in agreement." Indeed, our engagement was repeatedly postponed—first by Silas's finances, then by the cholera, and now this complication of having accepted Tilly in lieu of funds. "Tell me, is it true you do hair?"

I SENT THE CARRIAGE FOR HER THE FOLLOWING DAY, along with a missive explaining my plan to Silas. If the girl had an income, it might ease our way with James, the implication being that, by having failed to retrieve his fortune, Silas was ceding the solution to me.

I was careful to schedule the visit while Hatsepha was out for tea. When Tilly arrived, I was waiting in my room.

"I'll say one thing," said I, "you're not shy with your gaze."

"You said your hair needs fixing, ma'am."

"So how does Dr. Orpheus feel about my plan?" I flinched at my tone; my ruined engagement—if that's what it was—was no fault of Tilly's.

"I'd say he felt it was a right good plan seeing's he had no need of me today."

"You help him with his . . . research?" I tapped my foot. "Did he tell you that the summer before last we found a tumorous pancreas?"

She tucked her chin. I had the feeling she might have been embarrassed for me. "I do what he says."

Recalling my composure, I touched my hair. "Well then, perhaps you can help me with this mess?"

Two more times she came before Hatsepha got wind of our visits. After our first session, Tilly arrived with a kit and accompanied by Silas: who paced downstairs while she brushed out my hair.

"Mercy," I said. "That man is so nervous, you'd think we were delivering a baby." I adjusted the mirror to reflect Tilly's face and couldn't miss the smile. She was fair for a Negro. And those eyes. In certain light, they were green as moss.

"Tilly," I said, dropping the mirror to my lap and twisting around, "how would you like to move to Liberia? You're barely twenty. You could start your own life." When she did not reply, I said, "Oh, come now. Surely you have a tongue."

Tilly made a face. "And where was *you* born? I reckon not *here* with that accent. But *me*—I was born in Kentucky."

"You are right. Forgive me."

She placed her hand on my head. Her fingers felt like butterflies.

"This is fine, fine hair," she said. "But not so fine as Missus Bethany's." She picked up the hairbrush. Her thrusts were vigorous, but the sensation was not unpleasant.

As she twisted my scant tresses into a topknot, I said, "Tell me about Mrs. Bethany."

She said nothing.

"Eugene's wife?"

Again, nothing.

"Is she pretty?"

After a pause: "They say she is."

"But you don't like her?"

Tilly murmured something about it not mattering much either way whether she liked her since Mrs. Bethany was the missus and, as such, got her way, especially at her sweetest when they all had learned not to cross her. "And 'sides . . ." Tilly began, and stopped.

"Besides?"

"'Sides nothin'," Tilly said. "She's not my problem now."

I had so many more questions, but her lips were pursed. "Well then," I said. "Let's go show Dr. Orpheus how presentable you've made me."

SILAS MIGHT NOT HAVE NOTICED if Tilly had attached a dead raccoon to my head, but Hatsepha pounced after dinner.

"That's quite a fetching coil, Olivia. Have you been practicing?"

In fact, I told her, I had been auditioning a maid.

Her eyes narrowed. "Who?"

"Never mind. You would fear for your neck."

"Oh, Olivia! That girl?" She eyed my hair. She stroked her throat. "How is her touch?"

"She says she never worked in the fields."

We were nestled in the ladies' parlor. I could hear the servants clearing the dishes. William was tucked into bed.

"What are you up to, Olivia?"

I considered how to answer, but I was not fully certain. Surely, an additional income would benefit Silas. But beyond that, Tilly's situation nagged at me—the casual way in which she was a proxy for payment.

"Who knows?" I said to Hatsepha, my voice more carefree than I felt. "If Silas can make a little money off her, then . . . we'll see."

The next time Tilly came to the house to do my hair, she mentioned how nice it would be to have a hot iron. That, she said, and some satin ribbons for embellishment. "Some don't need it," Tilly said, "but your hair is flat."

With that, she reached into her kit and pulled out two sets of curls that she held to the side of my forehead, her brow furrowed as she gleaned the closest match.

"Tilly," I said, eyeing the clumps of hair she was maneuvering about my cheeks, "where did you come by those curls?"

She cast about her kit that was full of hairpins. "Thought I had a comb in here somewhere."

"The curls, Tilly. I know they do not come cheap."

Indeed, it was becoming de rigueur for young women to hack off their tresses and sell them, particularly when they had no other means of support. Flyers went out soliciting locks, countered by tracts that compared the practice to prostitution. The prices fetched, however, were compelling, and many a shorn head was concealed by hood or bonnet.

"Dr. Orpheus says it is neither here nor there if I keep the hair."

I narrowed my eyes. "Are you telling me this hair comes from a corpse?"

"No one need know, Miss 'Livia. These curls are as good as wasted. Why, I would whack off my own hair, though no white woman would want it even though I seen nappier on some of they own heads."

"I shall *upbraid* that man," I said, although I had to allow as how Tilly *was* resourceful. "You cannot go round robbing hair off dead people."

"Don't stop Dr. Orpheus from robbing them of everything else," she muttered. "Why the other day, I saw him cut a man's pecker clear off!"

"SHE NEEDS THE MONEY, JAMES."

"You have the wildest notions, Olivia."

At Hatsepha's encouragement, I had gone directly to my brother's workshop. "I am only asking you to invest in a venture."

"I would sooner give my money to that railroad scammer who came through last week."

I should have lied and told him the funds were for that Miss Beecher's school. Through the window of James's office, I watched the bank clerk haul in the bag of payroll. Should no children be born to James and Hatsepha, this would someday come to William.

Seeing the clerk unpack the bills, I was struck by an idea. "James, if you lend the money to Tilly and she builds her business, she can buy herself *and* pay you back. With interest! And then Silas's brother can pay *him*."

"Honestly, Livvie. What do you know of business?" I knew he was in a hurry to meet a maker of crates. "And why should you care about this creature?"

"So you *will* say yes?"

I AM SORRY TO SAY he did not say yes—at least not then. With most of his profits churned back into the business, James could brag without censure that he was lighting up Cincinnati, and not only Cincinnati but a good deal of northern Kentucky and no small swath of Indiana. Now he was eyeing the West. The problem was transportation, since most of the roads were wheel-breaking, shoe-throwing affairs and vulnerable to scoundrels. The best prospect, as James saw it, was with the rails, and so he huddled constantly with developers whose various schemes might crisscross the territory and expand the market.

I, in the meantime, continued to try to expand *Tilly's* market, much to Silas's amusement. "Why, Miss Givens, I believe you are on a mission."

"You do not see the benefit?"

Strolling with Silas on the raised walkway past a row of haberdasheries, silversmiths, hatmakers, and jewelers, we peered into windows to admire a shirt or a bolt of fabric, a hair clip or a ring.

"She could make even more money," I said. "Why in the North, a hired girl makes—"

"She's not a hired girl—"

"—and not from the North. I know." Chewing my lip, I looked down the street at the river.

"How about that one?" Silas said, pointing at a blue stone set in filigreed gold.

I shrugged. "Hatsepha has all the rings in the world," I said, touching my head upon which perched the locks of the deceased, "and nothing makes her happy."

"Is Hatsepha taking the medicine I prescribed?"

"She is practically a dipsomaniac." I touched his arm. "I do not wonder if you create more problems than you cure."

Silas tipped his hat at a couple drawing near, and I recognized Phinneaus Mumford and his bride, Ariadne Pritchard, the wretch who had absconded with my pantalette years before. Now she was wife to this rising politician whose platform was the improvement of sanitation after the last go-round with cholera.

"Looking at rings?" said Ariadne, and to my surprise, for it was generally assumed that Silas and I would never marry.

"I am ever hopeful," said Silas before turning to talk in earnest to Phinneaus Mumford about the disposal of trash.

Ariadne fixed her attention to me. "You are looking awfully well, Olivia." She eyed my head so intensely I feared my borrowed curls might go the way of my pantalette and end up on her person.

I leaned forward and whispered, "My new hairdresser. She is an alchemist, but do not tell anyone. I am trying to keep her for myself."

I had hit my mark. Ariadne looked rapacious. Clearly, James was not the only Givens whose métier was sales.

SLOWLY, WORD GOT OUT. Soirees, balls, teas—even debuts—were becoming more frequent in our former backwater. Though the streets remained muddy and swine-ridden, it was not uncommon to find an opera singer or an orator gracing parlor and proscenium. The growing fashionableness required the accoutrements of seamstress and jeweler, hairdresser and maid. One could barely leave the house without the help of staff.

"This girl of yours," said Hatsepha. "She's awfully good."

"As I have said."

"And what shall she do with the money?"

"She shall buy herself free."

"Are you sure of that?" said Hatsepha.

"Of course I'm sure," I said crisply. "A woman's got a right to buy herself."

But the next time Silas and I met for tea, I asked him straightaway.

"*Buy* herself? I hardly think so."

"But she brings in quite a stream."

"Which goes mostly to my brother." Silas looked at me with a mixture of exasperation and pity. "Like it or not, he still owns her." He signaled for the check before turning back to me. "But console yourself with this, my dear: enslaved or not, Tilly is better off with me."

CHAPTER 15

1834

Only October, and already snow—an early dusting that blanched the landscape. We ran outdoors to fling fistfuls of white into the air, roughhousing so joyfully that my hair came loose. Willy, too, was wild with play. We were in such a state when the rider came up the drive that we barely noticed the man, and had we done, wouldn't have known him. It was not until he called my name that I recognized the voice of my younger brother.

I pushed my hair back and squinted. I had seen him disheveled before, but this scarecrow bore little resemblance to Erasmus. So emaciated was he, so wan and long-haired and bearded, that had he announced himself as Our Lord Jesus, I shouldn't have disputed the likeness.

"Erasmus?"

I had been growing ever more uneasy at the lack of correspondence, wondering if he had taken ill or ended up incarcerated. Anything worse I refused to consider.

"'Tis your da!" I said to Willy, lifting him in my arms and rushing toward my brother, nearly knocking him off his mount.

Erasmus alighted, still holding the reins of a moribund mule that made his old horse Abel look like a thoroughbred.

"What steed is this?" I said. "And where have you been?"

"'Tis much to tell," Erasmus said, holding Willy and me to his chest. "Forgive me," he said. "Forgive me, forgive me, forgive me."

He had left us in the autumn of 1832 after the death of Julia. The leaves had turned, fallen. He had had no plans to speak of, just a vague notion of finding redemption. He ate what people gave him, gleaning ears of late corn, shooting rabbits. A month in, he had taken to boiling acorns. On the fifth week, he had walked into the river.

Sam Mutton, the preacher who had converted him, was on the shore when Erasmus floated by and yanked him out. What were the chances of that?

"'Twas a sign," said Erasmus. "On that you can count."

Erasmus had had some sense of where Sam Mutton lived, and my less charitable self wagered that Erasmus knew his "suicide" would draw attention. But Erasmus insisted God had handed him a miracle.

Over the next few months, he had worked alongside Sam at his encampment along the Ohio, manning two rowboats and a raft, meeting the steamboats, ferrying passengers who, for whatever reason, chose to disembark in the middle of nowhere. Some were interested in pushing into northern Ohio to settle and farm. Others preferred to jump ship short of Ripley or Cincinnati, where they might be noticed. Whatever their reasons for disappearing, Erasmus knew better than to ask.

Sam Mutton spent most of his time talking about the souls one met on the river, and how one should preach against slavery as those from the North would have it, or justify the institution, as many from the South would hear. Some would ask him for his sermon, delivered on the fly as they made their passage. Others received his wisdom unsolicited, merely as an aside from one riverbank to the other.

Mostly, I tell them what they want to hear.

When Sam died after a piece of venison got wedged in his gullet,

Erasmus stayed on in the encampment. Before long, he was in cahoots with whiskey runners that were siphoning off a still in Frankfort, paying Erasmus one barrel per ten he poled across.

There had been times—too many to count—when Erasmus would hear shots in the night. Occasionally, a patroller showed up and, seeing not Erasmus but a muddled inebriate on the threshold of middle age, his hair and beard badly in need of tending, shrugged and moved on. There was nothing to fear from this one.

Erasmus's nails grew long. Voices laughed from beneath the floorboards. He became aware that he was cold, and looked up to see red leaves clinging to branches that only days before were fulsome with green. What month was it? How old was the boy? He cried as he told me this, saying that never once had Julia accused him of abandonment. He would turn back the river if he could.

"I admit it now, Livvie. It was James she should have married. I knew it at the time."

Then Abel died, and this grieved Erasmus sorely. Burying the horse alongside Sam, he tried to collect himself and recall the days when a hundred people gathered to hear him preach. To offer up such a sermon again—*alleluia!* He tried and failed to recall the words. Something about glad tidings and the love of the Lord, but having no one to listen, he offered the Lord's love to Abel, saying, *Ye were a fine horse, and that's a fact. Would that I cared for my son as much as thee.*

Somehow the Lord, upon hearing these words, mistook them for a prayer, and Erasmus felt his heart fill and his mind grow steady in a way that was unfamiliar—like the first time he saw Sam and plotted his way out.

Go forth and sin no more.

It came to him from the rafters or the branches—not from beneath the floor where the Devil lurked. It sparkled like sunshine, and his face grew wet with tears.

The river. He had to get himself to the river.

Staggering toward it, he thought, *But what if I drown?*

And in the wake of that thought, *So be it.*

In he went. The cold waters of autumn surrounded him, his footing unsteady on the rocky edge, buttressed by the current. He plunged in as if he were a Baptist and came up choking, lungs full of river and laughter while he was carried downstream, his shoulder-length hair all about him. He waved at a steamboat. Everyone on the deck waved back as if he were an apparition borne by the flood. Then someone tossed him a rope and he grabbed it, and they pulled him in like a fish.

Praise the Lord, he said.

And everyone answered, *Amen.*

But when they offered him some whiskey to warm himself, he refused it. "I told them to just let me off at Cincinnati," Erasmus said, smiling at William and me. "It's time I retrieved my son."

HATSEPHA WOULDN'T ALLOW HIM into the house without a good scrub. Even then, she slipped a scrap of linen onto one of her petit point chairs. I sat across from him, while Erasmus repeated his talk of finding redemption and being baptized in the river.

"Well then," said Hatsepha, her eyes straying to the clock on the mantel.

Neither of us could bear to broach the subject of adoption, especially when Erasmus told us how he had preached on the landing for several weeks to scrounge enough money to buy the mule, professing that William was the reason for his return, having been called by God to do so, and that he meant to do right by the child.

Oh Lord, thought I. *There shall be such a tempest when James returns.*

"Tell me, brother," said Hatsepha, with a clear of her throat. "Do you have any society near your encampment?"

Erasmus blinked at her. He'd never had use for Hatsepha.

"Not so much," said Erasmus. I appreciated his effort to be civil. The confrontation would be arduous enough without being rude to the woman who had housed his son.

"No school?"

"None as such that you might recognize, though Sam owned some books."

"Twenty *miles* you say?"

"Depends if you go by horse or boat."

"Well," said Hatsepha, sitting back in her chair and shaking her hair, "James will never have it."

"JUST LIKE THAT?" said James when he returned that evening to find our brother in his parlor. "Gone for nearly two years and not a word? And now with a scheme that's little better than a squat?"

"'Tis land, and I own it," said Erasmus.

"Look at ye," said James.

Indeed, even cleaned up, Erasmus looked a sight. Not yet thirty and with silver in his hair. This plan of his (if you could call it that) of ferrying and preaching seemed daft—but not as daft as taking the boy away when Willy could be cared for and educated here.

"Why not ask the boy?" said Erasmus.

"The boy is barely five."

"He knows his father."

"I doubt that."

It was left to me to bring the child. Up till then, I had said nothing. My head and heart were not of the same opinion, but when I sank to my knees in front of William in the nursery, I whispered that his father had come for him, and that he should be very brave and good and kind. William was too young to know about the adoption or that James had consulted lawyers and tried to have Erasmus declared legally dead. It would be a difficult argument to make now that Erasmus had both a pulse and a desire to reclaim his son.

"He smells bad," said William.

"'Tis from the horse."

"That's no horse."

"Even so," said I.

We arrived in the parlor, and from the expression on my brothers' faces, I could see they had argued.

"There, then," I said. "Go greet your da."

And proud I was, too, of the lad, who marched right up to Erasmus and stuck out his hand as James had trained him to do when making the acquaintance of a stranger.

Look them in the eye, James would say. *Give a good grip so they shan't have the upper hand.*

William gave a mighty shake, but I could see he was crying. Then Erasmus, kneeling down, pulled from his pocket a smooth white stone upon which was the delicate imprint of a fish gill. William wiped his nose on his sleeve. "There now, my son, shall ye like to go up the river?"

And William, who had looked solemn and scared up till then, studied the stone and broke into a smile.

With a hoot, Erasmus grabbed the boy, tossed him into the air, and spun around. In that moment, the two of them swirling—father and son—I could see which way it would go.

Not for James, this boy, thought I. And I felt sad for James. But more than that, I was sad for me.

CHAPTER 16

1835

Erasmus stayed with us through that winter. For the sake of the boy, he and James were civil to each other. I cut my younger brother's hair, fed him, asked if he had any inclination to preach.

"It will take some doing before God wants to hear from the likes of me."

"Cheer up," I said, feeling compassion in spite of my views. "You speak of a loving God with infinite capacity for forgiveness."

"Forgiveness is not the same as fondness," said Erasmus. "Even the Catholics know this."

As soon as the snow melted, he told me, he and the boy would head back to the encampment to sow crops and ferry passengers in the hope that God might show His way. For all our sakes, I wished for a long winter, but the thaw came in March, and for once, Erasmus was true to his word.

James could not look at the boy when he was packed up and standing in the hallway, his hair wetted down as if he were going to church. I wondered when we would see him again, for twenty miles might as well have been a hundred, and Providence had a way of dividing families more often than not. It was a bitter wafer to be separated from that boy, but no more for me than for James. I had only seen him so wretched years ago when Erasmus returned married to Julia.

And what was I to do now that I was relieved of my charge? Since the cholera, Silas had barred me from autopsies, saying resurrections could carry risk. I was left to my needlework. At least my hair was presentable.

EXPECTING TILLY, I was surprised when Silas opened the door to his office.

"Olivia?" he said. "Do you have an appointment with Tilly? I thought she came to you."

I looked him up and down. "You don't look well," I said. Indeed, his whiskers were unkempt, his shirt unpressed. "I should think she'd be looking after you."

"I've been running an experiment . . ."

"May I come in?"

He stood back, saying something about a Negro with a missing spleen.

I pushed past him into his office space. There was no sign of Tilly or her hair basket. These days, she was frequently out ministering to ladies in their homes. "Dead or alive?" I said. When he looked at me blankly, I said, "The Negro?"

"Oh! Dead, of course. And most interestingly, his body seemed blackened with tar. It leads me to believe—"

"I've missed you, Silas. And the boy has gone with his father."

"Olivia . . ."

"What was it you once said? Something about having no time for a wife nor the means? Your being a man of 'limited interests and singularity of mind' was how you put it. You've insisted on no children. Well, I've thought this over, and frankly, it suits me, as does the fact you have no money. I no longer care what James thinks. I'm in need of being useful."

"I'm confused."

"I'm saying," I said, turning to face him, "let's get on with it."

LOSING THE BOY to Erasmus left James with little ardor for protesting my marriage to Silas. He even consented to our using their parlor for the ceremony with Hatsepha standing as my attendant, struggling between her disapproval at my marrying a poor man and her delight at showing off a new silk dress. I, in turn, felt quite giddy at the prospect of leaving Key's Hill. I had listened patiently to Hatsepha's marriage-bed advice that intimacies benefited from cloak of darkness, and that should I feel pain, do not blame the man, but with patient persistence, the results could be—"well, quite *pleasing*!"

This was the only time I blushed during her discourse. As for the rest, I refrained from mentioning that I had not only splayed open the womb of a corpse, but sliced through vagina and vulva.

The door to Silas Orpheus's office was, like all doors along that row of brick town houses, an impeccable, glossy black. Even the brass plate was respectable: SILAS ORPHEUS, MEDICAL DOCTOR. His flat behind the office was another story altogether. Stepping over yesterday's shirt and a pair of muddy boots, I stood in a parlor of shelves, and on those shelves, jar after jar of frogs, fish, even something with fur. Fossils and bones and pages of notes huddled upon the desk, the cramped space lit by candles burned to stubs, the discards collected in a pot for melting down and for use again as light or for fixing the corpses of insects.

And tools! Tools for hacking, for sawing, suturing, extraction. A mallet to test reflexes; a hammer to crack skulls. Even the bed was stacked with saws and books and newspapers and a few bloody rags.

"I'll need a place to sit," I said. "I could do with a chair and a cushion."

The room's one tall window faced north, away from the river. What few sticks of furniture there were—a pine table, a good mahogany dresser, a ratty needlepoint rug—were claimed by experiments in various stages: glass tubes, bottles of alcohol, instruments of bloodletting, of cupping, of measurement. There was not one book of poetry. Nothing upon which to make music. No flowers. No air.

"Dust, dust, dust," said Silas. He had removed his hat, but the room was cold, so he retained his scarf and coat. "Have you ever seen such dust?"

But his mattress promised a new frontier—as exotic and alluring as Illinois. My image was of Julia rushing from our room to my brother's bed, their exclamations and hushed laughter, their whispers of *Shh!* and *Darling!*

That my marriage bed might be otherwise had never occurred to me.

"And where does *that* lead?" I said, indicating a door on the other side of the room.

"That?" said Silas. "Oh, that's where I keep Tilly."

HATSEPHA HAD BEEN quite right about the pain, less so about the pleasantness.

Perhaps you should have a glass of wine? Silas suggested.

Perhaps you shouldn't have run off so quickly to wash, thought I.

After a month or so of this, we fell into a pattern of Silas asking me about my menses, showing ardor in the week that followed, abstaining during the second and third weeks and, of course, when I bled. The whole business quite embarrassed me, and I began to think I'd imagined those feelings of longing when I was barely fifteen.

Stitching with Hatsepha one afternoon, I cleared my throat. "This 'pleasantness' you spoke of . . ."

Hatsepha slowly lifted her gaze to mine, eyebrows raised, the hand holding the needle suspended over the canvas. Then she nodded. "I did quite think I was having a convulsion. And then it happened again. Well!" she said, stabbing her canvas and drawing through the thread. "I went straight to the minister. And you know what he said?"

I leaned in.

"He said"—she lowered her voice to assume pastoral authority—"'Dear lady, this is Jesus approving of your match.'"

It took me some time to broach the topic with Silas. We were picnicking on a low hill not far from the river. Tilly, as usual, was with us, sitting erect, her own parasol positioned to protect her skin from becoming even darker. She would study the opposite bank as if to solve a riddle. More than once I'd seen her toss a button or a ribbon into the current. When I asked her why, she shrugged and said, *You try crossing that thing without the Lord's help.*

Today, taking advantage of her distraction, I said, "Silas, do you believe Jesus—or God—keeps a ledger on people's marriages?"

Silas was lying on his side, propped on his elbow, reading a medical journal. For a moment, I thought he hadn't heard me. "A ledger?" I said. "Like the one James—"

"I heard what you said." With some care, he marked his page with a leaf and set aside the tome. "Surely you're not serious?"

"Well, you know I'm not . . . I don't . . ." I sighed. "It's not Jesus' pleasure I worry about. It's yours."

He stroked his beard. I felt like one of his cadavers. "Perhaps it is time for an anatomy lesson."

I glanced nervously at Tilly, but if she heard us, she gave no sign.

"There's a rather sweet glade just back on the path," said Silas. He almost smiled. "Perhaps we should take a walk." His eyebrow rose. "For the love of Jesus, that is."

"WHY'D YOU LET THE BOY GO?" said Tilly. We were discussing William and how, once he'd left, I saw no reason for staying on with James and Hatsepha. "Once you let a child go, you never get them back."

I was sitting in the chair in front of her as she combed and braided my hair in the corner of Silas's office.

"Erasmus is his father." Although I was in agreement with Tilly's sentiments, I felt obliged to model a sense of filial decorum.

"Don't see how that makes no never mind," she said. "Not all daddies want their chillun. From what you say, the boy's opportunity was up the hill."

"Let's talk about something else. *Your* opportunity, for instance. How much revenue have you brought in?"

Even Silas had to admit that Tilly's enterprise was impressive. He said as much when he begrudgingly conceded that it was a shame that she had to send most of the revenue back to Eugene in Kentucky. I fancied that Silas was changing his position on the subject of slavery and coming around to a more democratic view of human independence.

"Five ladies I done last week," said Tilly. "You'd think they was the Queen of Sheba."

"Humph," said I. "And where are they all going, I would like to know. Galas, I suppose. Or balls." I sniffed. "No one asks us," I added, thinking it would be lovely if Silas showed a little more interest in the living aside from our recent spate of affection. I still accompanied him to autopsies, but only at my insistence. He felt it was more expedient to take Tilly. I considered suggesting he should pay her for her assistance but decided not to press it as I didn't want to hear once more that her labors were part of the agreement with his brother. Many nights Silas would stay up late writing and experimenting, returning to our bed just before dawn, if at all.

"*I'd* like to go to a ball," said Tilly. "Dance all night. Wear out my shoes. Haven't you ever danced, Missus 'Livia? Why, they used to have dances down at the farm 'fore Missus Bethany went all strange, and they's neighbors stopped letting they daughters near Mr. Eugene."

I started to ask her what she meant, but she gave my hair such a tug, I cried out.

IN THE FIRST YEAR OF OUR MARRIAGE, Alexis de Tocqueville came to town, extolling Cincinnati as "a model of democracy." There was built a wax museum of such uncanny likenesses that Tilly and I swore we saw them breathe. So, too, the circus came, complete with fire-eaters and bearded ladies and a man with feet like fins. Eighteen thirty-five saw the charter of seven railroads, only one of which laid a road. Key's Hill was renamed "Mt. Auburn." And in 1837, the market crashed—the very same year that Silas took sick.

It started with a cough—a cough like any other, brought on by the increasing factory smoke or a malingering cold.

"You spend too much time in the basement," I said.

"It's nothing much."

"You should get some rest."

"I'll rest when I'm dead."

I regarded his pallor. "You shouldn't jest."

"Your concern touches me, Olivia. You are a better woman than you think."

"Oh, I consider myself fine indeed."

"And who is the jester now?"

Such was our banter. And then he was gone.

CHAPTER 17

1837

The veil on the bonnet I had borrowed from Hatsepha tossed in the wind. As the riverboat pushed upstream, every turn of the wheel swooshed like a year passing. Eighteen since our immigration; eight since William was born and I first met Silas. There were miles of shore, so many little settlements, an abundance of trees, an absence of landmarks, the feeling one has when something cherished slips from one's hands.

Closing my eyes, I was once again that girl of fifteen coming down this great river for the first time, awed by the enormous beeches and oaks, the flocks of birds, the body of the black man, bloated and abandoned, the view of Cincinnati in the distance. Decades had passed since Fulton's steam engine first drove a barge upstream, and still a sense of giddiness that one could span thirty miles in a day. Again, the turning wheel—this time whispering, *Get on with it! Get on with it!*

Tilly and I had tried to revive Silas with mustard poultice and mint teas. We stayed at his bedside, marking his breath and pulse. I touched his head; she held his hand. Together, we willed him to live.

Should we bleed him? I had asked.

I don't go in for that, said Tilly.

The cough became a rattle, became a gurgle, became a rasp.

There is no poetry in dying.

Now I was accompanying his body up the river. Every time we passed a small settlement or the merest wisp of an encampment, someone would be waiting in a rowboat, offering to take passengers ashore. Two young men on a raft just off the bow waved at me frantically. For a moment, I forgot my sorry cargo and waved back.

"Ferry off! Ferry off!" they cried, hoping to catch a fare. The captain blew the horn.

Occasionally, and much to my amazement, a passenger would alight onto one of the little rafts or skiffs. Though the road was clear and trodden on the Kentucky side, the Ohio shore was buttressed by trees so dense that I couldn't imagine any purpose other than the siren song of wilderness for jumping ship several miles ahead of Ripley.

"Ferry off!"

I looked down this time to see a boy and a man in a shard of a boat. I grasped the railing. How well I knew that hat, although the boy I barely recognized.

"Erasmus!" I shrieked, and hoarsely, too, but the blades and the cascading drip of water drowned me out. I pulled off my hat and veil, craning for another sighting.

"Ma'am?" A steward had heard my shouting and come to check on me. "Are you unwell?"

"That man in the boat," I said. "Do you know him?"

He squinted at the receding dinghy. "River preacher. Lives over yonder at Enduring Hope."

"Enduring Hope?" For three years, I had been sending letters and books to Erasmus Givens posted to New Richmond and Ripley, my own hope being that one or two would arrive.

Make the boy read, I wrote. *Don't reduce him to idiocy.*

I wanted to call out to the captain, *Turn around! Go back!* But it seemed our course was set, and half an hour later, we glided past Ripley.

FROM WHAT LITTLE SILAS HAD TOLD ME about his brother, I knew better than to expect mourning. Even so, I was unprepared for Eugene.

Disembarking from the steamboat, I scanned the crowd on the Maysville, Kentucky, landing, my hat pulled low against the glare of the midday sun. Everyone else seemed to scatter, and I was left quite alone.

Moments later, a Negro youth in homespun pants and oversized shirt hurried over. "Excuse me," I said as he hoisted my bag onto his shoulder. "What are you—"

"S'okay," said a familiar voice. "He's my boy."

The voice belonged to a man on a horse. I squinted up, and seeing a face I knew so well, I almost cried out.

"My dear sister Olivia," he said, dismounting, his voice thick with southern charm and irony. Like Silas, his tone was amused, but there was no affection in Eugene's voice. "May I call you Olivia?"

"Sir," said I, and held out my hand.

They had brought a hearse carriage for the coffin, and several horses. When I said I preferred to ride, Eugene whistled at the two boys loading the coffin. "Careful now," he said, lifting me up onto the sidesaddle, and all the while appraising me with that same familiar look.

Our procession through Maysville was somber. Merchants and customers came out of shops to pay their respects. Had it been another occasion, I would have spent more time admiring this town with its neat houses and stores and shaded streets. Whatever Eugene's faults (according to Silas, profligacy and gambling), the Orpheus family had standing. On the face of it, Eugene was dressed for the occasion in a frock coat and pantaloons, but on closer inspection, his loose cravat and brocade lapels betrayed evening clothes unchanged from the night before.

"I look forward to seeing your famous farm, Mr. Orpheus," I said, trying to conceal my discomfiture. "My husband told me all about it." The horse Eugene had given me was a chestnut with a gait not quite broken to the sidesaddle.

"You got to grip that horn with your knees," Eugene said when my horse shied at a passerby.

I tightened my legs as we ascended through limestone bluffs that gave way to fields of hemp, velvety soft and sultry. The buzzing in my ears seemed to come from a distant swarm of bees.

"How much longer?"

"I am forgetting myself, Miss Givens. You must be weary."

I *was* weary—brittle as porcelain. The next thing I knew, the ground was coming at me. A sharp pain in my arm, and Eugene was shouting, and I was being lifted. After that came darkness. I was aware of a rocking as if at sea. But the smell this time was of grass, not of salt water, and the box I was resting against was my husband's coffin.

"IMAGINE MY SURPRISE."

My fingers scrabbled at something lacy. The rocking had stopped, and when I opened my eyes, there were two faces staring down. One was a fair-haired woman, her hair in braids. The other was that of a black woman with cheeks plump as pincushions.

I struggled to rise, to regain myself, but my arm gave way, and the room spun. Hands pressed me back onto the pillow.

"When they opened that carriage," said the pale-haired woman, "I thought Eugene had brought along an extra body. It would be just like him."

The Negress wiped my brow. I was trying to say thank you when the two faces became three, the third being that of a child around seven. She was very pretty with green eyes and long lashes, plump lips, and dusky, wavy hair tied with a bow.

"Auntie?" said the girl.

"We're so glad you've come," said the straw-haired woman. She had a narrow, tattered face that reminded me of a Gainsborough portrait. If this was Eugene's wife, she looked older than her husband. "We've had nothing to talk about for weeks."

"My arm?"

"You've wrenched it badly. Mandy here has put on some salve."

I started to ask, *What kind of salve?* but the girl interrupted me. "I'm Elizabeth Mary Satfield Orpheus."

"Hush now," said the woman, who was presumably Bethany. "Don't bother her about that."

I touched my cheek. It had a tender, scraped feeling. I ran my tongue around my mouth, accounting for all my teeth. I said, "If you'd be so kind, I wouldn't mind a mirror."

THE FOLLOWING DAY, we buried Silas in the family plot just up the hill that interred four generations of Orpheuses dating back to 1787. The graveyard, twenty or so headstones, was laid out under a large oak surrounded by a wrought-iron fence. The family and a handful of friends stood within the perimeter while a dozen or more Negroes gathered outside. My eyes kept traveling to the group beyond the fence whose mood seemed more downcast than Eugene's. One youth in particular kept wailing, and some of the older slaves said to him, "Hush now, Grady. The Lord is listening."

I wasn't sure about the Lord, but Bethany surely was listening because she kept glowering at the young man, Grady, then at Elizabeth, who giggled every time Grady made a sound.

Barely listening to a eulogy that had little to do with Silas, I experienced a spasm in the back of my throat as the first clod of dirt hit the coffin and the cherubic minister in thick glasses and downy whiskers intoned, *Ashes to ashes*. It struck me that Silas would have preferred his body had been used for science.

A goddamn cold, he would have said.

I could imagine him in his smock and mask, scalpel ready to slice the lung, probing for the obstruction or the necrotic tissue that had interrupted his breathing.

You should have done it, Olivia. You had the guts.

I fought back tears.

Surely you are not sentimental, Miss Givens.

I practically jumped at the sound of his voice, but it was only Eugene thanking the young minister and inviting him for victuals.

"Dear, you look so terribly tired," said Bethany, who had come up beside me. She looked at my face, following my gaze to the face of her husband. She slipped her arm through my good one, careful not to jostle the sling. "So much to talk about, and there goes Eugene inviting half the county."

I SLEPT ALL THAT EVENING and well into the following day. When I finally rose, it was with the intention to return to the landing to catch the next boat to Cincinnati, but a week passed, the sling came off, and I remained, having succumbed to the entreaties of the girl Elizabeth, who, in spite of being done up in dresses and bows, was shockingly untamed, jumping up from the table, running into the pasture with the horses. In the girl's features, I could detect that trace of Orpheus.

"Tuh," I said. "Tuh," running the girl's forefinger along the shape of a *T,* then pointing to a picture. "Tree."

"Tree."

"What else?"

"Tobacco!" Elizabeth beamed.

"O," said I, tracing a circle. "Open."

"Oooo," said the girl, her mouth forming the exact shape. "Old," she said, peering slyly at me.

"Yes," I said. "Old Olivia."

Elizabeth reached out and hugged me—something I hadn't seen her do with Bethany—then rushed off to find Grady to play tag.

It must be one of Eugene's flusher times because everything seemed jolly, and both the girl and her mother had new dresses to show off. Although I agreed with those who naysayed slavery, I could detect no traces of the horrors I'd read about. Everything ran efficiently and with far more grace than what was offered by Hatsepha's German girls. Everyone I came into contact with seemed content enough—hardworking, surely—but no more so than those crow-backed settlers who'd hacked a patch out of wilderness.

I would study Eugene by candlelight, trying to glean debauchery, but he was mostly silent, and when he spoke, was alternately brusque and silky. Still, there was that appraising quality that made me uncomfortable to the point of blushing, and I would glance at his wife across the table, who didn't seem to notice anything but the child whom she one minute fussed after like a dust devil, telling her to brush her hair and pull it back from her face, then alternately ignored.

"We want to see your lovely eyes," Bethany said before turning away to study the lace on her sleeve.

They *were* lovely eyes. And as with her father's face, she reminded me of someone else.

It's awfully hot here, I wrote to James and Hatsepha. *But no more than Cincinnati, and at least there's a breeze,* adding, *It's not as ghastly as I thought.* What I didn't write was that I dreaded coming back to those empty rooms—empty except for Tilly, who was so busy with her clients she didn't need me anyway. Besides, I had a sense of Silas here—a younger Silas, whose life was simpler and less encumbered by the pathology of others.

At night we sat on the porch, counting fireflies and stars. If Eugene was with us, he leaned against a post, puffing on a cigar. If he talked, it was about horses and with such a passion that I thought I might actually come to care. Bethany, who knew horses herself, commented occasionally, but there was little true conversation between husband and wife, little show of affection. Bethany talked of her former life in Lexington as if she'd emigrated from a beloved country.

"Eugene only goes to Lexington on business," Bethany said. "He says business and wives don't mix."

Bethany was sitting in a rocker, her head thrown back, her eyes closed.

Eugene said, "Crop's just about done. We'll have to bring in some hands."

"And that boy? Grady?" I asked, wondering about the boy whom Elizabeth was teasing at the funeral.

"Grady?" said Bethany. "Touched little nigger. Must be near fifteen." Silas had set a leg bone for him when he was a small boy, she told me. "Or was it that arm? Either way, his bones knit badly."

"Grady's okay," said Eugene. "Weak in the head, though."

"I tell you he's been harassing Elizabeth," said Bethany calmly. "You've got to set him straight."

"The girl shouldn't be playing down there," Eugene said. "What's she doing down there, anyway? It's only going to cause trouble."

"Well, if *you* won't set him straight . . ."

Anxious to change the topic, I said, "Tell me about your dress, Bethany. The one you're going to wear to the cotillion."

Bethany wrenched her gaze away from her husband and laughed lightly. "Why, *that* old dress? You should know it's from last season."

THAT NIGHT I AWOKE, having the feeling that something was amiss. I swore I heard a rooster crowing, yet a short time later, the clock in the hall sounded three.

Perhaps I am too hot, I thought, pushing away the bedclothes. Dropping to the floor, I scrabbled around beneath the bed and pulled out the porcelain bowl, pulled up my chemise, and squatted.

The room was full of creaks and shadows. It was one of the better rooms with a fireplace connected to the central chimney. Turkish rugs blanketed thick planks of pine. Across from the bed, a vanity table held a mirror and an assortment of silver brushes. On the other side of the wall was Bethany's bedroom, but unlike the walls at Mrs. Humphries's, these were thick plaster, and sound didn't penetrate.

I shoved the chamber pot back under the bed with my foot, barely thinking about the dark hands that would remove it later. Something gnawed at me.

And then it came again—that reedy caw that wasn't a rooster.

One of the slaves must be sick, I thought, shuddering at the sound. *Just a slave . . .*

Then it occurred to me that, with my medical training, I could be of help. I lit a lamp and set about pulling on petticoats and a skirt, a shimmy and a morning coat, pushing my hair up into a cap. I laced my boots over thick cotton stockings, took the lamp from its base, and slowly made my way downstairs.

Even at this hour, the air was thick as cream. The gravel on the drive made a hushed crunch as I crossed toward the path that would lead to the slave quarters. An owl hooted. I could make out Sirius to the southwest. The mewling sound seemed to have stopped, then started up again. There was a rhythm to it that gave me tingles.

There. Clear. A swish followed by that ghastly yelp.

The cabins were in a row, maybe five altogether. I made my way between the buildings through the deep grass, the lamplight grotesque against rough-hewn logs. At the edge of the last building, I stopped. Another lamp was perched on a stump in a clearing, and in the middle of the clearing, a post, and tied to the post, a figure.

"And you shall not so much as *look* at her," Bethany was saying. And as she said it, she brought down the switch. The figure made a sound like, *"Lah."*

"Law, law," said Bethany. "Your only 'law' is your master." Her hair was loose past her shoulders. I could not see her face. Not wanting to be seen, I pulled back against the building and blew out the lamp, but no sooner had I done so than I realized I was standing close to a group of people, all of them watching silently.

Smack, went the switch.

"And when I'm done,"—*smack!*—"you shall be sorry you ever spoke to her, you hear me? You *hear* me?" Bethany threw down the switch. "Stupid boy." She picked up the lamp and wheeled around. Her face was devoid of passion. She might as well have been meting out instructions to the cook.

I shrank away and moved to disappear among the shadows. Bethany pushed past without seeing me. For a long time, none of the slaves spoke. They waited until she was well gone. Then the older man, the one called Handsome, said, "Cut the boy down."

I couldn't move, but the others did as Handsome said, and when he was down, Grady lay on the ground and whimpered. Someone lit another lamp. The boy's face was covered in sweat, and his eyes were wild. He cried, "I didn't do nothin'."

"There now, Grady boy, you go inside," said Handsome, giving him a hand.

"Here," I said, stepping out, "I can help dress those cuts."

The slaves stared with a combination of wariness and embarrassment. Some moved apart and made room for me to examine Grady.

A young man with a shaved head said, "Grady know better than to play with that girl. Every time he does, Missus goes wild."

"I wasn't doin' nothin'," said Grady.

"Go *inside,*" said Handsome. Staring at the ground, he said, "Ma'am, you shouldn't be here."

I felt the heat in my cheeks. "I heard a noise."

"You didn't hear nothin'. You should get back to the house."

I felt as though I were a schoolgirl being shooed from the yard. All those years ago when I'd sat at lectures, listening to Fanny Wright or the students at Lane Seminary talk about the abolition of slavery, it had been an abstraction, repugnant as leprosy, but little to do with me. It was like the tract on which you wipe off your hands. It was like that body in the river; something you caught out of the corner of your eye.

"TH," I SAID. "Like 'thumb.' See?" I held up my hand.

Elizabeth squinted at me. "Why?"

"Because that's what *T* and *H* do. Like 'thought' or 'thistle.'"

"Or stupid."

I tried and failed to match her look. "Or 'thick.'"

Elizabeth started smacking her feet against the table legs. We were sitting on the porch, the heat relentless in spite of the shade.

A little too harshly, I said, "Stop it."

Her kicking increased.

"You awful child . . ." I said with some impatience, and then stopped myself when I saw the hurt on her face.

"She called me an awful child," Elizabeth said when Bethany joined us, dressed to go out and with a radiance I had not seen.

"You *are* an awful child," said Bethany. "Look at your hands!"

Elizabeth made fists and dug them beneath her skirts. "Reading is silly," she said.

"Not so silly as sums, I daresay," said Bethany. She pulled on a glove and smiled at me. "You look tired, Olivia. I fear the humidity has made you wan."

"I am used to worse."

"Then come with me to town. They have the most beautiful hats in Maysville, and if you don't mind my saying, you could use with some sprucing up."

Elizabeth stared down at her fists. She had such long lashes, even for a child. "And what do you say, Elizabeth?" I said. "Since you have no more patience for literature."

Would she run off to find Grady? And in what condition would she find him? Perhaps she was used to seeing her friend brought low. She wouldn't look at her mother. Instead, she turned to me.

"Thimble," she said. "Thorn. Thread. Thoroughbred."

I closed the book on my lap. "Thank you," I said.

ON SUNDAY, the best carriage was brought up from the stables to carry us to church, where a visiting minister would be preaching. There seemed to be much excitement to hear a new voice. I noticed the lacquer on the brougham was flaking, the silk of the festoons faded. Still, the leather seat was deep, and I sank into it after the slave Handsome gave me a hand up. His eyes were averted, but I noticed the almost imperceptible shake of his head. All the way down the road to Maysville, I was aware of him standing on the coachman's strut.

The girl and I were squished between Eugene and Bethany. Staring ahead, I said to Eugene, "Business must be doing awfully well, sir, given your generosity toward my attire."

I touched the edge of my bonnet, one of the two purchased by Bethany. Just as Hatsepha had claimed years before, Maysville *did* have the most wonderful hats. The air reeked of mercury and tannin, the chemicals used for forming and setting hats. *Half the hatters lose their teeth,* Bethany had told me as we paraded past scores of shop windows. *The other half lose their minds.*

We had returned, each with a box carrying a straw hat that tied beneath the chin and stuck out so much you could scarcely see our faces.

"How curious you are, Olivia. I don't believe my wife has ever inquired about my business."

"And if I *did* inquire, he'd have my hide," said Bethany from behind her broad straw brim.

We rocked in silence the rest of the way to church.

The Orpheuses' pew was third from the front. With Bethany leading, we filed into our seats. Eugene hung back to exchange words with several gentlemen; only when Bethany said "Eugene!" did he saunter forward.

I clutched my cameo in the stifling heat, longing for the cool of the basement beneath the medical school, when the minister entered. *What a grumpy-looking man,* I thought. And then I recognized his face. It had been nearly ten years, but I knew that beaked nose and those unforgiving eyes. He had never reached out to his daughter, Julia, not once. After the revival and her marriage to Erasmus, he had forsaken her.

Now Ephraim Morrissey was going to preach to the good people of Maysville. I could barely sit still in the pew. The topic of the sermon, he told us, was the nature of actions and consequences.

"*If* little children are naughty . . ."—Ephraim Morrissey peered into the pews should they contain any said children—"they shall be cast out. I speak today of Noah's son Ham."

He stared straight at Elizabeth. I heard her catch her breath. I feared his eyes might fall upon me as well.

"When a child disrespects its parent," he continued, holding his gaze, "that child and the children of that child shall risk the curse of God." He opened his Bible, yet did not look down. "Lest ye think that by cursing His children, God might not be loving, I assure you that He makes this choice *only* because He is given no other. Our Divine Father loves us so much that He weeps for His cursèd children just as Noah wept for Ham."

On he droned in the most dismal way, recounting the story of Noah's son, the dark-complexioned one who had mocked his father's nakedness and was punished for his mockery.

And why should he not? thought I. Noah was a drunkard and frankly mockable; the streets of Cincinnati were strewn with the likes of Noah. According to the Reverend Morrissey, however, Ham's hilarity at his father's expense was ill-advised, for it resulted in not only him, but in *all* of his dark-skinned descendants being condemned to slavery.

"Japheth, Shem, and Ham," said the reverend. "Three brothers. Three whose blood shall *never* mix." He paused. "We . . ." He leaned forward, his face contorting. "*We* who are descendants of Japheth know that Ham was doomed to be a slave."

The white congregation nodded.

"Thus we shall reap what we sow," he concluded, slamming his Bible shut. The piano started. Bethany leapt to her feet and bellowed a full-throated, *Draw me nearer, nearer, blessed Lord, to the cross where thou hast died.* She jerked her head at Elizabeth and Eugene, who stood with less enthusiasm. *Draw me nearer, nearer, blessed Lord, to thy precious bleeding side.*

When I finally rose, I felt so spent I could barely mouth the words.

After the service, the congregation lined up behind the minister, who manned the doors to greet us. Bethany asked the reverend if he liked her bonnet while Eugene lit a cigar.

"And this is my sister," said Bethany. "Well, almost my sister. She was married to Eugene's brother."

"Mama," said Elizabeth, tugging on Bethany's arm. "Can we go?"

The minister's eyes bored into me with no hint of recognition. I held out my hand. "Olivia Givens Orpheus, Reverend. And I didn't agree with anything you said."

Did he even know his daughter had died?

"Olivia!" Bethany said, but Eugene let out with a loud, "Ho! Ho!" just as Silas would.

"Givens?" said the minister as we walked away, but just to spite him, I did not turn back. If he cared not to inquire after his truant daughter, he cared not for her fate.

Back in the carriage, Bethany asked if questioning the minister on the stoop of churches was acceptable in Cincinnati.

"You sound like my older brother," I said. "My father, too." The bow on the bonnet was strangling my neck. With a tug, I yanked it off. "Where do they find these ministers?" Elizabeth had fallen asleep, her head resting on my lap, her small body pushing me uncomfortably against Eugene.

"I was barren, you know," Bethany said, touching the dark curls of her daughter. "Until Elizabeth came along, I thought I was cursed." She turned to look out the window. "At least, that's what my husband told me."

The carriage rocked on with a motion that lulled the passengers, making all of us drowsy. I adjusted myself. My skirts were bunched up in the back, my petticoats clinging to my thighs.

"'Tis a terrible thing to want children and be deprived," said Bethany.

I opened my mouth to speak, but gave out a little gasp as I felt Eugene's hand insinuating its way under my skirt. Mortified, I said nothing.

"All of my friends had six, seven children, and there I was."

Eugene's hand crept onto the inside of my leg. I placed my bonnet in my lap and pressed down. Bethany stared out the carriage. We saw three slaves walking down the road. Bethany yawned.

"And then what?" I said, trying to quell the anxiety in my voice.

"Hmm?" said Bethany.

"The child?" This desperately whispered.

"Dear child," said Bethany in a distracted voice. She removed her glove and licked her fingers. Hypnotized, I watched as Bethany tried to smooth Elizabeth's curls with her spit. "Occasionally," she said, "the Lord needs reminding." Within a minute, she had nodded off.

Eugene was fingering the edge of my bloomers. Not daring to make a scene, I dug my elbow into his side. Yet when Eugene's middle finger started to achieve its mark, I pounded the ceiling and shouted, "I am unwell. Tell the driver to stop."

Bethany didn't rouse.

"Very well," said Eugene, abruptly withdrawing his hand. His voice was steady, bored. Perhaps I'd imagined the whole thing. Indeed, who would believe me? "Handsome!" he barked. "The lady needs to get out."

As soon as the carriage stopped, Handsome jumped down and was opening the door. With Bethany and Elizabeth asleep, I had to heft myself across Eugene.

"Whoa, now," he said, restraining me by grasping my waist. He removed himself from the carriage and went up to check the horses. Handsome held out his hand, helped me to the ground.

"I'll walk," I said.

Eugene tipped his hat as I passed. A covey of quail flew up from the field, startling the horses.

"I'll send someone to fetch you, missy," said Handsome. His eyes caught mine, seemed to say something, but interpretation failed me.

"Fine," I said. I replaced my bonnet. More than once I stumbled. The road shimmered in the heat. As the carriage lurched past, Handsome twisted around to watch me until they rounded a corner and disappeared.

IN THE DAYS THAT FOLLOWED, I felt suspended in amber while I pondered what to do. To stay was untenable. To return to Cincinnati with no husband meant I could no longer keep my grief at bay. And what would I do with Tilly?

I continued to tutor Elizabeth, cajoling her into reading, taming her enough to sit still for ten—then twenty—minutes before bounding up and shouting for her mother or Handsome or Grady. In truth, it seemed she might leap out of her skin. When I asked her if she was suffering from fidgetiness, she said, *Have you ever felt like you could run and keep on running as if you had someplace to go?*

"I really must go," I told Bethany at breakfast. "I've overstayed."

"'Tis only August!"

Casting about, I lighted upon a slim filial twig. "I promised my brother James."

That night, Eugene came into my room, drawing back the covers and staring down at me. He said, "I know you are awake."

I had extended no invitation that I was aware of—no surreptitious glance. He pulled up my nightclothes and held up the candle to examine my body. I could not speak. Eugene so resembled Silas, but a Silas whose paint was smudged. He seemed not to care that a lock of his hair fell aggressively forward, or that his collar had popped. His sleeves were pushed back. For a moment, I wondered if he had happened into my room by accident after too many brandies. I could smell them on his breath.

"Did Silas do this?" Eugene said, touching my breast.

I shivered violently.

"Poor Olivia," he said. "Married to a man who loved experiments more than women. How plucked you are," he said, touching my face. "So thin and hairless."

He took my hand, placed it on his crotch. "Could he do this?"

And with that, I yanked my hand back and bit him on the wrist.

"Christ!" he said, pulling back.

I sat up on the bed, grabbed the pitcher from the table, dumping water onto the sheets. Waving it at him, I said in a shaky voice, "Leave, sir, or I shall call the house!"

He rose from the bed, tucking in his shirt. "You think this house would care?"

"YOU'RE JUST A LITTLE BIJIBA," said Mandy the next morning when she came to see why I had refused to come down for breakfast. "Why this happens to Missus Bethany once a month. A bed warmer and a little medicine should do for you."

In less than an hour, she produced both along with some watermelon ice. The bed warmer eased my shivering, and the "medicine"—which I knew was laudanum—took me to a hazy place where nothing seemed to matter. For two days, I lay in the bed, speaking to no one, not even to Elizabeth, who came into my room early the second morning and stood beside my bed, staring at me with an intensity much like her father's. She said, "I am reading. What do you think of that?"

"I think that's fine," I said, but I closed my eyes and rolled over.

"Can I climb in with you?"

On the third night, I descended for dinner. Elizabeth was sprawled beneath the table with her plate. Eugene had pushed back his chair and was clutching a snifter of brandy. Bethany was dressed in white muslin, her hair in loose, colorless waves. I had the sense of peering through distorted glass where everybody looked like someone else. "Oh, lovely," said Bethany upon seeing me. "I am desperate for conversation. My husband hasn't spoken in days."

"I see," I said, for I could think of no other comment.

"He gets this way. 'The world looks dark,' he says. But what do men know of darkness? The world looks dark to *them* at the loss of a bet, while *we* are the ones to bear children."

Eugene regarded me over the lip of his glass. "You have my girl," he said, speaking, evidently, for the first time in days.

"Pardon?" I could barely look at him.

"My girl. Tilly."

"Honestly," said Bethany. "Let us not speak of her."

A cold broth was set at my place.

Bethany said, "We thought you wouldn't be hungry."

"You are pale, Olivia," said Eugene. He swirled his glass.

"Sit at the table, Elizabeth," said Bethany, lifting the cloth and toeing her daughter. "You are a little beast."

"Not until *she* tells me," said Elizabeth.

"Sit at the table like a young lady," I said so sharply it startled her. "Do as your mother says."

Elizabeth crawled out and started to take her seat, then ran over and climbed into my lap.

"I fear I've stayed too long," I said, stroking her hair. I needed to get back to Tilly.

Bethany squeezed her napkin. "But you've barely arrived!'

BY THE TIME I rose the next morning, Eugene had left for Lexington.

"You are a wretch for leaving, sister," said Bethany. She was still in her night chemise. "You must write me every week."

"I shall," I said, lying. I had packed as quickly as I could. If my cheeks looked flushed, no one mentioned it. "And you must get Elizabeth a tutor. She's exceptionally bright, and she should be better at reading by now."

"I hardly care for reading myself," said Bethany.

Handsome was waiting for me by the road cart. A basket of produce sat in the back along with my valise. I hadn't brought much clothing other than mourning garb; I had never meant to stay.

As Handsome helped me up onto the seat, the child came running from the house, her hair a-jumble.

"Auntie, let me go with you!" said Elizabeth, fetching with her long, dark curls. She grabbed hold of my hand.

Gently extracting her, I said, "The next time I'll see you, I shall scarcely recognize you. You'll be all grown up." I would miss her in spite of myself.

Handsome clicked his tongue. We started down the drive, the horse in a slow walk, the child tagging after us, her cheeks streaked with tears and dust. I had not dressed my hair. Loosed from its braids, it laddered past my shoulders like a washboard.

We were trotting at a decent clip now, Orpheus Farms receding in the distance. I was vaguely aware of Handsome talking to me as one might a child—histories about which I had not inquired, a balm of conversation that promised life would be fine. I asked about the fissure in his eyebrow that he said was split years ago in a ruckus he could barely remember. The size of his head might have been remarkable were it not hidden by the brim of a straw hat that he'd worn every summer since Mr. Eugene was forced to sell two of Handsome's children just to get by.

In the past few years, he told me, he'd taken more to tending the carriages than to plowing. Except for the time they'd tried to sell him off, he'd been generally well treated, even when he was sick and most likely dying (they'd lost three slaves to that fever), and Missus Bethany came down from the house and made them drink cherry liqueur she had made herself. Missus Bethany's cooking was a thing of beauty. Not like Mandy, who knew mostly biscuits, potatoes, and ham.

"Handsome," I said, "have you ever had any of Mrs. Bethany's watermelon ice?"

"No, ma'am."

I twisted a strand of hair around my thumb and forefinger. "Well, that ice was near the best thing I've ever eaten."

I was about to cry. If I started, I feared I might not stop. Holding my hand over my eyes, I squinted at a cornfield. The morning sun was just breaking through, the cornstalks tall and green. A mile down the road was the Harrises', and beyond that, the Dobbses'.

Handsome cleared his throat. "Missus Bethany is a real good cook when she tries her hand."

I had gone over and over Bethany's recipes for bourbon fancies, watched as she sugared the rims of crystal glasses or ground lemon zest into liqueur. *Just a breath,* Bethany said. *Won't do to measure.*

She had smiled at me in that Kentucky way that softened blades with butter.

"How far to the landing?" I asked.

"Just a little farther," Handsome said. "Just past town."

Soon it would be time for setting up jams and sorting rags for patching. All day long, the bees had been humming in the anise. Some early apples had fallen, their syrup beckoning the yellow jackets to swarm. I could smell the rising of sugar, feel the threat of stingers, sense the eyes that measured the hemp, awaiting more hands from the South when the work of harvesting would become fast and heavy. That year's crop was bumper, and there weren't enough men, women, and children. Just that morning, Elizabeth had seen Handsome from the porch, and put down her book and called to him.

I know how to spell your name, she had said.

Tha's really something, said Handsome, but he kept on moving.

He told me he'd heard from Mandy how I had stayed in bed for days and looked like death. And now I was wrapped in a blanket even though it wasn't cold.

"Will you look at that corn?" I said. "Why, if I could, I'd run right through it, and no one would find a trace."

He watched as I wrapped my hair around my fingers. Looking back over his shoulder, he said in an altogether different tone, "That man's a devil, missus. He pushed himself on my Delilah."

After a moment, I said, "I'm not in the least surprised."

He studied me. "Missus Olivia, might y'all know what's happened to my Tilly?"

This startled me. "*Your* Tilly?"

He nodded. "Second one of five. Grady's older sister."

"Oh, Handsome," I said after pondering his statement about Eugene pushing himself on Delilah and wondering if this had anything to do with Tilly. "Tilly is doing fine. She is prospering. Why, what that girl can do with hair . . ."

He laughed. "She always did like the hair." He looked at the corn as if he were seeing it for the first time. Cornfield gave way to farmhouse gave way to town. There, steamboats and every sort of vessel would be docked at the landing. Three mornings a week, the steamship *Fair Play* left for Cincinnati. Twice a day, a barge ferried back and forth across the river to Aberdeen. We didn't speak. There is a way in which a horse smells freedom. Could be the wind changes. Could be a sound. Something beckons, familiar, strange, forgotten; something more exotic than oats. Nostrils flare. Pace quickens. A horse can turn runaway fast. One minute docile, the brown eyes almost grateful for a carrot, and then white and wild with the itch of freedom.

CHAPTER 18

1837

A late-summer mist had settled on the river occluding the opposite shore. Sweat trickled down my neck, settled between my breasts. *Now I've done it,* I thought. *Now I've crossed the line.*

Almost twenty years before, we had sailed from Belfast, leaving our home for a strange land about which much was said. Each night beneath a twang of rigging as insistent as frogs, we had counted the stars, marking the North Star in particular. We watched our land disappear as the world tipped and the horizon loomed, a full week before the reek of our waste intruded upon our reverie of nostalgia and hope. We still had our treasure then. The distant shore did not seem far.

Not so the shore of Kentucky that Handsome and I could see as if backward through a telescope of time and place.

"You sure about this?" Handsome said, wiping his brow with his hat.

We had waited an hour in Maysville for the steamship before learning it had engine trouble. I had pitched a fit to think I might have to stay another night in Kentucky. As much to quiet as to deposit me on the Ohio shore, Handsome had hailed the barge. Once we were on the Ohio side, it seemed as natural as air to start down the road. Only now the sun was lowing, and we were a mile beyond Aberdeen.

We might not have stopped at the stable for oats. We might not have started down one road and, when we came to a fork, decided to proceed on the high one away from the river.

"You'll go back?" I said. "After what you told me about your wife?"

"I ain't saying I'll go back."

"What, then? Run? You can't run without me. You'll get stopped before you know it."

"I run once before." Handsome chewed his lip and stared at the top of the horse's head. "Woulda kept running, too, but there was this minister, see? Goes talking about Potiphar and Joseph, and how Joseph was a slave who walked away from his mastuh, so I got up in the overseer's face thinking *he* the one sassing my Delilah. All that done was get me slapped in the clamps."

One night while on the chain gang, he told me, Handsome had worked his shackles loose on a rock, shushing the boy beside him, and finally clunking him over the head with that same rock when the boy wouldn't shut up.

"I was wild, you know. I didn't know where I was going. We wasn't but a few miles out of Maysville. I knew about the North, but wasn't sure how to get there, or how I was going to saunter across the river like I had business on the other side."

"And you were caught?" I looked around as I said this, imagining the dogs, fearing the same fate for us.

"Not so much caught as returned." He was chewing so hard his bottom lip seemed to disappear. "Jes' my luck to run into that ol' preacher agin, and him as sick as a dog. Scared to death when he saw me. Probably thought the Devil had come, but all I wanted was something to eat, and a little money wouldn't hurt, but he had nothin'. Even his horse woulda been more use as meat than as a gitalong. Still, I aksed for help, and he turned me in. Tha's all she wrote for Potiphar and Joseph."

I could hear the bitterness in his voice and recalled the story Erasmus had told about returning a slave to his master. "You good at writing, missus. Maybe you could write up somethings says I'm free."

There was no denying it. The stories were eerily similar.

"Handsome," I said. "How far are we from Ripley?"

THERE WAS LITTLE SIGN OF LIFE along the river or at the Ripley foundry. A lamplighter moved slowly down the street, jostling his pole. The horse's head was drooping, its eyes covered with gnats, so we asked the lamplighter, a hunched old man of nearly fifty, for some water. Although I was jumpy, the lamplighter didn't seem to think it strange that I was riding in the company of a black man. He showed us the way to the pump, and I filled a cup. Only then did I realize how hungry I was, but Handsome said we best keep moving.

"Excuse me," I asked the lamplighter, "do you know a man named Erasmus Givens? Lives at a place called Enduring Hope?"

The old man shrugged. "There's all sorts of crazy camps along the river."

"Then perhaps you'll help us light our way."

We rode on for more than a mile, the road illuminated by the candle in a cracked and dented lantern affixed to the carriage post. The forest darkened. Hoots and shrieks replaced the trill of chickadee. Wondering if it was a possum's eyes glowing on a branch above us, I was about to give up hope, enduring or otherwise, when I saw the banner in the dusky light. There had been occasional signs and flags along the way, but this piece of rag—poorly made and betraying an unpracticed hand—stated in faded letters, ENDURING OPE. The *H* had gone missing.

"Stop here," I told Handsome, telling him to quiet the horse and to hide himself. Alighting from the cart, I wrapped my shawl around my head, gathered my skirts, made my way down a path, and came to a cabin perched at the edge of the river. "Hello?" I whispered. I could not see through the tiny windows, for the curtains were drawn, but I could smell smoke. Sucking in my breath, I banged on the door. There was no sound. I banged again.

I felt him even before the twig snapped and the gun barrel jabbed into my ribs. I turned, my hands reaching for the sky as a voice said, "Who goes there?"

"Erasmus?" said I.

A pause. Then: "Livvie?"

I lowered my hands and pushed back my shawl and said, "If you shoot me, Erasmus, James will hunt you down."

He lowered the gun, his eyes wide with surprise. For once, my brother was speechless, for I must have appeared to him as an apparition.

"You're not drunk," I said. "'Tis I."

"Holy smokes," said Erasmus.

I studied his face. "What's wrong with your teeth?"

He didn't answer, but put two fingers in his mouth and whistled. William came running out of the house. He was up to my shoulders now, and surely didn't know me. It was all I could do not to grab him.

"My goodness, Willy," I said. "You certainly have grown. Do you remember me?" He nodded, but I wasn't sure. Begrudgingly, I said to Erasmus, "It looks like you're feeding him."

"Livvie, how in God's name . . . ?"

"Light a lamp," I said. "I need some help."

I had left the cart back by the road. Blankets covered the bundles in the back, including Handsome.

"Did you ride here alone, then?" Erasmus asked.

"In these woods?" I threw back the blanket to reveal Handsome, who raised his head, squinting into the light of the lantern.

"What the . . . ?" said Erasmus.

"Handsome," I said. "You may recall my brother Erasmus. Is he the preacher you spoke of?"

"Handsome?" said Erasmus. "Handsome?"

Handsome unfolded and rose, swung his long legs over the side of the dray, and dropped to the ground. He rubbed his eyes and pulled on his hat.

Then he took a long, steady look at Erasmus. "You!" he said, and lurched toward my brother, grabbing him by the collar. Erasmus dropped the lantern. Little flames caught at the leaves.

"You that preacher!" Handsome said.

"What the hell . . . ?" Erasmus said just as Handsome's fist landed on his jaw.

AFTER THE FRACAS in which Handsome punched Erasmus, and Erasmus went down, with me shouting, *Sweet Jesus!* as Erasmus crawled like a sidewinder away from Handsome, who bore down upon him as though he were an avenging angel with ten years of recrimination at the loss of his wife and child and blaming it on Erasmus, William and I managed to break them up and even cajole Handsome into contrition. Now we were seated on the porch, our breaths steadying as we listened to the swish of water. The boy wouldn't take his eyes off Handsome in case he went for his father again. In spite of a cut on his cheek, Handsome had gotten the better end of the deal, for Erasmus was more of a runner than a fighter.

"I think my jaw's broke," Erasmus said. It came out, *I hink my yaw's roke*.

"Nonsense," said I, dabbing away the blood from his lips with a cloth. "You wouldn't be able to talk."

We were in the middle of nowhere, the night alive with the sound of crickets and frogs. I considered my situation, thinking of Eugene's sneering face. I had exacted my small amount of vengeance along with a slave who, from years of toil and grief, was good for little more than holding the reins to a third-rate livery.

"I can take him north," said Erasmus, jerking his head at Handsome, who was crouched on a log that served as a chair. "That is, if you're running." *Iffer 'unning.* To which neither Handsome nor I replied. Erasmus went on. "Ripley's just up the road. You know what they say about Ripley."

"Seemed quiet enough," I said, gazing at the bloody cloth in my hand. "What are you thinking?"

"I'm thinking we wait for a dark night."

William was too thin by half. I couldn't tell if those were freckles on his forehead or dirt. The river had turned to lead in the twilight. A rabbit scurried out from beneath the porch. The boy's eyes traced it hungrily. I wondered how often they had faced starvation with but a few stocks of corn and a rangy chicken or two. This was not what I had envisioned for the boy when I'd led him to the docks and said, *Look, Willy. Look at all the beautiful boats. Someday, these boats could be yours.*

"They'll come looking for you," Erasmus said to no one in particular.

"They's looking already," said Handsome, speaking for the first time in an hour.

Erasmus held his hand as if pointing a pistol and pulled the trigger. "Pow," he said.

The keening frogs crescendoed.

"They'll be looking for *you,* too," Erasmus said to me.

If they found me, I could be fined or jailed. Not for the first time in my life, I had disregarded the consequences. But this was far more dangerous than dissecting corpses or standing in support of secular virtue. Yet here we were. If I abandoned Handsome, his fate would be worse than mine.

"I've made a lot of mistakes in my life," Erasmus said to Handsome. "And you're not the worst of them." His eyes traced to the boy.

"Aksing *you* for help was the worst idea *I* ever had," said Handsome.

"This time," said Erasmus, "we'll figure out a better plan."

CHAPTER 19

1837

Tilly stared at me as if I were a ghost. Like me, she was dressed in black. "You've been gone for a while."

"You thought I'd been held captive?" I said, and breezily, too, dropping my bag and yanking off my bonnet. "You thought Mr. Eugene wouldn't let me go?"

That morning, Erasmus and William had ferried me to a steamboat that I boarded for Cincinnati. I had made Erasmus promise to shepherd Handsome to safety.

Tilly's eyes were ringed and red. She said, "Your hair could do with a wash."

Not that she looked much better. Normally immaculate in her own braids and twists, her hair fell below her shoulders in a bushy cascade. And her skin? So gray on her bones that I'd wondered if she'd eaten since I'd left. Surely, she'd tended her ladies, but now I wasn't sure. I had left so quickly to accompany Silas's corpse that I'd barely thought about the effect his death might have on Tilly.

That night, I sat straight up in bed and shouted, "Stop!"

A moment later, there was tapping on my door. "You all right?"

It took me a minute to realize where I was. My throat was dry. I had handed off Tilly's father to Erasmus, and yet I could risk no mention of Handsome. My heart pounded. I felt spent.

"Maybe some warm milk?" Tilly said. Her candle flickered along the bottom edge of the door.

"You fuss too much, Tilly. Go back to sleep."

But I lay awake long after she'd gone.

The next morning, sitting by the window at the table where Silas had scribbled out notes on gout and pleurisy, I fiddled with my tea. Tilly hovered, picking hair from a brush as if she were plucking a chicken.

"Tilly, you are staring at me as if I were Lazarus."

"You look queer."

I clinked my teacup. "I am not myself."

"I ain't passing judgment."

"'*Am* not,'" I said. "Passing judgment."

"Your clothes, Miss 'Livia. I unpacked your bag. Filthy, like you'd been rolling in hay. I'da thought they'd take better care of you."

A day and a half in a wagon; a night in my brother's hovel. "I'm sure they'll clean up fine."

She leaned in close, said, "I ain't seen you like this since you was got with child."

My belly gripped with the memory. A year into my marriage, my menses had stopped. I had agreed with Silas that we'd have no children, but for almost two months, I had felt a sweet fullness that was the closest my spirit had ever been to peace. I remembered the pity on Tilly's face when I'd doubled up with cramps, the blood seeping through my undergarments. Silas could not forgive me for becoming pregnant in the first place, but Tilly had tended me well.

"Well," I said, brushing away the pain, "no child now."

Tilly set the brush on the table, pulled out a chair. "You didn't like me much at first," she said. "You almost didn't get married on accounta me."

"It wasn't just you."

"But Mr. Silas? He was a much better man than his brother. Not perfect. But much, much better." Then, sitting across from me like an inquisitor, she changed her tone. "Tell me about Missus Bethany's girl."

It seemed a strange question. But remembering how Silas had taken Tilly back to Orpheus Farms about a year after William was born, I realized she must have midwifed Bethany's child.

"Pretty girl. Could do with a bit of tutoring. But overall, well dressed and clean."

Her hands clasped in her lap, she leaned forward. "How pretty?"

I thought of all the pupils I'd tutored over the years. "You must get attached," I said, "to the children you deliver."

She rose up, smoothed her skirts. "Some."

I studied her face as if for the first time. Narrow-nosed. Green-eyed. A brow that was so familiar. I could imagine Handsome's wife, Delilah, taken by Eugene. In the stable. In a field. And when Erasmus brought Handsome back, just to spite him, Eugene had sold off Tilly's older brother along with his wife and Tilly's mother, Delilah.

I set down my teacup, dabbed my lips with a piece of cloth. "I am so sorry, Tilly. And you are right about my hair."

I HAD BEEN BACK LESS THAN A WEEK when I heard the knock. At first, I thought nothing of it because there was a pounding from time to time—a patient who didn't know that Dr. Orpheus had passed (*six hours it took me to ride here, ma'am. Are you sure he can't fix this tooth?*); a solicitor of scraps; a census taker; a lame barker looking for work. When I flung open the door, I was half expecting to see that barker again because he'd been most insistent about his carpentry skills that, in truth, I would have welcomed were it not for that look in his eye.

"I said not to—!"

A caped man turned to face me.

"Mr. Orpheus!"

Eugene Orpheus removed his hat. "Ah," he said. "So I *do* have the correct address?" He leaned in ostentatiously to read the plaque.

"What are you doing here?" I asked, though I already knew.

"Madame?" He smiled an ingratiating smile. "I fear that we parted with ill feeling, for you left without saying good-bye."

Ill feeling? But I was determined to play along lest he suspect I realized he was here to inquire about Handsome. Tilly had gone out that morning to the market, leaving me alone wearing only muslin and with hair poorly suited to company.

"What do you want?"

"Will you not welcome your brother-in-law? You should, you know."

He pushed across the threshold into Silas's office and sat down in the Windsor chair where Silas would sit to consult with Mrs. Spencer on her rheumatism or Mr. Burgess on his liver. His hands were steady and his eyes clear, no sign of the drink. "I have never seen my brother's office," he said, looking about. "I regret that now. I should have come when he was living."

I inhaled deeply the scent of antiseptic. That something so astringent and unnatural should console me was unnerving. Eugene's eyes were on the labeled jars that crammed the floor-to-ceiling shelf. How many times had I told Silas to let me do the labeling, his penmanship was so poor?

"Ah!" said Eugene, getting up and crossing to the shelf. "And what is this?" He touched a large glass container. "Of course! A cat! He was horrible to cats. Good Lord, nothing much changes does it?"

I knew not what to say, so I waited, standing behind the chair that was used for patients. I did not want him to stay, and yet if I looked too discomfited by his presence, it might lead him to conclude . . . what?

That I was still upset about our incident in the bedroom? And why shouldn't I be?

But we both knew why he was here.

"It's a *stray* cat," I said, as if that explained it.

"Cut it up, did he?" Eugene laughed fondly, as one might respond to a precocious child. "He was always cutting things up. You can imagine the fuss. Chicken parts were one thing. But when my mother found a dog's head in his room . . ."

"He was a curious man, interested in physiology." I could see the room through Eugene's eyes—a dusty place attesting to the near poverty of his younger brother, who had shown no interest in farming, in land, in the owning of property other than dead things in jars; three sticks of shabby furniture; a widow.

"Physiology? Is that what it was about?" Eugene said, returning to his seat and crossing his legs. He looked quite at home and was clearly enjoying himself. And again, that eerie resemblance to his brother. "Cats?" he said, one eyebrow archly rising.

I cleared my throat. "*Why* have you come?"

His smile didn't waver. I felt my cheeks grow hot. In a placid tone, as if he were making a desultory inquiry about the weather, he said, "Where is he?"

Whatever color had infused my cheeks drifted away. I willed my voice to stay calm. I cocked my head. "Where is who?"

"My dear Olivia. You left five days ago. My wife and daughter are quite beside themselves. You left, and the slave who drove you never returned to the farm. What are we to make of that?"

"Handly, was it?"

"Handsome. He has been with us for forty years. Such disloyalty in a servant we've housed and fed all that time—well, it hurts a man."

"You don't look hurt."

"Don't I? And yet, I'm a man of strong feelings, Mrs. Orpheus.

May I call you 'sister'? May we resume our familiarity? I meant you no harm. I was overtaken."

Overtaken by what? By me? Drink? As I saw it, he was an opportunist who liked to prey upon the helpless and had misidentified me as such. Poor Olivia Givens—"so thin and hairless"—unable to resist his charm. He had mocked his brother, saying he was impotent. But Silas hadn't been impotent. Not really. True, his ardor was for his work, but our marriage had been consummated, if not passionately or frequently, at least dutifully and earnestly, though I confess thinking meanly that Silas felt more tenderness toward corpses.

"Even so," I said. "I can't help you with your man. He dropped me off at the landing, and I waited for the second packet after the first one did not come." How many times had I rehearsed this over the last few days?

Eugene looked at me sharply. "So you say . . . and yet I could find no witnesses. No one seems to recall your taking a ticket." He sighed. "Handsome's one of our own. Came to us as a boy. Not so young now. Scarred. Some would say problematic, though the last few years he's been docile. A good nigger, good with horses. You know how much a nigger like that's worth?"

"I couldn't possibly say, having never held with slavery."

"Your *husband* certainly held with slavery. Yes, indeed. 'Held' is one word for it. And yet *you*, Miss Givens—Mrs. *Orpheus*—you do not hold? I wouldn't have pegged you for a zealot. Only, perhaps . . . a bit naive?"

I gripped the back of the chair and forced myself to look assured. "I read the papers, Mr. Orpheus. Nothing more. My time in your state was perfectly pleasant, but this is Ohio, and you see how our laws hold differently."

"O-hi-o." He mimicked my accent in every syllable. He rose from the chair, took a deep breath as if an odor was pressing in against him, as if the fact of it made him very sad. He looked at me from beneath his brows, the way that Silas would when he wanted something, something he knew he could take but was trying instead to cajole.

"I'll ask again—"

"—and I'll deny it."

Eugene drew in close. From the depths of my soul, I stood my ground. He touched my face. "Such a pity," he said. He smiled mildly, but his eyes were devoid of amusement. "It would have been much easier. Are you absolutely sure?"

When I did not speak, he picked up his cape, his hat. His shoes were pointed, almost dainty. They'd be caked with mud by the end of the day.

When he got to the door, he stopped and turned, almost as if with an afterthought.

"One more thing, sister."

I stiffened.

"I believe we can agree that you still have *some* of my property?"

I swept my arms around the room. "Tissue in formaldehyde? Medical tools and bits of bone?"

"To the contrary," he said, repositioning his tall hat. There was no more flirtatiousness in his manner. "You have my girl. Little light-skinned thing? The girl who calls herself Tilly?"

CHAPTER 20

1837–1838

A month later, a letter came from Bethany saying how unhappy she'd been since I had left. Elizabeth missed me as well, and since my departure, wouldn't read a thing. Just stared out the window, sad as could be, and did I hear that a slave had run off? Never came back from taking me to the landing. I wouldn't know anything about that, would I?

I wrote her back. *Why no, sister. The man dropped me off as we had planned, though I had to wait for a later ferry, as the one I had intended to take had some problem with the engine. Perhaps he headed west?*

Oh, undoubtedly, was her reply. The man had given them problems once before, and though it pained her to say it, once a nigger ran, they were just as apt to do it again, having gotten it in their nostrils, that rank smell of running. All these problems, and Eugene creating such a fuss.

It seems he thinks you had something to do with it, sister, though I've told him he has misjudged your fine character. I'd be sorry if I were wrong.

Tra-la-la, I wanted to write, but when the next letter came, it was from Eugene.

"WHAT DO YOU MEAN, he wants her back?" said Hatsepha, her hands flying to her head.

We were sitting in James's library, the German girl having brought us tea. Books that James would have devoured as a youth in Ireland now lined the shelves in rectitude.

James's hair was threatening to break loose from its lacquer. "I do not understand. Is she or is she not his property?"

"For goodness' sakes, James, she's been living here for the better part of a decade."

"But what of her hair business?" James said. "You said she was to buy herself."

"Evidently," I said, and not with a little regret, "my husband sent all the money back to Eugene."

Sunlight filtered through casements struck the table. Anchored by a paperweight shaped like a ship was an essay by a man named Emerson.

James tapped his hand on the top of his desk. "If you ask me, this meddling with slavery is best left to others. We are barely out of a hole ourselves."

Earlier that year, the markets had crashed, triggering off a selling spree of land and shares, forcing businesses into bankruptcy and families into poverty. Were it not for James's ability to purchase materials at scale along with his insistence on paying in cash, Givens and Sons might have been another casualty, but the business was surviving thanks to the abundance of cheap labor and the bargain price of materials.

"Oh, I'm tired of hearing about it," said Hatsepha. "You'd think we could hold on to one little maid."

I raised my eyebrow at James. "So you think championing the girl is bad for business?"

James rose from his desk and paced. He studied a set of scales as if they might reveal the relative weights of morality, commerce, and

Hatsepha's hair. "Were I to intervene, it cannot be traced back," he said. He puffed his cheeks like thunderclouds. "I suppose Eugene, too, has been caught up in this infernal panic. Why else would he suddenly be interested in retrieving the girl?"

The panic had brought down a number of our finest, forcing the menfolk to gather wood for fuel or animal parts for rendering. Stately houses were put on the market, where they sat shuttered and owned by the banks that were themselves on the verge of collapse. Only last May, I had run into Ariadne Mumford, who looked quite deranged in last year's dress and a squashed hat.

"It's the girl's life," I said. When James showed no reaction, I added, "Not to mention your investment in Tilly's enterprise." For Hatsepha had prevailed and convinced James to back the girl so that she could buy proper supplies.

James twitched.

"There *is* an attorney," he said after some consideration. "You may have heard of him. Chase?"

"Salmon Chase?" He had conferred with Silas a number of times. "He has a problem with his teeth."

"Well, this Chase seems to relish making an issue of such cases. Remember that publisher fellow? Birney?" Birney had started the paper *The Philanthropist* to advocate for abolition. Twice his presses were destroyed during the riots a year before. "But first let us see what your Eugene Orpheus proposes to do." And with this, James offered his elbow to Hatsepha. She heaved herself from her chair and regally took his arm. I toyed with the idea of telling them I'd seen William, but it would beg the question of how I found myself at Enduring Hope, and it was better that they shouldn't know.

"Until that time," James added, almost as an afterthought, "you and Tilly shall move up here."

I WAS IN NO RUSH to move back into my brother's home. It felt like capitulation to Eugene and, in a sense, a betrayal to Silas, who had left me his small rooms and belongings.

I awoke in the wee hours to something that sounded like scurrying. I sat up in bed. "Tilly?" I was sure I saw candlelight moving along the threshold of the door. "Hello?" I said.

Alas, I moved too slowly. I pushed through the door in time to see the back of a man, his arms wrapped around the poor wretch whose eyes bulged with fear, her mouth silent beneath his hand. Too late I saw the second man who gave me a hearty shove back into my room so that I stumbled and would have fallen had I not caught myself on the bed. I rushed to the window and flung it open and called into the night for help. There were so few constables then, and had it not been for the passing vigilante in search of his cow, we would have lost her then and there, but the man interrupted the scoundrels' flight in time for others to rush from their homes in response to the ruckus that could well have erupted into a riot had not Mayor Davies arrived, clad in a topcoat and nightshirt to protest the outrage and to set it right, though not right enough, for it resulted in the arrest of Tilly.

THE COURT CASE that followed some weeks later riveted Cincinnati. Everyone rushed each day to read the headlines: "Colored Hairdresser Wrests Herself from Slavery" or "Escaped Slave Defies Law." Rumors abounded about who was behind Tilly's defense, with some saying it was the abolitionist banker from Indiana, others citing the First Congregational Church. It wasn't until someone's tongue slipped that suspicion fell on James. More rumors followed, including allegations that James was concealing runaways in empty boxes of Givens candles.

Soon the papers were identifying with certainty that James Givens, founder of Givens and Sons, was the benefactor funding one Tilly Orpheus, alleged slave, who had lived in Cincinnati since 1828 and was now a well-regarded dresser of hair, much esteemed by the fashionable ladies who thought it disgraceful that such a talented young woman should be snatched back into the jaws of the South after making herself so invaluable.

"Ariadne Mumford is particularly chagrined," Hatsepha said as she, James, and I promenaded along the shops by the landing. "She says if Salmon Chase loses Tilly's case, she will abscond with the girl herself."

"And with Phinneaus running for reelection?" said James, tipping his hat at a passerby. "I hardly think so. This prurient interest in abolition is only that. It will pass with the length of a hem and these ridiculous muttonchop sleeves."

I continued to refrain from mentioning Handsome, though I wondered what had transpired—if Erasmus had stolen him into the hills or packed him into the back of a wagon going north. Then again, Erasmus might have sold the poor man to the patrollers who were only too happy to pay the price, collecting it threefold from the owner who would beat the man to death.

"Oh dear," said Hatsepha. Two ladies and a man had crossed the street, braving mud and manure to accost James. I recognized Enoch Breckinridge and his two sisters.

"We read the papers!" said one of the sisters—possibly the one called Minna. "Is it true? Is it going to trial?"

There was no point in James's denying it. The best recourse was to stiffen his resolve and pretend that he had feelings on the issue.

"Ladies," he said. "Mr. Breckinridge." He nodded at Enoch, who was looking at James as if he were a specimen in a vitrine. "Lawyer Chase has advised us that a case can be made that the girl, having resided on free soil, is no longer subject to prior terms of ownership."

The two sisters beamed, for I suspect they, too, owed their coiffures to Tilly. Their brother, however, pointed his finger at James. "If that's the case, how are we to defend property held in another state whose laws may differ from our own? What about your family's mines, sir? I believe some lie in Kentucky. Can they be confiscated in so arbitrary a manner?"

James met his gaze. "You make a case, sir. And yet . . . well, this *is* a human life."

"You are on thin ice, Givens," said Mr. Breckinridge, clearly no appreciator of hair.

I started to say, *And here we are in 1838, and one would think we had come further,* but Hatsepha's fingers had clasped about my wrist like a vise.

"Let's walk, sister," she said, curtsying to the two women, who curtsied back.

"We think it's marvelous, Mr. Givens," said the one who was not Minna. "We think you are a Christian man."

Clearly, she had no idea how pale a compliment this was to James.

For the rest of the afternoon, James muttered to himself and glared at me. He knew it would only get worse, which, in fact, it did.

DURING THE TRIAL, Tilly was confined to a cell that had no mirror—just a pot and a mat along with one small window too high to reach. Without access to lanolin or sunflower oil, her hair looked so vexed that I wondered how I had ever thought she could pass as white.

The Negro inmates were relegated to the basement cells that dripped with runoff from the street. Only because James demanded it was Tilly given any privacy from the inebriates and one knife-wielding roust-about down the hall. Over and over again, I assured her that there was no finer lawyer than Chase, and that anyone with half a brain would see the common sense of her situation. The notion that she might return to servitude was laughable.

"Here," I said, removing my cap and handing it to her. "You can cover your head with this."

This was the second time I was allowed to see her. The first time, she had wept so fiercely that I doubted any possibility of conversation before she collected herself and inquired as to how her ladies were—Mrs. Ariadne and Mrs. Hatsepha—and had the Reed twins looked presentable at their tea dance?

But now she had a calmness that bordered on resignation. "You have been kind to me, Missus 'Livia," she said. "Kinder than you know."

"Don't be ridiculous," I said, taking in the ratty cot. "Heavens, but the smell."

She pulled on the cap, tucking in her hair. "You remember the first time you saw me?"

Quite vividly, I told her. She had been just a girl, but she had taken charge when Julia was in childbirth.

"And you remember the *next* time you saw me?"

Indeed, she had looked almost this poorly and quite deranged when Silas had brought her back to Ohio. Having met Eugene, I well understood her being in such a state when Silas retrieved her in lieu of his inheritance. Tilly had been skittish and unfocused, like someone who had toppled over in a carriage. But living with Silas and me had done her a world of good, even though people talked, saying it was strange that wherever Dr. and Mrs. Orpheus went, there was that girl. "I do."

"You ever wonder why I speak like a lady?"

"I do not. Your speech is appalling."

She ignored this. "That tatty dress you seen me in when you first came to get your hair done? You wouldn'ta known that I'd worn clothes nice as Missus Bethany's, seeing as they'd belonged to her and given to me when jes' slightly used. I was ten years old when my mother took me to the big house as a plaything. They'd cleaned me up, did my hair. By the time Missus Bethany saw me, I was pretty as a picture, and I smiled, smiled, smiled as if my life depended on it. Because it did, you know. 'Your life depends upon you being pretty,' my mother told me. And Missus Bethany, she loved me and played with me as if I was a doll. Told me I could touch her things and sleep by her bed and sometimes *in* it—like I was her child. It was Missus Bethany who protected me when my daddy burdened us by running. Did he tell you that he'd hit the overseer?"

"You're still pretty," I said.

"You're a bad liar, missus. With all due respect."

Now Tilly was imprisoned and possibly doomed, while Handsome, who had hit an overseer and run away, was finding his way to freedom.

"When Mr. Silas come and get me, I was more than miserable. Like one of those banshees you told me about. That was Missus Bethany's doing. She told me my baby died, but my baby was taken."

I shuddered, thinking of how the Orpheuses sold off their slaves, adults and babies alike.

Tilly sighed. "And Mr. Eugene would have gotten around to me either ways. He always did."

Something struck the grate of her cell and splashed on the floor. From the smell, I knew it wasn't water. All week long, a crowd had been gathering, as much to shout at each other as to harass Tilly. Then there was the jailer, who said to me as he'd unlocked the door, *You wouldn't be allowed in if it weren't for your fancy brother.*

"After this is over," I said, "James will help you out." I didn't add that a number of citizens had declared they would boycott James's products, which was difficult to do since he owned just about everything one needed to light one's house or business. "Perhaps we can move to Oberlin."

Only four years earlier, the Presbyterian college had admitted four colored students. And now they were accepting women.

"*Black* women?" said Tilly, incredulously. She had a point. "You are crazy, missus. Whose hair can I do in Oberlin?"

DURING THE THREE WEEKS OF THE TRIAL, James grumbled, but continued to pay Lawyer Chase. In court, I made out Birney the abolitionist, Burnet the canal-funder, the Merricks and the Mintons, the Hookers and the Hickenloopers. It was Indian summer and warmer than usual, harking back to the days we had gathered to hear Campbell vs. Owen. Then as now, the controversy brought forth assertions regarding the Mind of God, the Curse of Ham, the Blessings of the Chosen until many who had argued for condemnation rather than compassion were moved off their position by Chase's rhetoric that soared far higher than that of Eugene's oily, weak-chinned solicitor, who simply harrumphed in court, thinking the matter settled.

"Chase is quite impressive," said Hatsepha on the second day. "I think he's harboring ambitions."

"Then this case will surely end them."

"Have you not noticed how he looks at you?"

"Lord," I said, for Chase was no beauty, having a singular hairline well back of his brow. Still, he was tall, and with massive shoulders, fluid-tongued, and gifted in the law.

"Widowed," said Hatsepha knowingly. "Three years."

"Nor shall the Congress impose upon the state views that have no bearing on a treaty . . ." Chase went on.

"And so forth," said Hatsepha, yawning. "I told James he should just buy Eugene off."

Tilly wasn't allowed in the courtroom, she being not quite a person. I thought of her tiny cell, and for once had no quibble with Hatsepha.

"I am worried Chase's grandstanding could pose some risk to our girl," I said.

"He's trying to impress you," said Hatsepha.

"He's trying to impress his *constituents*," said I, for clearly the man was convinced that abolition was on the side of the angels and saw this as an opportunity to hold forth.

And so the day progressed. "How much longer must one endure?" said Hatsepha with a sigh.

Arms were draped across the backs of benches, affording views of exaggerated sleeves and bits of lace. Pin curls and loops were poised upon heads anxiously awaiting Tilly's liberation, while the men wore frock coats and waistcoats and sometimes showed up in britches. In spite of the temperature, the gay colors of summer were fading to winter cloth.

Chase, himself, appeared sober in a cravat and dark, collared coat. He strode back and forth in front of the bench, pounding his right hand into the palm of his left as he made the case for the freedom of those living north of the river, praising the Founding Fathers for their judiciousness in leaving treaties between individuals to the discretion of the states—in this case, Ohio, in which slavery was *not* legal, hence conferring upon Tilly the status of "freewoman" and under no obligation to her former master.

"She has lived for many years—eight to be exact—with Dr. and Mrs. Silas Orphcus, staying on after the death of Dr. Orpheus as a companion to Mrs. Orpheus and serving the community as a dresser of hair. She has made her own income. She has been a fixture in many of our homes. After all these years, are we to send her back with nary a pang of conscience, and to a less than happy situation in which families are broken up and tossed onto the block for sale?"

"He certainly seems to know the Orpheus household," whispered Hatsepha.

I did not tell her that Chase had been around to interview me, and that the conversation had veered off course.

I was a great admirer of your husband, Mrs. Orpheus, he said, after introducing himself and entering my flat. *A true pioneer.*

A man with little time, Chase shrewdly took in the books and bones, the journals and jars.

After my wife passed, he said, *I put all of her dresses into the wardrobe where I couldn't see them, but I didn't throw them out. Someday, my daughter might want to have them.*

How old is your daughter? I asked, understanding where this was headed and trying to avoid it.

Three. Only three. She was her mother's undoing, I fear. But then, I lost my *mother early. As did you, I understand. We are orphans, all of us. And yet we endure. Have you ever raised a child, Mrs. Orpheus?*

Only the children of others.

I ask too many questions, he said, noting my tone. *It's my profession, I fear. Now,* he said, taking a seat, *perhaps you will tell me about Eugene Orpheus.*

That had been three weeks earlier, and here we were in court, Salmon Chase armed with his interpretation of my domestic life, saying Tilly was my trusted servant—nay, a *friend!*—who had nursed me through the loss of a pregnancy (Hatsepha said, *You never told me!)* and, worse, the loss of my husband; that by rending us from one another and casting her back into slavery, I would be stricken, as would many women of our fair city who had enjoyed the skills of this remarkable woman who was compromised because of her race. In truth, Salmon Chase brought many to tears.

As for me, I burned with embarrassment.

Chase made his plea, catching my eye as he touched on every point of my relationship with Tilly, from the delivery of Julia's son, my short marriage, my widowhood, my promotion of Tilly's business, my interest in setting her free. Yet in the end, Chase's argument rested not on my personal relationship with Tilly, but on a state's right to dispute a treaty made between individuals.

When the verdict came, we all leaned forward, the pros on the right side of the court, the cons on the left. We were a divided city, and never so much as on that day when everything rested on the whim of a judge who smelled of brandy and whose moustache was the repository of crumbs. Perhaps that judge knew that he would lose the goodwill of half the town regardless, so when he found in favor of Eugene Orpheus and against Tilly, a collective gasp resounded, cries of victory and outrage, all of us rising to our feet, James taking my arm, the crowd so close that I couldn't hear Chase's protestations, Hatsepha grasping her hat, borne on a sea of gigot sleeves, pelerines, and flared skirts, everyone rushing, rushing toward the jail, some of us to bar the door, others to wrest it open.

"Careful," said James as I stumbled on a top hat and nearly fell into manure. "It's becoming a mob."

Indeed, it *was* a mob that arrived at the prison, shouting, *Tilly! Tilly!*

I tried to press through the tidal throng, making out grins and sneers as well as tragic eyes, fluttering hands, raised fists, but to no avail. When our girl was brought forth, I could not get near.

There stood Eugene's lawyer—that chinless inconsequent, consulting the jailer, who did not look displeased at the results. "I will come for you, Tilly!" I shouted. "Do not fear!"

But fear emanated from her like steam off a skillet.

Grasped by her jailer and the accompanying roustabouts who dragged her to a boat heading south, Tilly threw back her head and wailed. I have never before or since heard such a sound. The crowd fell into stunned silence as what was happening dawned on us all.

Whatever I had envisioned—rescuing her from Orpheus Farms, reuniting her with her father, setting it all to right—I knew from her wailing that it was not to be, for it wasn't back to Orpheus Farms that Eugene was sending her, but onto a barge bound for Natchez, deep in the South, where she would be beyond our grasp, gone forever, prodded by hands not our own.

CHAPTER 21

1838

When Hatsepha showed up unannounced, I cleared off a chair that I feared was inadequate to the task of supporting either Hatsepha or her billowing skirts. "You are not yourself," said Hatsepha, putting down her tea.

"And how would you have me be, sister?" said I, pushing a stack of papers to the floor. In less than a year, I had lost my husband, and now Tilly.

"You are even thinner."

Indeed, my clothes hung on my frame, but I had neither will nor means to alter them.

"And what has happened to your hair?"

Truly, it was lanky and ill-tended. Having considered chopping it off, I opted instead for a hasty bun or, as today, no style at all. If I walked out on the street, I would be pegged as a harlot with such hair, and though I was tempted to do so, I often yielded instead to convention and tucked the whole mess into a lace-edged cap tied securely below my chin.

Hatsepha clicked her tongue. "Not that mine is much better. My German girl may have a hand with a braid, but she is fierce with a pin."

"Your hair looks lovely," I said, though, for the first time, I noticed strands of gray.

She regarded me keenly. "You look stricken, Olivia. I don't think living alone suits you. I hear you're wandering about the streets and that you keep company with bones."

In point of fact, I had gone occasionally to the landing, but not so often as to deserve this comment. The river flowed toward the west, bucking over the falls in Louisville and turning south at Cairo, where it would spill into the Mississippi. I would stare at the water, remembering Tilly's little superstitions, how she had tossed in this or that: a lock of hair from a client, a glove that had no partner, a broken comb, an apple, a candle, a spool of thread. Votive offerings and trifles—things she would have cast off anyway. I consoled myself that everything that begins in one place ends up in another. Voyages could be endured. But if truth were told, I would have thrown myself in the river if I thought it would help.

"Well," said Hatsepha, rising and gathering up her reticule, "I shall tell James I tried, but you are as incorrigible as Erasmus. Why such insistence to live in squalor I shall never know. You came here for a better life, and what have you to show for it?" Her face seemed to wrestle with dimples competing with chins and a quivering lip. "It could be so lovely, you know. Having you live with us. You never minded living with Julia, but don't forget that I, too, am your sister."

THOUGH EACH DAY WAS A MISERY, I refused to move into my brother's house. Fortunately, I was given a reprieve, this time by Salmon Chase. It was nearly a month after the trial. The light gone so early in the afternoon, I had lit a candle that I might distract myself with reading, for I had taken to examining my husband's notes, and with no small interest, so that when the bell rang, I was annoyed, certain it was a vendor or a vagrant hoping for some food.

"Madame?" said Chase when I threw open the door. He removed his tall hat—to ill effect, given his forehead. Looking as though he was bracing for a scolding, he said, "May I come in?"

Tucking my hair into my cap, I said, "I was reading about the gout."

"May we all be spared." Adjusting to the dimness, he peered at the notes on the table. I waited. He seemed to be struggling—rare in a man so laden with words.

Unnerved by his reticence, I offered tea. He held up his hand so that I might not interrupt his worthy thoughts. Clearing his throat as if we'd been discussing the matter of the trial all day, he said, "You may fault me for pleading a technicality of the law, but no one cares about the humanitarian aspect. It didn't work for Wilberforce. It wouldn't work now."

"You think I 'fault' you?"

He pressed on. "Your passion on the subject is unusual. Northerners seem more squeamish with Negroes. I have *rarely* seen a friendship." He played with his cravat, fiddled with the bow of his shirt. For a moment, I feared he might disrobe, but it was typical of Chase to fiddle so, especially when cornered. "This case was a purely vindictive move on Orpheus's part," he said. "How *was* it he has come to have issue with you?"

"I fear it began with my husband."

"A rivalry, was it?"

"More of a test of wills."

"And the girl?"

"Oh, the girl *was* noticed," I said, "just as her mother had been noticed. Pretty girls always are, don't you think? It was a kindness that Silas finally fetched her back, though not so much a kindness to *me* at the time, for it forestalled our reclaiming his bit of fortune from Eugene."

"Which is why I'm here," he said, sounding relieved at finally having a subject with which to make traction. "It's the money."

Seeing my look of distaste, Chase went on. "You have a case, you see. The debt is still not settled. As his widow, you are entitled to Silas's inheritance." His fiddling became more feverish. "Now that the girl is sold, Eugene has the means to pay you."

Through the window, two chickens grubbing in the street pecked at each other and flew up in a dervish of wings.

"So I will profit on his sale of Tilly?" A cart rolled by, scattering the chickens.

"Think of it this way. *You,* at least, will have your independence."

IN THE END, I took the money, justifying it on the grounds that Silas would want me to claim it. One thousand dollars was quite a sum, and here I was, a childless woman who had come into a windfall. That winter, the river hardened, and the children of Cincinnati took to their skates. I sent a letter to Erasmus—several, in fact—but heard nothing back. This I explained away since mail in the best of weather was uneven and often dropped in a ditch, so when the thaw came and the river was cleared of snags, I purchased a berth to Ripley on the newly launched steamship *Moselle* that was notorious for its speed. I would have been rowed just as happily or ridden by carriage had the trace not been so muddy, but I shall not forget that boat, for the captain was overly warm to me as an unaccompanied woman perched on one of the better seats.

Erasmus lived about two miles to the west of Ripley along a rocky edge of the forest. Here and there was a stately house, but mostly there were cabins—dark, squat, clinging to a plot of tree trunks and unkempt barnyards, a fishing rod propped up on the porch, a tendril of smoke, a line of strung-up hides and unpatched britches, a sorry patch of tilling, of hammering and hope.

"Oh, dear Lord," I said upon arrival. The place was deserted but for a billy goat munching on some grass.

The carriage driver, who had carted me west from Ripley, took in this bleak destination on so wild a river and said, "Someone meeting you here?"

"Surely," I answered, though in truth I had no idea. Taking in the scene as the driver trotted away—that junk heap of a cabin; the half-built chapel; the barren orchard next to a barn—I wondered if my undertaking wasn't futile. But on closer look, the place *did* look better, as if an effort had been made. The last time I had found myself in this squalid Eden—nine months earlier—the porch had sagged and the doorjamb was askew. Clearly, there had been an attempt not only to shore up the place, but to embellish it as well. Sun-bleached antlers crowned the doorway. Rocks of every size girded the porch. A collection of something—was it stove legs?—crowned the eaves in improvised crenellation. As for the chapel, the windows were still unglazed, but the building now had a roof.

Seeing no one about, I sat down on my trunk that was packed mostly with books. The day was warm. A breeze drifted across the water, and I must have nodded off, for when a barking startled me, the sun was low, and the temperature had dropped. I squinted toward the river to make out a rowboat holding two individuals and a dog. Wanting to avoid being mistaken for some intruder and suffering a shotgun discharged in my direction, I rose up and called out, "'Tis I! 'Tis Olivia!"

"Hail, sister!" cried Erasmus, waving madly back. "Grab the line, Willy-boy!"

The boy scrambled up onto the tiny pier along with the dog, fixed the line to a wooden cleat, and rushed to embrace me. The last time he'd seen me was when I'd arrived with Handsome, after which he had rowed me to a steamship while I peppered him with questions. It was all I could do not to correct his constant "ain'ts" and "warn'ts" and other linguistic abominations that caused me to shudder.

"You must wonder why I've returned," I shouted above the dog's ecstatic barking, my hand screening against the glare.

"I got your letters," said Erasmus, climbing out of the boat and roughly tousling the boy's head.

And lovely of you to answer, I thought.

"Hush," Erasmus said to the dog, a mean-looking mutt of questionable heritage.

"You brought books?" said William, opening my trunk without asking, revealing uncut volumes by Hawthorne, Robert Montgomery Bird, and several installments by Dickens.

"Aye, Willy," said I. "We have much to read."

The billy goat had ambled up to the trunk, nosing the books for edibility. I clutched my shawl, wanting to ask about the fate of Handsome—whether he'd been ushered on or turned back as Erasmus had once before turned him back, sentencing the man to the loss of his wife and son. But before I could ask, Erasmus put his hand on my shoulder and said, "You must be famished, sister, after your journey. Rejoice, for we have caught a fish."

THAT EVENING, we sat by the hearth on rickety chairs as I told them of what had transpired with Tilly. Erasmus pulled on his pipe, his blue eyes fierce as embers. "'Tis a sad thing, and wrong that it should be so," said he as I described Tilly's wails as she was wrenched away to the departing boat. "For the day will come when God will sit in judgment upon the oppressor and find him undeserving of the pity of which he himself was lacking."

"And are ye preaching again?" I asked, for I hadn't recalled such flourishes the last time we spoke.

"I have once more found my voice."

He seemed sober enough, though I wondered how long it would last. The boy, I noticed, was staring at his feet.

"And what do you think of this, Willy?" said I. "Having your father preach?"

Knowing his father's eyes were upon him, William picked his words. "'Tis a comfort to some, I s'pose. Ain't many that cross who reckoned for a sermon."

Erasmus threw back his head and laughed. It was true, he said. He had become known as the River Preacher. "I may have no pulpit," he said, "but I have my raft."

A raft, I was to learn, that stayed mostly at the dock.

"You say you've come into some money?" Erasmus clicked his tongue after I told him that the money came via Eugene thanks to the efforts of Salmon Chase after the sale of Tilly. "These are ill-gotten gains, Livvie. But look around you. We could finish the chapel. Build a better road up to the trace. Maybe some lodging? Why, we could fix up this house!"

"I did not come to put your house in order."

"So why *have* you come, Olivia?"

It was a reasonable question. "We were under some duress when we last met," I said.

"Aye. Indeed."

"And since you would not write me, I've often wondered what happened to the man Handsome."

"You came all this way for that?"

"He was Tilly's father," I said. "I have some stake in this."

"Was he?"

"Was he what?"

"Her father."

I did not care for the direction of this conversation. I knew enough from having stayed at Orpheus Farms that slave breeders were not above espousing the principles of animal husbandry when it came to human chattel, and that blood merged more freely than we in the North might countenance. Besides, I had heard from Silas that Bethany could no longer abide Tilly, and what other explanation for that?

"Meaning there was more than dress-buttoning expected from the mother, Delilah," said Erasmus. "You know who Tilly looks like. She has Orpheus looks, and that's indisputable." Jerking his head at the boy, who had said nothing, Erasmus went on. "Now *me*—I'm clearly the father of this boy." He pointed at the boy's face. "Just look at his eyes."

True, the boy's eyes were blue, but they were calmer eyes, more intelligent.

"Got his mother's hair, though," said Erasmus. "Strange how that works."

"So where is he?" I said after Erasmus told me that many of the improvements had been achieved with the help of the runaway slave. "Handsome?"

Erasmus poked the fire. Sparks flew up like fireflies. The air was confounded with smoke, and I found it hard to breathe. In truth, I hadn't come back because of Handsome; I had come back for the boy. I told myself I was doing it for Julia or for Hatsepha and James. But I missed the boy with whom I'd traversed the woods, searching for stones and specimens. I coveted him as James had coveted him—as the promise of our future, as the assurance of our place.

"You told me you 'knew' someone," I said. "Someone who could help with Handsome."

"Aye," said Erasmus. "The Rankins. Stuck-up, the lot of them. Full of opinions. Of little help they were."

I had begun to fear he had returned the slave to the Orpheuses after all—or worse, taken a bigger profit by offering him to the traders. It wasn't beyond Erasmus to seize an opportunity, for in his own way, he was as entrepreneurial as our older brother, though lacking in discipline or drive.

"You sold him, didn't you? And after he'd already suffered once at your hands?"

Erasmus looked affronted. "To the contrary, I did exactly what Handsome himself requested."

CHAPTER 22

1838

It was a house of stick furniture and meager bedding, the one mattress assigned to me while Erasmus and William slept on a floor made prickly by straw. There was little crockery, and most of it chipped, a few misshapen pots fished out of the water along with the tub in which once a week we bathed. For all of our poverty, we did not lack for firewood or a diet of cow or goat milk and fish. We regarded the pig with an eye toward a late-summer slaughter that would yield ham and bacon, but in order to do so, we needed salt.

I was anxious to return to Ripley, especially once Erasmus told me what had transpired with Handsome, who was safe, if not entirely so. According to Erasmus, the Rankins had refused to shelter or move him, fearing they might be exposed as abettors, which rumor had they were.

A compromise to be sure, said Erasmus. *And yet I think it serves him.*

That Erasmus managed to shelter the man for several months was no small feat, for even on remote parts of the river such as this, patrollers checked the banks, especially in winter when the ice made a crossing possible. At first, he had kept him in a close-by cave, moving him into the barn when the weather grew cold. By February, Erasmus had found sanctuary for Handsome just north of Ripley in the

Gist settlement. Established as a refuge for manumitted slaves, the settlement was funded by the estate of an Englishman named Gist who owned land in Virgina, and who, upon his death, had freed his slaves, bestowing upon them property and means for their education. Like a tree into the forest, Handsome had melted into the free-black populace that, though frequently harassed by slave catchers in spite of their status, offered solidarity and more than sufficient cover for the occasional runaway.

For now anyway, said Erasmus.

That had been two months before my most recent arrival, and since then we had contended with a rising river that had nearly scooped up our cabin. One moment the flow could be as slow and calm as a conversation with an old friend, only to spike into a rage, unleashing water and debris. On those nights when thunder rattled the rafters and frightened the mule, the deluge came mightily.

"We need to go to market, Erasmus," I said one morning in June after our tilled field had drowned and the cow was looking sickly. "We are going to starve."

I still had money to buy dry goods and clothes for the boy. We hitched the carriage to the mule, riding most of the morning until, like a revelation, the town of Ripley appeared. After two months of living in the hinterland, I felt I was arriving in Carthage as I viewed the boat works, the mill, the tanneries and packing yard, the brick houses lining Front Street, the chestnuts flanking Main.

Erasmus pulled down his hat, and the boy imitated him—two mushrooms slinking up the road, followed by the dog.

"You look like you're hiding from the Devil," I said, hurrying to keep up. "Goodness, but all this refinement is a sight for sore eyes, and me with no one to call on."

Erasmus glanced from beneath his brim to see if I was joking, and I was, but only a little, for the past two months had wearied my bones and caused my hands to roughen. There was a time when Erasmus would have joined me in the jest; now he was sober and serious, on the lookout for potential enemies.

"Willy-boy," said Erasmus, "you go back to the carriage and give the mule some water. I'm going to sit outside while your aunt is in the store." William scampered off while I pushed into the shop that was filled with dry goods and provisions.

Linens! And such fine ones, too, made of cotton so smooth it promised a good night's sleep. There were pillows for sale, though I doubted our carriage could handle much more than the dog and the three of us given the quantity of flour, fabric, and salt we needed, not to mention a few twists of chocolate.

"I understand you have tea?" I asked the proprietress, a chubby but severe-looking woman whose clothing, while simple, was pressed.

"Homesteading, are you?" she said, eyeing my rumpled blouse. "In which here parts?"

I was about to say "just downriver," but since Erasmus was clear in his desire to remain elusive, I replied, "Just outside of Sardinia."

"Sardinia? We have friends in Sardinia. A pastor. Tell me, what church are you attending?"

"We are new arrivals," I said, quickly adding, "from Cincinnati. We are Presbyterians."

"Well then, you shall want to know Reverend Grayson. He is a fine Presbyterian minister. He is"—she paused and looked meaningfully into my eyes—"a respecter of freedom."

"As all Presbyterians should be."

"I don't suppose . . ."

I waited for her question.

"You'll be wanting extra beans?"

I FOUND ERASMUS on the walkway slouching against a horse post.

"That was an odd conversation."

"So you met Mrs. Beasley?" he said. "And what did you make of her?"

"Should I have an opinion? She sold me beans and flour. We did not strike a friendship."

"And yet if you had?"

"This town runs in riddles. It should be renamed 'Riddle-y.' "

"Trust no one," said Erasmus, scanning for his son.

IT TOOK WEEKS, but the garden revived so that we had spinach to go with our trout and a soft-boiled egg from the chicken along with a big chunk of bread and butter churned from the cow's milk. Once again, I had donned Erasmus's clothes in order to unshackle my limbs that I might prepare the plot, plant the seeds, shore up the fencing, hammer the shingles, sweep out the barn, preserve the berries, bake, salt, and cure.

With the longer days, William and I had time to read, and even into the lighting of candles we discussed the portrayal of the Shawnee by Robert Montgomery Bird, and whether Mr. Fenimore Cooper was better able to draw a portrait of the Indian. William allowed as how he wished *he* were an Indian, and Erasmus said, *A fine little scalper you would've made,* and all of us laughed at the character of Sam Weller in Mr. Dickens's *Pickwick Papers.*

So, too, we talked about religion, and whether God had preordained the course of our lives, and if there was a God at all. I confessed to my doubts, but Erasmus insisted that everywhere we looked, we could find examples of God's grace, the redemption of sins, of mercy on our souls, whereupon William added that God must love squirrels and crows very much, for there was abundance of each in the forest.

It was not yet a month after the solstice, the light still long on the day. It hadn't taken me long to notice the strengthening of my arms, and though I should have thought myself above this tough and menial work, it made me feel powerful. Free.

Soon the bats came out, dodging and darting, winging along the water's edge where the insects were thick. Mercifully, we had our own beds now thanks to several trips to Ripley, each odder than the last, Mrs. Beasley being markedly less friendly on subsequent visits to her store.

How goes it in Sardinia? she had asked, and crisply, too, so that I knew she had inquired and heard of no family named Givens in that town.

I was not entirely candid, Mrs. Beasley. I am not proud of our circumstances and did not want you to think unkindly of us for living so meanly down the river.

Many scrape by their first few years here, she went on, betraying little sympathy. Then, offhandedly: *Tell me, how long since you left Ireland?*

Is my accent still so noticeable? I said, feeling vexed. *You must think I'm recently off the boat.*

Are you not?

I realized she assumed I was Catholic, and almost laughed, for it seemed ridiculous to have been mistaken thusly, and yet how common to mistake others as being something they are not.

Twenty years. If you can believe it.

You don't say? And have you a husband?

Alas, he's passed. I live now with my brother Erasmus and his son, William.

The name "Erasmus" seemed to square the corners on our situation, emboldening Mrs. Beasley to sniff. *I know that boy William. He needs less supervision than the father.*

Now I sat with Erasmus and William as the first stars appeared. It was an inky night enlivened by cicadas and hoot owls as we readied ourselves for bed. There had been little time for study that day, so the boy and I read by the light of a lantern. We made our way through a passage of Hawthorne, each of us yawning yet wanting to persevere. The prose was stark and real, an elixir to a boy who had been raised on the Bible.

"'Tis bedtime," I said finally. "Your father is already snoring."

Half an hour later, we had joined him, but the night was not to last, for our sleep was suspended by the barking of dogs. They were distant at first, just enough to rustle me from a dream.

"What is it?" I hissed.

"Shhh," said Erasmus. "Listen."

Soon, our old hound was joining in. The barking grew louder until I could make out the shouts of men. Erasmus got up, put on his pants, touched a finger to his lips. "Stay in bed. I am going to check on the cow. If you wake before sunrise, and I'm still not back, light the lamp."

I pulled my covers up. The boy hadn't stirred. It took me an hour to go back to sleep.

IT WAS STILL DARK WHEN I WOKE AGAIN, though I could sense the dawn. Not wanting to wake the boy, I slid from my bed, pulled my shawl about me, grappled for the lamp. I struck a match and lit the room. It was then I realized that not only Erasmus but the boy, too, was missing.

"Willy?" I said, for he might have stepped out to relieve himself. "Willy?" I said more loudly.

I pulled on trousers and boots and went to the door. After a spring that had nearly drowned us, it had been a dry summer, and the river was low. It was quiet now. No more barking. I made my way to the barn, pulled open the door, held up the lamp, and was face-to-face with the cow and the goat, both of which looked at me expectantly.

"Erasmus?" I said.

Nothing.

I started to the shore to check the boat. It was rare that Erasmus might be summoned for a midnight ferry, but not unheard of. That he might have so stealthily vanished was not surprising, for stealth was his currency.

Then I heard a crash and wheeled around. "Who goes there?" I said, buttressing the lamp lest it expire. A form stood in the doorway of the unfinished chapel. Raising myself to my full height, I started to say again, "Who—" but was interrupted by the voice of my nephew saying, "Aunt Olivia! Come quickly!"

My hair tumbling about my shoulders, I hurried toward the open door. Inside, where the cross should have been, was Erasmus, lit by a candle and hunched over a form.

"Sister! Come!" said Erasmus with a tone more typical of James. "I fear she's broken her leg."

"She?" I held up the lantern to see of what "she" he was speaking of and was shocked to see a young black woman dressed in an enormous amount of soggy clothing, her leg akimbo, blood on her cheeks and bodice.

"Sweet Jesus!" I said.

I knelt down to examine the girl, those years of training with Silas holding at bay the floodgate of questions. Her shin was bruised and her ankle above her boot top swelled lividly.

"Willy," I said, "fetch some clean rags and water."

The girl's eyes were lowered, but I knew she was taking me in as if to see if I was worthier of trust than this white man who had tried to touch her naked leg.

"May I take off your shoe?" I said, holding my hands up so she could see they were empty. Her hair was full of brambles. "I am Olivia Givens," said I, choosing my maiden name in lieu of Orpheus. "What's *your* name?"

She said nothing, but her fingers clutched her skirt—one of four she was wearing—scrunching it up as if kneading bread, revealing ankle, shin, and knee. There were no visible breaks in the skin. I reached for her boot. It was damp and mud-caked. I felt her watching me as I unlaced it, though she scarcely could have run had I proved threatening. Her flesh quivered as I held her calf, examining her shin and her kneecap.

"There?" I said. "There?"

Each time, she shook her head.

I went back to her foot, started with the toes. "There?" I moved up to her ankle, rotated it. She screamed.

"Ah," I said. "There."

Remembering what Silas had taught me, I probed, following the line of sinew, palpating the swollen tissue. Gradually but firmly, I pushed against her foot. She flinched, but did not cry out again. "It's not broken," I said. "But it's badly sprained."

Erasmus leaned in, his hair falling forward, his blue eyes studying her dark ones. He rose and walked to the door. Turning, he added, "We will keep her for one day, Livvie. She must be ready to move on by sunset."

I asked no questions. That he had connections, I already knew. The way he slunk around Ripley, his secretiveness, his banter with those he ferried, his caginess about Handsome. My suspicion was that he was abetting; even more so, that he was sometimes paid.

After he left, I turned to the girl. "Your foot is going to turn black-and-blue, but I'll wrap it tight, and you'll be fine to ride. Would you like to take off your petticoats and skirts?"

Indeed, she was as layered as sodden cabbage in every conceivable garment that she—or more likely, her mistress—owned.

She mumbled something.

"Excuse me?" For the world, it sounded as though she'd said *Tilly*. The name was common enough.

"My name is Nelly," she said, and this time clear as day, and of course she was nothing like Tilly, this girl with her chocolate skin and wildish hair. I noticed her ear was clipped.

The boy returned, setting down the supplies and studying Nelly with concern.

"How in the world did you get across that river?" I asked as I bandaged her foot, trying not to look at the nails that were yellowed and curled like old cloves of garlic. She smelled as if she had soiled her underwear.

"Almost didn't. I cain't swim," she said. "I was up to my knees when the man come in the boat with that boy."

"That man is my brother."

"Don't look like you."

I tied up the end of the bandage, waiting for her to say how handsome my brother was in contrast to my homely self, but she did not. When the sun came up, I would cook up some balm of Gilead to ease the swelling and the pain.

"There, now," I said, smoothing the petticoats and hems. "Perhaps you'd like to go to the privy?"

She heaved herself up and leaned on me, both of us lurching across the floor. She said, "That ol' nigger said there'd be a pinch in the river. Little good a pinch does when that river is over your head."

I eased her down on a bench so that she might arrange herself. She started to strip. A layer of burgundy silk followed by gingham followed by calico, then crispy tulle. When she was down to her chemise, I made out the angry crisscrosses traversing her spine. She raised her chin. "I broke my back for my missus and give her two of my chilluns besides. That nigger said someone would be waitin' longsides the banks, but when I gots through the canebrake, there's nobody. That man don' know nothin'." She sighed with indignation. "'Sides, they dogs woulda got me sooner 'n I could learn how to swim."

"Dogs, snakes, slavers. Whatever possessed you?" I said. It was insanity, the likelihood of success being minuscule, the fact of our endangerment for helping her setting my nerves on edge. "And where did you come from?"

I could see her struggling with the truth. Nothing was straightforward in this world where steamboat flaunted current and voices carried from either shore. A bird picking berries on one bank could fly to the other side, drop its load, and seed a new crop like the wild juniper of the South rooting itself in the North. But this girl was forbidden stock, grafted or otherwise.

"I woulda drowned if it weren't for this boy," she said, jerking her head at William, who was braced against the doorjamb keeping a nervous watch. "This boy's eye is keen."

Stripped down to her bloomers, she was slighter than I'd thought. I supposed she'd come from one of the big farms in Augusta since that was the closest Kentucky town. Patrollers swarmed like ants, so she must have been a wily thing. I well remembered my own success at blending in to the point of invisibility years earlier when I had helped Silas in the morgue. Women become men; black becomes white. There is an art to disappearing.

"Where is he going to take me? Your brother?"

In truth, I did not know. Ever since Erasmus had taken Handsome to the Gist settlement, patrollers were regularly rousting out the settlers, asking them for papers.

The door opened and in came my brother, still holding the lamp. When he saw how scantily dressed young Nelly was, he turned away.

"They are looking for her," said Erasmus, his back to us. "If the dogs pick up the scent, they will know she's been here. There isn't much time, Livvie. As soon as morning comes, you've got to go to Ripley. Willy will take you. You will buy stocks and provisions." He handed a piece of paper to Willy. "Give this note to Mrs. Beasley."

"And what will you do with the girl, Erasmus? She can barely walk."

"She can sit in a boat, can't she?"

"They'll surely spot her."

"Not if she's wearing Willy-boy's clothes and powdered up white. No one will look twice. No one will think it strange. Just a boy and his father, rowing the river as usual."

WILLIAM TIED UP THE HORSE and unhitched the carriage, parking it in a vacant yard. Ripley, as ever, was bustling—the tolling clang of the ironworks, the hissing of boat stacks letting off steam. Tacked to the walls of Mrs. Beasley's dry-goods store were reward notices for runaway slaves, but none of the descriptions matched Nelly, who had run off only the day before. I had no doubt there were eyes on the town, even on me as I untied my bonnet and pushed through the door.

Mrs. Beasley was used to me now and begrudged me an ounce of courtesy since I seemed to have no shortage of money. The boy stood by the door with his hands in his pockets. I fingered the fabrics and imagined a new skirt, but our list was for items such as flour and a box of jars to lay up jams.

"You are looking passably well, Miss Givens, in spite of your circumstances," said Mrs. Beasley with a trace of disappointment.

I had returned to my maiden name since Tilly's trial, knowing that Silas would forgive me. Orpheus was too fraught a name in these parts, and it was easier to avoid explanation.

I thanked her for the compliment and thrust out the list. At the last two items, she raised her eyebrow.

"And what makes you think we have such face powder? And hair?" The tone in which she said this made it clear she had deduced I was a woman of loose morals. Who else would use cosmetics (although I well knew that many in Hatsepha's circle were doing exactly that to whiten their skin beyond the bounds of nature)?

"Surely I can acquire these in Maysville if need be," I said, throwing down the gauntlet. "But I am disinclined to travel, and Ripley is that much closer." And then, as if suddenly remembering, I fumbled in my reticule and extracted Erasmus's letter. "Oh, and this."

No raised eyebrow, just a piercing stare, first at the letter, then at me. "I'm not sure I understand," she said.

I shrugged. "It does seem quite inscrutable." Indeed, the content of the note sounded nothing like Erasmus.

I am in possession of a fine volume of Irrepressible Conflict *bound in black and wonder if you will trade for it.*

I knew that Erasmus had no such book, but before I could press the issue, Mrs. Beasley reached below the counter and set out what looked like a brooch along with a small silk bag. "You'll be needing these," she said. "And Mrs. Orpheus"—I jumped at her use of my married name—"tell that brother of yours we want no repeat of the last time." She nodded at William who was peering through the window. "Perhaps the young man can hoist up this sack of flour."

As William drove me home in the carriage, I examined my two packages. The brooch, when opened, contained a tiny white wafer. When I ran my finger across it, I picked up a ghostly trail of powder. To go with this was a bag of curls, not unlike the crown on William's head and no doubt lopped off some unfortunate corpse. We jostled along. Beyond the thick border of woods and hills lay fields of farmland, sparsely populated, the corn now high as my elbows.

By the time we arrived back at Enduring Hope, it was late in the day. Erasmus, chopping wood, barely looked up, but as soon as William unhitched the horse, he set down his ax.

"Well?"

"Mrs. Beasley seems to think I'm a prostitute."

Erasmus laughed a bit too hard.

"And Nelly?" I said. "Can she walk with that ankle?"

"If all goes well, she will not have to."

I told him about Mrs. Beasley's admonition about no repeat of the last time.

"You know what these people are like," said Erasmus, conjuring his twenty-year-old self, who shrugged off allegations.

"Did you not pay your bill?"

Erasmus picked up the ax, embedded it in a log. Running his callused palms together, he added, "These abolitionists are prickly. I suppose I should have warned them before I arrived with Handsome that day. But it's not as though they gave out a handbook."

"You showed up with Handsome at Mrs. Beasley's?"

"At the Rankins' house, as a matter of fact," he said. "How was I to know that patrollers were about? Certainly not because of Handsome. He'd cooled his heels here and been long forgotten. No, they were looking for some Joe or Jack that had already been run up to Chillicothe."

"No wonder they are less than sanguine about you," I said, imagining the scenario: Erasmus showing up with a runaway just as the Rankin family was warding off angry slave scouts.

He looked hurt. "Anyway, I found the man sanctuary in the end."

William had come out of the barn with a pail, approaching the cow and the goat for their nightly offerings. A baby goat had just been weaned and was now tagging after the boy, butting at his legs. William laughed and pushed him off.

"It would be nice if the boy had a friend," I said, watching the frolic between boy and beast.

"I need him here," said Erasmus. He looked at my reticule that contained some of the day's purchases. "I need you, too," he added, jerking his head at the chapel. "By tomorrow, that girl's got to look like Willy."

"You poor thing," I said to Nelly as I whitened her face the following morning before the sun rose. "Such are the indignities . . ." My voice trailed off upon seeing her clipped ear.

"Can I see?" she said. Her face flickered ghostly in the lantern light.

I told her we had no mirror.

She rolled her eyes. "In Augusta, I worked as an assistant laundress. And in a fine house, too. Plenty of mirrors in that house." This explained how she had access to her mistress's wardrobe.

William arrived with a set of bibbed trousers and a cotton shirt along with last year's boots that he had outgrown. Nelly regarded the ensemble with a queasy look. "I thought you was making me look pretty."

After she pulled on William's clothes, I affixed the curls to her hair, imagining Tilly critiquing my technique. Her skull felt small and fragile as a bird's. On went the hat, completing the effect. I sent William to fetch Erasmus, who joined us, seemingly satisfied with the result. "Sun's coming up," he said. "It's time."

"You'll pack up my clothes?" she said to me anxiously.

"You can't take them with you," I said, and then seeing she might cry and streak the powder, added hastily, "but we'll send them on once you are settled. You'll have the best wardrobe in Canada."

"Mastuh says niggers freeze they tails off in Canada."

"Mastuh says a lot of things, I'm sure." I kissed her on the cheek, dusting my own with powder. I looked at Erasmus. "Don't cross Mrs. Beasley, brother."

"Keep the boy out of sight," he said, whistling for the dog. "I'll be back by midmorning, God willing."

He loaded the limping girl into the boat, instructing her how to sit, how to duck her head just so. The mongrel jumped in after them.

"Let us hope no passengers will hail them," I said to William as we watched them disappear into the low mist. "It'd be just your father's luck to catch the first business he's had in weeks."

As Erasmus had instructed, I kept William out of view in the chapel while I kneaded dough in the summer kitchen. Although the humidity was oppressive, I stoked logs in the oven after the second rising so that we might have bread. A murder of crows shrieked from the treetops. The little goat, still pining for its mother's milk, mawed pitifully.

"Aunt Livvie," called William from the chapel, "might I come out now?"

"Stay inside, Willy."

"I have to piss."

"Oh, all right, then. But step behind the building and out of sight from the river." I started to add that I wanted to see his cursive practiced on the slate, but before I could call out, I heard the clop of horses on the path. I set down the log that I was about to put in the oven. Two riders came into the clearing. They looked harmless enough—early twenties, maybe. Beardless. One even had kindish eyes.

"Pardon us, ma'am, but we seem to have taken a wrong turn."

I pushed back my hair with my sleeve so as not to smudge my face with ashes.

"You must have seen our banner," I said.

"Enduring Hope?" said the one with the nice eyes. He turned to his companion, whose dark hair hung down behind his ears. "Now what can that mean?"

"There's no riddle here," said I. "We are but a sanctuary, and my brother is a preacher."

They sat on their horses, neither making a move to dismount, the one eyeing me, the lank-haired one glancing over the property, taking in the cow, the goats, the cabin, and the chapel. "And where is your brother now?"

"Seeking passengers to ferry off the boats."

"Off the boats? Or from the other shore?"

I glanced at my fire that was sorely in need of fuel. I had no weapon nearby and was unsure whether I required one, but we were off the beaten path and far from other neighbors.

"I could do with some praying," said the fairer one, dismounting. "As for my brother"—he jerked his head—"he is a reprobate."

"Then by all means pray," said I in as pleasant a voice as I could muster. "Our chapel sits here for the wayfarer and is ecumenically inclined."

At that, the darker one smiled, and not so nicely. "That's a mighty big word, ma'am."

"I am a schoolteacher," I said, imagining Silas saying, *Fine language for an atheist, Miss Givens.* I watched the back of the fair-haired one as he made for the chapel, and could only hope that William had heard the chatter and was hiding in the woods. "It merely means that all are welcome. Now, if you don't mind, I need to bake these loaves."

"Hot day for baking," said Dark Hair. "I sure could do with a drink."

"There is a well by the spring."

"Would you mind fetching it?"

He clearly wanted me away from the house, no doubt so he could see if there was anything worth taking.

"I seen your brother time to time on the river," said he. "Him and the boy."

"Well, then you know our business."

There was an awkward pause. His fairer brother reemerged from the chapel, but made no mention of having discovered William. Silently, I thanked God for the boy's full bladder.

"I'll get your water, then. But you haven't told me your names."

The nicer-looking one pulled off his hat and gave a rather silly bow. "Me . . . I'm Abner. And this here's Pate."

I introduced myself as Miss Givens, picked up a pail, and headed down the path. The artesian spring was away from the house and obscured by rocks and trees. I made a low whistle as soon as I was out of sight and immediately got a whistle back. Willy's eyes met mine from behind a large oak. I motioned at the outcropping of rock where they'd hidden Handsome in a cave. Stealthily, Willy moved that way as I banged on the pail, raising a racket. When I returned, both strangers were nowhere to be seen. I was unsurprised when they walked out of the cabin.

I said, "You are beyond your bounds, sirs."

Pate crossed his arms and leaned up against the door. Abner ran his fingers through his hair. His lashes, I noticed, were colorless. "Our apologies, ma'am, but we haven't been completely honest."

"Really?" I said, flatly.

"Thing is, we're on the lookout."

"Has there been a crime?"

"We've been losing inventory." He said it the way James might speak of a lost batch of candles. "And we're trying to plug up the holes."

"Speak plainly," I said, trying to keep my hand from shaking and spilling the water.

"Runaways, ma'am. Runaways taking advantage of kind people such as yourself."

"We harbor no runaways here. Why don't you check in the barn?" I said, filling the cup from the pail and setting it on the porch rail.

"Already have," said Pate, grabbing the cup and swigging.

"Well then. If you don't mind." I picked up a log, regretful that I could not wield it as a club.

"Those are some mighty pretty dresses you got in there, ma'am," said Abner, his lashes blinking like nervous albino caterpillars. "Seems like a sweet bit of finery for living in the middle of nowhere."

I forced a smile. "I have many friends . . ." I said, emphasizing the word, ". . . in both Ripley and Cincinnati, where society demands that I look my best."

"Looks like you've been trying everything on, the way those clothes are tossed in a heap."

Pate took another gulp and spat. He looked at his brother. "Where's the boy?" I must have looked dumbfounded because he sneered. "We know just about everyone goes up and down this river."

"Well then," I said, willing the boy to stay put, "you'll know the lad generally accompanies his father."

"Yep," said Pate. "No one here but you."

"And all those pretty dresses," said Abner.

"Not just dresses," said Pate, reaching into his pocket. "Lookie here."

There was no constable to call, no onlooker whom I could beseech. That this man had the brooch of white powder in his hand was outrageous, but no more so than the fact that they had entered our cabin while my brother was away.

"Are you in the habit of touching women's property?"

"We are great respecters of property. Which is more than some on this shore could claim."

The fire was burning hotly now. I picked up a stick of kindling and poked it.

"Don't let us keep you," said Abner. "Bake your bread."

"The fire's too hot."

"Put it in."

I lifted the board and slid the loaves into the opening.

Pate had opened the brooch. "Now why on earth would you have use of this?"

He smeared some on his cheek war-paint style.

"Only women I know who use this stuff are the girls at the cathouse. You catting for the River Preacher?"

Abner had turned and gone back into the house.

"I have money," I called after him. "Are you looking for money?"

Pate just stared at me. Abner came out of the house with a dress—the burgundy silk one, suitable for balls. He held it up to himself. "Mmm-mmm."

Pate said, "It'd look prettier on her."

"You can take the money and go," I said.

"Oh, we'll take the money," said Pate. He was close to me now. He was touching my face. I stood very still as he pressed the powder onto my cheeks, smeared it across my brow.

"Please," I said.

He grabbed the neckline of my dress and tore it from my shoulder. I could smell the alcohol on him. I thought of Eugene Orpheus, his drunken breath. I thought, *If only I had a pitcher.*

But these two wouldn't be as easily dissuaded as Eugene Orpheus, whose wife slept on the other side of the wall. The nearest neighbors were the Utopians who believed the Lord would come again. I wasn't expecting the Lord. I prayed only for the return of Erasmus.

There was a terrible ripping sound as the sleeve came off my blouse. Buttons fell to the ground.

Abner came toward me and shoved the dress into my face. There was no more kindness in his eyes. "You know who'd own a dress this fancy?" he said. "Mrs. LeFevre. You know what else? Her girl has gone missing. Loudmouthed bitch that don't appreciate its good fortune in working for a lady. Mrs. LeFevre . . . she's a lady. Not like you . . . some trash along the shore."

Pate had yanked down my skirt. I was wearing no petticoat, only bloomers.

Abner said, "Put this on."

Pate said, "It's too good for the likes of her."

"I'd like to see her in it."

Abner thrust the dress into my arms. I could not move. He said, "What are you waiting for?" Roughly, he yanked it over my head. I stuck my arm through an enormous sleeve. Abner fussed with a hook at my waist, but the dress was too small. "Hell," he said. "You know what else I'd like?"

Pate squinted at the river. "Get her inside."

After they'd gone, I lay on my bed in the ruined dress, my knees to my chest, the bread burning in the oven.

"Aunt Livvie?"

I turned to see William standing in the door.

"I stayed in the cave like you told me." The tremble in his voice told me that he had heard.

"Good boy." My voice came out raspy, though I had not screamed the entire time.

He came closer. "What's that white stuff all over your face?"

"Get me a cloth, Willy. Your da will be home soon."

He stared.

"Go on, then."

It was nearly evening by the time Erasmus got back. I had washed the white powder from my face, rearranged my hair, and put on a pair of Erasmus's trousers. William and I were sitting by the smoldering remains of the silk dress in a fire pit on the shore. Erasmus beached his skiff and leapt out.

"Well, *that* was a victory!" he said, his euphoria illuminated by the coals. He seemed to have completely forgotten that he'd asked me to keep the boy out of view. "Willy-boy, store the oars. And drag the skiff up, will you? Good laddie."

"He *is* good," I said flatly, but Erasmus did not notice my tone. "Is she safe?"

"Safe and on her way. My message to Mrs. Beasley worked."

Mrs. Beasley, he said, got word to Rankin after she'd hidden the girl in a secret room, and Rankin sent one of his sons to make arrangements. "They'll have her up the hill tonight and through the cornstalks by the morning."

His face held a flush that bordered on unhealthy. Waving his arms above his head, he danced a jig, singing, "'We are the light of the world! We are the light of the world!' Come, Willy-boy," he said, gesturing to the boy to join him. "Let your light shine that they may see our good deeds and praise our Father in heaven."

But William made no move toward his father, who twirled as if enraptured, the *alleluia*s rising and falling, just as Sam Mutton had taught him to excite a crowd, but there was no crowd now, and truly I was scared for him.

"Stop it, brother," I said. "Can't you see he's had a fright?"

"Ah, Livvie, you were always one to throw sand upon the flames. What're you burning there, anyway?"

"Trash."

"Well then," he said, his rapture now subdued, "what's for dinner?"

"I'm so sorry," I said, struggling not to cry. "But I've burned the bread."

CHAPTER 23

1838

After that day, I took a gun with me everywhere. *You're more than a little jumpy,* Erasmus said.

I said I'd seen a mountain lion. I suspected that if I told him the truth, he'd go off his head.

To both my relief and disappointment, Abner and Pate did not return, although I waited, sleeping lightly for two weeks, my finger on the trigger. More than likely, they had found others to harass. There had been an attack on an abolitionist in a church in Ripley, the man dragged from his pew. Not long after, a free black man from the Gist settlement had his head smashed in with a brick.

Erasmus still ferried passengers from shore to shore and from the decks of steamboats. The little money I had left—that which the brothers hadn't stolen—was running low, but our encampment began to prosper as word got out that we had a chapel. Each week, a new group of settlers arrived to pray. A few tithed. Many bought eggs or bacon. And when the route inland from Ripley was compromised after an abolitionist named Mahan from Sardinia was betrayed by a Kentucky slaveholder named William Greathouse and later arrested, several more runaways showed up at Enduring Hope.

Not one to let well enough alone, Erasmus decided to try his hand at further abetting. Giddy from his success in delivering Nelly to the Rankins, he angled to make himself essential to the operation of conducting slaves. In late August, he received a coffin from a steamboat that had embarked in Covington. Hoisting the coffin onto our carriage, he dropped it off at a cemetery just west of Ripley. When he later inquired of Mrs. Beasley as to what had happened to that coffin, and was the corpse still breathing, she gave him a withering look and said, *Whatever coffin do you mean?*

For Erasmus to be relegated to a mere link in a chain was nearly unbearable. Because each leg of the journey carried its own secret strategy, we seldom knew for certain who had made it from one station to the next before finally arriving in Canada. Like the man and two children whom Erasmus ferried down to Cincinnati, along with a load of tobacco. The last he saw of them, they were accompanying a tradesman with a wheelbarrow filled with the crop, heading away from the landing.

The worst thing, Erasmus said, *is not being able to tell anyone what I've done.*

Thinking there were worse things indeed, I said, *And didn't you preach that very virtue, brother? Shame on you for needing credit now.*

Nevertheless, I shared Erasmus's enthusiasm for our mission. This is not to say I wasn't worried, for I was in constant fear—but after Tilly and the fateful visit by the brothers, my heart had hardened against slavery.

Even worse, I discovered I was pregnant.

It was Mrs. Beasley, of all people, to whom I went for help the next time I accompanied Erasmus to Ripley.

She sat very still as I told her what had transpired that day. She was herself a widow, protected by neighbors, but she'd seen the violence. Just two weeks earlier, a woman had been shot in the back.

"And now this," I said.

"You did not hit or claw?"

I knew there would be no legal remedy for my outrage. I was no maiden, after all. The men were white. I had been alone.

"What do you want from me?" asked Mrs. Beasley.

"I am told your store has many wonderful things and for a variety of purposes."

I told her that I knew about abortifacients—that herbs such as tansy, pennyroyal, rue, and ergot could cause my bowels to constrict. I knew from my miscarriage it would not be easy—that it would be awful, in fact. Indeed, Silas and I had helped more than one woman desperate to end a pregnancy because of circumstances, poverty, transgression, or the burden of too many children. And I should never forget the freckled face of that woman who had died, trying to abort.

"Come back next week," said Mrs. Beasley.

The next week I made up a story about meeting a traveling doctor who had been a student of Silas's research. I would have driven the carriage myself, but it was seemlier if the boy accompanied me.

"Find lodging down at the mills," I said to William when we got to Mrs. Beasley's. "You know Mr. Rutger?" Indeed, Rutger had sent us an entire family early in August when it became apparent that there was inadequate transportation to usher them uphill. "Come back in the morning."

Mrs. Beasley looked up when I entered the store. "This is no small inconvenience. But given what you went through, I felt it was my duty."

She took me into her back room, pushed aside a worktable, undid two hooks obscured by a hanging cloth of embroidered Bible verse, and swung open a panel of beadboard wainscoting.

"Take this," she said, handing me a powder and a tincture along with a glass. "You understand the effects?"

Before shutting the wainscoting behind me, she added, "Take care you don't cry out."

The room was barely worthy of the name, furnished only with a cot and a basin. The concoction tasted like bile and took hours to act. In the middle of the night, my stomach heaved and then contracted as with a horrible bout of diarrhea. Everything released and, once released, persevered in spite of there being nothing left to expel. For the world, I could have been Julia in the final throes of cholera. Indeed, it was not until midmorning the following day that I could so much as sit. But the bloody sheets and the contents of the basin attested to the success of my endeavor. Thanks to Silas, I knew how to read the tea leaves of tissue, and though it pained me to have to do it, the suffering was worth it.

Mrs. Beasley looked in on me shortly after noon. It may have been my imagination, but she seemed a tad solicitous, asking if I'd like some clothing of her own.

"I'm a little faint," I said. "I'm sure it will pass."

"It usually does," said Mrs. Beasley. "As often as not, the mothers are younger than yourself. At least you lived. That's more than I can say for a couple of the girls."

I flinched at the use of the word "mother." Indeed, at thirty-five, I might have been a grandmother.

When Mrs. Beasley sent for the boy, it was late in the day. He arrived sprinkled with hay, regarding me with perplexity, for I looked white and drawn.

"You are a good boy, Willy."

By the time we got back to Enduring Hope, I was feverish.

"What's wrong with her?" Erasmus asked as the boy shouldered me from the buggy.

With a straight face, William said, "She's taken ill from a bad piece of fish."

"Then get her inside and cover her up. We must keep her warm and well drunk of water."

But no matter how much water I drank, I could not sit up without my head spinning. Whatever herb had been in Mrs. Beasley's recipe seemed more lethal than what it had cured. For three days I hovered and would have gladly been taken, so low was the sun, so thin the veil between here and there.

Erasmus wiped my brow with a cloth dipped in river water and fed me chicken broth. He scrambled eggs on a skillet over the open fire. He baked the bread that should have been mine to bake. But my stomach did protest.

"She needs a doctor," William said. He had stayed close to me, touching my forehead like a little nurse. "We should take her back to Ripley."

"'Tis best that I keep a light footprint in Ripley, given our activities," said Erasmus. "When dawn comes, we'll take her west."

AND SO IT WAS that I returned to Cincinnati in the company of my brother and my nephew—a weakened woman who had neither strength to live alone nor to protest against her brother's wife who insisted she move in.

"Finally you've come to your senses," said Hatsepha. "And goodness you're so thin!"

Thrice her maid came to change my sheets. I could hear the servants' murmured German as they discussed my plight, drawing Lord knows what conclusions. None of them wanted to get close to me in case I was contagious. I swam in the dull light of pulled draperies, tossing off the covers only to freeze. Food was brought in and taken away. And then one evening, I managed to drink some broth.

Hatsepha entered the room carrying a candle. "I don't know why you're having these problems, Olivia. You, a single woman. It reminds me of when I miscarried. I bled so hard, it ruined my woman parts, for, ever since, I do not conceive. Even when I think I might have, the bleeding comes." She blinked several times. "But then, you must know all about that."

"I'm sorry, Hatsepha," I said, for I hadn't known the full extent of her disappointment at her barrenness. Nor had she ever quite forgiven me for not confiding about my own miscarriage with Silas.

Before Erasmus left, I had heard raised voices, but could not make out the thrust of the dispute. Erasmus came to my door along with the boy, looking concerned.

"I won't tell James what you've been doing," I said, "if that's what you're worried about."

"It's *you* I'm worried about, Livvie. I've never seen you brought so low." But he did look immensely relieved.

"As for you, Willy," I said, extending my hand from beneath the comforter, "I expect you to keep up with your reading *and* your fossil collecting. I will return to test you as soon as the leaves turn red."

As Hatsepha rang for the maid to bring another change of bedding as well as a coal heater to warm the mattress, as she fussed with the hangings on the bed frame, tucked my hair into a cap, pushed on me a thick soup of beets, I swore I'd make my way back to Enduring Hope before the frost was hoary on the ground, but it was not to be. It took me years to return.

CHAPTER 24

1839–1840

The problem was, I did not get well. The bleeding stopped, but not the weakness. And worse, my eyesight began to falter. Whatever alchemy Mrs. Beasley's herbs had worked in my womb turned with a vengeance on other organs. I knew enough about the body to understand the symptoms of a compromised liver or kidney. The lower rims of my eyes turned yellow. I lost a good bit of my hair. Tilly might have said, *Good riddance to that mess,* but it made me sad to see my tresses come out in chunks, the red replaced by gray at thirty-six years of age.

Hatsepha read to me as I had read to William. We had moved on from Mr. Hawthorne (too puritanical, we agreed) to Mr. Dickens and Edgar Allan Poe.

"I'm afraid I'll have to take in my skirts," I said one day when the gingham slipped to my knees as we were walking in Hatsepha's garden. The late-summer vegetables were coming up—pale, delicate lettuces and tiny tomatoes the size of marbles and sweet as candy, so unlike the hearty vegetables suitable for winter that we grew by necessity at Enduring Hope.

"Nonsense," said Hatsepha. "We will commission a new wardrobe. Between the two of us—you so thin and me so fat—we have the perfect figure!"

And money to squander. Money that came from illumination such as God had created—only, according to James, *he,* James Givens, was better at it, first with his perfect candles, and now with gas for lamps.

"Candlelight is one thing, but gas brings consistency and durability. Gas brings the prospect of security and new horizons. People will have a new world once our cities are lit up with gas," James pronounced that night at dinner.

Orders were coming in, and already he was laying pipe in Clifton. The day would come (or night, rather) when walkways would glow in so modern a way that pedestrians could see their feet and one another.

"You amaze me, James," I said, recalling the first time he took me to the processing plant that extracted gas from coke. "I remember you practically falling into a vat of grease that you stirred yourself, and now—what?—a hundred men?"

"A hundred and twenty," he said.

He now hired with an eye for dedication and temperance and fortitude, blind to color and deaf to accent. Free blacks, Irish Catholics, Germans, Dutch—each found a job at Givens and Sons.

"But you," said James, "you must regain your strength."

If James—or Erasmus, for that matter—had any idea of what had set off my wasting, they did not let on. I was quite certain Hatsepha suspected because she went on at length about the deplorable nature of "women's problems" and how, as much as she'd wanted children, she thought it had gone far worse for her friends who had died in childbirth, or for those who had more children than they could count on both hands, these women forever on their backs, enduring a husband, issuing forth a child.

"We should count ourselves lucky," she said, patting me on the hand.

She never once asked who the father might be. Perhaps she thought that I, with no husband, would be desperate enough to make a misguided choice. And so I passed the summer of 1839 still ensconced in Cincinnati. In late August, I sent a letter to William commending him on his birthday and telling him how well I remembered his entry into the world. It was the night I'd met Tilly, the night before I met Silas. How my life had changed. Now I spent most of my time reclining, trying to read, occasionally making a trip into the conservatory, and receiving the occasional letter from Erasmus.

Dearest Livvie, he wrote in September,

> *It is already fall, the river so low that the steamboats are running aground. I am endlessly called upon to ferry passengers that have been waylaid by shallows and snags. The boy has grown beyond my shoulders and has become an expert shot. He often practices in back of the escarpment to the south, although he nearly took off the hat of one of the Utopians who was walking through the woods, and would have expedited the man's path to heaven, which, in the view of the Utopians, meant a swim across an ocean of lemonade escorted by angels so lurid they would make a Catholic blush.*
>
> *You would not recognize our little camp. I have secured another helper along with Willy, this time a young man whose wife died in childbirth. He has come here to pray and work off his grief. I told him about losing Julia, and he said, "At least you have a son." I suppose he's right on this, and I have sworn to thank God every day that I have the boy, and that if I no longer have a wife, at least I hold her memory in the expression of his face.*

After that, I heard nothing for months, and long months, too, in which my headaches grew worse, and I sat in the parlor by the thin light of autumn, a fire kindled in the hearth while Hatsepha read articles about exploding steamboats and arrests of runaways and a new contraption for pressing shirts. By the time Christmas rolled around,

I was in no mood to celebrate the birth of Jesus with jelly molds and a goose, though Hatsepha tried to stuff me with the latter, and so I took to my bed until they assured me that 1840 was well under way.

Dearest Livvie—

It turns out the young man who came to work here was a spy. As luck would have it, it was an uneventful autumn, but I thought it odd when he produced a bottle on Christmas Eve and got me to talking, then asked question after question about my other dealings. This is entrapment of the most perfidious sort, but also means that those holding with slavery are resorting to every description of trickery. I heard that someone tried to corner Rankin by using a man posed as a slave. Eyes are everywhere. My plan for now is to stick to ferrying wayfarers of a less controversial sort.

CURSED WITH ONE OF MY HEADACHES, I had begged off accompanying Hatsepha and James to church one late March morning, when Hatsepha's newly hired Norwegian girl knocked on the door of the library. I was curled up in a leather chair, covered by a rug, struggling to make out the print of *Nicholas Nickleby*.

"What is it, Mette?" This Mette was a superstitious girl, prone to hysterics whenever a misshapen root was dug from the garden, leading her to argue terribly with the cook about whether to worship the root as a spirit or toss it into the soup.

Lord protect us, said James. *We are becoming the last refuge for decommissioned saints.*

"There's a black man, lady," she said. "He says his name is Handsome." She put her hand to her mouth to suppress a laugh. "But I don't think he is."

I arose abruptly. The rug slid to the floor. "I will meet him in the cook's pantry."

She goggled at me for a second, thinking the whole arrangement odd—which it was, for I hadn't seen the man since the summer of our absconding and had only heard about him from Erasmus, who had been adamant about me not sending word to the man of Tilly's fate.

It's not as if the girl was so much in his life. She was a house girl, right? Erasmus had said, contending that if Handsome knew Tilly had been sold off, he might do something foolish. *Why should we burden him?*

I hadn't argued with his rationale. Who knew what Handsome would do? If he were to go back across the river to Kentucky to settle scores, he'd surely be picked up. *Furthermore,* Erasmus said, *Handsome can't read. He won't learn it from the newspapers. So unless someone tells him*—he shot me a look in the manner of James.

The cook's pantry was lined with baskets of onions, bottles of vinegar, cider, tubs of flour, sherry for flavoring and for the cook who took nips. I sat in a poky chair, wrapped in my shawl, while Handsome stood, hat in hand, before me. Although his hair was white, his face was much the same—the scarred eyebrow, the cracks around his eyes.

"Don't say it," I said. "I look ever so much older."

"Is it true?" Handsome said. "Tilly's gone?"

I had no choice but to nod. Indeed, it had been two years.

He didn't exclaim, but made such an expression that I felt cursed. Years before, when we'd made our escape to Enduring Hope, I had promised Handsome that Tilly would be safe in Cincinnati, protected by respectability and the esteem of so many ladies.

"Eugene came and got her," I said. "We hired the best lawyer to defend her."

"I'da liked to kill that Eugene," said Handsome. "And not for the first time neither. You know what he did to my Delilah?"

It didn't take much imagination.

"And I knows what he tried with you."

I said nothing.

"So now my girl's back with that devil?"

It took me a moment to realize he thought she was back at Orpheus Farms. "Oh, Handsome," I said. "Would that it were so."

I told him about the trial and the crowd, how they'd hustled her down to the river to an unspeakable fate. I told him about everything except how I'd taken the money. I could not tell him this.

Pots clanked as the cook got ready for Sunday lunch. The air was thick with frying onions and buttery biscuits.

I laid my hand on his arm. "Erasmus says you've got a good life in one of the settlements."

He stared out at the hills from the window. Whispers of green had appeared almost overnight.

"They started raiding the settlements," he said. "They's even stealing Negroes and selling them down. Maybe not so interested in an ol' nigger like me, but they's gonna come. Likes nothing more than a hangin'."

Neither of us said anything as the cook marched through the pantry, cross that we occupied her territory, glowering particularly at Handsome as if he offended her Irishness.

When she'd gone, I said, "Have you spoken to Erasmus?"

He shook his head. "Came a different way. 'Sides, that man don't know what he's doing."

I gave a quick look over my shoulder at the cook, but she was busy haranguing the Norwegian.

"He's got it down to an art," I said. "There's a network in Ripley."

"I heard it pretty much blew up this last year on accounta Mahan's trial."

"What about here? Do you have any contacts?"

"I was thinking *you* might, missus. Your older brother? I'm told he backed my Tilly."

"Oh my goodness, he'd be the last one to ask. Yes, there was Tilly, but that was personal. James is the picture of propriety. I'd suggest the Birneys."

"I see." He fiddled with his hat brim. "Oh, and missus, if someone *was* to go to Kentucky to steal off slaves, there's some others down on Orpheus Farms you might want to know about."

"And put ourselves right back into hot water?"

"There's Grady," he said, ignoring me, naming the boy whom I had seen flogged so viciously by Bethany. "And there's my other girl, Sticks."

"Sticks wasn't four years old," I said. "She's your girl?"

"Grandchild. And probably seven by my count."

Seven. The age my child with Silas would have been.

"And my other granddaughter. Sticks's cousin? She'd be pretty hard to get at, being up at the house 'n all. Best probably to leave that one alone, though it was cruel when they snatched her. Drove her mother crazy. Well, *you* saw her."

Just then, Cook dropped a pot and I jumped. I was about to ask him exactly what he meant when the Norwegian girl ran into the kitchen and yelled, "Mr. Givens is back, and there's not even soup on the table!"

"Go to the carriage house, Handsome," I said. "Tell Rutherford I've given you work brushing down the horses."

I went up the backstairs to my bedroom and popped my hair into a cap and pulled on a housecoat. When I entered the dining room, I saw that we had company for Sunday lunch.

"Ah," I said, "Ariadne. And Phinneaus!"

They both smiled, but neither could hide their shock at seeing me. For once, I was glad that I seldom left the house.

"We heard you let your apartments to that young doctor," said Ariadne. "We heard you were unwell."

"Much better, thank you," I said.

"Next spring," said Hatsepha, who had just entered the room, adjusting her bows after ridding herself of her hat, "Olivia and I are going to take the waters. We might even go to Saratoga!"

"As far as that?" said Ariadne. She sniffed and glared at her husband. "Phinneaus insists that Mays Lick will suffice for us."

"James will send me anywhere I want," said Hatsepha. "I believe he likes having me away." She gave a little laugh as James stepped through the French door from the garden. "And where have you been?"

"At the stable seeing to the horses." James shot me a look. "We've had some turnover in the hands, and I thought it best to examine their work."

"And?" said Hatsepha.

"You get what you pay for," said James.

As soon as the lunch was over—a two-hour affair in which Hatsepha and Ariadne sparred over the virtues of coral versus amethyst in setting off the complexion—I said my good-byes and hurried to the library to search for a scrap of letterhead. Finding a sheet, I scribbled out a quick testimonial about Handsome and begged that the recipient help him along. I addressed the envelope to James Birney.

Slipping out the back, I made my way to the stables. Handsome was curled on top of a pile of hay, snoring. There was no sign of the groomsman Rutherford, who must have departed for his own Sunday meal.

"Handsome," I said, shaking him. He sat up. A bit of straw clung to his hair. "I want you to take this letter to the Birney house on Walnut Street. Tell them you work for Givens and Sons."

"That's a terrible plan," said a voice from behind me. I turned. James stood in the doorway, arms crossed. "And who, may I ask, is Handsome?"

Handsome rose to his feet.

"James," I said, choosing my facts carefully, having never actually admitted that it was I who had absconded with the man. "Handsome used to work for Eugene Orpheus." James wore the unreadable face that made him so good at his business. I was prepared to dig in my heels and summon arguments to counter his objections.

"Birney?" James shook his head. "You do not think that every colored person, man or woman, who goes into Birney's house isn't watched?" He clicked his teeth. "I assume you have no papers?"

Handsome held up two empty hands.

"And you, Livvie. Why would *you* get involved?"

Playing a precious card that I hoped would move James's heart, I said, "Handsome is Tilly's father."

Handsome cleared his throat. "I thank you, sir, for what you tried to do for my girl."

James raised his eyebrow and, in feigned exasperation, said, "But can you do hair?" When Handsome did not respond, James added, "Don't worry. I only jest. Look, man." He straightened and pointed his finger at Handsome. "You showing up here puts all of us at risk. The good news is that my sister hasn't already sent you down to Birney's, where you'd be grabbed before your hand touched the knocker."

"How would you know this, James?" I asked. "From what I hear, Birney is a devout abolitionist and outspoken for our cause."

"Exactly," said James. And he was right. Even after his press was destroyed, Birney had persisted in publishing his abolitionist newspaper, *The Philanthropist*, and thus invited scrutiny. "And please do not say 'our' cause, Olivia. Your recklessness pains me." Again, to Handsome: "Can you steer a pair of drafts?"

"It's what I've been doing all these years."

"We could use another driver in the company yard. And the name of Givens keeps the patrollers away. But if you go outside the yard, I will not be able to protect you."

"With all due respect, James," said I, "that all sounds a bit shaky."

"With all due respect, Olivia, Handsome here doesn't have many choices. Unless I want to call the constable, which I don't. I've seen enough colored people dragged back into slavery to keep me ill for a lifetime." James looked at me and said, "And why the amazement, Livvie?"

"It's just that . . . It's a very kind offer, James."

"Sometimes you see me narrowly."

"You are *very* kind, Mr. James," said Handsome. "You and your brother, though he was the one who sent me back to—"

"Well, then, Handsome," I said, cutting him off. "What do you say? Are you going to work for the great company?" It wouldn't do to have him bring up his connection to Erasmus, and I didn't want to step on James's charity.

"If it's all the same to you, ma'am, and to you, Mr. James, I think I'd best try my luck in Canada."

"But how will we get you to Canada?" I said.

"Well," said James, and quite jovially, "let's go into the library and write another letter. This time"—he jerked his head at the letter in my hand—"we'll write to Mr. Dean. Now *there's* a man who can help you."

HANDSOME SLEPT IN THE LOFT above the stables that night and the following. On the third night, a dray pulled up stacked with candle crates.

"Evidently, Livvie," James said as he filled out the paperwork in his study, "we are reaching farther markets. These candles are going all the way to Cleveland. Now let's go talk to your friend Handsome."

We went out to the stables, James holding forth about Mr. Dean, his crate maker. "An ingenious fellow! Knows a lot about a lot."

"Crates?" I said cautiously, but James seemed delighted.

"Crates. Pallets. You name it." He whistled for Handsome, who peeked out of the loft. "C'mon down!"

Handsome descended the ladder and stood while James explained his scheme as if he were pitching investors rather than speaking to an audience of two. He took us to the dray that was stacked high with crates stamped with the label "candles," but with the name of Givens omitted. As he dropped to the ground and crawled beneath the wagon, James said, "I've commissioned Dean!" He beckoned us to follow, so we, too, ducked down and scrabbled forth. Soon we were beneath the platform of the dray as James unlatched two hooks, allowing a trapdoor above us to fall open. "Look inside," he said to Handsome. "You'll have plenty of air, but not much light. You might get a sore joint or two, but it shouldn't be too uncomfortable. There's a place to sit, see? Dean was only too happy to build some cabinetry besides crates. There's a man waiting for you in Cleveland."

"Well, I'll be smote," said Handsome, standing up and craning his neck into the cunningly fashioned compartment that, from the outside, was concealed by stacked-up candle crates. He would have said more, but we heard footsteps across the yard, so the three of us crouched very still, assuming it was one of the servant girls. We could hear the sound of a skirt sweeping along the cobbles. Suddenly Hatsepha bent down and peered at us.

"Dear?" said James. "What are you doing here?"

"Eleven years of marriage?" said Hatsepha. "Surely you know I read your mail?" She gaped at Handsome, whose eyes were wide and who looked as if any minute he would bolt. "So this is the man you are ushering?"

"You intercepted my note to Dean?"

"And to that man in Cleveland."

James and I braced for the tirade—the ignominy of this endeavor, the prospect of jail, the loss of our good name and business.

"Well, he has to eat something," said Hatsepha. "I had the cook make up a basket. Oh, and a blanket. It's still cold at night."

James, Handsome, and I crawled out from beneath the dray and brushed off the straw.

"I ain't got words," said Handsome, taking the basket.

"Nor I," said I.

"We loved Tilly very much, Mr. Handsome," said Hatsepha. "It was an outrage what was done to her."

Handsome took the basket and gave a little bow. James said, "You might want to use the privy. It's an all-night ride."

"WELL, I HOPE THAT TAKES CARE OF THAT," James said before we went to bed. "Your little foray into abolition."

"James," I said, "what made you think of using crates?"

We were in the library. James was paging through a book of Mr. Emerson's lectures, and furtively, too, since Hatsepha had pronounced Emerson "too heady," and worse, an atheist.

"Interesting what this man Emerson says," said James, marking a line with his forefinger, "about being part of something larger. This notion of us all being one."

"You didn't answer my question."

"Ah," he said. "Crates. Well, I overheard Dean going on and on about abolition and . . . well, Dean makes our crates."

"So who gave you the man's name in Cleveland?"

"Dean, of course. Seems to know everyone," said James. He tapped his finger on Emerson's essay. "I've often wondered . . . had I been a scholar . . ." He wrestled with the words, his eyes drifting back to the page, lingering on the essay until he came to the end and snapped the book shut.

CHAPTER 25

1841

Dear Livvie—

Now with the snow upon us, one would think our life would quiet down, but not so. First, the mule ran off on Christmas Eve. For once, I felt blessed that the nag was slow, for I caught up to her just up the road at the Utopia settlement, where, I believe, they were eyeing her for a meal.

And then a flock of blackbirds—you know of what I speak—decided to fly over a frozen river. Half of them went through the ice. How wrenching it is to hear their screams and know that if I went out in the skiff, I might join their frigid Purgatory.

Lastly, the boy had a spell of fever, but seems to be recovering

I set down the letter on the settee in my sitting room and rubbed my eyes. *The boy needs a mother,* I thought to myself. *And Erasmus needs a wife.* I knew there were women he visited—the kind who live on the edge of town and who weren't averse to a penny. But he needed a partner, and since it wasn't to be me with my compromised vision, he should seek someone out. Perhaps the third daughter of some farmer.

In the meantime, I had my books and my notes. Often, I would inscribe my own observations in the margins of Silas's conclusions. I would, for example, add a few lines about the benefit of peppermint along with chamomile for a cold. At the *escritoire,* I scribbled on a sheaf of paper that rice, when heated in a silk bag, could ease menstrual cramps or even the contractions that followed the aborting of a fetus. I had noticed, too, that corsets caused bruising and constrained a woman's ability to laugh.

My own health was finally improving. The most difficult to endure were the headaches, and I squinted at everything—words on a page, stitches pricked by my needle, a bird in a tree.

The week after receiving Erasmus's letter, Rutherford took me into town in the gig to see the oculus maker, a German Jew named Krauss who also practiced phrenology.

"Really?" I said when he placed his hand on my skull as if to fathom my myriad ailments and quirks. "I fear it's my eyes that are giving me fits."

"And your head, yes?" Krauss said in a thick accent. "What is this here? Did you fall down?"

Abner—or was it Pate?—had slammed me into a wall.

"It was a mishap," I said.

"And yet when I press here"—he dug his thumb in painfully—"it goes all the way to your stomach, *ja*?"

Indeed, I felt quite nauseated.

"Your skull has known some violence."

Not only my skull.

"My eyes?"

"Ah," he said. "We try some lenses."

He brought out a black lacquer box lined with velvet and filled with rows of crystal disks. Holding up one after another, he instructed me to gaze toward a painting on the far wall and tell him when I could see the cow.

"The Holstein?" I said on the fourth lens.

"Actually, a Friesian," said Krauss, sounding immensely pleased. "Now, on to the close vision," he said, producing a second box of crystals. He handed me a book and asked me if the letters were clear. It took me some time before I could distinguish an *O* from a *Q*.

"Bifocals would be best," he said, "but not so pretty, I think. So heavy with the frames. You need to wear glasses like jewelry, so a set of lorgnettes. One for reading, one for scenery."

"Bifocals are fine," I said, well aware that I was lucky to have glasses at all, and only thanks to James. Then there was the matter of my sensitivity to light, but Krauss said that he had a solution—dark crystals the color of amber. "I show you mine," he said, leaving the room.

The table by which I was sitting was covered with papers, so I experimented with the lenses for closer reading, pecking among the sheaves. Rejecting various Cincinnati papers and flyers, I snatched up an old copy of *The Liberator* dated February 1, 1839. I had read William Lloyd Garrison's works, but was no subscriber. Now with a new lens, I found myself regarding his reasoning with keener focus.

> There has never been, as far as we know, in all the free states, a single meeting of colored people in favor of Colonization. Surely they are more interested in a right decision of the matter than any others. And he who should say they are not competent to inquire and judge wisely in the matter needs only to attend one of their meetings on the subject to blush at his own ignorance and prejudice.

That Krauss would openly display the work of an abolitionist like Garrison betrayed the naïveté of one so recently immigrated. When he reentered the room, I tapped my finger on the page. "Is this your customary reading?"

"Ja, ja," he said. "This terrible situation. No German would hold with it. And even the English have said *genug*. Enough. But here in America—" He clicked his teeth. "Freedom, democracy, and incredibly—this."

"You are openly an abolitionist?"

He leaned back his head and laughed. "I suppose yes. Only two years ago, I was just a German. I get here to Cincinnati, and I am nothing. Now I have a business and I'm an abolitionist. What a wonderful country, no?"

"Enslave the liberty of but one human being and the liberties of the world are put in peril," I said, reading aloud the banner head.

"We know this to be true, *ja*?" said Krauss as he ushered me to the door, promising me glasses by the following week, adding, "And are you sure no lorgnette?"

"Heavens, no."

"But you are a pretty lady!"

I laughed. "Maybe once." Indeed, my hair was turning white.

"Mrs. Orpheus?" he called after me as I descended the stairs to the street. "Please take care that nothing further hurts your head."

THE GLASSES, INDEED, were unbecoming, but my headaches diminished. I could spend more time reading and writing, though I still found stitching excruciating.

"Truly, Olivia," said Hatsepha, "you might have done with the lorgnette."

"These free up my hands. Perhaps I shall take up the piano again."

Hatsepha stared out the window and sighed so heavily that I could only imagine she was overcome by longing for a time when we had played duets, unburdened by husbands and the passage of time. "Do you suppose he made it?"

"Pardon me?"

"Handsome?" she said. "I hear the cold in Canada is fearsome." She began to thread a needle. "I wouldn't have thought I'd care so much, but Eugene Orpheus was dreadful and not in the least like your Silas. Perhaps I feel quite spiteful."

Bolstered by a sudden sense of solidarity, I said it would be a worthy venture to spirit off each and every slave, and not just Handsome, whose flight to freedom had been inadvertent from the start.

"Goodness!" said Hatsepha. "Where would you put them?"

"*You* told me to suggest Liberia," I said, and accusingly, too.

"I changed my mind on that subject." She shuddered. "Or rather, Tilly did. She said, 'Miss Hatsepha, I no more speak African than you speak Chinese.'"

"What if we could spirit just a *few*?" I said. "Tilly has a brother named Grady. And there's a little girl named Sticks."

"Tss!" she said. "The names they give their children. Well, we can't exactly *parade* a fleet of Givens candle crates into Kentucky, can we?"

I dared not tell her that Erasmus had transported a man in a coffin, for evoking my brother's name had an ill effect on Hatsepha. *That madman,* she called him. *That abductor of children,* she would say, ignoring that William was, in fact, Erasmus's child.

"You're absolutely right," I said. "The idea is mad. Silly for me to even put into words. And yet . . ."

Hatsepha licked the end of her thread. "And yet, we *could* get a bit of revenge."

The poor woman had no idea how appealing revenge was to me—not only against Eugene, but against those brothers, Abner and Pate, the whole damn lot of slaveholders. And yet we would find few friends on this side of the river, regardless of abolitionist ardor. *Tut-tutting* about slavery may have been an acceptable posture, but worse than slavery was the thought of actually *ending* it, for too much was at stake—livelihoods, property rights, not to mention the exquisite indignation derived at the expense of slaveholder and slave alike. We whites of the North could slip from our pews to sip at the cup of disapproval tendered by our minister and still return to our Sunday meals of self-satisfaction and demiglazed duck.

And so I would have limited my experience of ushering slaves to my episode with Handsome and my stint at Enduring Hope, and would have done so happily had not I received another letter from my brother.

Dearest Livvie—

It has been some time since you left us. New Richmond is turning into a metropolis. More people settle all the time. I've heard little from our friends in Ripley, who have been spooked by the aggressiveness of the patrollers and undone by Mahan's tribulations. I've turned my attention elsewhere. We have cleared more forest, and though the soil is thin, I am hoping to grow apples.

He went on to complain about insects and birds picking at his crops, and worse, the Utopians upriver who had laid in no provisions but who, from time to time, poached what they could from his land.

The boy continues to shoot and maintains his interest in rocks. He is a good lad, but prone to fevers, the last spiking high enough that I sought the council of Mrs. Beasley, who gave us a tonic that was so foul, the boy got well for fear that I'd force him to drink more of it.

How I longed to go back and abscond with my nephew so I could nurse him to health, but here I sat on the veranda of James's house, myself an invalid, a throw upon my lap, a cup of tea, welcoming confinement the way I once welcomed the torpor of Orpheus Farms.

Never had I conceived that I would be so suited to dependency—I, who came from people who had raged against the Crown, against war, against embargoes set, then lifted, raising our fists and voices against the Catholics and the limits of our prosperity, enduring seasickness and the threat of drowning in order to drive our stake into a new land that, to our minds, seemed boundless.

My tainted eyes confused a horse grazing on the far end of the pasture with a cow. And was that Hatsepha waving at me from the window, or a bit of curtain seeking a breeze? I reached for my amber lenses that gave me the appearance of an insect. When the dray came up the driveway, I could not make out the faces, even with the lenses. It was clear that there were two people, but man or woman I could not say. Only the jerky motion of the driver when dismounting alerted me to his identity, the fact ascertained by the ridiculousness of his hat.

"Livvie!" shouted Erasmus, taking the stairs two by two and embracing me. Dropping the letter and gaping at the embodiment of its author, I stood shakily as he took my hands. He smelled of sweat and last night's whiskey. And as always with our reunions, I leaned into him.

Nearly three years since I'd seen him and the first thing out of my mouth: "Please tell me the boy is all right!"

He took me by the shoulders. "Why, you can see for yourself!"

He took my hand and led me to the dray, where sat William, wrapped in a blanket. The boy's lips were pale, his eyes hollow. "Aunt Livvie," he said through chattering teeth. "I'm a bit het up."

"HE'S FILTHY," said Hatsepha as we stood outside the bathroom door while William scrubbed himself in a tub. "I imagine it's been ages since he's seen water from a pipe."

"I imagine it's been ages since he's seen soap," said I.

Hatsepha leaned toward the door and listened. “He’s having quite a party. I imagine we shan’t recognize him when he emerges.”

Indeed, the young man who came out in the clothes Hatsepha had given him looked little like the Willy of the river.

“Off to bed,” said Hatsepha.

That night at dinner, I turned to Erasmus. “How long has he been ill?”

This seemed to stump Erasmus, who had a talent for losing track of time. The boy’s symptoms, however, fitted malaria.

“You were right to bring him here, Erasmus,” said James. “Indeed, you cannot take him back.”

“’Tis true he’s of little use to me in so sickly a state,” said Erasmus. “But once he’s well, he can help me with the ferrying.”

“Such a future!” said Hatsepha. “Perhaps he will aspire to be a barker.”

“Ha!” said Erasmus. “And what would you know of work?”

IT WAS I WHO CAME UP WITH A PLAN. I waited until I had Hatsepha alone.

“You must offer Erasmus something in exchange for the boy,” I said as I walked arm in arm with her viewing the buds on the espaliers. “Set him up in business. Give him a purpose. Finance him.”

“He will drink up all the profit.”

“What if the profit is to his soul?”

Her eyes narrowed. “What are you getting at, Livvie?”

I tucked a thorny rose into the trellis. “You said yourself you wanted revenge for Tilly.”

Hatsepha placed her hand on mine and smiled. “Careful,” she said. “You’ll prick yourself.”

Over the next few weeks, Hatsepha and I plotted, and all the while Erasmus paced, checking on William, remarking that the boy was showing improvement from the quinine I'd administered, and yet still finding time to pinch the cheek of the Norwegian girl.

Once we had developed every detail of our plan, we called on James in his study.

"Another venture?" he said upon hearing of our proposal to sell used hats. "Do you think I'm made of money?"

To which I said nothing.

Hatsepha cleared her throat. "Remember how Olivia once asked you to finance Tilly in her hair business, and you refused? In the end, Tilly did quite well. Or was doing until they stole her away."

James waved this off. There were profit margins to consider. Overhead and liability. "And who's going to peddle these hats?"

I pounced and placed my hand on his forearm. "That's the beauty of this, brother. It shall be Erasmus who plies the trade."

"Oh, this is even richer than I thought."

"Dearest," said Hatsepha, and evenly, too, for I knew she was quivering with purpose. "If you set up Erasmus in this business, we can extract from him certain terms."

James snorted. "What? That he never come back?"

Not breaking her gaze, Hatsepha said, "Exactly."

On a Tuesday afternoon, Hatsepha and I went to James's factory to call on Mr. Dean, the crate maker and carpenter. Balding and squat, with muttonchop sideburns and woolly brows to match, he had come to America as an indentured servant, having lost his wife to the cholera. Now he was a freeman and skilled not only in carpentry but in smithing as well.

"If it weren't for your husband," he said to Hatsepha, "I'd be a poor man. He treats his workers well."

"He speaks highly of you, Mr. Dean," said I. "As a matter of fact, we saw the special crates you built for him some time ago. Those that set upon the wagon and surrounded a compartment adequate for importation."

After a long pause, the crate maker said, "And what would you be importing?"

"Hats," said Hatsepha in a barely contained whisper. "The hatmakers in Maysville are ever so much superior to the ones in Cincinnati."

"Ah," said Dean. He looked down at his tool bench that was covered with neat rows of hammers and chisels, clippers and benders. It reminded me of Silas's autopsy table. He cleared his throat. "And if these hats are quite large?"

"Certainly we must provide room enough that they not be crushed."

"And breathe," said I. "Hats need to breathe lest the feathers start to smell."

"And your husband, ma'am?" he said to Hatsepha. "He is investing in your hat scheme?"

"Why, yes, although he is less inclined to fashion and disinterested in certain details. Such as air holes."

In the end, Dean agreed to participate, and with some ardor, as if hats were ever so interesting. No one uttered the word "slave" much less "runaway" or "concealment."

"And will we be needing separate compartments," he asked, "for accessories and the like?"

He seemed quite besotted with Hatsepha, telling her that she reminded him of his dear departed wife, God rest her soul, who was a warmhearted woman who enjoyed her meals. "Not like some of them," he said, glancing at me, "like sparrows upon a twig."

Hatsepha pressed her hand on his and promised we would return to inspect his handiwork. As we left, she gushed with optimism. "Oh, I think we have an enterprise! Tilly shall be avenged. And James, who thinks he has dispensed with Erasmus and financed millinery, shall never be the wiser."

"HATS?" SAID ERASMUS. He was perched on a tufted slipper chair in Hatsepha's sitting room, his knees nearly to his chin, his hair gathered into a rather untidy ponytail.

"You'll be far more convincing as a salesman," said Hatsepha, "than you are as a preacher."

Erasmus leaned back in the chair. Hatsepha flinched as the cabriole legs creaked. We had presented the idea of going into Kentucky to lure away slaves—an enterprise far riskier and with far greater consequence than merely harboring runaways on the northern shore, an endeavor already rife with peril but not as apt to result in hanging.

"I don't know much about the hat trade," he said. "Feathers and such."

"You didn't know much about godliness, yet you ran off and became a preacher," said I. "Besides, I've spoken with someone who knows Birney. He says he'll meet you. Just don't tell James about the contraband. It's all he can do to suffer hats."

This last statement had a happy effect on Erasmus, who was both flattered that the well-known abolitionist might take an interest in him and gratified that the true nature of the project should be kept secret from our brother.

Hatsepha rose and went to her boudoir. Flinging open the doors, she revealed shelves and shelves of hats, bonnets, and caps. "I am happy to purge my possessions, brother, that you might have an inventory."

I would have been impressed by her beneficence, but I knew she was angling for a new wardrobe from James.

Entering the boudoir, Erasmus snatched from a shelf a straw hat encrusted with shells. Placing it on his head, he pivoted with passable grace in front of the mirror. "Does it suit, Livvie? Shall I convince them of my calling?"

Trying not to look at Hatsepha, I said, "There's just one requirement, brother. If you set out on this adventure, you do not return to Cincinnati unless invited. In addition, the boy stays with us."

To Erasmus's credit, it was not an easy decision. Though an unreliable husband, he was not an indifferent father. While he knew the boy's prospects were better with James and that the lad had proved to be more introspective than was useful on the river, William remained my brother's last true bond with Julia.

"You see her in the boy," I said later that evening as we watched the summer gloaming from the window.

"I expect we all do," Erasmus answered. "Especially James."

In the weeks that followed, Erasmus shadowed his son. We worried he was having doubts.

And what should I do with these curséd hats, Livvie?

Find a way to undo what you did to Handsome and his family.

And when I'm done?

James guarded the boy with the greed of a miser. He touched his hair. He moved a coin between his fingers to entertain. He showed him his collection of rocks.

William touched each stone the way a priest might touch a relic. "Trilobite," he said, reverently. "Brachiopod. I got one of those."

"Do you, now?" said James. "They're not all fossils. See this one? This one's mica. Fool's gold. Don't be tricked by this one."

Hatsepha and I waited to hear from Dean that the contraption was completed. When word came, we sent for the carriage at once, along with a new horse to replace the bedraggled mule. The conveyance was indeed a magnificence of polished mahogany, wire-glass window, sheered curtains, and ingenious, adjustable shelves that we set to stocking with Hatsepha's cast-off hats.

The day he left, Erasmus headed toward the stable at dawn. As far as James knew, he was setting off on his new career as a hat peddler with his mobile storefront cleverly designed by Dean. As to the extent of the cleverness, James had no idea about the voids and compartments concealed behind cabinets that could store excess inventory and yet were large enough for a person.

How many times had Erasmus left us? But the finality of this exodus felt unlike any prior departure. When I was a girl of eighteen, my father had bid adieu to his children while shouting instruction from the deck of a steamship. Now, as the sun rose, it was Erasmus's turn to give his son advice. I hoped he might extol the value of literacy, of learning a business, of living in a home so fine as this, but Erasmus barely looked at the boy as he readied his fresh horse, hitching it to the carriage purchased by James. Just before climbing up on his fancy, new rig, he leaned down to whisper something to William, who nodded. Once in the seat, Erasmus clicked his teeth. As the horse began to trot, Erasmus doffed his old black preacher's hat and threw it into the air. It spun high, caught the sunlight, seeming to hover, until the boy broke loose and ran to catch it.

CHAPTER 26

1842–1844

During those years, I received a letter once again from Bethany Orpheus. I read with little surprise to find that Eugene's financial problems continued to press upon the farm, that he was as much of a brute as ever, that slaves were being discarded like last season's dresses, and that their daughter, Elizabeth, was flourishing. *A pet, but hard to tame,* were Bethany's words that I took to mean the girl had a mind of her own—and good for her, with that awful father, and Bethany herself so distractible and with her inclination to cruelty. *You must be strong,* I thought, remembering the child who was so proud at sounding out her letters.

She can manage the silver, wrote Bethany, *and a do-si-do, but to me she is not warm.*

It took some time to screw up the inclination to answer Bethany's correspondence with a brief reportage of how I was now living with my brother and his wife, who had enlisted me in various committees and good works having to do with, of all things, the church. This, I knew, would make Bethany smile, for she had borne witness to my heresies and indifference to God.

I cross my fingers during the pieties but am happy to sell some lemonade if it raises a dime for the poor, I wrote to Bethany, who soon wrote back about her own travails, saying they should themselves be selling lemonade, so disappointing was the hemp crop, and now Eugene was talking about ripping it out and replacing it with tobacco.

Thank goodness, she wrote, *the slaves have so many babies.*

"Oh, do not tell me," said Hatsepha when I read her the letter in the carriage on the way to a temperance meeting. "That you should be married into such a clan I cannot bear."

I reminded her that, though she might find them offensive, the Orpheuses did hail from an august line of Virginians, at which she sniffed, saying the landed gentry's time had come and gone, and it was people such as James and her father who were industrious and who looked to the future upon whom Fortune smiled. Finding no argument from me, she added, "And this silly Bethany, I supposed, has spoiled the girl to a fault."

"It's been years," I said. "Though I recall the child as more neglected than spoiled."

"Well, we can't all have daughters to spoil," said Hatsepha, with a sideways glance. "Some of us can't even have sons."

As we entered the hall, we braced ourselves for a long evening fanning ourselves and discussing strategies for the discouragement of inebriation, when across the room, a hat caught my eye. I knew that hat. I had seen it on my sister-in-law's head. And yet there it was donning the coiffure of Mrs. Danspierre, a woman of such prestige that approaching her would require genuflection of a sort that would elude most Presbyterians.

"Oh my land," I said, nudging Hatsepha.

Hatsepha screwed up her eyes and let out a whoosh. "Dear me," she said. "That's my hat two seasons ago." She pressed my hand and stifled a laugh. I knew it pleased her greatly to think that so grand a matron had been brought so low.

"Don't gloat just yet," I said, for it had occurred to me that the appearance of this hat signaled more than a reversal of fortune. "I warn you, say nothing unless she mentions it."

We approached Her Highness, who was in deep conversation with a collared gentleman who moments earlier had addressed the gathering about the sorry spectacles he had seen in Bucktown—spectacles that were unfit for our eyes, but worthy of our ears, every pair of which was pricked to the lurid details that were supposedly beyond our experience.

"He died, you say?" said Mrs. Danspierre.

"But only after much suffering, most of which was inflicted upon his family."

Mrs. Danspierre clicked her tongue ostentatiously to indicate that no matter of circumstance would force *her* to endure such ignominy. And yet here she was in Hatsepha's hat.

We curtsied. She nodded back, then smiled at the minister, indicating that his presence in the conversation was no longer required.

"Mrs. Givens," she said, turning back to Hatsepha. "Mrs. Orpheus."

"You look quite dashing, Mrs. Danspierre," said Hatsepha.

"Ah! You have noticed my hat?"

"I could not fail to do so," said Hatsepha. "Why, I was just telling Olivia—"

I interrupted. "How much we support the idea of temperance," said I. "Hatsepha says it is her favorite cause."

"Really?" said Mrs. Danspierre, smiling tightly. "I would not have marked you for a supporter of causes, Mrs. Givens. You seem so concerned with . . . well, your clothes. In fact, it is of such that I seek your opinion."

Had I not known Mrs. Danspierre by reputation as being one of the most formidable examples of *ton* or fashion in Cincinnati, I would have sworn she looked mildly amused, even conspiratorial.

"My hat, you see," she went on. "Would you say it looked somewhat frayed?" She leaned forward and whispered, causing us to lean in, too. "Bedraggled, even?"

"Oh no," said Hatsepha. "It looks quite fresh."

"Indeed?" said Mrs. Danspierre, straightening. "How disappointed I am. For you see, this monstrosity has been worn before."

I coughed into my hand. "There is something about the flounces . . ."

Mrs. Danspierre's eyebrow rose, her voice taking on the stentorian quality for which she was famous. "I care nothing for flounces. Why would I? But I will have you know, there is quite a market for such hats, a market with significance far beyond that of temperance." She gave us two knowing jerks of her head, then pivoted and strode off.

"Well!" said Hatsepha. "If she thinks that wearing my old hand-me-downs is supposed to impress me . . ."

"Don't you see?" said I. "She knows! She knows exactly where her funds went from buying that hat!"

Hatsepha gaped. "Surely you don't think?"

I CAN'T SAY that suddenly the drawing rooms of Cincinnati were festooned by Hatsepha's hats. From time to time, we recognized a cap or a bonnet—or thought we did—but we were reassured that Erasmus was proceeding in his enterprise by Erasmus himself, who wrote more frequently than he used to, perhaps because he was curious about his son.

> *I have quite a knack for salesmanship* [he wrote]. *Indeed, it takes me back to the days when I was scavenging animal parts for James. You have to know how to talk to people, women especially. I have yet to meet a woman who doesn't like to be told that she looks fetching in this or that, and though I know nothing about hats, I know well how to appreciate a pretty face, and this is to my advantage, for I have*

made more selling hats in a week than I have in years of preaching the gospel.

"Isn't he supposed to be"—Hatsepha dropped her voice—"smuggling people?"

Our original scheme was that Erasmus would consult with Mrs. Beasley and her associates as to the particulars of whom to abet. Few knew all the details of the network, but Erasmus was supposed to make himself available, and when instructed, go across to Kentucky. After familiarizing himself with a town or village, he would establish trust and blend in. At a predetermined time, he would collect his cargo and conceal the person in the compartments of his carriage. The proceeds of his actual hat sales were to be used for purchasing further inventory as well as to support himself. That hats now were appearing in Cincinnati, however, indicated that he was selling into a market other than the one we had intended.

Hatsepha smacked the parchment. "He says nothing about conducting runaways!"

I scrubbed the letters for a clue. Something about the popularity of a certain style of headdress that was easily shipped, for instance. But the letter was inscrutable, and we were left guessing as to the efficacy of his enterprise.

Years passed, and we heard less and less from Erasmus. By then, William's voice was changing, and he had grown a foot so that he met me eye to eye. I spent most of my time tutoring my nephew, exploring not only literature, but the natural world as well. We even familiarized ourselves with the sages of the time—Emerson and the like—discussing the limits of democracy, the responsibilities of the educated man. Indeed, I hadn't been this intellectually engaged since I was married to Silas, and had to remind myself that the boy was not my peer, but rather a lad whose views were not yet formed.

"That's my boy," said James, marveling at William's ability to solve an equation.

"Be careful," said I. "He is ours only temporarily." Even if Erasmus never returned for him, the boy would grow up.

James accused me of discouraging William from his training at Givens and Sons. As for William, he liked history, but was most alive when talking about rocks—a not altogether inconsequential talent when pertaining to the business of mines. When he was thirteen, we took him by carriage to eastern Ohio, where were located most of the mines whence James extracted his gas for lighting.

"Never become a miner, Willy," advised James. "'Tis a dirty thankless job that results in infirmity. Own a mine if you must, but better still, be rid of the headache and own the leases to the gas that is easily rendered from coal. 'Junk,' they said, just as they said pig fat was junk. But from this junk comes light."

And so continued William's education in the absence of Erasmus, whose presence dimmed before an incandescent life with James, the memory of a campsite by the name of Enduring Hope, a half-built chapel, the slowness of rural life along the river, a father who wrote intermittently and vaguely about selling hats in this village or that south of the river, none of which seemed compelling.

CHAPTER 27

1847

The house was in a state. Trunks had been purchased—mostly for books—but Hatsepha insisted the boy have new vestments, particularly if the winters were cold. I reminded her that, though Oberlin was farther to the north, it wasn't so far—not nearly as far as if he'd gone to Princeton or Harvard or Columbia College's School of Mines.

"Nevertheless," she said, "we don't want him taking a chill."

"I'll be fine, Aunt Hatsepha," said William.

She gave him such a fond look that who would have remembered this was the baby whose squall had disrupted her wedding, who persistently reminded her of Julia, who came to us unkempt and ill-educated, but whom she and my brother now regarded as their son?

"You *will* write," said Hatsepha, brushing some lint off his shoulder.

"And with beautiful grammar," he said, gracing me with a glance.

I was afraid to smile lest my whole countenance dissolve. This boy who had to be taught how to hold a teacup, to dip punch from a crystal bowl, to dance a square at a cotillion, to fashion his cravat, to whom to bow, from whom to turn away, when to remove his hat. He did all this as if learning the customs of a foreign land, finding them charming but irrelevant, something to be indulged.

It had been seven years since Erasmus had brought him to us.

Though Hatsepha may have seen it as charity, we had in fact traded for the boy, ridding ourselves of Erasmus, who now was absorbed as an itinerant peddler into northern Kentucky where he could observe the comings and goings of commerce.

Hemp, mostly, he wrote. *And lately, a zeal for tobacco.*

His letters spoke of a maker of tools so fine that farmers came up from Versailles, and an ironworker whose banisters were famous. And of course there were hats, along with all variations of fashion, including footwear, the leather for which had come from north of the river, but whose final incarnation rivaled those of Paris. Livestock, especially horses, but occasionally cows and sheep, the rare exotic such as a zebra once making an appearance upon the auction block and causing quite a stir.

But it is in human flesh they mostly deal, wrote Erasmus:

> *the trading of which would curdle your blood. I tell you, Livvie. It's as if these people had no heart or mind or sense of pain. I would deny that this was the very country to which we came so long ago, and with the highest of expectations.*

About the true nature of his enterprise, he wrote more opaquely, such as the time he ushered to Ripley a woman fleeing the paws of her master. So coded was the text that I could not be sure if it was the girl's body or soul that had been scarred (the line read "a parcel damaged but reparable") or if she was a child of fourteen or a woman of forty-one (both numerals appearing in a sentence describing the cost of said parcel). That she was a female, we had no doubt, and hailing from Augusta, transported by wagon to Erie.

> *As Dante described hell, such is the auction block. It could well bear the placard "Abandon all hope, ye who enter here." The slaves know it, too, Livvie. You can see it in their eyes.*

In the first few years after Erasmus left, William had run away twice, once after arguing with Hatsepha, and once after a small dustup when I insisted he complete an essay before hiking up the hill. I had known where to find him . . . down on the quay, having taken a horse from the stable. Having no money of his own, he was prevented from accessing passage upriver, but it took my explaining several times that his father was no longer at Enduring Hope but instead making money in Kentucky.

Hats? William had blurted in disgust. *Da's a riverman.*

I had leaned into William's face—this when I still stood taller—and said, *Your da is doing important work, and there will come a day you'll be proud of him.*

Whether he had believed me and held on to this vision or sloughed it off as the memory of his father faded, the boy turned to literature and his rock collection and, in what would have made Erasmus happy, a love of hymns. He seemed reasonably but not particularly pious, a trait in keeping with our family, Erasmus's convenient sanctimony notwithstanding. He attended teas with young ladies—the Isabelles and the Mauds, daughters of landowners and of shipbuilders, regarding them courteously but with detachment.

You care more for your fossils, I once chided him.

And you, *Aunt Fossil,* he said with that smile.

How much I loved the boy.

And now we were sending William off to college. He stood a full head taller than I and had grown into a sort of handsomeness that I associated with English poets, though my eyesight was unreliable. He was accepted in church and town and workshop as James's heir and sat next to Hatsepha in the carriage.

Of his father, he had ceased to speak.

He was getting into the carriage now. Late summer, but one of the maples already red. Five slaves had been hunted down in Bucktown the week before and dragged back across the river. The pulpits were heating up. I did not know whether to wish for rains and a turgid river to stanch the flow, or a dry autumn and shallow waters that might ease the passage of runaways.

I ran to the carriage. "You shan't strain your eyes by staying up too late? The books shall wait till morning."

William leaned out the window and took my hand. I wanted to touch his curls. "I have a case of candles, Aunt Livvie. And a lamp from Uncle James."

James approached from the house, behatted and caped. He would escort the boy to school, the first of our family to go to college. Even with my dreary eyes, I could see the pride in my brother's face, and for a moment, I recalled *him* as a young man eagerly selling candles, determined that fortune lay ahead.

"Good-bye, William," called Hatsepha, producing a lavish hankie from her sleeve. Soon she would be blubbering, so I took her arm, and together we watched the trunk-laden carriage amble away, the hand of our nephew waving with all the optimism and confidence of that earlier Givens, my father, as he'd set upon the Ohio River on a flatboat, his future sure as the current, so close he could feel it, the promise of a new land right around the next stand of trees.

CHAPTER 28

1848

It wasn't until the course of buttered sole that the subject was broached. Hatsepha had laid out all her finest linens, most of which were embroidered *HGP* in a lovely cursive, the enlarged *G* in the middle denoting "Givens," the sponsor of the feast.

The occasion was the visit of our cousin Samuel who hailed from Enniskillen. It was Cousin Samuel's father who had appropriated the family estate after the end of the Napoleonic Wars when the embargo lifted, he being the first son and the favorite of our grandfather. At the time of our emigration, Samuel, along with his parents and siblings, had stayed in County Crom, raising hops and cattle, fetching whatever the market would bear, smoking, drinking, praying to a Protestant God while assiduously avoiding the Catholics.

Now it had behooved Samuel to sail to the States to see how his cousins fared, although, as James pointed out, no one had seen fit to inquire until now when commodity prices had dipped again and word of the American Givenses' success had drifted across the pond. It was early spring, and the centerpiece featured daffodils wedged so tightly into corsets of silver that they threatened to explode. Cousin Samuel twisted his water glass, gold-rimmed and enhanced with the Givens crest—a griffin surrounded by flames. In an Irish accent unmarked by famine or suppression of any kind, he addressed the assemblage gathered by his cousin's wife. "A parson, you say?" he said, nodding to the Reverend Boland. Turning to Phinneaus Mumford: "And *you*, sir. A politician? Better a politician in America than in Dublin, where you'd fear for your hide." Upon seeing the alarm on Phinneaus's face, Cousin Samuel assured him that the constabulary in Northern Ireland was inclined to favor Protestants.

"Still bickering with the Catholics?" said Phinneaus Mumford. "Why, in America, it suits us to get along."

"And yet," said Cousin Samuel, "is there not some disquiet hereside when it comes to this slavery business?"

Silence, punctuated by the clink of fish forks upon plates adorned by the portraits of ancestors, real or imagined.

Ariadne Mumford spoke up. "All we talk about these days is slavery. Goodness, you'd think we were *steeped* in it, but we'd be hard-pressed to find a maid." Ariadne patted her hair that had been dented by her hat, one that was all too familiar for having been one of Hatsepha's staples two years earlier. "Of course there *was* our Tilly. Terrible scene when she was dragged off, and screaming, too." She laughed lightly. "Sadly, she was the only one who could make sense of this mess." She indicated her sorry hair as well as giving mine a piercing look.

At that moment, I regretted my earlier restraint when Ariadne arrived wearing a hat—pleated moiré lavishly lined in pink—and looking haughty as a cat wearing a castoff, oblivious to the destination of its proceeds.

"Sold to a brothel, no doubt," said the Reverend Boland, speaking of Tilly, and with more relish than was seemly as he cut into roast beef garnished with horseradish.

"Fascinating," said Cousin Samuel, chewing zealously. He pinged his crystal goblet as if to make a toast, then tapped on the dinner plate with a spoon that also bore the Givens crest. "Truly fascinating," he said, bringing the spoon close to his eye. "You Americans fought a revolution and still manage to set a table fit for a lord." Waving his napkin like a handkerchief of surrender, he said, "Does nothing escape the Givens mark?"

Ariadne Mumford looked forlornly at the napkin in her lap, and for a moment I suspected she was fixing to purloin it, much as she'd done with my pantalette so many years before when it had shown up at her neck.

Phinneaus Mumford could not contain himself. "This abolition business. Terrible for commerce. Why, ask James."

Hatsepha eyed him beadily. "And what would my husband know of abolition?"

James dabbed his mouth with his napkin, smudging the *G* with gravy. "You must think I have my head in the sand, wife."

Said I, "We all know you are too preoccupied with work to bother with the controversy. And thankfully, I might add, for without you we would starve."

It had taken some years for James's business to recover after he'd paid for the defense of Tilly. Apart from the risk he took with Handsome, we saw no need to sully him any further by tying him to the topic. In this I was thankful, for he seemed uninterested in Erasmus's whereabouts or whether his business was successful. Erasmus was displaying a surprising aptitude for discretion, covertly moving about Kentucky, though lately I had seen signs that he'd ventured back to Cincinnati in spite of our admonitions to stay away. That Ariadne had bought a hat without recognizing this peddler as our younger brother spoke to the efficacy of his disguise as well as his change in demeanor. True, she had not seen him for years, but that Erasmus had taken such a chance infuriated me. Indeed, his last letter had bragged of his successes, implying that he was not only carrying out his mission, but was thriving economically as well.

I see another Givens venture in our future, he wrote. *One that might dwarf James's enterprise.*

"Slavery more than abolition," said James, who was still considering Phinneaus's statement.

"Excuse me?" said Cousin Samuel.

"You ask what causes instability in business. I fault the Peculiar Institution more than those who would remedy it."

Hatsepha waved to Mette, the Norwegian girl, to take away the plates and bring the dessert.

"It is such a pleasure having you visit, Cousin Samuel," said Hatsepha as we settled into the sherbet. "James and Olivia were just children when they left Ireland. How would they find it now?"

"More refined than here," said Cousin Samuel. "Though not without its problems."

"Starvation, for one thing," I said under my breath.

"There are those who *would* starve," said Cousin Samuel, sucking on his spoon. "And the Crown does little to help. But then again, we're not fighting savages on the prairie. Ha! Ha!"

After dessert was done, James spirited Cousin Samuel, Phinneaus Mumford, and the Reverend Boland to the study for a smoke.

"Awful man," sniffed Hatsepha as we retired to the parlor. "I'll wager he's looking for a wife."

But the following day, Cousin Samuel confided in me the real purpose for his visit. We were promenading upon the quay admiring the steam vessels.

"Why, you could take a boat all the way down to New Orleans," I told him, hoping he would take the hint.

"Alas, boats bring me no pleasure, though a marvelous thing they are. So many are leaving Ireland. 'Tis a sad thing, emigration."

"As I recall."

"You were sixteen?"

"Fifteen."

"Barely a woman. And sailing to Lord knew what."

I told him I couldn't remember such solicitousness ever expressed by his father.

"But now you've created such a prosperous household—"

"James has. Not I."

"—that a new generation of Givenses need not suffer such uncertainty."

A horn tooted, and a roar rose up from a crowd as a brass band burst into a waltz to hasten the embarkation of a new batch of travelers. There was always a sense of hurry-up about the landing, speed being an American virtue. Boats would race to see which was the fastest to Louisville, blotting out all memories of a decade earlier when the steamship *Moselle* had overtaxed her boilers and exploded. I should never forget the gruesome aftermath that littered the shores. It was the very vessel I'd taken when I'd returned to Enduring Hope.

"What are you saying?"

"To be blunt, Cousin Olivia, I am impressed by the wealth of the American Givenses, the only drawback being the lack of issue." We paused as a passel of Germans pulling their children and a crate of chickens hustled toward the docks. "And so I have a proposal . . ."

Surely he didn't think? And at my age?

"I am one of nine, Cousin Olivia. And while I have never wed, my siblings have not only married, but have many children of their own. Thirty-three descendants at last count, and my older sister Edith thrice a grandmother."

I nodded, but a woman wearing a coal-scuttle bonnet trimmed with lavender lace and a satin bow had caught my eye.

Cousin Samuel went on. "This dearth of children must pose a true problem to your brother . . ."

I could not see the woman's face, but when she reached up to adjust her hat, I saw the color of her hand.

". . . that he might relish the prospect of adoption."

I had missed most of what Cousin Samuel was saying, but that statement jarred me away from the black woman wearing the coal scuttle, and I returned my attention to him.

"Adoption?" Evidently, the refinements of Enniskillen were not enough to compensate for the lack of food or prospects.

"So that he might have an heir."

"But he *has* done," I said.

"Ah, you mean the boy William?" Cousin Samuel gave me a sympathetic look. "But isn't his own father still living? The reprobate? And James has said nothing about formally adopting this boy."

Trying to keep one eye on the coal scuttle that I was sure was the one I'd donated to Erasmus's effort at the inception of his business, I said, "You must understand, everything he . . . we . . . have worked for, and *still* work for . . . it is all for William."

"I see." Cousin Samuel chewed his lip like a man who has lost a wager. Then he brightened. "Well then," he said as we resumed walking. "This William of yours. I daresay *he* will be looking for a wife."

"Excuse me," I said, laying my hand on Cousin Samuel's arm, "but I have an appointment with the oculist."

Leaving my cousin openmouthed, I hurried across the street. I had been quite proud of that hat. The woman headed south on Elm, crossing the creek at Meeker. By the time I caught up to her at the edge of Bucktown, I was gasping for breath. "Pardon me," I said, "but your hat."

When she spun around, I half expected to see Tilly, but this one was taller and darker. Raising her chin—in indignation or sartorial pride—she said, "What of it?"

"Who is the maker?"

She touched the lavender lace and narrowed her eyes. "Hatter come down by way of Maysville. Who's asking?"

"And where," said I, my heart pounding, "might I find this man?"

"DID YOU THINK, brother, that we would not notice your presence in Cincinnati?"

I had flown like a banshee into the brothel. The red-haired girl next to Erasmus rose up bleary-eyed. "La, who is this old lady?"

Which did not soften my mood. "Get out of bed," I said. "Ingrate."

"You can accuse me of indiscretion, sister, but not lack of appreciation," said Erasmus as he stood up with the sheet held in front of him that I might be spared his shame. The girl laughed and ran behind the screen to fetch her jumper.

"I shall wait outside," I said, turning toward the door.

The morning air was bracing even in this part of town, where slop and night soil were flung with abandon from third-story windows. There was barely a plank to avoid the mud. One might think that five decades had brought no improvements to the Cincinnati streets. Certainly, James's vision of a city lit by gas stopped well shy of Bucktown.

"So, Livvie," said Erasmus, joining me, his hair trimmed short, his beard quite elegant beneath his too-blue eyes. He beamed at me like a suitor. It had been seven years since we'd seen each other, but this time there were no embraces.

"You look ridiculous," I said to him as we walked toward a fresher neighborhood. "And why are you in Cincinnati? Did we not tell you to steer clear? What if James had seen you? Or William?"

But Erasmus insisted that no one would recognize him, for he was playing the part so beautifully, and even if they did, what fault was there in James Givens's brother having gone into business of his own?

"Besides, there's quite a lucrative market right here in Cincinnati. Especially if you suggest to the ladies that their purchase might help finance the goal of emancipation. They'll stop shy of soiling their hands, but their vanity blooms with the thought of their own goodness."

I remembered Mrs. Danspierre's smug, knowing look.

Erasmus went on. "And in case you hadn't noticed, sister, I must actually sell hats to be convincing. In fact, I have a few that would look lovely on *you,* Livvie. A bit of buckram with a picot ribbon?"

"You take nothing seriously."

Erasmus took my arm, tipping his hat at a couple passing by. We had returned to brighter streets of gaslights and candles behind casements. Erasmus started talking. Did I know that most runaways fled with no plan at all? The lucky ones found people like him to help them, but it didn't always go according to plan. One woman showed up with all of her mistress's silver, forcing Erasmus to chuck it into the river lest the boat sink. Every day he walked a tightrope. "And yet you consider me unserious."

He did not have to elaborate. Hatsepha and I had followed the various "trials" of those accused of helping runaways—convictions resulting in long incarcerations and exorbitant fees, not to mention the backwoods hangings.

We had arrived at the stable where Erasmus had parked his wagon. A young boy sat whittling on a crate, chewing tobacco and spitting at a cat.

"They break up families, Livvie. They sell off the children without blinking an eye." Erasmus ruffled the hair of the boy, who spit again, this time in my direction. "I suppose James will be expecting him to learn to ledger."

I realized he was talking about William. Perhaps the true reason Erasmus had drifted back to Cincinnati from time to time was his hope to get word of his son. I started to tell him that William, who was off at college, preferred paleontology to numbers. Instead, I said, "Our cousin Samuel is visiting from Ireland. Do you remember him?"

"I remember a prig who threw a stone at me and tried to kiss you."

"It wasn't Samuel I kissed." It hadn't even been a boy. I eyed the lad on the crate. At one time, William was just this scruffy. "Evidently he wants to adopt out some of the Irish Givenses or, barring that, marry off a niece to William."

Erasmus told the boy to fetch his horse. Scrambling up, the boy muttered about getting paid. Erasmus tossed him a coin, and the boy ran off, returning with the mare. Erasmus pulled himself onto the horse, tipped the tall hat that had replaced his preacher's cap. He started to say something, and then ducked his head, his lips tightening. Finally, he drew a long sigh, and when he spoke, it was with a thicker voice. "'Tis a terrible thing," he said, not meeting my eye, "to give up one's child."

TWO WEEKS LATER, a letter arrived from Maysville via the Birneys. I stood in the hallway, fussing with my glasses, trying to read the words. In the parlor, the Norwegian girl rubbed wax into the wood.

Dearest Livvie, it began, *I find myself incarcerated.*

CHAPTER 29

1848

It had been eleven years since I last touched foot in Kentucky. The steamer chugged to Maysville, the river shouldering a mist more common to autumn than spring. For ten days it had rained. Everywhere was talk of flooding and, once again, the drownings of souls desperate to cross.

We cannot have our name dragged into this, James had said after Hatsepha and I told him what had transpired with Erasmus being accused for abetting slaves. James had turned quite red and thundered and paced, accusing us of conspiring against him before turning to me and saying, *Well, I suppose you'll require funds*.

Knowing I would need to conceal my identity, I had already answered an advertisement for a teaching position at a school for young ladies. I looked the part—spinsterish and in need of money, but not so needy that I couldn't pay for a room and spend a day or two gazing into store windows while applying for a job.

It was a short carriage ride from the ferry landing to the town of Maysville, where Erasmus had been arrested. I checked into the hotel across from the post office and, knowing that the names "Orpheus" and "Givens" might draw attention, registered under Hatsepha's maiden name of Peckham.

Maysville was a lovely town, and I found myself thinking—as I had many years before—that I shouldn't mind living among these fine houses and wide streets and shops full of every kind of merchandise. It did not take long to pick up the gossip. All one had to do was stop in at one of the many hatters to glean talk of the itinerant who was liberating slaves across the county. *And selling styles three years out-of-date,* said one dandy hatter who reeked of castor oil and minted brandy, and this at only ten in the morning. I took pains to fuss with the netting while asking just how this man Givens had been captured. How could they be sure? Had they caught him in the act?

According to one hatter, one of the Dobbses' slaves had expected a ride across the river, but when passed up for a boy from another farm, had exposed the abetting rogue in hope of a reward. In spite of the fact that no slave had been found in the culprit's company, there was a pattern of chattel vanishing coinciding with new but slightly dated hats appearing on the matronly heads of Maysville.

I had just come out of a shop and was patting my hair back into place when a carriage pulled up, and the passenger leaned out and said, "Why, I thought it was you, but you're so changed."

My heart sank, for I had not considered that I would be spotted since no one knew me other than Eugene Orpheus and Bethany. I looked over my shoulder and approached the carriage to come face-to-face with my former sister-in-law. I had not seen her in years. Nor would I have easily recognized her, for she, too, had changed, her hair graying, her lips lined. But it was her general effect of having shrunk that startled me. Had I walked away quickly, I might have fooled her into thinking she had seen a bespectacled ghost. Instead, I climbed into her cab.

"A teacher?" Bethany said after I told her the reason for my presence. "And you weren't going to let me know that you were passing through?"

"Well, given the circumstances of my last encounter with your husband, I hope you will not tell him of our meeting."

Bethany sniffed. "I never see my husband. He has taken to living in Lexington with his mistress, and everyone knows. 'Poor Bethany,' they say. 'She might as well be dead.' Well, I just might be, and who would watch his farm, then?"

Surely Eugene had told her how he'd sold our Tilly down the river.

Bethany looked me right in the eye. For a moment, I doubted her sanity, but she seemed to read my mind. "That girl Tilly was nothing but trouble. I told your husband to take her. The last thing I needed was a hysterical housemaid, and me with the baby and all. 'Silas,' I said, 'get her away from me before I strangle her myself.'"

Seeing the proprietor of my hotel coming down the walk, I slid down in the carriage that I might not be seen in Bethany's company.

"Her mother was no better. Eugene got rid of *her*, too. Good riddance to both of them. But that's neither here nor there," Bethany said, adding that I must come to tea.

"Promise me! Promise me!" she called out the carriage window as she pulled away, her gloved hand waving. I hadn't asked why she looked ill.

AFTER THAT, I fairly cowered whenever I went out, but it remained my mission to discover what was happening to Erasmus without appearing unduly concerned.

As chance had it, I was perambulating around the jail—a high-windowed brick pile with a sign reading MASON COUNTY JAILHOUSE—glancing at the posts for the upcoming slave sales, when a woman appeared at my side. Though my eyes were poor, there was no mistaking it—the very headdress that Hatsepha had worn to debates back in the thirties. I myself would have done without a hat before donning such a monstrosity, but women often wear things that recall a certain fashion, however unbecoming. I cleared my throat and addressed the girl—for a girl she was, by all appearances, and of a simple face smattered with freckles that spoke of too much sun.

"That is quite a lovely hat."

She beamed like a sunflower and adjusted the side bow with coquettish flair. "Ain't nothing like it from here to Ver-sales," she said, presumably naming the town in Kentucky, not France. "Bought if off a man who knows his way around a woman's head," she added. "And that's not all." She leaned in, and I thought to myself, *She's not so young after all*. "Sad part is, they arrested him." She looked vaguely familiar.

"For selling hats?"

"For stealing slaves. I went to see him in the jailhouse, and that jailer says, 'You stay away from that one. He's like the Pied Piper. Everywhere he goes, darkies disappear.'" She made a sucking sound. "I don't believe it, though. Man like that ain't got time for darkies. It's the ladies he likes, and if nothing else, he might steal off someone's daughter."

"But surely someone has come to help him?"

"And that's another thing. Every time they go arresting someone for abetting, whole bunches of ministers and abolitionists rush to their aid." She leaned in and whispered. "But this fella's got *no one*."

As she talked, I finally placed her. I had met her years before with Silas. Bella Mason, the daughter of the Orpheuses' overseer. I remembered Silas saying that if Bella were anything like her mother, she would be brimming with information.

"Such a sad story," I said. "What do you think will happen?"

She shrugged. "I'd say his business is pretty much finished either way. You want a hat like this, you gotta go to France."

"LETTER CAME FOR YOU," said the hotel proprietor when I returned that afternoon. He seemed more indifferent than suspicious, but he gave the envelope a second look and said, "Seems she confused your name."

"Do you mind?" I said, holding out my hand, wondering if I would need to offer an explanation to preempt the speculation of why the letter was addressed to Olivia *Orpheus*.

"Come from Mrs. Orpheus up at the farm," said the proprietor. "Must've been in a hurry when she addressed the envelope."

"Ah," said I. "Of course." I gave a laugh to imply that this was a silly mistake that women made when jotting off ideas, and who knew why Mrs. Orpheus, the wife of Eugene, was reaching out to me, Olivia *Peckham*. Perhaps her daughter required tutoring.

I sashayed to my room and tore open the letter.

My dear sister—

How auspicious that we met. Would that we had more time to talk, for there is so much that I want to tell you. I forgive the sorry business with that man, Handsome. If you had any agency in his disappearance, all is forgotten. He was not of much use to us anyway.

It is of Elizabeth that I am writing. You were always solicitous about the child. Indeed, I confess that I was perplexed by your interest, for what was she to you?

But it is upon your continued interest that I must rely, though I can say she is of modest accomplishments, being only fair at the piano and passable at French. You taught her to read, and from then on, she read with so much zeal that I was taken aback but secretly pleased, for Eugene wouldn't have countenanced it if he'd had the choice. You know he is of a mean spirit and seldom supportive of our sex. I had hoped he would be moved by paternal feelings, but clearly he was not.

And so I write that you might consider Elizabeth as you move about in a world that is out of my reach. Please be aware of her well-being, for I fear that she may be in need of advocates should anything happen to me which, sadly, I suspect it will.

Yes, yes, I thought. The offspring of my nemesis who might be in need of a friend should she want to be more than a debutante married to the highest bidder. In the meantime, I had an appointment to interview for a position.

THE LIMESTONE ACADEMY FOR YOUNG LADIES was a Palladian manse commissioned as a home by one of the early families of Kentucky. One wing housed the dormitory for the girls who boarded, the other held classrooms and the additional spaces for living. The cab wound its way up the bluff on a graceful drive lined by beech trees and dropped me by the stairs. I knocked the heavy brass handle, and a shy girl who wouldn't meet my eyes led me to the headmistress's office.

Theodora Winslow rose from her desk. She was backlit by the morning light coming through the French doors, but I could see she was a woman of impressive height, her graying hair still abundant and quite probably her own.

"You are Irish?" she said, holding my hand after we'd made our introduction.

"Scots-Irish," I said. "Long ago immigrated."

"We are all immigrants," she said kindly, but I had the feeling that her ancestors predated mine and, indeed, the Republic.

She asked what brought me to her school, and why I might want to teach young women, and all the while I answered with rehearsed lines, glancing from her to the view of the river and across to the opposite shore. So transfixed was I that it took a moment to sink in that she was repeating a question.

"Your family?" she said.

"Ah!" said I, coming to. "None, really. I am free as a bluebird."

"Free," she said, her smile widening. "Lovely."

THEODORA WINSLOW AND I spent the afternoon discussing what literature to teach, and if music should be more emphasized than language in a classic education. Soon I'd forgotten that my application had been a mere ruse. She had such merry eyes and a soothing way of speaking that I found myself wanting to have her as a friend. It had been so long since I'd had someone who truly knew my mind (Silas and maybe Julia, both gone) that when she told me the terms of my employment, I could not refuse.

But first, I told her, noticing how beautifully her pearl bobs offset her complexion, I had to return to Ohio to get my affairs in order.

WHAT HAVE I DONE? I thought as I jostled along in the carriage. Still, it was a job for which I was well suited, and the thought of having my own income gave me no little satisfaction. I had lived with James and Hatsepha long enough.

Stopping at my hotel, I told the proprietor that I had secured the position and wanted to send a note to Mrs. Orpheus. I scribbled off a missive to Bethany about visiting at a later date and that I'd be residing at the school. Having done my best to brush her off, I rode in a cab to the river to catch the ferry to Aberdeen.

Not forty minutes later, I was back on the free soil of Ohio and climbing into another hack to carry me down to Ripley. It had been years since I'd been there, and then under the unhappiest of circumstances that had resulted in my poor eyesight. But now I had a different purpose and, knowing of the sympathies of Mrs. Beasley, was headed once again to her store. I calmed my breath before entering, but as soon as I was inside, I could see that not much had changed except the colors of the bolts of fabrics and a display of ladies' gloves alongside buckshot and bins of barley.

Mrs. Beasley, more hunched than I remembered, retained the visage of a cactus in James's conservatory.

"Mrs. Beasley? It is I, Olivia Givens."

"Ah," she said, squinting at me. "I was wondering when you'd show up."

I SPENT THE NIGHT in her extra bedroom. When she showed me to the room, she said, "You look exhausted," in response to which, and to my horror, I began to cry.

"We know all about your brother," said Mrs. Beasley.

"Then why in heavens aren't you helping him?"

"We will help him if we can," said she, "but there are Negro hunters everywhere trying to glean abettors. Do you think it would be in your brother's interest to be supported openly by abolitionists when there is at least some doubt about his guilt?"

The next morning, one of the Rankins' sons was the first to arrive in response to Mrs. Beasley's summons. He was introduced to me as Lowry.

"I have heard of you, sir," said I.

"And I of you," said Lowry Rankin with some admiration that did not altogether displease me.

By that afternoon, ten or more people had come into the store. Mrs. Beasley locked up and pulled down the shades. There was John Collins, who made coffins, and the freed slave John Parker, who was an ironsmith, McCoy from up by Eagle Creek, and Wilsey and Makepeace and Huggins, and one or two others, including a minister named Shands.

Said Lowry Rankin, "Your brother's case is good. But he needs to keep his mouth shut except to protest his innocence."

"He needs to lie low," added John Collins, whose coffins were used to hide runaways. "Is there anybody you know who might visit him and not draw attention?"

I said I knew of one.

Together, we designed a letter to Erasmus so opaque and yet so clear that if one was searching for meaning, one would comprehend that, even if he was convicted, Erasmus's debt would be settled. In any case he should retain an uncharacteristically humble posture and be frequently seen in prayer.

"You say you've been offered a position?" said Mrs. Beasley.

When I said that it was at the Limestone Academy to work for Mrs. Winslow, a glance passed among them, and Mrs. Beasley turned to me. "I think you'll find yourself perfectly situated."

ONE DAY LATER, I was back in Maysville. It took few queries to locate Bella Mason at her humble house off Main Street. She was swinging on a porch swing and drinking lemonade, one leg dangling just enough to rock herself while she shouted at a towheaded child, dirty with snot, that may have been hers or the neighbor's. When she saw me stride up her walk, she cocked her head as if she couldn't place me. Then her dull gaze narrowed to eyes of cunning. "You come to buy the hat?"

I told her that I'd come to ask for a favor and that I hadn't been altogether truthful.

"You don't remember me, Bella, but we met once before. Oh, not the other day. It was back in '32 when Silas Orpheus and I ran into you in Cincinnati."

I recounted how we had met on the street, and how Silas had asked about her father, who had been the Orpheuses' overseer until he was fired. Bella had told us about Bethany Orpheus's "anemic pregnancy" about which Silas had been unaware.

"I don't remember any of that," said Bella, pushing the porch swing harder. "You say you're an Orpheus?"

"By marriage. But now I am a widow." Still, I told her, I had sympathy for how badly her father had been used. "Something about a slave named Handsome?"

"They was always blaming my father."

"And who do you suppose was responsible for retrieving Handsome when he ran off from the chain gang?" She stared at me dumbly. I threw up my hands. "Why, the very man, Erasmus Givens, who sold you the hat and who now sits in jail for abetting slaves."

Bella scrunched up her face as if solving a riddle. "Then why doesn't he just tell them he's no abolitionist seeing's as he *returned* a slave to the Orpheuses?" Studying me, she chewed her lower lip violently. Then: "I seen you staring at the jailhouse. Don't think I haven't. What's your interest in the hatter?"

I swallowed. I was taking an enormous risk that Bella could be trusted. "The hatter," I said, "is my brother."

THE NEXT DAY was an agony of waiting. I paced the parlor at the hotel, trying to read a book, casting it down, picking up knitting, looking at the clock. At last I spotted Bella through the casements strolling up the street. I rushed to the porch.

She walked up the steps and plunked herself down in a rocking chair. "Law, but your brother is pretty."

"Bella, did you pass him the letter?"

"He read it. He says he has a lousy lawyer, and was hoping to get Henry Clay. 'My, my,' I said. 'Henry Clay!'"

"But you gave him the message?"

"Oh, I told him. And he gave me an earful about your fancy brother having to disavow him. I told him sure as soot that if *I* had a fancy brother, I'd let the whole world know." Giving the rocker a violent push, she almost toppled over.

The following day, I wrote James and Hatsepha telling them our friend was doing well, all things considering. He appreciated our support and understood our reluctance to claim kinship. In the meantime, I had secured myself a position and would be staying for the time in Maysville.

THEODORA WINSLOW took me in as a sister. My charges were the daughters of the prominent Kentucky families of Maysville, Washington, and Augusta—young women of curiosity and accomplishment, some with an intellectual streak. Wary of being seen as urging them to progressive views, I nevertheless smiled at every sign of intelligence such as questioning a large family or confessing a passion for novels.

"*Jane Eyre,*" said one of the girls, a redhead named Polly. "Have you read it, ma'am?"

"I have not," I said. "Who wrote it?"

"Why, the sister of Emily Brontë!" exclaimed another girl, sending her compatriots into lascivious giggles about Heathcliff.

Evenings I spent with Theodora, reviewing the day, discussing the girls, sharing our favorite passages of Shelley or Keats. We sipped tea and sometimes sherry, and she soon confided that, though she was a Kentuckian by birth and with slaveholding parents, she had changed her views about human bondage. As a child, she had watched from her window as a boy rushed back and forth to the well to fill her bath, and it occurred to her that this boy would never have any choice but to do what he was told. "I was only twelve and already unhappy about anyone telling *me* anything, so I could only imagine how *he* felt."

One evening, after two glasses of sherry, she led me to the drawing room in her quarters. From here, the windows commanded even better views of the river. On the opposite was a tall bookcase. Theodora removed several tragedies by Shakespeare, exposing a knob that she grasped firmly and yanked, swinging the bookcase open to reveal a narrow, circular staircase. I followed her up, our steps lit by a candle. At the top was a garret holding five narrow cots as well as a table and chairs. I didn't have to ask her to explain.

Because of our common friendship with Mrs. Beasley in Ripley, I confessed my true reason for coming to Maysville. I told Theodora that Erasmus Givens was my brother, and that we had conspired to abet slaves across the river. I told her about Handsome and even about the girls we had hidden in the barn. But I couldn't bring myself to tell her about what had happened afterward with the patrollers.

"You have many secrets, Olivia," said Theodora with her lovely gaze that now I claimed solely as my own. "It seems we are to be the best of friends."

EACH MORNING, we scanned the local paper for details. Unlike me, Theodora had indulged in a lorgnette that, when not in use, dangled fetchingly in a golden case from her bodice.

"It says here that the trial is proceeding," said Theodora, holding the glasses to her eyes. She leaned toward me. "I have *never* known the word of a slave to be given any weight against the word of a white man." She returned to the print, and then startled me with a gasp, stabbing the paper with her finger. "Listen to this!"

> Bethany Orpheus, née Boothe, whose father bred some of the finest racehorses in Kentucky, has succumbed to pleurisy brought on by a cold she contracted last Christmas. She is survived by her husband, Eugene Orpheus of Orpheus Farms, and has been buried in the Orpheus family plot. According to her husband, there was no service.

I was stunned that Bethany could go so quickly, in spite of her obvious infirmity. Downstairs, one of the girls was practicing piano, and badly, too.

"You're shaking, Olivia."

"May I see the article, please?"

She handed me the paper. Twice I scanned the text.

"What is it?" she said.

I took off my spectacles, feeling suffocated as if by a miasma on the river. "The article," I said, "does not mention a daughter."

BY JUNE, school was nearing a conclusion, as was Erasmus's trial. I continued to stay away from the courtroom and the jail, using as my scout Bella Mason, who was caught up in the ruse and quite enthusiastic about spending time with my brother. Crowds had gathered for the closing arguments. If he was convicted, Bella would pass along James's money to satisfy his fine.

But on the week before the judge was due to hand down the verdict, word came out that Tuesday's slave sale was not to be the ordinary auction of field hands and their offspring. It was to feature Orpheus slaves—the "best-bred slaves in Mason County."

Strollers passed by the slave pen for days, peering through the slitted windows, asking to see this one or that so they could give it a poke. That one of these persons might be Grady, the boy I'd seen take such a whipping from Bethany over ten years earlier, sparked my curiosity, but I was not going to indulge in such prurience. Indeed, I hesitated to go into town.

The evening before the closing argument, Bella called on Erasmus at the jail. I waited on her porch, ignoring the prying eyes of the dim-looking child who prowled around the corner like a cat.

When Bella got back, she sat down in the rocker next to me and crossed her arms. "Well, you won't believe it."

By then, I was used to just about anything coming out of Bella's mouth. She had given me specific details about Erasmus's lice problem, and where he was sorely afflicted. So, too, had she described the judge as "a breeched son of a bitch who musta kicked his way out of a mule's ass."

She smiled in a way that scared me.

"I seen your brother, and you know what? He ain't the only prisoner of interest in that ol' jail. Maybe the only *criminal,* currently speaking, but he has company."

"Speak English."

"We-ell, *he* being a kind man and a purveyor of hats, had to inquire, the wretch was wailing so pathetically. Beat by her husband, you'd think. Or a whore got too drunk and picked a fight. When he sees her in the opposite cage, he asked her to hold her candle up and beholds not just any creature, but a chit jes' as 'lovely as the day is long.' And passably white, he says, but when I think about it, we could've all said the same, ever since we seen Mrs. Bethany parading her about at church. So now the rooster's come home. Thing was, pretty much everyone knew Mr. Eugene couldn't have children, him kicked by the horse and all." Bella started rocking. "Why, they say she can even read!"

When the day came to hear the verdict on Erasmus Givens, who had been accused of abetting slaves on the soil of Kentucky, it was to the auction platform, not the courthouse, that the crowds flocked, including Theodora and me. I had veiled my face for fear I should encounter Eugene Orpheus ensuring his chattel received the highest price.

Bella pushed into the throng and came up beside me, her hair twisted into a braid on the top of her head. She was wearing her best frock for the spectacle, though the fabric was poorly printed and frayed.

"You need to go to the courthouse, Bella," I said, and severely, too. "Come and get me when the verdict is read."

Clearly disappointed to miss the sale, she strode away with a head toss. Had I not paid her one hundred dollars, I doubt she would have complied.

I had nearly two thousand dollars from James in my reticule at the ready to pay off Erasmus's fine. Standing next to Theodora, I craned to see each sorry soul as he or she was paraded upon the platform, the first being a boy and his sister who were crying for their mother. The auctioneer—a beady-eyed, thick-necked, scraggly-haired Frenchman, twisted the girl's arm and said, "This one's young and can still be taught. And the boy? See the back of him? Clean. No marks. Healthy children ready to be groomed."

Many of the people in the crowd were local and more interested in gloating over how low the Orpheuses had fallen than in buying slaves, but a number of people had come from out of town—bidders and agents from Lexington who represented plantation owners and collectors from the South. I remembered the man who'd bought Tilly, and wondered again at her fate.

"Four hundred," bid a man old enough to be Methuselah.

"Each," said the auctioneer. "You mean four hundred each?"

In the end, the two children went for a total of nine hundred dollars and were hauled off, gripped by a man who told the agent he was going to split them up.

After that, a mangy-looking field hand and two women missing teeth were auctioned for a fair price. The field hand was marred, said the auctioneer, marking him as uppity. But that was when he was a boy, and by now the fight was out of him. Indeed, there was no spirit in this creature. I started to turn away, then glanced back for a second look, wondering if this could be Grady, now grown and beaten. And where was Sticks?

Next to me, Theodora sighed.

One after another was auctioned off—twenty or so altogether—to settle Eugene's debts. If Eugene was in the vicinity, he wasn't showing himself.

"And now," said the auctioneer, "what you've all come to see."

I hadn't laid eyes on Elizabeth since she was a fat-cheeked girl with curly hair. The petite young woman standing on the platform, her dark hair pulled tight, her eyes squeezed shut, looked little like the child I'd known back in 1837.

"This fine thing can pass as white," said the auctioneer. "Indeed, she is only one-thirty-second Negro, and would be *une belle* mistress for any man."

People had started to mutter among themselves—little tremors of shock that this was the very girl who'd come to their teas.

"Open your eyes, girl. Let them see your face."

"Let us see your legs," called out one man in a pigtail.

Whispers gave way to the clicking of tongues and the shaking of heads, but no one stepped up to intervene. Elizabeth slowly lifted her eyes. I strained to spot Eugene, who'd raised this girl to call him Daddy. But the look on Elizabeth's face betrayed no hope of rescue.

"Eight hundred," called one of the agents from Lexington.

"Eight hundred?" said the auctioneer in a mocking tone. *"C'est un objet d'art, celle-là."*

Indeed, she *was* beautiful. And I had little doubt as to why. The cheekbones of her mother—not Bethany's, but Tilly's. It was obvious. Tilly, who was half out of her mind when Silas had retrieved her, substituting her for the money owed him. *They have taken her child,* Silas told me, trying to convey her anguish. *Tell me about Missus Bethany's girl,* Tilly had asked when I returned from Maysville. *How pretty?* Tilly herself, who had been dressed up as a doll and taken to the big house. Even Handsome said it was cruel when they snatched her. *Drove her mother crazy.*

And those Orpheus eyes. In all likelihood, Tilly was herself an Orpheus from the wrong side of the blanket and not the child of Handsome. It was ridiculous to think of Tilly as Silas's half sister, but if the stories about his father and Delilah were true, the case *could* be made for Elizabeth to have claim upon the farm had there been anything left to claim, and if she weren't part African.

"One thousand," said another voice from the back. I tried to make out the bidder, but the crowd seemed to convulse like one mighty organism at the sight of the girl upon the block.

"Do I hear eleven hundred?" said the Frenchman. Silence. Who had made the offer? I remembered Tilly screaming as she was carried toward the river.

"Eleven hundred!" said I.

Theodora gripped my arm.

"We hear eleven hundred. Eleven hundred. Ees nothing for this beauty. Look at her!" The auctioneer grabbed Elizabeth's chin and turned her face from side to side.

Theodora moved away. From beneath my veil, I could see her whispering to a minister who was standing near us in the crowd. I recognized him as the man named Shands whom I'd met at Mrs. Beasley's.

"Look at her magnificent shoulders!" said the auctioneer as he tore her blouse away from her neck. A gasp went up from the crowd.

The vein in my neck pounded, and for a moment, I felt as though I should faint. Then Theodora was beside me. "It is arranged. But you must not bid again."

Minister Shands took off his hat and raised it high. "Twelve hundred," he called out.

"For shame," said a woman behind me.

"Fifteen hundred!" came the same voice from the back of the crowd. *Mississippi*, I thought.

Said the Frenchman, "Think of this beauty by your side. Or by the side of your client."

With this, he tugged down her shirt, exposing her breasts. He reached down and lifted her skirts. "Turn around," he said to Elizabeth.

She stared back at him coolly and did not move, and though I hadn't seen her in over a decade, I felt proud.

"Sixteen hundred," cried the minister.

"You shall not have her," said the southern voice from the back.

"By God, I will," said Minister Shands.

And so the bidding went until it reached almost two thousand, the voice in the back growling in chagrin, the auctioneer exultant as the hammer came down. "Nineteen hundred dollars for this magnificence," he shouted. Men were staring at the ground. Some of the women were crying.

Theodora leaned over to me. "Now hand that minister your purse."

"What?"

There was a moment of confusion as Elizabeth straightened her skirt, pulled at her blouse, and spit into the face of the auctioneer. Through my shock, I felt Theodora wrest the purse away from me, and the minister was striding toward the stage, bowing and holding out his hand to Elizabeth. In the distance, someone cheered.

At the edge of the crowd, I caught sight of Eugene Orpheus—bearded, caped—as he turned on his foot and stalked away.

CHAPTER 30

1848

That evening, we rode back to the school, and wildly, too—that we might escape questions and any return of my good sense. I was once again Olivia Givens, the woman who had stood in defense of Reason so long ago at debates and lectures. Now as then, I was the woman who had lost her mind.

"Where will I go?" said Elizabeth, who was wrapped in the minister's coat and bunched into a tiny ball in the carriage seat beside me.

"Quickly," said Theodora, once we arrived at the school.

She hurried the girl into the building and left me standing in the hall. I would wait until morning to think about my lightened purse and what I would tell James.

"The attic?" I said when Theodora came downstairs and told me that she'd ushered the girl into the garret behind the bookcase. "Didn't we just buy her freedom?"

"You don't know these people," said Theodora.

Sighing, I said, "Oh, yes I do."

WHEN BELLA MASON showed up at our door the following morning, I was poorly rested and ill-humored and even less ready to hear what she had to say.

"Ain't it come to a pretty pass when a fine man like that goes up against a nigger, and for what?" Bella said, pushing past me. "'Least he won't get hanged."

"Tell me."

"And don't think I won't wait for him," she said, after telling me that Erasmus had been sentenced to six years with no parole nor option for a fine. "I have all the time in the world."

Any decent lawyer should have shot down the case. The only credible witness was a slave who claimed Erasmus had approached him with a scheme to steal off another Negro named Grady from an adjacent property. Flaunting precedent, the judge allowed the testimony of this ingrate named Dollar, who felt it should have been *he* who was stolen away.

And how was he planning to steal you exactly? asked the prosecutor.

Dollar hadn't been exactly sure, saying that Erasmus implied he had magic means to conceal people, but what that meant exactly, he couldn't tell. Still, he'd hung his hat on the notion of piggybacking on the flight of Grady once he'd help get word to the slave to meet Erasmus down by Dobbs's creek.

According to Dollar, he waited in the brush, but saw no meeting transpire.

Then how do you know this man absconded with this slave? said the defense lawyer, a walrus of a man and prone to belching. *Were they rendered invisible?*

Huh?

Did the accused actually make them disappear?

They's gone, ain't they?

Erasmus averred he'd never met this Dollar, but Dobbs's foreman claimed otherwise. And there was the matter of a mother with two children gone around the time that Erasmus was loitering in Maysville. Finally—and more damningly—there was Erasmus's carriage and its suspiciously large compartments.

You look about the state of Kentucky these past few years, said the prosecutor to the jury, *and you'll see a trail of old hats and vanished slaves.*

That Dobbs's foreman was white and attested to Dollar's account was the final blow to Erasmus.

"That's preposterous," said Theodora after Bella finished telling us of the trial. "They are blaming him for every slave that's run away."

"I'm sure he's flattered," said I, agreeing that it was Erasmus's bad luck to have a judge who was itching to make an example.

"He's lucky not to hang," said Bella. "Say, you hear what happened yesterday down at the slave market?"

HAD THE CIRCUMSTANCES BEEN DIFFERENT, Elizabeth might have stayed on and become one of Theodora's students. Indeed, by posing her as such, we were able to remove her unobstrusively from Mason County. Theodora was well known as the headmistress of Limestone Academy, and I would plausibly pass as the chaperone for a girl being returned to her family. We dressed Elizabeth in clothes suitable for one of our young charges and hid her face under hat and veil. Together, we rode in the school's carriage to the landing whence Theodora bid us adieu as we boarded a ferry ostensibly for Covington but actually planning to disembark in Cincinnati. Once there, I would explain to my brother and to William why I hadn't secured Erasmus's freedom and had returned instead with this "orphan."

The captain of the vessel blared the horn as we pulled away, the big wheel reprimanding the water. Elizabeth said, "I've always wanted to take a boat ride."

But Bethany had hidden her away in Maysville, jealous that her pretty child might be fingered by others and snatched. Had Bethany known that the girl would be sold off along with the silver?

The story Theodora and I came up with was this: that the girl had been a student whose parents had died, leaving her a pauper. It had fallen upon me to help her out. As to the loss of James's money, that would require another lie: that a fee had been charged along with incarceration lest Erasmus be hanged.

I prayed that James wouldn't read the Maysville papers.

"You'll like Hatsepha," I told Elizabeth. "She's always longed for a daughter."

"Why can't I live with you, Auntie?"

"You must never call me that."

I had already decided not to linger in Cincinnati. Instead, I would stay on with Theodora while Erasmus served his time.

"You are safer in the North," I told her.

It had rained and blown that day as we steamed down the river. I had held on to my hat, scanning the Ohio shores for the little cabin that belonged to Erasmus, but the area around Enduring Hope had flooded. Indeed, Utopia, just upriver, had all but washed away.

We alighted at the landing in Cincinnati just as the sun came out, the throng of people pushing and hollering, hauling feed and logs behind whinnying horses and sullen mules. We ducked under lines and made our way around stacks of crates to cabs tethered to nags who would be unenthusiastic about climbing up a hill.

I hustled the girl into a carriage.

The muddy streets clutched the wheels as we wended our way up to Mt. Auburn. I had tried to explain my family to Elizabeth, to remind her of her uncle Silas.

"I don't remember him," she said.

"I brought his body back the summer that I met you."

"I wonder where *I'll* be buried," she said, looking out the window.

I SHALL NEVER FORGET the look on Elizabeth's face when we pulled up to the Mt. Auburn house that clearly outranked the fine but smaller manse on Orpheus Farms. Nor shall I forget the faces of my family when we were announced into the dining room without first sending word. It being summer, the crystal bowl at the center of the table was piled with figs about which flickered candles from James's workshops. Overhead, a magnificent gaslit chandelier glowed with Givens gas, and around the table, Givenses of every sort, including, to my amazement, Cousin Samuel from Ireland.

It was William who rose and offered his chair to Elizabeth, who hadn't eaten all day and looked as though she'd faint at the appearance of all that food.

"My apologies," I said. "We seemed to have interrupted your festivities."

"Sit! Sit!" said Hatsepha, fussing at the Norwegian girl to add places.

"This is my ward, Elizabeth," I said. "Elizabeth . . ."—I flailed about, recalling one of her middle names—"Satfield." It was the only name I could conjure, having so recently woven a history for the girl while forgetting to change her name. I expected they would ask a million questions, but they sat there dumbly until William cleared his throat and indicated another young woman sitting at the table.

"This is Cousin Margaret," he said. "It seems we are to be married."

Now I understood their distraction, for we had walked right into the celebration of William's betrothal to Cousin Samuel's niece from Ireland.

Said Cousin Samuel, "It seemed appropriate given William's circumstances and his imminent graduation."

James cleared his throat.

Everyone gawked at Elizabeth. With her hair pulled up and her borrowed lace collar, she was quite a picture, her dark eyes an indictment of the pale, insipid Irish girl who'd just crossed the ocean and who still looked faintly seasick.

So many years since we'd left Ireland because there wasn't enough to go around. Our father on the deck of the flatboat whistling Beethoven. And now the family we'd left behind was turning to us to regain their fortune.

"How remarkable," said I.

HATSEPHA CLOSED my bedroom door behind her. "Well?"

"Well what?"

"Is he . . . emancipated?"

We hadn't been able to discuss any of this at the dinner that consisted of six courses, each including a toast to the young couple.

"No," I said, dizzy from so much wine. "Anything but." I stared at Hatsepha miserably. "And why are you marrying off William to this girl?"

She sighed. "I suppose it's not a bad thing that William gets established before going into the business. I can't say the girl is enthusiastic. Plucked out of obscurity in County Crom to be shipped off to Ohio. I expect the whole thing's quite a shock."

"As I well remember," I said. "But you have a very nice house."

"And no children," said Hatsepha, flatly.

"Which brings me to Elizabeth."

Because of our mutual scheming, I should have been inclined to tell Hatsepha everything, but my intuition told me to avoid revealing the whole story of Elizabeth's tortured lineage, the fact that she was Tilly's daughter. Instead, I told her how the girl's parents had perished at sea returning from the Continent, how they had left her penniless but accomplished.

"And since *you've* never had a daughter . . ."

"I would do well to consider this Margaret my daughter, but her accent's so thick I can't quite warm to her. Your charge, Elizabeth, seems much more amiable."

"Oh, she is," I said quickly. "We find her very much so."

In the end, Hatsepha acquiesced. And not only acquiesced, but bought Elizabeth a wardrobe within weeks of her moving in. If any gossip floated down the river about a white girl sold as a slave from Orpheus Farms, it did not reach the heights of Mt. Auburn. Elizabeth, now more beautifully dressed than any debutante, sat at the piano as I once had—playing haltingly but with enjoyment. A few young men came to call, but she concentrated on my brother James, asking him questions about his books and his business so that he, too, grew fond of the girl.

And when William came home that Christmas and spent more time with the orphan from Kentucky than with his betrothed, no one complained, least of all his fiancée, Margaret, who had taken a liking to the son of Phinneaus and Ariadne Mumford. James assured Cousin Samuel that the Mumford boy was an equally good match and certain to make his niece happier than William, who was prone to rumination and a fascination with rocks.

I had returned to Limestone Academy. I liked the company of my young students, and the company of Theodora even more. At last, I had found my sister and partner. All through that spring and summer, after the passage of the dreadful law that hunted down Negroes regardless of their status, we kept a lantern in our window for any soul who needed shelter.

But over time, something continued to nag me. It was what Bella had said about Eugene not being able to father children, along with my dim recollection of Silas mentioning during a dissection that Eugene had been kicked by a horse as a boy in such a way as to compromise fertility.

When I mentioned it to Theodora, she blushed and grew flustered in a way that was out of character. In a town the size of Maysville, very little escaped the wags.

Theodora cleared her throat and fingered her lorgnette. "There were rumors, Olivia. He couldn't . . . you know . . ."

"Dear God," I said, filling in the blanks.

"Probably idle servant gossip. But it does tend to drift upstairs."

Rumors, like the one about Bethany Orpheus's "doll," who seemed immaculately conceived and who, just as miraculously, had passed as white.

But if Eugene hadn't fathered Elizabeth, who had?

CHAPTER 31

1890

William and Elizabeth married in 1851 just after William's graduation from Oberlin. The world was changing, and quickly. In 1850, the Fugitive Slave Act had passed, forcing the return of any black person suspected to have escaped. We called it the "Bloodhound Law." In 1854, William Lloyd Garrison sponsored a freed slave from Canada to return to New York to claim forty acres and a mule. The man, who called himself Handsome Orpheus, told the story of how he'd ushered himself to freedom with the help of Erasmus Givens.

Erasmus, who by then had served his time, was prone to fits of coughing, but was still strong enough to find his way back to Enduring Hope, where he once again took up ferrying, telling his story to anyone who would listen about the part he'd played in the moral imperative that was abolition. By the time Abraham Lincoln delivered his speech in our fair city in 1859, Erasmus had achieved a small bit of notoriety. Mr. Lincoln declared that there was not a public man in the United States who had not opined as to whether slavery was right or wrong, and Erasmus, having suffered sorely for abetting, was proud to take up the mantle of hero thrust upon him by Handsome, after which he was harassed not only by patrollers and anti-abolitionists, but by the advocates of emancipation, who perceived him as a saint.

Although he relished the credit, so poorly was he cut out for this role that, according to Hatsepha, he showed up at their door accompanied by a woman "not fit for society"—namely Bella Mason, whom I defended to Hatsepha as more loyal than the rest of us, having sat through Erasmus's entire trial and imprisonment. Erasmus, who had set out to save souls, had saved his own in the end.

As for Eugene—having sold off his chattel and eventually his farm, he was spotted from time to time at a floating card game or at the watering holes of Saratoga and Salt Sulphur Springs. It was while at Saratoga that cholera swept through again and took him out. No one shed a tear, least of all Elizabeth, who never spoke of him and only occasionally of Bethany as a woman who'd taken her in as one might a cat.

She'd dress me up, Elizabeth told me. *Then lock me in my room. I had no friends my age. It was as if I was a leper.* After Eugene died, she said to me, *I'm glad I've become someone else.*

In 1855, another year of riots and the same year my old friend Salmon Chase became governor, Elizabeth, having lost her first child to diphtheria, gave birth to Mary. My nephew, William, Mary's father, succumbed to duty over passion, assuming his responsibilities in James's company along with Absalom, the son of Ariadne and Phineaus Mumford, now married to Cousin Margaret, who bore him seven children. When James passed away on the eve of the Civil War, William stepped into the chairmanship, but it was Absalom who had the presence of mind to corner the market for rosin—a key ingredient in the making of candles and soap—just before the Confederacy blew up the southern rails, resulting in the Union army encampments lit nightly and exclusively by Givens little wicks.

Hatsepha outlived James by almost twenty well-dressed years, and when she passed eight years ago, no one wept more than I. She would have been so pleased at Mary's consolidating all the Givenses in Spring Grove Cemetery designed by Frederick Law Olmstead—not just the height of fashion, but the nearest approximation of immortality one could enjoy in death.

Tell me about our family, Auntie, Mary asked me a month ago when describing her plans to dig us up and reinter everyone in the beautiful plot bought by her father, William, on the top of a knoll. William himself picked the stone from which to fashion the obelisk—a gorgeous specimen of Kentucky limestone riddled with fossils. *Tell me about the Givenses.*

Hatsepha and James lie in the cemetery at the First Presbyterian Church. Mary's parents, William and Elizabeth, rest there, too, and Mary's grandmother Julia as well. Sadly, Mary's great-grandmother, my mother, lies in a pauper's grave whereupon a music hall now stands. As for Erasmus, William's father and Mary's grandfather—well, he was swept down the river, and though marked by a gravestone and redeemed, is, alas, irretrievable.

I never expected to outlive them. Certainly, I had hoped to die before William. But fevers are capricious, and the one that took first William in 1888 and then Elizabeth a month later spared me, just as the cholera spared me when it stole away our Julia.

That, of course, is the Givens side. What do I tell Mary about the Orpheus side and her mother, Elizabeth, whom everyone thought was an orphan?

First, let us go back to 1828, Erasmus leading Handsome, the escaped slave who had rescued him, back to Orpheus Farms, back to his wife and children, oblivious to the fact that the institution of marriage, like literacy, did not exist for slaves.

Handsome, who had asked Erasmus for help. Handsome, who had never tried to run away, but who had been giving his master, Eugene, trouble because of Delilah, who, at fourteen, was purchased by Eugene's father from the grandson of a Frankfort man who had bought a shipload of slaves from Angola. I suspect it was to Delilah that Eugene had gone when it was time to lose his virginity. Eugene, who had been kicked hard by a horse in the bollocks when he was only twelve. He would not have cared that his father had used Delilah thusly, nor that Delilah had born a child that came eight Decembers earlier in 1814, a child that was noted in the ledger as "Girl," later to be called Tilly.

Tilly, a half sister to Eugene and Silas, born of their father and Delilah.

I imagine Eugene stopping his horse and looking at Delilah, assessing her figure. Her hair would be wrapped up in a scarf, her bosom ample beneath the shift. *Hey now,* he might have said as she drew water from a pump, *I hear my daddy's mighty pleased with you.*

Yassuh, said Delilah, her eyes not meeting his. She had a life with Handsome that was good, and if her firstborn child, a girl, had an Orpheus look about her, as did the youngest, well that was the Devil telling her never to forget these Orpheus men.

Eugene could have taken Delilah in a stall at the rear of the horse barn. While he was pumping away, he would lean in close. *You do this with Wilbur?* Wilbur—the overseer and Bella Mason's father. Delilah, her checks wet, would shake her head. Since she had been cast off by Eugene's father, there was only Handsome in her life, and now this shame.

Over the next month, Handsome had started to act up. Wilbur, the overseer who had run the preacher off the fields for exhorting slaves to run away, mentioned it to Eugene. *He won't pick up a broom when I set him to muckin',* said Wilbur. *And he looks me straight in the eye.*

For Handsome knew something was wrong. Delilah wouldn't tell him, but Handsome knew how white men were, even though he had been well treated. Delilah wasn't the same when he held her. And when he touched her privates, he found blood on his fingers.

The preacher who gathered them on the edge of the field had mentioned Potiphar, who had freed his slave Joseph, and Handsome had listened with only one ear. The white people had a fine place to gather—he'd seen the spire—but why should God be interested in a bunch of niggers whose church was a cluster of stumps behind their cabins? Still, the preacher had made an impression, and after Wilbur drove that preacher off, Handsome decided to confront the overseer.

You've been harassing my woman.

And Wilbur had laughed, saying, *That ugly thing?* For Wilbur preferred light-skinned girls, like the firstborn of Delilah named Tilly, who was only fourteen and whom Delilah watched like a hawk.

Handsome struck Wilbur in the face.

And so Handsome was sold on the block when the trader came through, sold as one of the Orpheuses' famously fine slaves, who were in good condition as well as docile and sweet-spirited, having been treated so well by the Orpheus family.

It was a not-so-docile Handsome who broke from the chain gang, only to encounter a feverish Erasmus one day later.

Thou are truly saved, were Erasmus's departing words to Eugene Orpheus after he returned Handsome. My brother—Mary's grandfather—left feeling gratified, for he had seen Delilah rush from the little cabin into the arms of her husband. That Eugene went on to sell Delilah at a bargain price—and not only Delilah, but also her youngest son—Erasmus would learn years later, and this from Handsome himself, who blamed Erasmus for the outcome, wishing Erasmus had done what Handsome had asked in the first place and helped him to escape, seeing as Delilah would have done better had she been allowed to stay, and not only Delilah, but Tilly, the daughter whom Delilah was protecting, for without her mother, Tilly was left on her own, and it wasn't just Wilbur who had noticed the pretty young thing with the eyes that were almost green.

Erasmus, William's father, Mary's grandfather. Mary's other grandfather, an Orpheus.

I invite you to my wedding night. Recall that I was thirty-one years old when I entered Silas Orpheus's rooms as his wife—not so old that I shouldn't have been eager, not so blighted by cholera's toll that I shouldn't have found comfort in my husband's body. He unlaced my chemise and undid my pantelettes, kissing me here and even there, and though I much admired him, I had to will myself not to recoil. He was no virgin. Unlike me, whose only experience had been that fumbling kiss at fifteen, and this with another girl. Who knew that an adolescent memory would eclipse the consummation of my marriage or that I would feel the happiest in my later years in the company of another woman?

That joyless night that should have drawn Silas and me together only pushed us apart. And though we enjoyed that brief period of carnal contentment before he died, Silas seldom pressed himself on me. I had fleeting thoughts that he might be seeking comfort in the brothels, but I knew better. It was not to brothels but to the other bedroom that he went. I felt gratitude to Tilly, and not just for fixing my hair.

Tilly. The green-eyed girl. The birth mother of Elizabeth. Like the begats in the Bible—Nebaioth from Ishmael; Ishmael from Abraham. The Angolan and the shipmate begat an Augusta slave girl who begat a daughter with the overseer, who, with her master, begat a daughter named Delilah, who, with a master named Orpheus, begat Tilly, who, while assisting Silas Orpheus, begat Elizabeth with him. And in a strange way, I have been happy all these years knowing that William's wife, Mary's mother, the lovely Elizabeth, was *not* the progeny of that hideous Eugene, but the daughter of my husband, Silas, who never wanted children of his own.

The monument in Spring Grove sounds lovely and so like William to select limestone of the sort he would have studied, not only as an owner of coal and gold mines, but as a connoisseur.

Becoming a fossil is no small feat, William once told me. *You must be buried quickly lest your remains be eaten or washed away.*

The fossil is the imprint of the hard stuff. What was soft, mutable, quick to decay leaves no trace, yet with fossils, as with history, it is the tender tissue wherein the story lies. A fin hints at the ability to swim. Find the remnant of a wing, and one can assume flight. But how these creatures spent their days, if they were light-loving, God-fearing, ruthless, or blind, one can only guess, just as one can only guess at conversations long ago evaporated except for the reminiscences of a now-ancient aunt.

There is no earthly trace either of Tilly that I know of, or of Grady, or Delilah. I'm sorry I shan't be buried next to Theodora, and sorry, too, that Silas shan't be reinterred in the Givens plot. But Mary seems determined. I don't know which grandfather she takes more after—my brother Erasmus, who cajoled animal parts as renderings, or Silas Orpheus, who cajoled human bodies for science. Or perhaps there hovers within Mary, my great-niece, a trace of Angola, however faint, that flashes across her face at certain moments, such as when she concentrates on a book as her mother, Elizabeth, did, or when she swore to fight the Confederacy when they briefly threatened our city back in 1864.

I am not long for the world. Mary's husband, Percy, has bought a ranch of some description in Northern California that used to belong to the Mexicans. Though the train trip sounds far easier than our ocean passage of 1819, I can't abide with moving west.

Seventy years since we Scots-Irish Givenses washed down that river. Cincinnati is now a mishmash of railroads, not to mention the coming streetcar. I understand that young Mumford-whatshisname, who runs James's company, has put a wager on electric lights. Even if my vision were good, I shan't live to see it. I am surprised and not a little sorry that it's fallen upon me and not Erasmus to eulogize the Givenses and the Orpheuses and even the unfathomable ancestors of Tilly. But I shall try to rise to the task. What may I ask, other than that our trespasses are forgiven?

Bury us deeply. Bury us well.

Acknowledgments

With gratitude to my agent, Carole Bidnick, and my fine editor, Jennifer Brehl, who waited a long time for this one. And to my writing group and our decades together: Sherri Cooper Bounds, Phyllis Florin, Donna Levin, Suzanne Lewis, Mary Beth McClure, Alison Sackett—writer-whisperers all, stalwarts of encouragement.

I want to thank Greg McCoy and Shane Meeker at the Procter & Gamble Corporate Archives and Heritage Center, the Cincinnati Historical Society, the Cincinnati Museum Center, the National Underground Railroad Freedom Center, and the Kentucky Gateway Museum Center.

As always, I owe a debt to the support of my husband, Peter, and my children, Chapin and Anna, who believed in this project, and to my ancestors George and Mary Gamble, along with their children, who had the courage and faith to emigrate.

Insights,
Interviews
& More . . .

About the author

About the book

About the author

Meet Terry Gamble

Cristiana Ceppas

Terry Gamble is a Phi Beta Kappa graduate of the University of Michigan. She lives with her husband, Peter Boyer, in Sonoma and San Francisco, California.

Reading Group Discussion Questions

1. Early in the novel, the narrator, Olivia Givens, draws attention to the fact that her family is Protestant, saying, "We were Ulster Plantation Irish, which is to say that we were Scots" and citing her father's "tepid Calvinism." She goes on to imply conflict with the Catholics. How does religion play into the narrative arc of *The Eulogist*? Discuss how religious beliefs affected social standing, business prospects, moral outlook, and political views as depicted in the novel. How does religion inform these aspects of society today?

2. *The Eulogist* begins with the Givenses emigrating from Northern Ireland because their farm can no longer sustain the whole family due to crop losses and dropping prices after the Napoleonic Wars. Seeking new opportunity, they risk everything to "come to America to pray and to prosper. Come to America because America wanted us—this too-new country with land and trees to spare but not enough people." Under what circumstances did you or your ▸

Reading Group Discussion Questions
(continued)

ancestors immigrate? How were they received in their adopted country? What hurdles and challenges did they face?

3. It is unlikely that the Givenses, coming from Northern Ireland, have ever seen a black or indigenous person before arriving in America in 1819. Olivia says of indigenous people, "America—where it was said that the Indians were cannibals," and says of black people, "Hottentots. That's what they were to us." Yet when the Givens family arrives in Cincinnati, most of the indigenous people have been driven out or eradicated. Across the river in Kentucky, black people are enslaved, while those who lived in Ohio are either freed or runaways. With the subsequent waves of white immigration, race wars break out in Cincinnati, including a fateful eruption on the night when Olivia's nephew William is born. How do these earlier examples of racial conflict continue to express themselves in present-day America? Where do you see examples of progress and resolution?

4. Early nineteenth-century America embraced "The Cult of True Womanhood," characterized by "piety, purity, submissiveness, and domesticity."* Olivia chafes under these limitations. She is intellectually curious and longs for adventure. How does she assert her independence? What price does she pay for it? How do these earlier attitudes toward the role of women inform today's societal expectations?

5. Several new technologies upended commerce and society in the early nineteenth century: the cotton gin that led to a growth in slavery because of the demand for pickers and processors; and the steam engine that revolutionized river traffic, workshops, and factories, and presaged the railroads. What technologies have altered your life? Your parents' lives? Your grandparents' lives? What advantages did they yield? Did they destabilize as well as raise the standard of living? ▸

---

* Barbara Welter, "The Cult of True Womanhood: 1820-1860" (*American Quarterly*, Volume 18, No. 2, Part I), 151.

Reading Group Discussion Questions
(continued)

6. None of the Givens siblings—James, Olivia, or Erasmus—starts out with the intention of addressing slavery. While they may find it annoying, distasteful, or even shocking, they initially see it as the status quo, a fact of this new country in which they are hoping to succeed. By the end of the novel, all three siblings have taken some action against slavery. What compelled them to do so? Why did they change their minds? About what issues have you changed your mind? Have those issues spurred you to activism?

7. Laws banning interracial marriage or "intimacy" (anti-miscegenation laws) existed in America starting in Colonial times and were not overturned until the Civil Rights movement in the 1960s (*Loving v. Virginia,* 1967). Such laws were intended to maintain "racial supremacy." But America isn't alone in having such laws in its past. Think of some other examples of the criminalization of or taboos against interracial or interreligious marriage. Do they still exist?

8. By the end of the novel, Olivia is eighty-six years old and has outlived many of her relatives. In "eulogizing" them, she recounts some surprising turns in their genealogy. Have you researched your own family's genealogy? Any surprises? What legacies are you most proud of? What questions remain?

Behind the Book: Digging Up Ancestors

It started with receipts for the bodies. My sister and I were sorting through the detritus of our parents' lives—commendations to my father from Rotary, my fifth-grade essay on beetles, our mother's set of twenty finger bowls, ash trays, pink lipsticks from the sixties, photos of sailboats and cocktail parties, golfers in plaid shorts, and one of my father with Governor Edmund Brown, both of them looking pained. By the end of the weekend, we barely examined what we were pitching out. It was only because of the hand-drawn rendering of a stone obelisk attached to a letter that I took a second glance at the correspondence from a monument maker to my great-great-uncle James Norris Gamble, dated 1890.

"That's the family plot," my sister told me when I showed her the letter. "In Cincinnati."

I had been to weddings in Cincinnati, but never funerals, so I hadn't seen the towering marker that came to reside on the knoll in Spring Grove Cemetery that was designed by Frederick Law Olmstead, who also designed Central Park and Golden Gate Park in San Francisco where I now live.

"Let's save it," I said.

"What else?"

I studied a wad of papers. "Receipts," I said. "Oh, wait." I read them again. "Holy cow," I said. "They're receipts for exhumations."

EACH FAMILY HAS its creation myth. Ours was the Scots-Irish Gambles coming down the Ohio River on a flat boat and settling in Cincinnati. They had intended to go to Illinois. The father, George, a farmer, hoped to preach as a Methodist minister, but his son James fell ill with cholera. Resting in Cincinnati while James recuperated, they decided to stay. We know the rest: how James became a soap-maker using the byproducts of pigs from the slaughterhouses; how during the Crash of 1837, he teamed up with his brother-in-law, William Proctor, who made candles to buy in bulk and survive tough market conditions. Religious men, they built their company on honesty and integrity as well as steely ambition. But what most interested me was that they lived on the Ohio River, right across from the slave state of Kentucky.

We still feel the tremors from nineteenth-century America. Like today, it was a time of rapid industrial and technological changes that displaced ways of life and forced culturally diverse people together, created vast and concentrated wealth, saw an emergence of the Second Great ▸

Behind the Book: Digging Up Ancestors ***(continued)***

Awakening in which religious zeal pushed back against the Enlightenment, pitted families and friends against each other over slavery, suffered race riots and segregation, planted the seeds for suffrage and public health, medical science, transportation, lighting, roads. While Mary Lincoln was consulting spirits using Ouija boards, Charles Darwin was publishing *The Origin of Species*. While Mark Twain and Charles Dickens were capturing the imagination of the masses, it was a book by a Harriet Beecher Stowe that drove a stake through the complacency around slavery.

I was well aware of our creation myth, but there were unanswered questions. What, for instance, did those ancestors whose names were on those receipts think of slavery? I began to resurrect their views like bodies from a churchyard, starting with visits to Cincinnati, Ohio and Maysville, Kentucky, lurking in historical societies and museums, especially the Cincinnati Museum Center in the Union Train Station from which my father departed for World War II. I talked to historians and librarians. I talked to re-enactors. I read Francis Trollope, and de Toqueville, and the medical pioneer, Daniel Drake. I attended Civil War Round Tables in dingy motel conference rooms. I joined a tour at the Underground Railroad Freedom Center focused on women and slavery, everyone on the tour a black woman except for the docent and me. At different points of the tour, we read aloud from Sojourner Truth and Rosa Parks and the poetess Phyllis Wheatley. At the end, we shared about our ancestors. Several couldn't recall more than one or two generations, but one woman knew that her great-great-grandfather had killed his overseer and escaped to freedom, and that out of that act of desperation, their family went on to thrive. As for me, I had the privilege to trace my roots back to the 1600s—our family's migration to Ireland from Scotland under King James, their two hundred years of farming, their plight at the end of the Napoleonic Wars that sent them to America, this new country that was eager to accept them and offer a path to prosperity. My white family came voluntarily, their history documented in ship logs and letters and diaries and photographs and commendations from the Rotary Club. Not so most African Americans whose families descended from slaves.

More reading. An account by a free black hairdresser named Iangy that may be one of the first books in print authored by a person of color: ▸

Behind the Book: Digging Up Ancestors ***(continued)***

A Hairdresser's Experience in the High Life by Eliza Potter, a free black woman. And then there's Ann Hagedorn's *Beyond the River*, a marvelous account of life in Ripley about the people who fought for the end of slavery and who secreted runaways to freedom. But the real treasure trove was a piece of 1940s apologia called *Slave Times in Kentucky*. It was in that book that I read how a mixed-race young woman was raised as a daughter in a white household, only to be sold off when her mother died. The girl could pass as white. So outraged were the people of Lexington to witness this beauty being sold at auction that the appetite for slavery began to wane. Fortunately for her, she had caught the eye of Calvin Fairbanks, a Presbyterian minister whose mission was ushering slaves to freedom. Purchased by the minister, the young woman was later married into a Cincinnati family of consequence. Who was that family? Even our family, with its predominantly Scots-Irish coloring, has its share of aunts and cousins of extraordinary beauty and dusky skin.

In the summer of 2010, I traveled to Ireland and the town of Omagh where I saw a re-creation of how Protestant-Irish farmers lived. There, in an emigration museum, I saw the kind of ship my family would have sailed on and found in the ship's log of the *Lucretia* the recorded names of my ancestors: the Georges and the Jameses, the Marys, the Elizabeths, and the Olivias—two generations of Gambles that had made it across the sea.

I hadn't intended to write about the Underground Railroad or about race or religion, about children separated from their parents, or the challenges of being a woman in the nineteenth century. I just wanted to understand. But at some point, the research faded into the background, and story and character emerged. Erasmus heading into the wilderness trying to find God. James working in his workshop, building an enterprise to sustain the family. And most of all Olivia, whose hair, like her temper, tends toward the red. Into "this mosquito-infested backwater" she alights, a woman "of unremarkable countenance" determined to think her own thoughts, form her own opinions, possess her own body, associate with whom she pleases. "You're a radical, Miss Givens," the doctor Silas Orpheus says to her.

In digging them up, I discovered my own ancestors to eulogize. My great-great-aunt who perished nursing the freed black soldiers who had volunteered for the Union Army. ▸

Behind the Book: Digging Up Ancestors
(continued)

My great-great-great-grandfather, the state supreme-court judge who refused to honor the *Dred Scott* decision. My great-grandmother Mary whose appetite for travel, visionary architecture and social progress informs my life today. As I hope the descendants of Olivia will come to realize, I owe my ancestors, now replanted in Spring Grove, a debt for their courage to immigrate, to dig in, to stand up. ~